W9-AXS-886

Praise for Janet Tronstad
and her novels

"*A Baby for Dry Creek* shows how losing a parent
can affect a young child for a lifetime. This sweet
romance is both suspenseful and entertaining."
—*Romantic Times BOOKreviews*

"Janet Tronstad's quirky small town and witty
characters will add warmth and joy to your
holiday season."
—*Romantic Times BOOKreviews* on
A Dry Creek Christmas

"Janet Tronstad pens a warm, comforting story
that brings joy to its characters."
—*Romantic Times BOOKreviews* on
Shepherds Abiding in Dry Creek

"Amid angels, Christmas pageants and
unknown danger, Ms. Tronstad creates a very
enjoyable story about learning to believe and
love again."
—*Romantic Times BOOKreviews* on
An Angel for Dry Creek

JANET TRONSTAD
A Baby for Dry Creek

A Dry Creek Christmas

Steeple
Hill®

Published by Steeple Hill Books™

If you purchased this book without a cover you should be aware
that this book is stolen property. It was reported as "unsold and
destroyed" to the publisher, and neither the author nor the
publisher has received any payment for this "stripped book."

STEEPLE HILL BOOKS

Steeple
Hill®

Recycling programs
for this product may
not exist in your area

ISBN-13: 978-0-373-65125-2
ISBN-10:   0-373-65125-2

A BABY FOR DRY CREEK AND A DRY CREEK CHRISTMAS

A BABY FOR DRY CREEK
Copyright © 2004 by Janet Tronstad

A DRY CREEK CHRISTMAS
Copyright © 2004 by Janet Tronstad

All rights reserved. Except for use in any review, the reproduction
or utilization of this work in whole or in part in any form by any
electronic, mechanical or other means, now known or hereafter
invented, including xerography, photocopying and recording, or in
any information storage or retrieval system, is forbidden without
the written permission of the editorial office, Steeple Hill Books,
233 Broadway, New York, NY 10279 U.S.A.

This is a work of fiction. Names, characters, places and incidents are
either the product of the author's imagination or are used fictitiously, and
any resemblance to actual persons, living or dead, business establishments,
events or locales is entirely coincidental.

This edition published by arrangement with Steeple Hill Books.

® and TM are trademarks of Steeple Hill Books, used under license.
Trademarks indicated with ® are registered in the United States Patent
and Trademark Office, the Canadian Trade Marks Office and in other
countries.

www.SteepleHill.com

Printed in U.S.A.

CONTENTS

Books by Janet Tronstad

Steeple Hill Love Inspired

*An Angel for Dry Creek
*A Gentleman for Dry Creek
*A Bride for Dry Creek
*A Rich Man for Dry Creek
*A Hero for Dry Creek
*A Baby for Dry Creek
*A Dry Creek Christmas
*Sugar Plums for Dry Creek
*At Home in Dry Creek
**The Sisterhood of the Dropped Stitches
*Shepherds Abiding in Dry Creek
**A Dropped Stitches Christmas
*Dry Creek Sweethearts
**A Heart for the Dropped Stitches
*A Dry Creek Courtship
*Snowbound in Dry Creek

*Dry Creek
**The Sisterhood of the Dropped Stitches

JANET TRONSTAD

grew up on a small farm in central Montana. One of her favorite things to do was to visit her grandfather's bookshelves, where he had a large collection of Zane Grey novels. She's always loved a good story.

Today, Janet lives in Pasadena, California, where she works in the research department of a medical organization. In addition to writing novels, she researches and writes nonfiction magazine articles.

A BABY FOR DRY CREEK

For I was hungry and you gave me food;
I was thirsty and you gave me drink;
I was a stranger and you took me in.
— *Matthew* 25:35

This book is dedicated with many fond memories to my forty cousins, both the Norris side of the family and the Tronstad side of the family. Thanks for the good times!

Prologue

Chrissy Hamilton figured her life couldn't get much worse. On the morning of what was supposed to be her wedding day, she had found another woman in her fiancé's bed. And that wasn't even the worst part. After she'd stomped out of Jared's bedroom and driven almost all the way to Dry Creek, Montana, in her cousin's truck, she'd met a man who made her knees melt so fast she wouldn't have cared if an entire cheerleading squad had been camped out in Jared's bed.

Of course, nothing could come of her attraction. She was two and a half months pregnant and just about as confused and miserable as an eighteen-year-old in trouble could be.

Besides, if Chrissy couldn't trust the man she'd loved since she was fifteen, she certainly wasn't going to risk trusting some Montana rancher she'd just met.

It was too bad about the rancher, though. With his black hair and sky blue eyes, Reno Redfern was the sexiest man she'd ever seen. Which was one more reason to leave Dry Creek.

Seven and a half months later

Dry Creek did not have a postmaster. It didn't even have a post office. Everyone knew that. Still, the letter addressed to the postmaster sat there on top of all the other letters the mail carrier had left on the counter of the hardware store this cold spring morning. The mail carrier hadn't even looked at the letter before crawling back into the postal truck and heading down Interstate 94 to the next small Montana town on his busy route.

The hardware store sold everything a rancher needed, from weed killer to waterproof gloves, and most of it was sitting on long wooden shelves that lined the walls. A stack of ceramic mugs stood on a cart beside the stockroom door and the smell of brewing coffee welcomed customers every day of the week except Sunday, when the store was closed.

Of course, not everyone was a customer. The hardware store served as an informal community center, and some retired ranchers, like Jacob, spent most of their waking hours there arguing about cattle prices and waiting for the mail.

"Who'd be writing to our postmaster?" Jacob

asked as he lifted the first envelope and read the address. He had been a rancher for sixty of his seventy-seven years, and his gnarled fingers showed it as he held up the letter.

"We don't have a postmaster." Mrs. Hargrove also waited for the mail. She didn't sit, like the men, preferring to stand on the rubber mat by the counter so her muddy boots didn't dirty the wood floor as the men's boots were doing. She would rather distribute the mail herself, since she could do it more efficiently than Jacob, but she was a fair-minded woman and Jacob had gotten to the mail counter first.

In addition to Mrs. Hargrove, a half dozen ranchers were waiting for their mail, and the door was opening to let more into the store. Each time the door swung back or forth, a gust of wind came inside. As usual, spring had started out cold, but everyone had expected it to warm up by now. Most of the ranchers said they could still smell winter in the air and they didn't like it. They should be planting their fields, and it was too muddy to even plow.

"We might not have a postmaster, but we got us a letter," Jacob said as he put the envelope up to the light and tried to see through it before lowering his eyes and looking around at the others. "From a law firm. In California."

"What would a law firm want with our postmaster? We haven't broken any laws." Another retired rancher, Elmer, spoke up from where he sat by the black woodstove that stood in the middle of the hardware store. The morning was chilly enough that a small fire was burning inside the stove.

As he was speaking, Elmer stood up and frowned.

The inside of the hardware store got quiet as Elmer slowly walked toward the counter. The people of Dry Creek had a large respect for the law and an equally large distrust of California lawyers. They also knew that Elmer had an instinct for trouble, and if he was worried enough to leave his chair, they were worried, too.

"I keep telling folks we need to get a more regular way of sorting the mail," said a middle-aged rancher, Lester, as he looked up from the bolts he was sorting along the far wall. He scowled as he took up the old argument. "You're not supposed to see other folks' mail—it's not legal. The FBI can get involved."

"The FBI has better things to worry about than who sees your seed catalogs," Elmer said as he finished walking over to Jacob and looked down at the letter the other man still held. "Besides, no one in California would care how we sort through our mail. Would they?"

"Well, open it up and read it to us," Mrs. Hargrove finally said. She had a raisin bread pudding baking in her oven and she didn't want the crust to get too brown. "We haven't got all morning."

Jacob took out his pocketknife and used it as a letter opener. Then he cleared his throat and carefully read the entire letter aloud word by word. Jacob had always been proud of his speaking abilities, and he hadn't had many chances in his life for public performances. If there hadn't been so many people gathered in the hardware store, he probably would have listened to what he was saying instead of just focusing on getting all the words spoken correctly and loudly the way Mrs. Baker, his first-grade teacher, would have expected.

> Joseph K. Price, Attorney-at-Law
> 918 Green Street, Suite 200
> Pasadena, California 91104

Dear Dry Creek Postmaster,

I'm writing to request your help in locating a man who lives in your community. Unfortunately, I do not know the man's full name, so I cannot write to him directly. The nature of my business is this man's relationship with a young woman, Chrissy Hamilton, and her new baby. It is the paternity of the infant that I wish to establish.

Miss Hamilton was in your community last fall. I am hopeful you will know the young man who spent the night with Miss Hamilton in her cousin's truck. The man's first name is Reno. If you can supply me with the man's full name, I assure you that my client, Mrs. Bard, will be happy to reward you (you have no doubt heard of the family—they own the national chain of dry cleaners by the same name). I realize this is an unusual request, and I want to assure you that no one is asking the man to assume financial responsibility for the baby. Quite the opposite, in fact. Mrs. Bard is anxious to adopt the baby should it be proven to her satisfaction that her son, Jared, is the baby's father. I apologize for the unorthodox nature of this request. It would not be necessary if Miss Hamilton were more cooperative. But she is young (eighteen, I believe) and does not yet see the full advantage to herself in this arrangement. I look forward to hearing from you soon.

Yours truly,
Joseph K. Price, Esq.

The whole store listened and then stood still in stunned silence for a moment.

Finally Elmer spoke. "Our Reno?"

"Nothing says Reno's the baby's father," Mrs. Hargrove cautioned, and then her voice softened. "Imagine, a baby."

"Where is Reno, anyway?" Elmer looked around. "He's usually here to get his mail by now."

Chapter One

Reno Redfern stopped his pickup in front of the hardware store in Dry Creek. He was late and splattered with thick gray mud. Hopefully someone would have sorted the mail by now, and he could quietly pick up his few bills and get back to the ranch and shower. If he had been paying more attention to the road, he wouldn't have slipped into the ditch and ended up with the wheels of his pickup stuck in the mud.

Reno shook his head. He'd made it a point to thank God repeatedly for the rain—what rancher wouldn't?—but he was working on being honest in his dealings with God, and so far he hadn't been able to say anything polite about the mud. The mud just lay everywhere, making the ground look forlorn and generally being a nuisance.

Reno had liked the first part of spring well

enough. The cold of winter had eased up a little and he could walk from the house to the barn without pulling his cap down over his ears. But later, for some reason, everything had turned to mud. The mountains were no longer covered in snow, but the grass hadn't taken hold yet either. Gray clouds hung in most of the skies, and the air was wet even when it wasn't raining. The worst part was the deep clay that trapped everyone's wheels.

Reno frowned as he opened the door to his pickup. The one good thing he could say for the mud was that it matched his mood these days. If it had been a normal Montana spring with endless blue sky and those tiny purple wildflowers blooming beside the gravel roads, he wouldn't have been able to take all the love and sunshine flowing around the Redfern Ranch now that his sister, Nicki, had settled into married life.

At first Reno had wondered in alarm if he were jealous of Nicki's wedded bliss. But that wasn't it. He just missed the way things used to be.

There was such a thing as too much happiness, Reno finally decided, and his sister proved it. Nicki was so sweet these days it made his teeth ache. If she weren't so sweet, he probably wouldn't miss the old Nicki so much.

But as much as he tried to bring Nicki back to her senses, he couldn't. He couldn't even get her going on a good argument about cattle prices and fertilizer, and those used to be her favorite topics for heated discussion. But now all she wanted to talk about was curtain fabric and love. She had a perfectly good rancher's brain that was turning to sentimental mush, and he was powerless to stop it.

And she wasn't content to limit her new sentimental thoughts of love to herself and her new husband. Oh, no—she had started to speak of marriage with a missionary zeal that made Reno nervous. He had seen the speculation in her eyes several days before she came right out and asked him if he'd like her to set him up.

Set him up! Reno still couldn't believe it. He and Nicki had had a pact. Neither one of them was going to get married, at least not for love. Of course, they'd made that vow when they were ten and twelve, a good four years after their mother had left their father and they'd heard every day since about the damage love could do from their father's own bitter lips.

Besides, even if Reno decided to take leave of his senses and look for a wife, he didn't need his sister doing the looking for him. There were plenty of women who wanted to date him. Granted, he wasn't exactly in touch with any of them at the moment, but that was only because he was busy feeding the new calves and, well—things.

"I'm getting around to it." Reno had set his glass of water down on the kitchen counter when Nicki asked her question. "You don't need to worry about me. I'm doing fine."

"Really, you've met someone you want to date?"

Reno scowled. She didn't need to sound so surprised. "Well, no, but I will—"

"When you have time," Nicki finished for him, and shook her head. "I know as well as you do that there's never any extra time when you're ranching— you have to make time for what's important."

"Getting the alfalfa planted is important."

"With mud like this, you can't even plow. That's why Garrett and I decided to go to Denver. There's nothing to do right now."

"I can change the plugs on the tractor."

"Or you could do something fun for a change, like maybe go down to Los Angeles and pay a visit to Chrissy Hamilton."

Reno was struck dumb. Chrissy was the cousin of Nicki's new husband, Garrett Hamilton. "Why would I do that?"

"Because you've been, well, morose since Chrissy visited here last fall. That's not like you."

Morose? Ever since Nicki had married her trucker husband, she'd started learning a new word every day. Reno didn't like to discourage anyone who wanted to learn. Still… "That's not because of Chrissy."

Well, Reno admitted to himself, it might be a little bit because of Chrissy, but it wasn't in the way his sister thought.

Chrissy had come to Dry Creek last fall looking for Reno and Nicki's mother. Before Chrissy moved back to Los Angeles, she had been a waitress in the Las Vegas casino where their mother worked. The two had become friends, and Reno could understand why.

If Chrissy was upsetting to him, it was only because she reminded him of his mother. Both women had that high-wattage, bright-color sway that went with a place like Las Vegas. They wore fancy sequin dresses with the same ease that women in Dry Creek wore their aprons.

It was clear that neither his mother nor Chrissy belonged in Dry Creek, and that's why Chrissy had bothered him. Really the only reason she still bothered him, he told himself.

Nicki looked at him as if she didn't believe him. "You're not still afraid to get married, are you?"

"Huh?"

Nicki had the grace to blush. "I know we both said we would never get married, but we were kids. What did we know?"

"We knew what Dad told us."

"Ah, well, he only saw one side of being married. If he'd known there were people out there like

Garrett, who can really love someone, he wouldn't have wanted us to stay single all our lives."

Reno decided he shouldn't argue with his sister on this one. "I suppose he might have been okay with *you* marrying."

Nicki looked relieved. "And you, too."

Reno doubted all of it. He had known his father. But he held his tongue.

"Anyway, here's Chrissy's address and phone number," Nicki said as she pulled a piece of paper out of her jeans pocket and set it on the kitchen counter. "You could at least call and talk to her—or write her a letter or something."

With that, Nicki turned and walked away.

She might as well have left a stick of live dynamite on the kitchen counter.

Reno just stared at the paper.

He didn't tell his sister that he didn't need to call Chrissy or write her a letter to find out if the two of them were destined for some kind of wedded bliss. For even a little bit of bliss to happen, the woman would have to like him, and it appeared the very thought of dating him made Chrissy Hamilton want to cry.

Even someone as lovestruck as his sister would have to agree that was not a good sign. Fortunately, no one knew about him and Chrissy.

When Chrissy had been at the ranch last fall, he'd

decided to invite her to eat dinner at the café in Dry Creek with him. He hadn't thought it was any big deal. He'd spent the afternoon convincing himself that just because her green-gray eyes made him want to take up painting storm clouds, that was no reason to think he was interested in anything but getting to know someone who could tell him more about his mother.

He'd even stopped himself from wondering about Chrissy's lips once he decided they looked as soft as they did because of some sort of Las Vegas beauty trick.

No, he'd put all that aside. Dinner was just a logical thing. Hamburgers and fries for two hungry people at the café in Dry Creek. Maybe spaghetti and garlic bread, if they had it. He'd started out by saying there was no reason to go to any trouble and change clothes and they both had to eat, so would she like to come with him to eat at the—

That's as far as he'd got before she'd given him a stricken look and started to cry. He hadn't known what to do but take her in his arms and let her sob against his last clean shirt. After the first burst of tears had ended, she'd pulled back and looked embarrassed. Her cheeks had been pink, and her eyes had dared him to ask about her tears.

Before he could say anything, she'd thanked him for the invitation in a businesslike voice and added she was sorry she couldn't date him. She was also sorry about the shirt, she said, and added that a little bleach should take the mascara out.

By then he couldn't say he hadn't been asking her out on a date, so he'd just thanked her for the laundry tip. He hadn't added that he was surprised. He'd never figured someone like Chrissy would know anything about laundry.

Fortunately, no one knew about any of this, and Reno wasn't about to tell anyone. He picked up the slip of paper from the kitchen counter, intending to crumple it up and throw it away. He should be glad Chrissy wasn't interested in him.

Reno was cautious when it came to women. Even if he hadn't had his father to remind him of how fickle women could be, his mother had taught him that some women just weren't meant to live on a ranch.

Life on the Redfern Ranch could never compete with the excitement of a big city. Ranch life was plain, good living, and that was all Reno wanted, but he knew there was no theater, no fine dining, no museums, no upscale shopping.

A Vegas cocktail waitress like Chrissy would never stay in a place like Dry Creek any more than his mother had. Oh, Chrissy might think it was quaint and amusing enough for a week or so, but in the long term she'd leave. Dry Creek would never be enough for her.

Yes, throwing away that piece of paper his sister had left on the counter was the only sensible thing to do. Reno said those words to himself, but for some strange reason he didn't listen. Instead, he folded the piece of paper into a small square and put it in his shirt pocket.

He told himself he'd throw it away tomorrow. When tomorrow came, he told himself it wouldn't hurt to wait until the next day.

That was two weeks ago Monday, and he no longer even bothered to lie to himself. Every day when he changed his shirt, he moved that piece of paper to the new pocket.

Reno shook his head. This past Saturday he'd actually looked at a map to see which freeways he'd need to take if he drove down to Los Angeles. He'd gone so far as to remind himself he'd never seen the Pacific Ocean and had a good reason to drive down to Los Angeles, quite apart from seeing Chrissy. A man ought to see the ocean some time in his life.

Reno scraped his feet on the porch of the hardware store. At least no one in Dry Creek knew about that slip of paper in his pocket or the foolish thoughts going around in his head. He wouldn't have had any peace if they did. Sometimes it felt as if he had a dozen grandparents, each one of them anxious for him to date someone so they could plan a wedding and then begin the more serious business of knitting baby booties.

Reno didn't know why the seniors in Dry Creek were so set on babies. But all he heard these days were wistful remarks that, given all the marriages in Dry Creek lately, it sure was a shame there weren't any babies.

No, he didn't want the people of Dry Creek to know he was even thinking of visiting Chrissy. They'd start putting their hopes on him, and he'd only let them down.

Chapter Two

Reno opened the door. The hardware store was silent, and for a brief second the light was such that Reno thought no one was inside. Then he saw all his neighbors, and they saw him. It was a toss-up as to who was more startled.

"It's that clay mud," Reno finally said as he stepped inside. They were looking at him as if he were covered with tar or something toxic. "I guess I look a little odd."

"You look just fine," Mrs. Hargrove declared stoutly as she smoothed down the skirt of her checked gingham dress. Mrs. Hargrove had to be eighty years old, and she'd worn the same set of gingham dresses since the late 1950s. She had one in every color of the rainbow. A good dress, she told folks, never wore out as long as you took care of it. Over the dress she wore a black wool sweater that had been stretched out by too many washes. She had rubber boots on her feet and a paperback mystery stuffed into the pocket of her sweater.

Reno stopped and stood still. If Mrs. Hargrove had to defend him that strongly, he must look worse than he thought. She'd been his Sunday-school teacher years ago, and she was loyal to her students. He'd been in the first grade when he'd realized that she fussed with her hair or her dress on the few occasions she was nervous. She'd done it when Randy McCall asked where Eve got her babies from, and she was doing it now.

Mrs. Hargrove reached up and patted her gray hair to make sure her bun was secure. She could have saved herself the effort. Mrs. Hargrove's hair wouldn't dare misbehave, any more than the first-grade boys would have years ago.

"If someone will just hand me my mail, I'll step back to the porch," Reno offered as he looked down. He must have left giant tracks on the clean floor or something, but the floor was already muddy, and not with his footprints. "I'll have to remember this one for April Fools' Day. I don't think Lester got this much of a reaction when he dressed up like Elvis and went to the café for breakfast. Who would have thought he was that much of a clown?"

Lester stood up from where he was kneeling

beside the bottom bin of the nail rack. He was a short, wiry man who seldom spoke, and he cleared his throat before he started to talk. "I may be a clown sometimes, but at least I would financially support a baby if I had fathered one."

"Huh?" Reno wondered if he had missed something. Lester was Reno's closest neighbor, and he looked as if he'd screwed up all his courage to speak. "Since when do you have a baby?"

"Sometimes a man can have a baby and not even know it."

At least six people in the room sucked in their breath.

"Hush, now," Mrs. Hargrove finally managed to say. "It's none of our business. Just because we're all used to seeing everyone's mail as it comes in, it's no reason to meddle."

Reno wondered what she was talking about. Everyone in Dry Creek meddled. It was one of their most endearing traits. It meant they cared.

"That letter was addressed to us," Jacob said indignantly. "We weren't reading anything but what was meant for us. We're the ones who take turns passing out the mail in Dry Creek. We're the postmaster."

"Still," Elmer muttered as he walked back to his chair by the stove, "it's not our business. Of course, in my day a young man was raised to do the honorable thing and marry a woman he got with child."

"Lester got someone pregnant?" Reno finally asked. The last he knew, Lester had been courting Nicki. That was before she married Garrett, of course, but still Reno didn't like to think of Lester playing his sister false. "I thought you were planning on marrying Nicki."

If Reno's voice rose a little, he figured no one could blame him. A man was supposed to defend his sister's honor, even if she was off being a trucker along with her new husband.

Lester took a step forward. "Not me, you fool. You're the one with the baby."

Lester could as well have said that Reno had a castle in Spain or a boot growing out of his head. *"What?"*

"Now, remember the letter didn't say that Reno was the one," Mrs. Hargrove cautioned. "For all we know, he didn't even have those kinds of thoughts about Chrissy Hamilton. The Reno I know is a good boy."

Reno choked. He wished he had a little more mud covering his face so no one could see his guilty flush. How did you tell your old Sunday-school teacher that you'd stopped being a boy a dozen years ago? He sure didn't want to start telling Mrs. Hargrove about the jumble of thoughts he had about Chrissy Hamilton.

Even though he knew Chrissy wasn't the one for him, he still found her attractive. Well, maybe more than attractive, if he was strictly honest about it. Something about Chrissy reminded him of the time as a boy he had been fascinated by a picture of cobras in some catalog that had come to the ranch.

Not that Reno was worried. He had been smart enough not to order a cobra from that catalog when he was nine years old and he was smart enough now to avoid Chrissy. Just because he was drawn to both of them in some mysterious, crazy way didn't mean he had to do anything about it.

Besides, Mrs. Hargrove was right about one thing. It wasn't anyone else's business anyway.

"Chrissy is a fine-looking girl," Elmer volunteered as he sat down in his chair by the stove. His voice was thoughtful. "Reno would have to be blind not to see that."

"Well, that's true," Mrs. Hargrove conceded before she turned back to Reno. "But that doesn't mean he's the father of her baby."

"Chrissy has a baby?" Reno felt the streak of mud start to dry and crack on his face. His voice had grown hoarse and he had to clear his throat. He felt a strange disappointment. "I suppose she's married to that Jared fellow by now, then."

Jacob frowned as he looked down at the letter in his hand. "Doesn't sound like she's married to anyone."

Reno had known Jacob all his life. The man had

taught him how to rope a calf. But Reno didn't believe him on this one. Chrissy might have been mad at her boyfriend when she was in Dry Creek, but Jared had significant money, and a woman like Chrissy would weigh that in the scales before she called it off. Reno figured there was some misunderstanding. He held his hand out for the letter. "Let me see."

Jacob handed him the letter.

There was silence for a minute before Mrs. Hargrove said, "You know, maybe one of us should write to Chrissy and invite her to come to Dry Creek with her baby."

Reno snorted. He didn't want to hurt Mrs. Hargrove's feelings, but Chrissy would probably rather move to the moon than to Dry Creek. She likely thought it was the backside of nowhere, and she was right. Just because the people of Dry Creek liked the middle of nowhere didn't mean Chrissy would. "We don't have any shows or nightclubs or anything. Shoot, we don't even have a proper post office."

Reno returned to reading the letter.

"We have the café," Jacob answered. "And the Christmas pageant every year."

"Pastor Matthew's sermons have been downright entertaining lately with some of his stories about the twins," Mrs. Hargrove added. "I think he's almost as funny as that guy on the television everyone talks about. Any new mother would enjoy that."

"She could play with those calves of yours, too," Jacob added. "They're pretty cute—especially the ones you're feeding with that fancy bucket of yours."

Reno looked up from the letter. He had finished it. "Well, she should be happy. Sounds like she's going to get a handsome payment."

"Reno Redfern!" Mrs. Hargrove said. "I can't believe you think that sweet girl would give her baby up to that lawyer!"

"Well, she wouldn't be giving it to the lawyer. The baby would go to Mrs. Bard. How bad can living with your grandmother be?"

Reno couldn't help but wish he'd had a grandmother who would have taken care of him when his mother left. "She probably bakes cookies and everything. The baby will be fine."

Mrs. Hargrove drew herself up indignantly. "Don't you know anything about a mother's love?" Then she gasped and put her hand over her mouth. "I'm sorry. I wasn't thinking."

Reno forced himself to smile. "That's okay."

It wasn't Mrs. Hargrove's fault his mother had left him and Nicki when she left their father. It wasn't anyone's fault. Not all women were good mothers.

"I should have insisted that father of yours bring

you to town more often when your mother left,"
Mrs. Hargrove muttered. "Just because the two of
you looked fine, I shouldn't have assumed your poor
little hearts weren't broken."

"Nothing was broken," Reno said. "Lots of
people have it worse in life."

Reno had made his peace with the fact that his
mother had left when he was six. He'd had his father
and he'd had Nicki. He'd done just fine.

"But still—"

"I'm sure Chrissy and her baby will be fine."
Reno wasn't sure which topic he wanted to discuss
less, his mother or Chrissy.

Mrs. Hargrove nodded. "Still, if they were to
come here—"

"I'm sure she doesn't want to move here," Reno
repeated.

"Well, still, there's the baby to think about. It's
our Christian duty to at least invite Chrissy.
Someone needs to write her a letter and ask. It's the
hospitable thing to do for someone in trouble and—
and—I'm beginning to think that's what God would
want. He always said we should offer hospitality to
the stranger who's in trouble."

Reno looked at his former Sunday-school
teacher. She was eyeing him the way she had in the
first grade when she wanted volunteers to answer a
question. She wasn't playing fair by bringing God
into this, and she probably knew it.

"I think God was talking about feeding strangers when they show up in town and are hungry. So far every person who drives through Dry Creek seems to be pretty well fed. But if they're not, I'll leave word with Linda and Jazz at the café to give them something to eat and add it to my bill."

Mrs. Hargrove frowned. "Hospitality is about more than food—God also told us to take in people who are in trouble."

"Well, God usually brings them to your doorstep. Chrissy is thousands of miles away."

"I didn't think of that," Mrs. Hargrove said. "We can't just write a letter. How will she get here?"

"She's not coming." Reno ground his teeth and searched for a change of subject. "Lots of mud outside, isn't there?"

No one answered him.

"You know, Reno has a point, though," Jacob agreed. "Usually God would do something to give a person a clue. Even Reno can't just go driving down there to bring her and the baby back here. He doesn't have the poor girl's address."

Reno reached up to make sure the pocket on his shirt wasn't on fire. Keeping quiet wasn't exactly a lie, but he didn't want to deceive anyone. "Well, even supposing I did have an address for her, people in Los Angeles move around all the time. How long would an address be good, anyway?"

Jacob frowned as he pointed to the letter Reno still held. "Come to think of it, I bet that attorney would have her current address. Sounds like he's keeping a close eye on her."

Mrs. Hargrove nodded. "It's settled, then. Someone will have to go see if Chrissy wants to come here."

"I'll go," Lester volunteered from where he stood counting nails to put into a brown paper bag.

Reno looked at Lester suspiciously. The man had an eagerness about him that Reno didn't trust. "It's a long way down to Los Angeles."

Lester grinned. "Yeah, but it's a long way back, too. If she says she'll come back here, I figure it'll give me time to court her."

"What? She's half your age," Reno said. "You can't date her."

"She's single." Lester looked surprised. "I'm single. What's your problem? She's not that much younger than your sister, and you didn't object to me dating Nicki. Besides, some women like older men."

"No, Reno's right," Mrs. Hargrove said. "We can't be sending some man down there who's going to make her nervous. We need to send someone safe. Like Reno. He wouldn't ask her out. Why, he's almost family, now that I think of it."

"Almost family—" Reno choked.

"She's Garrett's cousin," Mrs. Hargrove explained patiently. "Garrett is married to your sister. That means Chrissy is almost your cousin."

Almost cousins. Reno groaned. It wasn't fair. Family was the cornerstone of the Redfern Ranch and it had been for generations. Mrs. Hargrove knew he'd never refuse to help someone who could claim to be family. If he did, he'd be breaking one of those family rules that the Redferns had held on to since the turn of the past century.

Reno gritted his teeth. Usually he was proud and grateful to be part of a family that had lived on the same land for so long. But sometimes, like today, the rules of the family were not ones he wanted to keep.

"And she's got that poor little boy with only half of his rightful parents," Mrs. Hargrove continued, as though she were just chatting.

This time Reno did groan aloud. He had a weakness for babies who didn't have a full set of parents. This wasn't a family rule; it was all his own.

"All right, I'll go," Reno said before his good sense kicked in.

"What about those calves of yours?" Lester asked. "With your sister and that new husband of hers gone, there won't be anyone there to feed them."

"Oh." Reno had forgotten about the calves.

Usually when a set of twin calves was born, one of the two was a runt that was visibly smaller and weaker than the other calf. The mother would often ignore the runt and feed only the stronger calf. The Redfern Ranch had a bumper crop of twins this year, and it took Reno four or five hours a day just to keep the runts fed.

Some ranchers figured the runts were too much trouble to keep alive and left them to live or die as nature saw fit. But Reno didn't agree with nature on this one. He always brought the runts into the barn and fed them a special formula from a bucket he'd made that had an agricultural nipple so the calves could nurse easily.

Keeping those calves healthy was one of the most satisfying things he did as a rancher, and he'd long ago realized that he identified with the poor motherless things. He couldn't leave them. They'd die without regular feeding.

"I can see to them," Mrs. Hargrove said. "Do me good to get out on a farm again."

"There's no need. I can feed them," Lester said reluctantly. "If I'm not the one that goes to get Chrissy, I can do that much. That's what neighbors are for—especially when it's too wet to plow. Besides, it'll give Reno a chance to tell Chrissy what a good neighbor I've been."

Reno forced his lips into a smile. "You're the best."

"Good." Mrs. Hargrove nodded as if it was settled. "Then Reno can bring Chrissy back."

"She might not want to come." Reno felt he should remind everyone of that fact. He certainly didn't intend to give Chrissy a sales pitch. He would make the offer to satisfy Mrs. Hargrove, but he didn't expect Chrissy to actually agree to it. "Los Angeles is her home."

"Oh, you'll convince her." Mrs. Hargrove smiled. "You could always get the other kids to do whatever you wanted."

"That was in the first grade."

Mrs. Hargrove nodded. "A boy never loses that kind of charm."

Reno grunted. He felt about as charming as the mud on his feet.

Mrs. Hargrove's smile wavered and she looked a little uncertain. "Well, at least you will be sincere. And tell her we have free sundaes at the café on Friday nights."

Reno doubted there was a woman anywhere who would move across three states just to get a free sundae. He turned to leave the store. He'd go back to the ranch and show Lester where the milk buckets were. "I'll be on my way in a couple of hours."

"Good." Mrs. Hargrove nodded and then cleared

her throat. Her face went pink and she patted at her hair again. "You know, Reno, it's none of my business if you and Chrissy—you know—if you're the baby's father. I just want you to know that even if you and Chrissy got off on the wrong foot, God can still make a good life for the two of you if you let Him."

Reno pushed his cap down on his head. He didn't need to look around to know that every man in the hardware store was staring at the floor. They were all used to talking about calves being born and cows artificially inseminated. They weren't a delicate group. But none of them was comfortable talking about any of those activities with Mrs. Hargrove. He decided to spare everyone further speculation about his love life. "I'll call when I get down to Los Angeles. My pickup should make it in three days."

"Your pickup?" Mrs. Hargrove frowned. "You can't take your pickup. You need a back seat with seat belts for the baby's car seat. You'll have to borrow my car."

Mrs. Hargrove drove a 1971 Dodge compact the color of old mustard. It smelled of foot powder and wouldn't go faster than fifty miles an hour. The junk dealer in Miles City had given up offering Mrs. Hargrove cash for the car and grumbled he'd have to charge her a tow fee when she finally came to her senses and gave up on the old thing. Still, the car never refused to start, not even in thirty-below weather, and that was more than some of the newer cars did.

"I could rent a car," Reno said as his mind began to calculate the cost. Three days down and three days back. It was the price of the feed supplements he was giving those runt calves. Some years that would be fine. But this year money was tight.

"Don't be foolish. My car's sound as a tank. It'll get you there and back."

Reno frowned. If he had any lingering hopes that Chrissy would surprise him and want to move back to Dry Creek, Mrs. Hargrove's car would remind him how unlikely those hopes were. A stylish woman like Chrissy wouldn't go to her own funeral in Mrs. Hargrove's car. She certainly wouldn't pack up her belongings and ride across three states in it. "I'll take it. Thanks."

"Tell Chrissy she's in my prayers," Mrs. Hargrove said.

Reno nodded as he walked to the door. "I'll do that—if I get a chance."

He doubted he would be given a chance. Chrissy had not seemed drawn to the church when she was here last. He was pretty sure prayers would fall into the same category as mustard-colored cars when it came to women like Chrissy.

"I know she's never gone to church much," Mrs. Hargrove continued. "But now that she's a mother she might want to—be sure and tell her there's a good Sunday school program for the little one."

Reno had a sudden vision of Chrissy sitting beside him in a Dry Creek church pew and it made his mouth dry up with the shock of it. He shook his head to clear his mind. He didn't need something like that vision rattling around in his head.

The church in Dry Creek was a place of peace for him. After his mother visited the town last fall and Reno had started the process of forgiving her, he had been drawn to the church he'd last attended as a child.

Reno had never really stopped believing in God during those years when he didn't go to church. He'd just stayed home to keep his father from drinking. For some reason, his father had insisted Nicki attend church, but he'd given Reno a choice. When he'd realized his father was drinking when he was alone at the ranch, Reno had found reasons to stay home on Sunday.

Until now he hadn't thought about what it would feel like to sit in church with a wife beside him. Reno had a sudden empathy for the loneliness his father must have faced on those Sundays long ago after his wife left.

Reno cleared his throat. He was as bad as Mrs.

Hargrove. He needed to keep reality in mind. "She might decide not to come."

"Use your charm."

Reno grunted as he opened the door and stepped back out into the cold air. Fortunately he didn't need to worry about charm when it came to Chrissy. He wasn't likely to be given the chance to talk to her long enough to be charming. All he hoped was that he had enough time to give the invitation from Mrs. Hargrove so that he could honestly tell everyone he'd asked the question. That's all Mrs. Hargrove and God could expect.

Chapter Three

Chrissy looked out the big windows of Pete's Diner to the busy street outside. Something was making her edgy today, and not even the steady pace of orders from Pete's regulars could keep her mind focused. It must be because she'd seen that funny cap this morning. The man wearing the cap had told her he was from North Dakota. She smiled, because it was the same kind of cap that Reno wore in Dry Creek, Montana.

Whatever possessed her to remember that cap she didn't know. She also didn't know why the cap was so appealing. She'd always thought a Stetson on the head of a cowboy was the only kind of hat that would make a woman's heart race; but that farmer's cap that Reno had worn made her question all she knew about men's headwear.

If someone had told her she'd fall for a man in a cap, she would have said they were crazy. Especially a forest-green cap that advertised a yellow tractor, of all things!

But the cap sat on Reno's head, and that made all the difference. Reno had the chiseled bone structure of a Greek statue and the smooth grace of a man who was used to working outdoors. He wasn't just tanned, he was bronzed. He didn't need a cap to make him look good. *He* made the *cap* look good.

Chrissy caught her reflection in the small mirror the other waitresses kept by the kitchen door. She wished she could say the same for herself. These days she didn't make anything look good. She wondered if Reno would even recognize her if he saw her again.

Reno had known her when she still glimmered with her carefully applied Vegas look. Back then, she'd worried about whether her nail polish matched the dress she was wearing that night. She had regular manicures and pedicures and facials. She worried about the bristles in the brush she used to apply just the right shade of blush to just the right area on her cheekbones.

She always looked as much like a fashion model as an ordinary woman could.

At Pete's Diner, she'd stopped wearing blush. The heat from the kitchen gave her cheeks more than enough color. As for nail polish, she'd given up worrying about what color would even go with the fluorescent-orange uniforms Pete insisted his waitresses wear, and so she left her nails unpolished. Instead of a facial, she was lucky to get a good session of soap and water before Justin woke up.

Now she used lip balm instead of lipstick and kept her hair pulled back. In short, she was a fashion disaster and couldn't muster up enough energy to even care much about the fact.

She'd actually debated dyeing her hair to match her natural color and letting it grow back brown just because it would be so much easier to take care of that way.

Funny how having a baby can change what is important, Chrissy thought as she picked up a salad order for table number eleven. She'd applied for the job at Pete's because it was close to her mother's house and she could use her breaks to walk home to nurse Justin. She hadn't even cringed at the neon-orange uniforms. She'd have worn a chicken suit if it meant she'd be close to her baby.

Besides, she'd never liked the flash of Vegas all that much. Her whole time in Las Vegas had been spent trying to be the woman Jared wanted her to be. Not that Chrissy blamed Jared. She knew a man liked to have a glamorous woman on his arm, and she had been determined to please Jared. She'd never been a natural beauty, so she knew she had to work at looking good. She'd spent hours at cosmetic counters talking about the latest eye shadows and lip liners.

Now she didn't have time to do what it took to be fashionable. It was enough if her slip didn't show. The important people in her life—her baby and her mother—cared more about her smile than her makeup, anyway.

Chrissy's mother had been more supportive throughout Chrissy's pregnancy than Chrissy had dared to hope. Chrissy knew from the moment she knew she was pregnant that telling her mother about the baby would be harder than telling Jared.

Chrissy had been a problem to her mother since the day Chrissy was conceived. She was in the first grade when she first heard the word *illegitimate*. She couldn't even pronounce the word, and she had no idea what it meant. When she asked her mother about it, her mother had told her it meant Chrissy was a special gift from God and that she shouldn't worry about that word.

The next month her mother had decided they should move.

Until Chrissy was thirteen, she and her mother had moved almost every year. It was small town to small town to small town. In each town her mother talked about going to the church there, but they never did. Chrissy didn't know how old she was when she sensed her mother was actually afraid of churches.

Finally her mother decided they'd move back to the Los Angeles area. Big cities, her mother told her, were more forgiving of unmarried mothers on welfare.

In Los Angeles her mother found the courage to go to a church she'd gone to many years ago, and she was happy. She repeatedly invited Chrissy to come to church with her.

Chrissy had refused. She'd finally figured out that her mother had been afraid of churches because of the way people had treated her when she was pregnant with Chrissy. Her mother might be ready to forgive church people, but Chrissy wasn't.

The closest she'd been to a church recently was the time she'd walked up the steps of the church in Dry Creek looking for a place to sit while she waited for the café to open one morning.

Ah, Dry Creek.

Dry Creek had occupied her mind since she'd left there last fall. She supposed it was unfair to fantasize that the place was her real home, but she did nonetheless.

For some reason, Pete's Diner had reminded her of Dry Creek. With its worn vinyl booths and fluorescent lights, it looked as solid as the café in Dry Creek. The diner sat squarely between two retirement homes and it had a loyal group of customers. Business here would never be bustling, but it was steady.

When she got the job, Chrissy felt she'd finally landed on her feet. Her mother could stop worrying about her. Chrissy didn't need to ask to know the worries that were going through her mother's mind. Her mother didn't want her to be a welfare mother. She didn't want Chrissy to have to accept the pity of others because she needed their charity. So the job at Pete's was important. It showed she could take care of herself and Justin.

And then two minutes ago, one of the other waitresses had told Chrissy that Pete wanted to see her in his office.

Don't think it's bad news, Chrissy told herself as she knocked on the door outside the office. Just because she'd been caught in the rush of layoffs at other restaurants lately, it was no reason to panic. There had to be a dozen reasons that Pete might want to talk to her. Maybe the fry cook had told him it had been her idea to offer a shaker of salt substitute on the table along with the regular salt and pepper.

"Come in."

Pete was probably grateful that she was concerned about his customers' health, Chrissy told herself as she took a deep breath.

"Please sit," Pete said as he looked up from some

papers. Pete had been a semipro football player before he bought the diner thirty years ago and, even with the gray hairs on his balding head, Chrissy thought he still looked as if he would be more comfortable on a football field than behind a desk.

"You wanted to see me?" Chrissy sat down on the folding chair opposite Pete's desk.

Pete nodded and then swallowed. He opened his mouth and then closed it again.

"Is it about the salt substitute?" Chrissy asked. She couldn't stand the silence. Please, let it be the salt substitute. "I haven't heard any customers complain. Except for Mr. Jenkins. But he thought it was sugar and put it in his tea."

"Oh, yes, the salt substitute." Pete looked relieved. "It's never too early to pay attention to good health. I should have thought of offering a salt substitute years ago. Someone mentioned it to the dietitian at the retirement home down the street, and she recommended us to some of the residents who'd never been here before."

"So business is good." Chrissy was starting to feel better.

"It's never been better. That's sort of what I wanted to talk to you about. You see, I—"

Chrissy's cell phone chose this moment to ring. She told herself to ignore it. But she'd gotten the phone only so that Mrs. Velarde could call her. Mrs.

Velarde lived across the street from Chrissy's mother and was baby-sitting little Justin temporarily. Chrissy was having as much trouble keeping baby-sitters as she was keeping jobs. She knew the call was about Justin.

"Excuse me," Chrissy said finally as she reached around to unclip the phone from her belt. "I need to get this."

She turned her shoulder slightly and said a low hello into the cell phone.

"There's a man," Mrs. Velarde almost shrieked into the cell phone. "You told me to watch out for a man prowling around, and he's here!"

"Jared's there?" Chrissy was shocked. When she had warned Mrs. Velarde to watch out for Jared, she had never expected him to make the drive down from Las Vegas to see Justin. The bond that had held her and Jared together in high school was no longer even a thread.

Jared had learned that money could buy friends since he'd gotten access to his trust fund, and he no longer needed Chrissy. With his new friends, his life had unraveled even further in the months since Chrissy had left him. He'd told her he was glad she was gone, because now he could date women who really knew how to party.

Chrissy had told him that he was a fool and she was sorry he was the father of her baby.

No matter how isolated Chrissy had felt in high school, she had never turned to the drug crowd for friends. Jared was using drugs, and he had made it very clear he wasn't interested in being a husband and or a father.

But as much as Jared wanted to avoid the baby, Jared's mother was adamant in her desire to know more about Justin. She had given up on Jared ever entering the family business, but she obviously had hopes she could start over and train a baby to be a more obedient heir. So far Jared had refused to tell his mother that Justin was his son, but if Mrs. Bard offered Jared enough money, he might decide to confirm what his mother already suspected and help her try to claim custody of Justin. "You're sure it's him?"

"Well, I don't know what Jared looks like, but there's a man parked in front of my house who keeps looking over at your house. He even went up and rang the bell once, but no one answered, of course, with you and your mom both at work."

"You're sure he isn't a deliveryman or some-thing?"

"There's no uniform. Besides, he's young and good-looking. No one else comes to your house who is young and good-looking."

"I guess it could be Jared. Or someone else his mother has hired."

Mrs. Bard made Chrissy nervous. Mrs. Velarde had already told her that a private investigator had been asking questions about Chrissy in the neighborhood. It had to be someone working for Jared's mother.

"You want me to call the police?" Mrs. Velarde asked.

"He hasn't done anything yet, has he?"

"He sits out there."

"Does he look like someone on drugs?"

"No. He just sits."

"That's probably not Jared, then. Maybe he's a salesman and will go away in a minute or two. Just keep Justin inside until I get home."

Mrs. Velarde grunted. "I'll keep my baseball bat by the door, too. Nobody comes to see our Justin without his mama here."

"Call if you need me." Chrissy said goodbye and flipped her cell phone shut before she saw the concerned frown on Pete's face.

"Trouble at home?" Pete asked.

Chrissy didn't bother to deny it. He knew that much already. And the trouble would only get worse. Mrs. Velarde was scheduled to leave for Florida next week to move in with her daughter, and so far Chrissy had not found someone else to take care of Justin while she worked.

"My neighbor who is watching Justin is worried.

I may need to leave for a few minutes and go home if she calls again."

"You're welcome to use the delivery car to drive home. Take as much time as you need." Pete rubbed his hands over his head. "I've never been able to offer the best salaries in the business, but I've always tried to be flexible."

"I appreciate that."

"I've always looked at the staff as family, which is why it's so hard to—"

Chrissy wanted to put her hands over her ears. She didn't want to hear what was coming next. "But business has been good."

"Business has never been better," Pete agreed. "And your idea with the salt substitute is one of the reasons."

Chrissy decided she didn't need her hands over her ears after all. Maybe the reason Pete had called her into his office was to thank her for the suggestion.

"It was a simple idea," Chrissy said.

Pete nodded. "But it has made all the difference. That's why I wanted you to be the first to know the news."

Chrissy felt a sudden unease. A thank-you would be nice, but it wasn't actually news. "Are we changing the menu again?"

Pete chuckled. "I don't think I'd live long enough to do that even if I weren't moving to Arizona."

"*What?*"

Pete winced. "I didn't mean to just blurt it out like that. I never was any good at things like this. Actually, I wanted to thank you. The extra business we have because of the salt substitute must be what finally made the diner look attractive enough to find a buyer. A real estate agent called me last week."

"I see."

"The offer is just too good to turn down."

"Will the new owner keep the place a diner?"

"They're thinking along the lines of a tea shop. Crumpets. Scones. That kind of thing."

"I see."

"They've promised they'll have a job for every one of my staff. I wouldn't sell otherwise."

Chrissy started to breathe again. She'd already lost two waitress jobs because business was bad; she didn't want to lose another because business was good. "Do the others know?"

"I'm going to tell them when the shift changes at three this afternoon. That way, everyone will be here."

Chrissy heard a bell in the kitchen. "That must be my last order. I better get out there."

Pete nodded.

For the next hour Chrissy was too busy with hamburgers and chicken strips to worry. And then she got a second call from Mrs. Velarde.

"I've got to go," she said to Pete as she walked to the door of the diner.

He nodded and tossed her a set of keys. "Take the delivery car."

Reno decided everything he had ever heard about crime in Los Angeles was true. Here he was in broad daylight, parked in a residential area, and it sounded as if a dozen police sirens were all going off at once. It had been enough to wake him up from his nap, and he was tired enough to sleep through an earth-quake.

Tonight he'd check in to a hotel by the ocean and get a good night's sleep before he left to go back. He'd pulled into Los Angeles early this morning and had gone directly to the office of Joseph Price, Esquire. Reno didn't know why he'd decided to visit the lawyer. Maybe he just wanted to be sure Chrissy hadn't already accepted the offer before he went to the trouble of trying to find her with the address he had.

He hadn't been in the lawyer's office five minutes before Reno regretted stopping. Chrissy was no match for the man, and Reno would have been happier not knowing that fact.

Reno's distrust of the man only deepened when the lawyer talked about the educational opportu-nities Mrs. Bard was hoping to give Chrissy's baby.

"She's prepared to pay the costs for a private education, from military boarding school to graduate school at Princeton or Yale—she's even got her eye on some kind of exclusive kindergarten for the gifted in Boston," the attorney said as he offered Reno coffee in a china cup.

"No, thanks," Reno said. "I thought Mrs. Bard lived in Los Angeles. Is she moving to Boston?"

"She doesn't need to move to Boston." The attorney set the cup of coffee on his own desk. "Fortunately, the school is a live-in situation. Twenty-four-hour care and mental stimulation. The baby will grow up to be a genius."

Reno grunted. "Even a genius needs a home."

The attorney took a sip of coffee. "The Bards own a house in San Marino and another in Vail. The boy won't lack for a place to visit during his school breaks. And there'll be adequate supervisory care."

Reno didn't like the sound of this. What kind of grandmother was this woman? "It takes more than a house to make a home. Isn't Mrs. Bard going to bake him cookies?"

The lawyer laughed. "Mrs. Bard doesn't bake anything. She's a very busy woman."

"Too busy for a little boy?"

"Don't worry. Mrs. Bard is hoping to make the boy her heir. That should tell you how she feels. Her only concern is that the baby is Jared's son. That's why she hired our firm. She's paying us a handsome bonus if the baby is Jared's son, so of course, we're hoping it is."

The lawyer started to lift the cup again.

"How much of a bonus?" Reno asked.

The attorney stopped with his cup halfway up in the air and looked at Reno. "You certainly ask a lot of questions. Why are you so worried about this baby, if you've never even seen him?"

Reno smiled slightly. He could see the lawyer was beginning to think that Reno might really be the father of Chrissy's baby. It was the first time in the conversation that the question had even seemed to arise. "Let's just say I want to make sure everyone is happy."

The lawyer studied the cup he held in his hand. "I see. Well, I can assure you Mrs. Bard will want to share her happiness with everyone if we prove to her the baby is Jared's son. So if she's happy, we're happy. Of course—" he paused "—if someone else had reason to believe he could be the baby's father, we would want to make him happy, too."

"You'd pay me off?"

The lawyer shrugged. "I didn't say that, now, did I? I'm just pointing out that there's no way to really prove who the father is without a blood test, and Miss Hamilton refuses to agree to that. I'm afraid Chrissy is both stubborn and foolish. She refused to list Jared on the birth certificate or even to say he's the father, so she can't press for child support. At her age, with only a high school education, she'll never be able to support the baby herself, not working as a waitress like she does."

"But—" Reno started to protest.

The lawyer waved his hand. "Oh, I have to admit she's a gutsy young woman. She bounced back real fast when she lost her last two jobs. But how much longer can she move from job to job? It might be okay now that she's living in her mother's house, but how long will that last? She won't find a decent place to rent in Los Angeles on her salary. And that's just now. She'll certainly never be able to afford private schools and college. We're really doing her a favor to help her recognize that the baby is better off with Mrs. Bard. It'll save Miss Hamilton years of hard work and heartache. Mrs. Bard is even willing to pay her enough so that she can go to college herself and make something of her life."

"She *has* made something of her life." Reno stood up to leave. "She has the baby to prove it."

Reno left the lawyer's office with a sour taste in his mouth and drove to the west side of Los Angeles. The lawyer had at least confirmed Chrissy's current address. After Reno knocked at the house's door and no one answered, he went back to the car to wait. It was hard to get comfortable in the compact space of

Mrs. Hargrove's car, but he managed. His waiting had turned to napping when the sirens penetrated his sleep.

Reno saw the woman open her door and wave a baseball bat at him at the same time that the police cars came around all the street corners and headed straight for him.

Reno woke up all the way. People in Los Angeles sure knew how to get a man's attention.

"Come out of your car with your hands up," the loudspeaker on top of one police car blared out as the cars pulled to a halt and turned off their sirens.

Reno counted four police cars blocking him in.

Reno hadn't trained a half-wolf dog without learning when to move easy. He put his hands up in plain view and nudged the car door open with his elbow. He couldn't even guess what law he'd broken. Maybe people didn't park in front of houses in Los Angeles, especially not in rusted-out cars with red plastic balls on their antennas. Mrs. Hargrove had put the red ball on the antenna one winter when the snow was particularly high, and she hadn't bothered to take it off.

"I can move the car if you want," Reno called out as he shouldered the door open and stepped out. "And that red ball, it's just a plastic thing from some gas station."

"Keep your hands where we can see them," the

voice on the loudspeaker demanded. Apparently the police in Los Angeles took their parking tickets seriously.

Chrissy's heart stopped when she saw the police cars parked in front of her place. Four cars! Whoever was in that car must have tried to take Justin. That was the only thing that would make them send four cars. She knew Mrs. Bard had hired an attorney to try to take Justin away from her, and Chrissy had begun to wonder if Jared's mother would try kidnapping the baby if she got frustrated enough.

Chrissy knew Mrs. Bard could offer her baby all of the advantages money could buy. Sometimes Chrissy felt selfish for even refusing to consider the woman's offer—until she remembered that Jared had had those same advantages, and look how unhappy his childhood had been.

Chrissy pulled her car up behind a police car and got out to rap on its window.

"What's happening?" she asked.

The policeman inside looked up from the report he was writing and rolled down the window. "What do you think you're doing? Keep your head down. He could be armed. Get back to your car and wait."

Chrissy saw the police put handcuffs on some man standing beside an old car. They were all on Mrs. Velarde's lawn. Chrissy could see only the

back of the man the police had cuffed. It wasn't
Jared, but the man did look familiar. Mrs. Bard must
have hired one of Jared's friends.

"I'm not going back. My son's inside that house."
Chrissy pointed to the house where Mrs. Velarde
lived. Chrissy thought she could hear Justin's cry
from here. She was glad to see that the baby-sitter
had drawn the drapes to the house.

As Chrissy checked the house she saw Mrs.
Velarde standing on the porch with the baseball bat
in her hand. She had a housedress on, and her hair
was in curlers.

"Go back inside!" Chrissy shouted.

Even though she was watching Mrs. Velarde on
the porch, Chrissy also saw the man who was being
handcuffed turn at the sound of her shout and look
over at her. It was enough to make her eyes turn
from the sitter.

Oh, no! Chrissy looked at the man in astonishment. He had a cap on his head that hid his face from
the sun, but she didn't need to see his face to know
the man who stood there was the last man on earth
she wanted to see. Or, rather, it was the last man who
would want to see *her*.

She hadn't realized until she'd been seeing her
physician for a while that spurts of idiotic tears were
perfectly normal for a pregnant woman. She'd never
cried before in her life, but when she was pregnant,

she'd cried over everything, even dinner invitations from handsome men that she couldn't accept.

"What's he doing here?" Chrissy whispered.

"Dealing drugs, we think," the policeman answered from inside the car. "Or maybe just using them. We don't know."

"Reno Redfern?"

The policeman nodded. "That's what he said his name is. I'm running his plates now to check it out. Do you know him?"

Ten minutes later Chrissy poured Reno a cup of coffee in Mrs. Velarde's kitchen.

"I'm so sorry," the baby-sitter repeated as she wiped her hands on her apron. There were open cardboard boxes sitting in the kitchen with pots and pans in them.

"It's my fault," Chrissy said. "If I hadn't been so paranoid about Jared showing up, I wouldn't have kept asking Mrs. Velarde to keep an eye out for a man on drugs."

Chrissy tried to ignore the boxes. What was she going to do with Justin when Mrs. Velarde moved to Florida?

"Well, I guess most people don't park in front of your house and then go to sleep," Reno offered.

"I thought you were out on some overdose," Mrs. Velarde admitted as she drew a circle around her head with her finger to signify "crazy."

Reno took another gulp of his coffee. "No harm done. I'm glad you're suspicious of strange men hanging around." He turned to Chrissy. "I don't know if you're aware that Jared's mother has hired a lawyer to investigate you."

Chrissy nodded miserably. "Don't tell me she sent someone to Dry Creek, too."

Dry Creek was the one place that she'd felt was beyond Mrs. Bard's reach. Not a day had gone by since Chrissy left Dry Creek that she hadn't thought about that little town. She'd go to sleep at night with the picture of it in her mind. She'd even made up a little lullaby about the town that she sang to Justin.

Chrissy looked up from her hands. "I'm a good mother, you know. I might be young, but I love my son and we're going to do just fine."

Chrissy knew she'd never give up her rights to Justin. She didn't know much about rashes and formulas. She didn't make much money, but she'd find a way to avoid welfare. Maybe someday she could save enough to buy a small restaurant. She'd be a respectable member of the community. Justin wouldn't regret that she hadn't given him to his grandmother to raise. Besides, she knew how to make Justin smile, and she intended to devote her life to seeing that he was happy.

Reno nodded. As it turned out, he hadn't needed to worry about what to say to Chrissy when he met her. The police had sort of taken care of that. But he couldn't seem to get the conversation into position so he could ask her about moving to Dry Creek.

"It sure looks like you have everything under control." Reno nodded his head in the direction of Mrs. Velarde. "You've got someone to take care of Justin if you want to go out to dinner after work—" Reno swallowed. Now, why had he mentioned dinner? That had nothing to do with moving to Dry Creek.

"Work!" Chrissy set down her glass of water and looked at Reno. "I've got to run. But I'll be back— my shift ends in two hours. Can you stay till then?"

Reno nodded. He'd driven over a thousand miles. He needed to ask the question. "I could even take you out to dinner when you get back."

Reno saw the surprise in Chrissy's eyes. He couldn't tell if it was a good surprise or a bad surprise.

"Oh, there is no need to eat in a strange place," Mrs. Velarde offered. "I'm making meatball soup."

Chrissy left Mrs. Velarde's kitchen before the tears could start. Reno had asked her to dinner again. Of course, this time it might not be a date as much as it was a way for him to find something to eat in a strange city, but it still made her want to cry. She wondered why that was. The doctor hadn't said the tendency to tears would continue after Justin was born.

Chapter Four

When Chrissy got home, Mrs. Velarde announced that the soup was not enough for dinner. "Better you should go out to eat with Reno. A nice man like him, he needs a full meal. Maybe some fish. I'll watch the baby until your mother gets home."

Chrissy didn't like to rely on her mother for child care. Her mother had made enough sacrifices all her life for Chrissy.

"Mom's working late tonight," Chrissy finally said. "Some last-minute meeting. I should take Justin with us."

"Nonsense." Mrs. Velarde shooed her out of the kitchen and into the living room, where Reno stood holding Justin. "The baby will be more comfortable here. Mr. Reno—he has been so kind, playing with the little one and cutting the onions for the soup so

I don't cry the onion tears. And me—I almost had him arrested. Now he must eat."

Mrs. Velarde stopped to beam up at Reno.

"But I'm not even dressed for dinner." Chrissy looked down at the orange uniform she still wore. Pete had the eye of a football player, and he believed a uniform should be seen from a distance. The orange dress was obviously not something to wear on a date—if Reno was in fact asking her out on a date, and not just looking for someone to guide him to a good restaurant.

"You look fine," Reno said as he handed Justin to Mrs. Velarde. "I hear there's a great seafood place at the end of Mullen Drive. Matt's Galley. Mrs. Velarde said it's a favorite of yours."

Chrissy knew enough about men to know that they would at least look at a woman before saying she looked fine if they were heading out on a date. Well, she supposed that was her clue. This wasn't a date. They were just two people who were hungry for seafood.

"How was work today?" Reno asked.

Chrissy noticed the candle at the table cast shadows on Reno's face, but it did nothing to dim the startling blue of his eyes.

"They're going to turn the diner into a tea shop." Pete's announcement had been hard for most of the staff. Some of the waitresses had worked for Pete for ten years or more. "But Pete assures us we'll all have jobs with the new owners."

Chrissy found it hard to concentrate on talking about her job.

She wondered if Reno could be any better looking. Back in Dry Creek when she'd been out at the ranch, Reno's good looks just sort of matched the scenery. The sky had stretched from east to west with nothing but the Big Sheep Mountains to stop it from reaching down to level ground. The ground itself had been golden with fall colors. Even the air had smelled rich with the promise of moisture. Reno's good looks had just blended into the countryside, and no one seemed to particularly notice them any more than they noticed the sky or the mountains.

But here…Chrissy knew it was unusual for three different waitresses to ask if they needed more water within the space of five minutes. It was clear that Reno was getting plenty of notice. Not that he seemed to be paying any attention. Chrissy was glad he wasn't, even if this *wasn't* a date.

The waitresses at Matt's Galley wore snappy shorts and black nylons, which made Chrissy feel even more dowdy in her orange dress. The dress didn't even fit properly, since it was a size too big. She'd bought the uniform secondhand from one of the other waitresses rather than buy a new one of her own. Tonight she wished she'd spent the extra twenty dollars.

Reno frowned. "Mrs. Velarde told me you've lost a lot of jobs—"

Chrissy flushed. "The restaurant business can be unpredictable." The two restaurants she'd worked for before Pete's had both gone out of business.

"All I meant was—well, when she told me that, I wondered if Mrs. Bard's attorney was behind it."

Chrissy was amazed that the thought hadn't occurred to her. "Would he do that?"

Could he do that? Chrissy asked herself. The first restaurant had closed after they lost most of their business to a sandwich truck that parked outside their doors and practically gave away gourmet sandwiches to anyone who wanted one.

The next restaurant had been closed when someone left a lit candle on a table near the stack of folded napkins.

"But one of the restaurants burned down— wouldn't he lose his law license doing things like that?" Chrissy protested. "I've never met the man, but he can't be that foolish."

"I *have* met the man," Reno said, "and I think he'll do whatever he can to collect the bonus Mrs. Bard is offering. I have the impression the amount is very generous. And all he really has to do is convince you Justin is better off with Mrs. Bard than you. He's talking Princeton and Yale. And I'm sure he's not breaking any laws personally. He probably knows people who arrange things."

"Justin would never be better off with someone else." Chrissy grabbed hold of the only thing she could in the swirling thoughts around her. How could she compete with Princeton and Yale? She'd be lucky to afford community college. Still… "I'm his mother and I love him. I'll never let him go."

Reno hadn't realized he was holding his breath until he felt the tension slowly leave his body. He was glad Chrissy sounded so adamant. "Then you'll need to come back to Dry Creek with me."

"What?"

Reno frowned. He hadn't meant to say it so bluntly. He hadn't shown a glimmer of the charm Mrs. Hargrove thought he'd shown in first grade. "That is, if you want to come."

Chrissy was still looking startled.

"We have free sundaes in the café on Friday nights," Reno added. He swore the temperature inside the restaurant had just risen twenty degrees. "They have eleven kinds of toppings."

"No one has eleven kinds of toppings."

"They count the sprinkles and the nuts."

There was silence for a moment, and Reno began to think the impossible was happening.

"I don't accept charity," Chrissy said.

"It's only a sundae." Reno told himself he shouldn't be disappointed. He hadn't really expected her to agree.

"I mean coming back to Dry Creek. I don't need anyone's pity. Justin and I will do fine."

"What's pity got to do with anything? It's an invitation."

Reno remembered Mrs. Hargrove's advice to be charming, so he did his best. He relaxed his frown and smiled with all his heart.

Chrissy blinked. Reno should warn a woman before he smiled like that. His smile made her lose her place in her thoughts, and she had a feeling she needed to think. "From you? Is the invitation from you? Are you asking me to come?"

"Well, yes."

Chrissy felt as if she'd fallen down a rabbit hole. Reno was sitting there and asking her to—to what? Had he seen her looking at him and admiring his eyes? Was he suggesting she move back to Dry Creek so they could live together? Or was her mother right? Chrissy's mother had cautioned her that men would think she was more—what was the word her mother used— *available* because of Justin. Chrissy hadn't believed her. But here sat Reno, with a heart-stopping smile on his face, asking her to move back to Dry Creek.

"Babies are a lot of work. I don't have much time for fun."

"I know what you mean," Reno said. He looked relieved that she had changed the subject. "I have a dozen or so calves that eat up a storm. I don't get much done except feeding them this time of year— and I need to get to the plowing if the mud ever dries up."

"What I meant is, I don't go out like I did before Justin was born."

Reno wasn't looking as distressed as Chrissy thought he should be if he was getting her message.

"I'm not going to have sex again unless I'm married." Chrissy finally decided she might as well be blunt. "So there's no reason to ask me to come live with you."

"Oh," The surprise on Reno's face couldn't have been anything but genuine.

"Oh." Chrissy echoed. She wondered if she could hide under the table in her orange dress or if it was hopeless. "You weren't asking me that, were you?"

"I never thought you would—" Reno took a deep breath. "I mean, not that if I had thought you would—I'd—of course, I'd not—"

"Would you two like more water?" a cheerful blond waitress inquired as she stepped closer to the table.

Chrissy said, "Yes."

At the same time Reno said, "No."

The waitress glanced at Reno's face and hesitated. "I'll come back."

Chrissy didn't blame the waitress. She would have run away, too.

"I never would suggest that you come live with me in that way." Reno said the words slowly. Chrissy only had to look into his eyes to know he was sincere. "Of course, you probably know that I find you attractive, so it's not that I wouldn't want to—"

"Really?" Chrissy was feeling better already. So Reno found her attractive.

"I asked you out," Reno said indignantly. "You were the one who refused."

"I was pregnant."

"Pregnant women eat."

"So you thought I needed help and you decided to ask me to move to Dry Creek?"

Reno nodded.

"Well, I still don't need your charity." Chrissy crossed her arms. She'd already thought about moving back to Dry Creek, and she'd gone over in her mind any possible jobs. There were none that she could see.

"Who mentioned charity? I'm offering you help."

"I don't take handouts. I need a job to support myself and Justin."

"Mrs. Hargrove thought you could stay with her."

Chrissy blinked. "Mrs. Hargrove? Does she know about Justin?"

Reno nodded. "She's the one who started this idea."

"Mrs. Hargrove wants me to move there and stay with her?" Chrissy had liked Mrs. Hargrove when she met the older woman at Thanksgiving dinner at the Redfern Ranch. But Mrs. Hargrove was clearly a churchwoman, and Chrissy had always thought churchwomen looked down on unmarried mothers. She knew they had looked down on her mother years ago. "And she knows about Justin? Isn't she worried that I don't have a husband?"

"Not that she's mentioned."

"Why?" Chrissy crossed her arms. "Why would she want me to come stay with her when you and I both know she has to think I'm one of those sinners?"

Reno smiled. "Mrs. Hargrove teaches first-grade Sunday school. She thinks everyone is a sinner."

"Well, if she thinks that, then why—"

Reno interrupted her softly. "She also knows about forgiveness and grace. She knows life isn't always easy."

Chrissy relaxed her arms. Maybe there were people like Mrs. Hargrove who weren't set on judging her. "Well, if I had a job—"

"We'll worry about a job when we get there."

Chrissy's cell phone rang. She kept the phone clipped to her waitress uniform, so it was still in place. Chrissy reached down to unhook the phone, and she put it to her ear. "Hello?"

"There's a fire!" Mrs. Velarde said breathlessly. "I called the fire department, but it's still burning."

"Grab Justin and get out of the house!" Chrissy stood up from the table.

"Not my house," Mrs. Velarde said, and then she took a deep breath.

Chrissy relaxed. "Just stay inside, then, until the fire department gets there."

"It's your mother's house," Mrs. Velarde continued.

Chrissy turned to Reno.

Reno had already stood and laid three twenties on the table. "Let's go."

As Reno drove faster than he should down the street toward her mother's house Chrissy reminded herself that her mother was working late. *Please, let her be working late,* Chrissy added, and realized in surprise that it was the first time in her life that she could remember praying. It must be all this talking with Reno. She hoped Mrs. Hargrove's God was listening to her.

The sharp, hot smell of burning wood grew stronger as Reno drove the car to the fire truck parked in front of Chrissy's mother's house.

"Was anyone inside?" Chrissy called out to a fireman before Reno had pulled the car to a stop.

The fireman shook his head. "Didn't look like it."

Chrissy slumped against the car seat. "If she had been there, she could have died."

"They would have gotten her out."

"I need to go to Dry Creek with you," Chrissy said softly. "If he will set fire to my mother's house, he will do anything. My mother's not safe with me here, and neither is Justin."

"I'm sure they'd never hurt Justin."

Chrissy grimaced. "I know. All they want to do to him is take him away from me."

Chrissy turned at the sound of another car driving down their street much too fast. The car braked and her mother stepped out and started running toward the house. "Chrissy!"

"I'm over here, Mom," Chrissy called from the car window.

Then she stepped out of the car and into her mother's arms.

Reno watched Chrissy hug her mother. So Chrissy was coming back to Dry Creek with him. He wished it hadn't taken a fire to make her decide. It sure hadn't been his charm that had swayed her in the direction of Dry Creek. Still, he'd feel better knowing she and Justin would be where he could keep an eye on them. Strangers would be easy to spot in Dry Creek.

Reno remembered the interstate that ran past the Dry Creek exit and frowned. A car could pull into the town at night and no one would notice. Chrissy and Justin would be a lot safer at the Redfern Ranch than in Dry Creek. His dog, Hunter, would frighten off any trouble from the city. Maybe once he got Chrissy and Justin to Dry Creek he could mention the safety of the ranch.

Chapter Five

The smell of burned wood and rubber hung in the air as Chrissy put a box into the trunk of Mrs. Hargrove's car. The car was parked in the Velarde driveway, and Chrissy's mother was inside at the Velarde kitchen table. Most of what Chrissy owned had been burned in the fire, so Mrs. Velarde had given her a cardboard box to pack what was left. Quite a few of Justin's things were all right, because they had been with him at the Velarde house.

The only other things that Chrissy still owned for herself were several sequin-dresses from her days as a cocktail waitress in Las Vegas. She'd given the dresses to Mrs. Velarde to keep for the Salvation Army truck when it came by for donations. Now she'd need to wear them sometimes, even if it was only when she had her orange waitress uniform in the washing machine.

The small box fit into the trunk beside the spare tire. It wasn't much to start a life with, and Chrissy was glad Reno had sounded as if he felt she could find a job. If she had a job, she could buy some more clothes and a few toys for Justin.

Her mother had surprised Chrissy by urging her to move to Dry Creek.

"The Lord knows you're used to moving. I'd feel better knowing the two of you are safe," Chrissy's mother said as she looked over at Reno and smiled slightly. "Besides, I'll know you're with family there, and that makes me feel better."

Reno frowned. "We're not really related. Just by marriage. We're not cousins."

Chrissy's mother smiled more broadly. "Oh, I know that. I meant Garrett. He'll be there, won't he?"

"Oh, yeah, in a few days."

Chrissy's mother nodded. "Chrissy has always been fond of Garrett. Besides, I may be able to move up there, too, when I wrap things up here with the fire."

Chrissy had told the fire captain about her suspicions, and he had written everything down, even Mrs. Bard's full name and Jared's phone number. The captain said the fire looked as if it had started on the outside wall by the garage. There was nothing electrical around, and although they wouldn't know for sure until they did some testing, he thought the fire had been started with gasoline. Of course, he added, whoever set it was probably only intending to scare Chrissy and her mother and not actually burn the house down. If someone had been home, they would have smelled the smoke long before the house burned.

The streetlights made shadows on the asphalt, and Chrissy was glad Reno had agreed to leave tonight for Dry Creek. She got nervous every time a car drove down the street. Would that lawyer send someone to see if she was still there?

Once, a black sedan stopped at the end of the street, and she didn't relax until she heard the music being turned up loud. It was some old sixties music that she hadn't heard for a long time. She recognized some Beatles songs and a Carpenters song. Then she heard the Mrs. Robinson song. It was odd music for teenagers, but who else would turn the music up like that? The black sedan wasn't a kid car, but it might belong to one of their fathers.

Chrissy shook her head. She wasn't used to feeling spooked, and the more miles she put between herself and Los Angeles, the better she'd feel.

"You'll call Pete's and explain?" Chrissy reminded

her mother. Ordinarily, Chrissy wouldn't leave a job without giving notice, but she knew Pete would be relieved to have one less employee to worry about in the sale of the diner.

Chrissy's mother nodded. "And you call when you get to Dry Creek. I'll be staying with Mrs. Velarde for a few days."

It was past midnight before Chrissy strapped Justin into his infant seat and crawled into the back seat herself. "Let me know if you want me to drive."

"Maybe you can get some sleep." Reno came around the side of the car with a blanket and handed it to her.

"I'm happy to help drive." Chrissy hugged the blanket to her. It smelled of peppermint, and she couldn't wait to snuggle into its warmth. "You haven't had any sleep either."

"I had a nap this afternoon with Justin." Reno slid into the driver's seat and checked the mirrors. He frowned a minute and then opened the car door again. Standing outside, he twisted the red ball off the antenna. "This car is odd enough, but with that red thing sticking up like that, a blind man could follow us to Dry Creek."

Chrissy fell asleep before Reno got on Interstate 15. He noticed her stir at the first sound of Justin's crying at dawn. There was desert on both sides of the car and a string of cars behind them on the single-lane highway.

"Do you want to stop in Vegas? We're coming up on the city." Reno looked back at Chrissy and held his breath. It had occurred to him somewhere around Barstow that Chrissy might want to stop in Vegas and stay there with Jared or at least visit him and show him their baby. Reno knew she'd said she wasn't returning to Jared, but sometimes people didn't know what they wanted until it was in front of them.

"If you don't mind," Chrissy said sleepily. "Any gas station will do. I should nurse Justin."

Reno started to breathe again. "No problem."

The casinos of Vegas stood straight ahead on the road like giant cartoon buildings. In the gathering dawn they looked almost eerie with their flashing lights. Reno pulled into the next gas station that he saw also had a pay phone.

He'd decided to call Mrs. Hargrove so she could post a sign in the café asking for someone to work as her housekeeper. As proud as Chrissy was, she wouldn't accept a job that she thought was created just for her. A sign on the bulletin board in the café when she got there should convince her that Mrs. Hargrove's job was legitimate. Chrissy wouldn't need to know Reno was the one paying her salary.

Chrissy sat in the back seat of the car while Reno

made his phone call. She was glad he'd decided he had some things to do so that she could nurse Justin in private. She loved these moments with Justin, even though being this close to Las Vegas made her nervous. When Justin was satisfied, she rearranged her blouse and looked around.

Chrissy rolled down the car window and glanced at the other cars in the gas station. Was it her imagination, or could she hear the same songs that she'd heard when she packed up earlier to leave with Reno? Yes, there it was—the faint sound of the Mrs. Robinson song.

She looked around more closely. None of the cars at the pumps looked familiar. Besides, the music was probably from a CD, and there could be millions of copies of the song. She looked over the cars at the pump again. She didn't see a black sedan, and that's what had been in her neighborhood.

Chrissy was glad when she saw Reno walking toward the car. He'd gone into the minimart and was carrying a white bag and two cartons.

"I got us some milk and donuts." Reno slid the items through the open window and into Chrissy's waiting hands.

"Thanks. What do I owe you?"

"Don't worry about it."

"I can pay." Chrissy had about thirty dollars in her purse. Her mother was going to send the check from Pete that would cover the hours Chrissy had worked this week. "I might need to owe for the gas, but I can pay for the food as we go."

"You don't need to pay for the gas. I was coming this way anyway."

Chrissy couldn't think of any reason Reno would drive to Los Angeles. When she'd visited him on his ranch, he'd made a point of telling her that he never traveled.

"I don't take charity," Chrissy reminded him, reaching into her purse and pulling out two dollar bills. "Here."

"I'm not that poor." Reno frowned at her in the rearview mirror as he started the car. "I can pay for everything."

If Chrissy had been looking around instead of arguing with Reno, she would have noticed that the music she'd heard had gotten a little louder, and that a black sedan pulled out from the other side of the minimart before backing up so it was no longer in view.

"We'll split the cost of the gas," Chrissy finally said. "I'll pay you back when I get my check."

Reno grunted in response as he drove the car out of the gas station area.

"You never did say what brought you to Los Angeles," Chrissy said a few minutes later. Surely he hadn't driven that far just to give her a ride back to Dry Creek. Of course not. He hadn't even known she would want to move back there.

"I went to see the ocean."

"Oh, and did you like it?"

"I don't know yet."

"You mean you didn't stop and see it?"

Reno shrugged. "I'm young. I've got lots of years to go see the ocean."

"I wish I'd known that's why you came. I could have stayed in Los Angeles another day if you wanted to go to the beach."

"It's all right."

Chrissy shifted in the back seat. "It would have been fun to show you the ocean. We could have gone to the pier and ridden the old carousel."

"I bet Justin will like that in a few years."

Chrissy tried to ignore the picture forming in her mind of her and Reno and Justin going on a beach vacation. That was something that would never happen. He hadn't even said that. She knew Reno was being kind. But by the time Justin was old enough to ride a carousel, Reno would have grown tired of befriending a single mother. That was another lesson she had learned from her mother's past. The occasional man who had wanted to date her mother was usually not interested in being an instant father, and so he hadn't lasted long as a friend to her mother, either.

* * *

Chrissy could tell the difference in the air as soon as they drove into Montana. Justin was sleeping, and the inside of the car was peaceful. They came into the state on Interstate 15 and turned off on Interstate 90 at Butte to head east.

The farming area smelled fertile with rain and wild grass. Clouds gathered ahead of them when they passed the downtown area of Miles City and began the last miles leading to Dry Creek.

Chrissy felt her whole body relax as she watched the space around her. Now, why had she never noticed how little space there was in Los Angeles? Everywhere you looked in L.A. something stopped you from seeing very far. But here in Montana nothing stopped a person's gaze except for the Rocky Mountains to the northwest and the gentle slopes of the mountains to the east that she knew were called the Big Sheep Mountains.

"Are there any sheep?" Chrissy asked. "In the mountains."

"Not for years since the cattle took over," Reno replied as he made the turn off the interstate to go into Dry Creek.

Chrissy took a deep breath. She was really going back. She hoped Reno hadn't exaggerated the welcome she would receive. She kept pushing her nervousness to the back of her mind, since it was too late to turn back anyway. "Are there a lot of cattle in Dry Creek?"

"More cattle than people." He paused. "I hope that doesn't bother you."

"Bother me? Why would it bother me?"

"Some women might find Dry Creek lacking in excitement after life in the big city."

"Oh, look—" Chrissy pointed to the curve in the road. The gravel road widened a little at that point. Instead of snowbanks there was wild grass on the edge of the road, but Chrissy recognized the place anyway. "That's where we met."

She blushed. That hadn't come out right. "I mean the night when your truck broke down—"

"—and you gave me a ride." Reno finished the sentence for her as he slowed to a stop. "I remember. That was some night."

Chrissy remembered that night, too. If she hadn't been so angry, she never would have decided to drive her cousin's truck to Dry Creek, even though Garrett had left the keys with her and given her a couple of lessons on how to shift the gears on the sixteen-wheel truck. But the minute she'd discovered Jared with another woman—in the most "with someone" sense possible—she hadn't been able to stay in Las Vegas.

Her instincts had told her to go to Dry Creek to find her cousin, and that was all she'd wanted to do.

"When I was in trouble, I always looked for Garrett."

"He's a good man."

Chrissy wondered if Reno even knew that it wasn't Garrett who had eased her pain on that trip. Reno had given her all the sympathy she needed, until by the time she left Dry Creek last fall, she'd realized she didn't need so much sympathy after all.

That night they met, she had managed to drive the truck fine on the interstate, but once Chrissy had turned off on the gravel road into Dry Creek, the truck started to cough. She'd never seen a night as dark as that cloudless, moonless one.

She'd been half spooked by the lights of a stalled truck ahead, but also half relieved. Maybe the other driver could tell her what to do about that coughing in the motor.

Chrissy had pulled the truck as far to the shoulder of the road as she could before she'd opened the door and climbed down from the cab. She'd left Vegas in such a hurry that she hadn't changed her dress or grabbed a coat. She was still wearing the short glittery white dress that Jared had picked out as her wedding dress.

The night air had been cold enough that her arms were covered with goose bumps. Her hair, bleached a champagne blond to please Jared and curled to sweep away from her face, had lost any sense of fashion around Salt Lake City and become so wind-blown that it looked as if she'd taken a fan to it instead of a curling iron.

At first Chrissy had thought the other truck was deserted and her heart sank. Then she'd seen the long denim-clad legs lying on the ground under the truck's engine. When the rest of Reno slowly crawled out from under the truck, she'd stopped in her tracks.

She had expected to meet a short, stocky farmer with thinning hair who would be shy and happy to help her. Instead, she'd seen a guy who should be plastered on every month of some hunk-of-the-year calendar, and her heart had sunk even further. Good-looking men, in her experience, really didn't even try to be as helpful as plain-looking ones.

Bringing herself back to the present, Chrissy glanced up at Reno in the mirror. She had to admit that he was confusing for a good-looking guy. He didn't act as if he was superior. And he had certainly been helpful to her. "I'm usually not as crazy as I was that night."

"I thought you were an angel," Reno said simply.

Chrissy glanced up again and saw Reno looking back at her. Since she was in the back seat to be close to Justin, she and Reno had carried on long conversations through the mirror for two days now.

Chrissy kind of liked the flirtatious way it made her feel.

"It was dark out."

Reno grinned. "And you sparkled with all that glitter on your dress. It was an honest mistake. I didn't think to check for wings."

"Not many angels pull up in a sixteen-wheeler truck."

"They do when your own truck is dead and it's cold enough outside to freeze your toes off." Reno paused. "I never thought of it, but I owe you for the ride that night."

"Of course you don't owe me," Chrissy said a little more sharply than she'd intended. Justin moved in his sleep and lifted his fist up to his mouth.

"You keep saying you owe me for this trip we're taking right now. If you owe me for *this* ride, then I owe you for *that* ride."

"It's not the same," Chrissy said softly.

"You might have saved my life. It was cold enough that night for a man to freeze to death. So I owe you for more than just the ride. I owe you for— preventive medical services."

"You would have found a way to keep warm."

Chrissy blushed. She suddenly remembered the way Reno had kept them warm that night. He'd wrapped blankets around them both individually and then wrapped himself and his blankets spoon-fashion around her on the small bed in the back of the cab of her cousin's truck. Chrissy couldn't ever remember feeling so warm and safe.

"Well, I'm willing to call it even between us if you are," Reno said. "I won't pay you for that trip and you won't pay me for this one."

"I can't pay you anyway until I get my check or find a job," Chrissy pointed out as she reached over to rub Justin's back. He was starting to wake up, and she liked him to know she was there. "So until then we can call it even."

Reno grunted as he turned the car's wheel to the right. "We'll call it even—period. I don't want you giving your wages to me."

As Reno made the wide turn, Chrissy saw the small town of Dry Creek come into view in the distance. "We're almost there."

The sky was partially cloudy, but there was no wind. She could tell because someone had white sheets hanging on a clothesline and they did not move. The snow flurries that had covered Dry Creek most of the time she was here last were gone. In their place were broad stretches of mud. Someone had put wooden planks around so people could walk without stepping in the puddles. She noticed two extra-wide planks in front of Mrs. Hargrove's house. No doubt someone had put them there so the older woman would be able to walk more easily.

The planks were an act of kindness that touched Chrissy. Dry Creek wasn't a dressed-up town like Las Vegas, but the people here cared about each other. Chrissy wondered if they could care about her and Justin, as well.

She didn't want the trip to end. She'd been comfortable thinking about going to Dry Creek, but she wasn't so sure she was comfortable actually arriving here.

Reno had entertained her with stories of what had been happening in Dry Creek since she'd been there last. She learned about his new calves and Mrs. Hargrove's arthritis that was sometimes so bad she couldn't peel potatoes. He told her about Lester dressing up as Elvis on April Fools' day and the Friday sundae night at the café.

He even told her about going to church again and what that had meant to him. He talked about forgiving his mother for leaving the family all those years ago. He told her he'd never quite understood about grace when he'd been a young boy, but now that he was a man he felt humbled by it. He wasn't so much forgiving his mother, he said, as trying to see her as she was, the way God might see her.

Chrissy didn't quite understand what he was saying, but she couldn't doubt his sincerity.

For the first time ever, Chrissy began to wonder if God could be real. She'd had people talk to her about God before, but never with the matter-of-fact directness Reno had. He talked of God as naturally as he would the sky or the mountains. Chrissy knew beyond a doubt that God was real for him, because Reno didn't make a big deal of trying to convince her of anything. Reno talked about God with the same warmth he used when he talked about Mrs. Hargrove or his sister, Nicki.

As Reno was telling her about the different things that were happening, he'd pass along greetings to her from various people in Dry Creek. He said that Elmer had asked him to tell her he'd buy her a cup of coffee when she came to town. And Linda from the café had asked Reno to tell her she was looking forward to Chrissy coming to town.

During all the days when they talked, Reno had not indicated anyone had a negative thought about her coming to the area. But Dry Creek was a small, conservative town. She was sure she'd find her share of turned shoulders and unwilling welcomes. It had been just eighteen years since her mother had had a bad experience in a small town because she was an unmarried mother, and eighteen years wasn't that long ago.

"I should comb my hair," Chrissy said. As she recalled, churchwomen were big on combed hair. "Or roll it into a bun or something."

"Your hair looks fine," Reno said.

"You're right. It's this orange dress they'll think is strange. No one wears an orange dress this bright. They'll think I'm nuts."

"They know about the fire. Nobody cares what you're wearing. Besides, Linda wears those kinds of colors all the time."

Chrissy reached for her purse anyway. A touch of light lipstick couldn't hurt.

"We're here." Reno slowed the car to a crawl. "We might as well get something to eat at the café."

Chrissy forced herself to look out the windows of the car and take a deep breath. The people of this town had been friendly to her when she'd been here last fall. If the fact that since then she'd had a baby without the benefit of marriage made any of them treat her any differently, then they were the losers, not her.

"There's not as many houses as I remember." Chrissy forced herself to concentrate. She could do this. "The town's smaller than I thought."

"Yeah," Reno said curtly. "One café. One store. Seventeen houses. Seventeen and a half, if you count the Andersons' basement. One church. That's it. No growth expected. Not even a post office."

Chrissy lifted her head. She'd taken on bigger challenges and done fine.

Reno watched Chrissy get ready to face Dry Creek and his heart sank. She looked as if she was getting ready to walk the plank. Was it really that bad to live in a small town like Dry Creek? "It's not like you'll need to be here forever."

"Huh?"

"I mean, the lawyer is going to give up sooner or later. Then you can move back to Las Vegas."

"Oh."

"Or L.A. if that's where you want to go," Reno said as he parked the car in front of the café and took the keys out of the ignition.

"But I don't have a job in L.A. anymore." Chrissy reached over to unbuckle Justin from his car seat.

Speaking of jobs reminded Reno that he hadn't called Mrs. Hargrove since he'd talked to her when they stopped in Las Vegas. He hoped she had remembered to put a notice on the bulletin board in the café asking for a live-in housekeeper.

Reno opened the back door for Chrissy. "Here, let me hold Justin while you get out. And he'll need a blanket. It's a little chilly out here." Reno had held Justin many times over the past couple of days, but he continued to be surprised every time Chrissy handed him the baby at how small Justin really was. This time was no exception. Chrissy had assured Reno several times that Justin was a healthy weight for his young age, but Reno still wanted Dr. Norris to check Justin out.

"Remember, if you take a job, you need to ask

for this Thursday off so we can take Justin to the doctor in Miles City."

"I can't ask for a day off the first week of the job." Chrissy stepped out of the car and stretched. "We'll have to postpone the doctor's visit until the next week."

"Well, we'll wait and see." Reno didn't say that Mrs. Hargrove wouldn't care what day Chrissy took off. After all, he wasn't supposed to know about the job that was posted inside on the bulletin board.

"He sure is an agreeable little guy," Reno said as he looked down at the baby. "Look at him smiling."

"Babies that young don't smile. Its just gas. It says so in the baby books."

"Those books don't know everything. I can tell by the look in his eyes that he's smiling at me." Reno hated to give the baby back to Chrissy. It suddenly hit him that this was probably the last time he would get to hold the little one. "He knows I'm the one who taught him how to make a fist."

"I think that's pretty natural. So he can suck his thumb."

"Yeah, but I showed him how to hold his fingers so he can get a good grip on a baseball when he's older."

Chrissy smiled as she held out her arms for Justin. "He'll appreciate that."

Reno gave the baby to her. "If you ever need someone to watch him, let me know."

Reno figured he was due some visitation rights. After all, he'd changed Justin's diapers several times on the road. That should give him *some* rights.

"Thanks. I'll remember that."

Chrissy squared her shoulders as she cradled Justin to her. Reno figured she was preparing herself to face Dry Creek. He only hoped she would give the place a chance.

Chapter Six

Chrissy stepped through the door that Reno held open for her and entered the Dry Creek Café with her baby cradled in her arms. She took a deep breath. It was midmorning and she'd made it home. She remembered the smell of baking biscuits and coffee from when she'd been here before. And the black-and-white checked floor had been in her dreams on more than one night. Six or seven tables were scattered around the café like before.

But something was different. Three tables were pushed next to the large window overlooking the street. Lace half curtains covered the bottom of the large window and matched the white tablecloths covering each of the three tables. In the place where bottles of ketchup sat on the other tables, silver vases stood filled with pink silk flowers. Matching pink napkins were placed beside the silverware on those tables. A wide aisle separated the three tables from the rest of the more casual ones.

Chrissy nodded. That was clever. It made the place feel as if had two restaurants instead of just one.

"Linda thinks we need more class," Reno said as he turned to leave the café again. "I'm going to bring in the diaper bag in case you need anything. I'll be right back."

A delighted shriek made Chrissy look toward the door that led to the kitchen, and she saw Linda stand still for a moment in the open doorway before she came rushing toward her. "You're here!"

Chrissy felt her heart smile. It sounded as if she had one friend in Dry Creek besides Reno. With the two of them by her side, she'd be fine.

"Oh, I can't wait to see the baby!" Linda whispered as she stopped about a yard from Chrissy and then tiptoed closer. Linda had a butterfly tattoo above one eye and a copper-red streak in her dark hair. "Is it sleeping?"

"No, he's awake."

"So it's a boy."

Chrissy nodded. She decided she had no reason to feel self-conscious about her orange dress here. Linda was wearing a purple velvet dress and a large pink apron.

Linda just stood grinning at her. "And you! How are you? You know, I meant to write, but I lost your address and then I forgot to ask Garrett for it again and, well—" She stopped to take a breath. "You're here!"

"It's good to be back," Chrissy said. "I thought about writing you, too, but there was the baby and then I was working and—well, it's good to see you."

Chrissy knew Linda and her boyfriend, Duane "Jazz" Edison, were running the café to earn enough money to buy a farm of their own so they could get married. Unless Linda had had a birthday since Chrissy was here last, Linda was twenty.

"Now, sit down and tell me about the baby," Linda said as she motioned to one of the tables with the flowers on them. "What does he like to do? Are you nursing him or is he on the bottle? I want to know everything. I love babies."

The door to the café opened again, and Reno came in with the diaper bag.

"Well, Justin eats good, so he'll be growing fast," Chrissy reported.

"He's going to be a baseball player someday," Reno added as he set the diaper bag on the floor at Chrissy's feet. "He's got a good grip in his fingers. Don't you, big fella?"

Chrissy watched as Reno ran his thumb softly over the smooth skin on Justin's tiny hand. "I can feel him practicing his pitches already."

Justin gurgled in response to Reno's words.

"That's right," Reno murmured.

Chrissy's throat went dry and she had to swallow. Where had she been for these past days? She hoped Justin wasn't becoming too attached to Reno. Was it possible for a baby to even do that? Chrissy remembered how painful it had been for her when she was young and her mother's boyfriends would leave. The first few times it happened, Chrissy didn't understand and thought the men had disliked her for some reason. She didn't want Justin to have that same hurt in his life.

"The baby seems to like you," Linda said quietly to Reno.

"Yeah." Reno grinned as though he'd been given a first-prize ribbon.

"Justin just likes the sound of men's voices," Chrissy added quickly. She was beginning to see just how complicated this all was.

She had more to worry about than whether Justin was becoming attached to the sight of Reno. She also had to worry about the hurt Justin could do to Reno.

Reno might not recognize the speculative look in Linda's eyes, but Chrissy did. Linda was wondering if Reno was Justin's father. Of all the things Chrissy had worried about in coming to Dry Creek, this was one that hadn't occurred to her. Reno had told her about the letter that had come to the Dry Creek post-master, but she didn't believe anyone in Dry Creek would seriously believe Reno was the father of her baby.

"The baby's father is still in Las Vegas, you know." Chrissy would rather talk about almost anything than Jared, but she wanted the record to be straight in this small town. If she had to talk about her past with someone here, she'd rather it was Linda than anyone else.

"That's got to be hard," Linda said as she reached over to give Chrissy's shoulder a squeeze. "So it was the guy you were engaged to…"

Chrissy nodded. "But it's all right. We'll be fine, Justin and I. Just as soon as I get a job."

"Oh, that's right." Linda jumped up. "Getting a job won't be a problem in Dry Creek. We have a bulletin board over here for jobs."

"Really?" Chrissy asked as she turned to Reno. "Will you hold Justin for a little bit while I look at the ads?"

Reno nodded as he put out his arms and accepted the baby.

If he hadn't been distracted by Justin, Reno would have noticed right away that something was odd. As it was, it took a few minutes of the excited chatter over at the bulletin board before it dawned on him that Mrs. Hargrove's posting for a house-keeper wouldn't generate that much enthusiasm.

Reno stood up and walked closer to the bulletin board that was on the west wall of the café. He couldn't believe his eyes. There had to be a dozen notices scribbled on index cards and tacked to the board.

"Here's one that looks interesting," Chrissy was saying. "Dancing instructor wanted for gentleman. Twenty dollars an hour."

Linda nodded. "Jacob put that up. He said he was thinking he'd like to be able to dance the next time someone has a wedding in that barn south of town."

"We did line dancing at that wedding," Reno interrupted. "There's nothing to learn. You just put your foot where the caller tells you to put it. In. Out. Whatever."

"Before you got there, we had waltzing," Linda said.

"I can waltz." Chrissy was still running her fingers down the cards lined up on the board. "Here's one that calls for someone to do some mending."

"Elmer swears he's got a dozen shirts with no buttons on them," Linda said. "He said he's flexible on the timing of it, too. He's lived without buttons for a while now. He just wears a sweater over everything. But with summer coming, he wanted some shirts to wear that don't require a sweater."

Reno looked at the cards in astonishment. Had everyone in town listed a job on the board? It sure looked like it. What were they doing? Everyone knew there were no jobs in Dry Creek.

"Ah, here's one for a cook/housekeeper," Chrissy said. "That sounds promising."

Reno relaxed. Finally she was looking at Mrs. Hargrove's notice.

"But where's the Wilkerson place?"

"Lester's?" Reno's voice came out so loud it made Justin start to fuss. Without thinking, Reno started to slightly rock the baby where he stood.

"Now, now." Chrissy turned and started to coo. "It's all right."

Reno wasn't sure if Chrissy was cooing at him or Justin. "Why's Lester advertising for a cook?"

"Well, he is alone out on his ranch all the time. He could probably use some help," Linda said as she gave Reno a look that said he shouldn't be making this so difficult.

Reno grunted, but didn't back down. "The man eats from cans. All he does is heat it up. Hash. Chili. Soup. It's all the same. A cook would be wasted on him."

"I don't know," Chrissy said thoughtfully as she held out her arms for Justin. "He did seem to enjoy that pie at the big Thanksgiving dinner at the ranch last fall. I make a pretty good apple pie, and I think that's his favorite."

Reno frowned as he handed Justin to her. He didn't like the thought of Chrissy making pies for Lester. "If he wants pie, he can come to the café."

"We don't serve pie," Linda reminded him.

"And it's a live-in position," Chrissy said as she cradled Justin upright against her breast. "That way I wouldn't have to pay rent anywhere, and Justin will have a place to play."

"Justin can't even walk yet. It'll be a good six months before he needs a place to play," Reno protested, and then thought a minute. "How long do you plan to work for Lester, anyway?"

Chrissy leaned in to see the card better. "I don't know. It doesn't say what the salary is. All it gives is a number to call."

"I'll call him," Linda offered as she walked toward the kitchen. "You just keep looking."

"There's got to be a better job there," Reno said as he started to scan the notices to find Mrs. Hargrove's. "Something closer to town."

"I don't mind being out of town."

"You say that now. But the wind blows something fierce out there on the ranches. And the solitude. Some days you don't see another soul. Just horses, with a few chickens thrown in for excitement."

"Well, I'd see Lester," Chrissy reminded him as she rocked Justin against herself. "Three times a day at least for meals."

Reno ground his teeth. "Lester doesn't talk much, though. You'd be bored in no time. He doesn't have a television. He doesn't get any magazines except for the *Farm Journal.*"

Linda opened the door from the kitchen and came back into the room. "The job pays eighty-five dollars a week and room and board."

"That's not enough," Reno said firmly as he went up close to the board and scanned the notices. When he found the one he was looking for, he put his finger right next to it. "There. That's the job for you. A housekeeper for Mrs. Hargrove. Room and board included."

Chrissy walked over to look up at the small, neatly penned notice that Mrs. Hargrove had tacked to the board. She Chrissy shifted Justin in her arms so she could read the announcement better. "But her job only pays seventy-five dollars a week plus room and board."

"I'll pay the extra ten," Reno said. Lester must have read Mrs. Hargrove's notice and decided to outbid her. "That way you won't lose money by working for Mrs. Hargrove."

Chrissy tipped her head up at him suspiciously. "Why would you do that?"

"Yeah, why would you do that?" Linda asked along with Chrissy.

"Ah." Reno ran his hands over his hair. He was guessing Mrs. Hargrove hadn't told Linda about their plan. "Because Mrs. Hargrove is an older lady and she needs the help more than Lester does."

Reno hoped Mrs. Hargrove never heard about this conversation. She didn't think of herself as old, and she'd snap at anyone who implied she was not able to take care of herself.

Chrissy was still looking at him funny.

"And I know Mrs. Hargrove can't afford to pay you any more herself because she's on Social Security, so I want to help." Reno smiled. "She's been good to me, and I want to do something for her."

"I noticed the other day that her porch needs fixing," Linda offered.

"Thanks. I'll go take a look at it." Reno gritted his teeth. Whose side was Linda on? "I should have checked the porch myself before I headed down to Los Angeles. Those old boards usually have problems about now."

"She said you usually do it and don't take any money for it," Linda said.

"In the past we've settled it with her giving me a plate of her homemade chocolate chip cookies."

"Well, of course, if all she has is Social Security,

she can't afford to pay anyone," Chrissy said thoughtfully. "I wouldn't feel right taking any money from her, and I don't need cookies. I'm sure I can help her with what she needs when I'm not working at Lester's."

"But you can't work at Lester's," Reno said. He could see the question in Chrissy's eyes and knew it was on the tip of Linda's tongue. He needed to focus. Ah, he had it. "He's a single man, and it wouldn't be proper for you to live in the same house with him alone."

Chrissy's face turned red. "I hope you're not suggesting I would do anything but bake pies for the man."

"No, I didn't mean that at all." It had to be about sixty degrees inside the café. There was no reason for Reno to be sweating. "I just mean you have to think of Justin."

"I'm perfectly capable of taking care of Justin," Chrissy said coolly.

"Besides, you're talking about Lester," Linda said as though he'd suggested Chrissy was willing to date a troll.

Reno bowed his head in defeat. "I'll pay you a hundred dollars a week plus room and board to work at the Redfern Ranch."

"Doing what?"

"Well, I like pies, too—and there's the house."

"You don't need a housekeeper. I can't take a job that's just charity."

"I have the calves to feed." Reno looked up and thanked God silently. Yes! That was it. "The poor things need someone to take care of them, and I'll have to start plowing any day now. Who's going to take care of them?"

"Don't they have their mothers to take care of them?" Chrissy didn't look convinced.

"Not these calves," Reno said mournfully. "They're all alone in the world. No mother. No father."

Reno hoped his prize bull forgave him although it was true that the animal had never shown any interest in his offspring, so the calves actually had no father when it came to having someone care for them.

"Oh, the poor things," Chrissy whispered as she glanced down at Justin, who was sleeping in her arms. "It's bad enough not having a father, but not having a mother, too, would be just awful."

Chrissy broke off with a stricken look at Reno. "I'm sorry, I forgot about your mother."

Reno stopped the triumphant war whoop that wanted to come rushing out of his mouth and he managed to wince instead. "It is hard. Not everyone understands."

"Of course they don't," Chrissy said soothingly.

"So you'll take on the feeding of the calves?"

"Well, I suppose it is more important than baking pies for Lester," she agreed. "Although his would have been more convenient, since it was room and board."

"My job includes room and board, too," Reno offered.

"Oh, no, you convinced me that wouldn't be proper."

"Oh, it's different with Reno," Linda said smoothly. Reno thanked her with a smile until she added, "Mrs. Hargrove was saying that he admitted in the post office the other day that he feels only family feelings for you on account of the fact that you're almost cousins."

"Almost cousins?" Chrissy asked faintly.

Reno could see Chrissy was surprised. He was shocked himself. "I don't remember saying anything quite like that."

"Oh, well, Mrs. Hargrove goes for the essence of what a person says," Linda said with a wave of her hand. "You know how it is—sometimes you're not even sure what you mean, and then Mrs. Hargrove sums it up for you and it's right on the nose."

"I see." Chrissy swallowed. "Well, I've never had an almost cousin before…"

"What about Garrett? He's your cousin," Linda said as she adjusted the salt and pepper shakers on a nearby table. "Just pretend Reno is Garrett."

"I could do that, I guess," Chrissy said.

Reno frowned. He didn't like the fact that Chrissy could make a promise like that so easily. He sure couldn't promise to see her through the eyes of a cousin any day soon.

"I don't see why you're looking for a job anyway," Linda said as she moved to another table and swung out a chair for Chrissy to sit down. "If that guy in Vegas is the baby's father, shouldn't he be paying enough child support to take care of you both? I thought you said he had a trust fund or something."

"He does," Chrissy said as she sat in the chair. "But it's complicated. To get child support, I need to claim he's the father, and if I do that, I'm worried Jared's mother will have a better case to get custody."

"But you're the mother. She can't just take your baby away from you."

"She's already got some attorney trying to find out things about me so he can say I'm an unfit mother."

"And if that doesn't work, he's trying to scare her into giving up Justin," Reno added. "Someone set fire to Chrissy's mother's house just before we left L.A."

"You're kidding?" Linda said as she looked from Reno to Chrissy. "Some lawyer would do that?"

Reno nodded. "He might not do anything himself, but he'd pay people to cause some damage."

"Wow." Linda frowned. "He's serious. I thought he was just some kind of crazy guy who wrote letters to stir up trouble."

"I still have the letter," Reno said as he patted his shirt pocket. "I'm keeping it in case we want to get a restraining order on him or something."

"It's not the lawyer I'm worried about—it's the people he hires that scare me," Chrissy said. "I'm glad Justin isn't old enough to walk or crawl. I'd be a nervous wreck every time he went out to play."

"Oh, surely the lawyer will give up after a while. He can't care that much," Linda said.

"It's Jared's mother who cares. And she never gives up. Oh—" Chrissy stopped in surprise and turned toward Reno. "I never thought about that—that's why you didn't want me to take the job at Lester's and stay at his place, since he's not married. You were worried Mrs. Bard might use it against me in a custody battle."

Reno grunted. He should have thought of that. "You can never be too careful."

"Well, you don't need to worry about Mrs. Bard when you're in Dry Creek," Linda said firmly. "We'll take care of you and Justin. We keep an eye out for strangers." Linda paused. "Well, except for a few times when things have gotten out of hand."

Reno grimaced. He could tell from the look on Linda's face that she was remembering the time a stranger had come to Dry Creek and dressed up as Santa Claus so he could get close enough to the woman who was playing the angel in the church Christmas pageant to try to shoot her. Come to think of it, Linda had felt sorry for the man in the Santa Claus costume and given him a free spaghetti dinner from the café before the pageant.

Linda looked at Reno. "I guess she'd be better off out at your ranch."

Reno nodded. "My dog, Hunter, doesn't let strangers get too close unless I give him the all-clear sign."

And I'll be there, Reno thought. He remembered that what had saved the angel was that Pastor Matthew had risked his life to save hers. Even Reno had been touched by their story of love and happiness.

"I don't really think the lawyer would send someone up here. Do you?" Chrissy asked as she looked from Reno to Linda. Justin seemed to sense his mother's fear, and started to fuss.

"Of course not," Reno said quickly as he scowled at Linda.

"You're perfectly safe here," Linda added when Reno finished.

"It's just that I keep hearing that music playing

in my head," Chrissy said as she put Justin to her shoulder and looked over at Reno. "Remember after the fire, there was that black car with a few guys in it, and they were playing those old songs from the sixties—it sounded like a CD or something. I remember because they were playing that song— how does it go…the Mrs. something one—"

"Mrs. Robinson?" Linda asked as she stood up from the table. "I don't believe it. They've called here."

"Who?" Chrissy asked as she started patting Justin on his back.

"Some guy called asking how to get to Dry Creek, and he had that music playing in the background. I think he was on a cell phone—we don't always get good reception here if someone is on a cell. Usually we don't even get the call, but sometimes it comes through and sounds faint like this one."

"They called here?" Chrissy looked over at Reno.

Linda nodded. "We finally got the phone for the café listed under Dry Creek Café, Dry Creek, Montana. We thought we should ask for reservations for our new dinner section." Linda motioned to the three tables in front of the window. "I'm so sorry. We never would have gotten a listing if we'd known."

"Did he say where he was when he called?" Reno

walked over to the window and looked out at the road leading into Dry Creek. He saw a puff of dust in the distance, but it looked like a pickup.

"He asked for directions from Salt Lake City," Linda said, and then looked over at Chrissy. "And I invited him to try the café while he was in town. He said they would, so he must have someone with him."

"We should call the police," Chrissy said, and then bit her lip. She stopped patting Justin on the back, and he started to cry. "Of course we can't do that. No one's done anything. It's not a crime to play sixties music."

"We'll tell our deputy sheriff anyway. He can keep an eye out for strangers," Reno said as he held his arms out to take Justin. "And we'll tell the men at the hardware store. Not much gets by Elmer and Jacob."

Chrissy gave the baby to Reno, and she stood up and started to pace.

"You're safe here," Linda said. "We have a neighborhood watch program going—well, not the official thing, but we watch who comes and goes. Not that there're many strangers anyway."

"I do feel safer here than in Los Angeles," Chrissy admitted. It made sense that there would be fewer strangers here and fewer chances for mischief. "My nerves just need to settle down."

Chrissy stopped pacing at the window. She could see the Dry Creek church across the street, and the Big Sheep Mountains were in the distance. The Montana landscape didn't offer many places for a criminal to hide. She should feel safe here.

Then she glanced over at Reno. He was rubbing Justin's back.

Maybe she was relaxing too soon. The lawyer wasn't the only man she needed to worry about while she was here.

Chapter Seven

Reno was just about as content as a man could be. The midday sun was shining in the café window with enough force that it might even be drying up some of the mud outside. If it did, Reno would have an easy drive to the ranch.

Not that mud was on his mind too much. Chrissy was sitting across the table from him, and she had a happy flush on her face. They had both just eaten a couple of the best hamburgers Reno had ever tasted.

Life didn't get any better than this, Reno decided as he leaned back in his chair.

Everyone had calmed down after Linda decided that maybe the man who had called on the phone was Jacob's nephew, who was planning to visit the old man in a couple of days and be there for Jacob's big birthday party.

"I'd forgotten he might call," Linda said again as she held Justin up and smiled at him. "Pastor Matthew told me they wanted to have a birthday party at the Elktons' barn and asked us to provide the food, so of course Jacob's nephew had this number."

"If you need help with the party, let me know," Chrissy said before she took one of the last French fries from her plate and dipped it in ketchup. "I can help you handle a hungry crowd."

"Oh, that's a relief," Linda said. "I wasn't sure how I was going to manage everyone, even though we're going to have a limited menu. Grilled steaks and baked potatoes mostly, since that's Jacob's favorite dinner. Besides, it's a good menu for cowboys, and they're inviting the whole crew at the Elkton ranch."

Reno frowned. He wasn't sure he wanted those cowboys to get a close-up look at Chrissy. "Maybe I should help instead. You know how those cowboys are when there's a party."

"I've worked in Vegas," Chrissy said as she picked up the last French fry. "I can handle anything."

"Maybe you can both help," Linda suggested as she laid Justin over her knees and started to rub his back. The baby gurgled in delight. "We'll even be able to pay decent salaries."

"Oh, you don't need to pay me," Chrissy said. "It'll be fun to have a party."

Some of the joy went out of Reno's day. He supposed Chrissy's disappointment in Dry Creek was inevitable, but he didn't like to think about it. "This might not be your usual party. Besides, we don't have parties very often around here, so you wouldn't want to get used to it. Mostly it's a pretty boring place."

"I don't know about that. We've had a lot of weddings in the last year." Linda eyed Reno suspiciously. "I don't know if those are exactly parties, but they have sure been fun. You don't want to sell this place short."

"Well, I guess there have been the weddings," Reno acknowledged. Maybe if he was lucky, there would be another wedding to help keep Chrissy entertained. Women sure liked weddings. He looked over at Linda. "I don't suppose you and Jazz are planning to get married any time soon?"

Linda's smile tightened. "Jazz and I are no longer engaged."

"What?" Chrissy said. "Why didn't you say something? Here we've been chatting away about all my problems and—oh, I'm so sorry."

"Don't be sorry," Linda said. "We just realized we have incompatible goals. It's really for the best that we found it out now, before we went to the trouble of getting married."

"How incompatible can your goals be?" Reno had always pictured Linda and Jazz as a sensible engaged couple who agreed on what they wanted out of life. "I thought you two were planning to buy the Jenkins place and raise cattle. Isn't that what this café is about? Saving up enough money for that ranch?"

Linda lifted her chin and then bent to rub Justin's back some more. "There's more to a marriage than which piece of land to farm and what cattle to buy."

"Well, of course, but—"

Reno was interrupted by the sound of a loud scraping that came from outside on the porch.

"What's that?" Chrissy said.

Reno could see the shape of a man through the glass on the café door. Something about the shape looked familiar, but it didn't look quite right.

The door opened, and Lester Wilkerson stepped inside the café.

"What's with him?" Reno had never seen Lester in a suit before. He didn't even know the man owned a suit. Yet here he was, wearing a black suit and a tie. He was holding a metal bucket. Lester had slicked his red hair back and shaved his face so close he'd nicked his chin. The metal bucket was dented in a few places and obviously old, but Lester was holding it out in front of him as if it was a grand bouquet.

"What's this?" Reno asked. Now that he'd gotten a closer look at the bucket, he could see it held what looked like a small bush.

"Flowers," Lester announced as he took a deep breath and smiled. "Well, not yet, but Mrs. Hargrove told me there will be some soon—geraniums."

Lester held out the bucket to Chrissy. "I know women really like their flowers and there aren't any blooming in Dry Creek right now because of the rain—well, and winter, of course—but there should be some flowers on this plant soon. They'll be red, according to Mrs. Hargrove." Lester paused as though to remember something Reno figured he had memorized, and then continued after clearing his throat. "The way I see it, if one flower says welcome to a woman, a whole plant should say it ten times better—so welcome to Dry Creek, Chrissy Hamilton."

"Why, thank you," Chrissy said as she accepted the bucket and held it in her lap. "I'm touched."

Reno wasn't touched. He was astonished.

"I know women like them fancy bouquets," Lester continued. "But I figured you might like a plant to keep in the kitchen window. Sort of a homey touch."

Chrissy blinked. "I think that's the sweetest thing anyone has ever done for me."

Reno wondered if she had forgotten he had just driven over two thousand miles to bring her and

Justin back to Dry Creek. "Yeah, it's sweet. That's Lester for you. As sweet as they come."

"I just wanted to welcome you to Dry Creek," Lester said again nervously. Now that he didn't have the bucket to hold, he used one hand to smooth back his hair. "I'm sure you and your baby will be happy here. I heard you're thinking of taking the job I posted for a cook—"

"She's not taking the job," Reno interrupted. "She's going to work on the Redfern Ranch bottle-feeding the spare calves."

Chrissy moved the bush so she could give Lester a soft, apologetic smile. "It's only because I think family should stick together, and Reno says we're practically cousins."

Lester grinned. "Oh, well, that's okay then. I can see why you'd want to help out your cousin. Cousins, huh?"

Lester turned to Reno and winked before turning his smile back to Chrissy. "And I bet your cousin told you what a good neighbor I am."

Reno forgot Lester had asked him to put in a good word for him. "He's the best—but about this cousin business. Actually, it was Mrs. Hargrove who said—"

"Ah, yes, Mrs. Hargrove. Wonderful woman." Lester grinned even wider. "Besides, my place is just next door to the Redfern Ranch. I'll be seeing you almost every day as it is. I usually pick up the mail for both places and bring it out from town."

Justin was starting to cry. Reno didn't blame him. The little one couldn't see his own mother through all the leaves that went into that plant. Linda moved the baby so he cradled against her shoulder and could see everyone.

Reno frowned as he turned back to Lester. "I thought you stopped getting our mail when Nicki got married. I haven't seen you around, and the mail's always on the counter when I go to town."

"Yeah, well." Lester shrugged. "I've decided I should be more neighborly, so I'm starting up again. The Bible says to do unto others you know."

Reno had never heard Lester quote from the Bible before.

"It also says it isn't good for a man to be alone," Lester added as he dipped his head for a pause. "I used to enjoy those morning visits with Nicki before she got married. She'd always cut me a big piece of her coffee cake and pour me a cup of coffee." Lester managed to look forlorn. "It was more than the food. I kind of miss that womanly touch—being a man on my own isn't easy."

Reno wondered when the violins were going to start.

Chrissy had a sympathetic look on her face.

"Well, you'll have to stop and visit when you

bring the mail. I'm not sure I can promise you coffee cake. But it'll be good for you to visit. I'm sure you and Reno have lots to talk about."

"Reno's usually out working in the fields by the time I bring the mail." Lester grinned.

Reno grunted. "I'll make a point to come in and say hi—since you're so lonely and all."

"Now, won't that be nice." Chrissy beamed.

Reno wondered if Chrissy had any idea what Lester was up to.

Chrissy told herself she had never been happier. She was lying in a bed with crisp white sheets that she had put through the ranch's washing machine yesterday and then hung out to dry on the clothesline that had been strung years ago outside the bunkhouse. When she took the sheets off the line late yesterday, they smelled like the outdoors. She'd cuddled in their scent all night. She'd never had a sheet that had been dried outside in the sun before, and she hadn't known what she was missing.

Yes, it was a good life, she said to herself as she opened her eyes and looked around. Speaking of the sun, it was just starting to shine in through the windows she had washed yesterday. She took a deep breath. The air still smelled from the lemon floor polish she'd used on the hardwood floor. Her arms still ached, but her heart was happy.

Justin was in a makeshift crib beside her bed. And they were both in their own home. Well, as close to their own home as she had ever had. Reno had agreed to let her use the bunkhouse as her own while she worked on the Redfern Ranch.

And it was all because of that geranium. Chrissy needed a place to keep the plant, and she didn't want to move a plant in a bucket into someone else's kitchen. And where else could she keep it, since she didn't have a front door to set it beside?

Something about the plant made Chrissy want to have her own place. Granted, the bunkhouse needed some work, but the building was basically sound. She had curtained off the bottom half of the main room to make a private bedroom. Reno had helped her put up a single bed frame and then brought over the mattress from Nicki's old bed.

"You may as well have this single," Reno said. "Nicki and Garrett have a queen bed now in the new house they've built. We've got a spare dresser you can use, too."

Reno had mentioned earlier that, in addition to building a new house on the knoll about a half mile from the old ranch house, Nicki had also insisted on buying two washing machines and putting one in the ranch house for when she wanted to do any wash over there.

"And maybe I could put up a plank table like the

ones we set up for the Thanksgiving dinner last fall," Chrissy suggested. She had decided to sign up for as many as possible of the jobs that she had found on the bulletin board at the café. She had already called Elmer and said she'd be happy to sew buttons on his shirts. A table would be useful while she mended.

Reno nodded. "You can use the rocker from the ranch living room, as well. You'll want that when Justin can't sleep."

Reno said that as long as he was bringing the rocker over, he might as well bring the television in from the barn, too. The small black-and-white television was one Reno used during calving season, but it would get a strong picture if he hooked the antenna to the roof.

"Don't go to any special trouble," Chrissy said as she moved her plant. She'd set the geranium's bucket inside the front door to the bunkhouse, but then decided maybe it should go by the rocker on the small rug there.

"Oh, I'd do this for any hired hand," Reno said, and Chrissy believed him. "The Redfern Ranch has a reputation to uphold."

Chrissy started to lift the bucket, but Reno stopped her. "You're not supposed to lift anything."

"Why?" Chrissy blushed as she realized why. "Oh, that's before the baby is born. It's okay afterward."

"Still," Reno said as he moved the plant to where she wanted it. "We have a reputation."

"Oh—you mean the ranch's reputation." Chrissy swallowed. "As I remember, your ranch has been here since the turn of the century." The stories Linda had told Chrissy last fall about the ranch's history had been very entertaining. "I'd love to hear more about those days."

The first Redfern had been a young Englishman who had came west and worked on a cattle drive. After the drive, he bought this ranch in southern Montana and stocked it with Texas longhorns. As the ranch grew, the bunkhouse filled up with a whole assortment of cowboys.

Chrissy was hoping Reno would tell her more stories about the ranch, but he changed the subject to floor wax. Since he didn't have much to say about floor wax either, she decided he must not want to talk about the ranch.

If Chrissy had that kind of a family history, she would be telling stories about her great-grandparents to everyone who would listen.

As it was, she had very little family history. Her mother's parents had died when she was still a baby, and her one uncle, Garrett's father, had never been very friendly toward her and her mother.

Her mother refused to say anything about Chrissy's father other than that he had died in an accident before she was born. The only relative Chrissy had, besides her mother, was her cousin, Garrett.

Oh, well, she told herself as she yawned and stretched in the bed. She'd been on the Redfern Ranch for only a day so far. She could be patient to learn all its stories. In the meantime, it was six o'clock and she should get up and go to the main house to fix Reno breakfast.

Reno had not asked her to make breakfast, but it was her first official day on the job and she wanted to make a good impression. She'd even rinsed her waitress uniform out last night and hung it out on the line so it would be ready for her first day working with the calves.

Chrissy was determined to be a good calf feeder. She hoped the calves weren't afraid of orange. She knew red was upsetting to bulls, and the bright orange of her uniform was a little too close to that color for her own comfort.

But Reno had told her she didn't need to worry. He planned to be with her the first few times she fed the calves to make sure everything went all right.

Chapter Eight

Reno didn't know it was possible to burn instant oatmeal. It wasn't as if he'd never thrown a packet of flakes into a pan of boiling water before. Of course, the other times he'd made oatmeal, he hadn't also attempted to make biscuits, so he had remembered to turn the gas burner off when he put the flakes into the water.

But this morning those biscuits had distracted him. Well, the packet said they were supposed to be scones, but they had looked like biscuits, at least when he put them in the oven.

Oatmeal hadn't seemed enough to feed Chrissy, and he thought eggs and bacon might be too much like plain old ranch food. That's when his eyes had fallen on the packet of scone mix. He wondered when Nicki had bought that packet, but he was thankful she had. He'd decided to fix the scones and a pot of tea in case Chrissy shouldn't be drinking coffee yet on account of Justin.

The scones promised to have dried cranberries and orange peel in them, and they had looked suitably lumpy when Reno dropped them by teaspoon onto a cookie sheet just as the directions said.

He thought the dried cranberries and orange peel would have that civilized touch that would let Chrissy know she wasn't at the earth's end.

How was he to know the gas oven would decide to turn blazing hot? For the past decade that old oven had been taking twice as long to cook meat loaf as the recipe promised it would. Why did it need to change its habits now?

Reno had decided to do all the cooking yesterday when Chrissy asked about using the washing machine. Thankfully, there was a new washing machine in the ranch house because Nicki had just bought one, but that was the only thing in the kitchen that wasn't forty years old.

Reno didn't want Chrissy to discover how hopeless the rest of the kitchen was. Women judged a house by its kitchen. He knew he shouldn't care what Chrissy thought about this old house, but he did. It was his home. He expected to bring his bride here someday. Of course, the bride he would bring would be grateful for an old gas stove, because she would understand the sacrifices a young ranching couple generally had to make.

He didn't feel like explaining all of that to Chrissy, however, and he wouldn't have to if he did all the cooking. Of course, he couldn't expect a city woman to like the kind of bachelor cowboy breakfasts he usually made of fried potatoes with onions and plenty of baking powder biscuits and eggs over easy. But he was willing to try some new recipes.

How hard could cooking for a city woman be anyway? Reno had asked himself yesterday when he made the decision.

He was afraid he was getting the answer this morning.

Reno slid the main window up and propped the door open. The sun was just beginning to top the mountains behind the ranch, and there wasn't so much as a breeze coming through. Reno shook his head in disgust. It was always windy here except on the day when a man wanted to blow the smoke out of his kitchen.

Reno looked out the door at the wood boards on the porch. Yes, they were wet. There had been the usual drizzle of rain last night, and so there would be more mud today.

Reno lifted his eyes to the gray sky that backed the mountains. If he had any doubt that God had a sense of humor, mud would convince him otherwise. But then, Reno had read some of the book of Job already this morning, and he guessed life could be worse. At least Job hadn't mentioned any mud.

Chrissy looked at the mirror in dismay. The bunkhouse bathroom had a long mirror that was so old the surface bulged a little and gave a distorted image. At least, she hoped some of the way she looked was due to distortion in the mirror.

She had made a mistake by leaving her orange dress outside on the clothesline to dry overnight. How was she to know it would rain? Her dress wasn't just wet, it was also cold and stiff. Even when she brought it inside and laid it out by the small wall heater in the room, she knew it wouldn't be dry for breakfast. She'd be lucky if it would be dry by lunch—or dinner, as they called the noon meal here.

She had only three other pieces of clothing in the box she'd brought from Los Angeles. One was a strapless black evening gown that probably didn't fit anymore since she'd had Justin. The next was the white almost-wedding dress that Reno had said made her look like an angel. The third and final choice was a dark blue evening gown that not only had straps, it had a good solid front and back. It might have sequins, but it did look respectable. She had bought the blue gown in Vegas, hoping Jared would like it and she could stop wearing the black one. He didn't like it, but she had kept it anyway.

Chrissy shook her head. It was either the blue gown or her old wedding dress.

It wasn't even the blue gown that was making her look funny in the mirror. She looked more closely. Something was wrong with her complexion. She looked a little yellow around the eyes and green around the mouth. If she hadn't felt so good, she'd have thought she was sick.

Thankfully, she had makeup in her purse. Although she'd been too busy to wear much of it lately, she'd also been too busy to clean out her purse, so she had everything she needed: eyeliner, foundation, lipstick, blush and eye shadow.

Chrissy used the mirror as she put her makeup on, and by the time Justin woke up she decided she looked pretty normal. After all, she wouldn't want to scare the poor calves on her first day as their feeder. And she was sure they'd like the blue dress better than the orange one. And as for Reno, all the men she had ever known liked a woman who was dressed up enough to step off the cover of some magazine. She doubted Reno was any different from Jared when it came to that.

Yes, it's all under control, she told herself as she looked at her watch. It was only six-thirty. Most people didn't eat until seven, so she'd have plenty of time to scramble some eggs and make toast for Reno. It'd be the perfect way to let him know she intended to earn her salary.

Reno forgot all about the burned scones when Chrissy showed up at the kitchen door with Justin in her arms. He must have missed explaining something to her about working on the ranch. They'd never had a dress code at the Redfern Ranch before—well, unless you counted the fact that every cowboy was required to have a bandanna around his neck if he was riding into dusty territory—but Reno wished he could pull out a sheet of policies related to how a ranch hand should dress.

Chrissy was as pretty as a greeting card. Her brown hair curled up into fluffy blond tips that were tucked behind her ears. Her green-gray eyes looked even more mysterious than he remembered them from yesterday. Her lips shone with a raspberry color he figured was a Vegas special. He could say for sure none of the women in Dry Creek wore a lip gloss like that one, not even Linda.

But it was the dress that stopped him cold.

"You look great," Reno said, and swallowed. The dress reminded him of that time just before midnight on a clear night when the stars were all out. It also reminded him of all the reasons that Chrissy didn't belong on the ranch. She was fine china, and most days on the ranch they used paper plates. "New dress?"

Chrissy winced. "Not really. It's just that I washed the orange one last night, and I put it on the line to dry."

"And it rained," Reno finished for her in relief. It wasn't as bad as he feared. "Well, that's easy to fix. I can give you some old shirts or something."

"I couldn't take your clothes."

"Oh, I know they'll be big, but we can fix you up with a belt."

"I mean, I make it a rule never to accept charity. That goes for clothes, too."

"It's not charity. It's just being practical. I have plenty of work clothes, and you need some."

Chrissy lifted her chin. "I take care of myself and Justin."

She walked right past Reno into the kitchen. "Now, I came to fix breakfast for you, since it's my first day on the job."

Reno was grateful the kitchen was still dark enough that the smoke didn't show. If Chrissy wondered what had been burning, she was too polite to ask about it.

"Oh, I already fixed breakfast for us. You don't need to worry about meals. And before you ask, meals are not charity. They're part of your wages."

Chrissy nodded. "We had a meal included at the diner when I worked there. That's a nice benefit. Thank you."

Chrissy hated to admit it, but she was relieved. She realized she might have overstated her cooking abilities just a tiny little bit when she'd talked about her apple pie. She'd been so enthused about getting the job at Lester's, she'd forgotten a few things about that pie.

She'd remembered them yesterday as she was scrubbing the floor. It had been several years ago, and she had bought canned filling and refrigerated piecrusts from the store. All she'd really had to do was unfold the crust into the pie tin and add the apples from the can. Her mother had even crimped the edges.

Of course, the pie had tasted good, but something told her a rancher would expect her to know how to crimp the piecrust herself. Besides, she didn't see any grocery stores around where she could buy a handy piecrust. People around Dry Creek probably made their own crusts.

Still, she didn't want to take advantage of Reno. "I'd be happy to help with the cooking. Feeding the calves doesn't seem like enough to do if the job includes room and board."

"No, that's fine. Feeding the calves is all you were hired for—you don't want to spend all day working."

"But that's hardly like work at all." Chrissy had gone with Reno yesterday to meet the calves she was to feed. She had noticed that Reno moved through the livestock with comfort, and the calves came running over to him as if he was their mother. Reno rubbed the calves' ears, and Chrissy petted each one individually and assured each one that she would take good care of it.

"Well, you also have to see to Justin."

"Yes, but that's not my job here. I want to do a good job, too. I need to work to earn my salary."

Reno had never known a woman so desperate to make sure she earned every penny of her salary. If he hadn't been trying to keep the true state of the kitchen a secret from her, he would happily have let her do the cooking just so he wouldn't have to think up other tasks. But he knew women set great store by kitchens, and he didn't want her to know that nothing worked right in the one he owned.

"You're fixing up the bunkhouse," Reno finally said. "Nicki and I sort of let things go down there, since no one has been living there. That's worth something."

"But I'm doing that because I live there. I really feel I should do something more."

Reno had a flash of inspiration. "You can do the shopping." That should be safe. All women liked to shop. "For the groceries, that is."

Reno felt as if he'd solved his problem. She'd never realize that the refrigerator in the ranch-house kitchen went clunk in the night or that the gas stove was so old the burners needed to be lit with a match.

Reno didn't know why he wanted to keep the truth of the ranch kitchen from Chrissy, but he did. He supposed some stubborn part of him wanted to think that she might someday decide that it would be all right to live on the ranch.

Of course, he assured himself, he was only trying to prove to himself that his mother could have endured living here in peace if she hadn't left all those years ago. Or maybe that his own bride wouldn't dislike this old kitchen too much when he got married.

"It's very comfortable here in the kitchen," Chrissy said as she sat down at the breakfast table and settled Justin on her lap.

Reno eyed Chrissy suspiciously. She didn't look as if she was being sarcastic, but now that she'd brought it all up, he had to confess. "It's old, but I have plans to replace some of the appliances someday. I have to start with the farm machinery first, before I work on the house."

Reno half expected the look of protest that grew on Chrissy's face.

"Well, you can't get rid of those old appliances. They look like they're from the fifties—they're probably collector pieces by now."

Reno was taken back. He didn't know anyone who would want to collect the old things, unless it was the junk dealer in Miles City. "You're not upset because I said the farm equipment came before the kitchen?"

"No, why should I be?"

Yeah, Reno thought to himself. Why should she be? She was clearly only staying long enough to find the appliances quaint instead of frustrating. "I will admit there's nothing like those old gas stoves for baking bread."

Reno had decided as long as he'd made the kitchen sound old-fashioned, he should continue. And what he said was true. He could still remember his father talking about the bread Reno's grandmother had baked in those old stoves. Reno had always wished she'd been alive when he was born.

Chrissy looked at him. "Were you baking bread this morning?"

"Ah, no," Reno said. "And don't worry about it. I was hoping you like cornflakes with peach slices."

Chrissy smiled as though she was happy.

"I could also make some toast." Reno remembered that they had bought a new toaster and coffeemaker several years ago. He'd given the coffeemaker to Nicki for Christmas, and she'd given him the toaster. "We even have some homemade jelly from Mrs. Hargrove. I think its chokecherry. There's nothing like chokecherry jelly on toast."

"I've never had chokecherry jelly."

Reno had been counting on that. If he had any hope that Chrissy would be content on the ranch until they figured out what was happening with that lawyer, Reno would need to keep her entertained. Tasting a new kind of jelly wasn't much, but at the moment it was all he had.

"Did Mrs. Hargrove make the jelly?" Chrissy asked after she'd eaten a bit of the toast Reno had made. "From berries?"

"Why, is something the matter?" Reno didn't think there could be any problem with jelly, but maybe he was wrong.

Chrissy shook her head. "It's just that I didn't know anybody made jelly anymore. I've only seen people buy it in the store."

Reno thought Chrissy looked a little worried. He stood up. "Oh, we have the store-bought kind, too— in the cupboard—if you'd rather have that. It's grape, I think. Let me get it for you."

Chrissy shook her head again. "No, thanks. I like Mrs. Hargrove's jelly better than any other jelly I've ever had."

Reno sat down. One thing was perfectly clear to him. He was never going to understand women. He would think that, since he'd had a sister all his life, he should know more about women. But then, Nicki had always said she didn't like all the things other women liked, like nail polish and shopping. Reno stopped. That was it.

"After breakfast we'll need to go shopping."

There, Reno told himself, that news should cheer her up. It seemed to work.

Chrissy beamed. "I can do that."

"It's on your job description." Reno nodded. He wasn't doing so badly, after all. A little shopping. Some different jelly. All of their problems would be solved.

Chapter Nine

Reno wondered what was wrong with him. He'd remembered his wallet, since they were going to do some shopping. He'd remembered the tire chains, since, even though the day was sunny so far, the mud was still thick on the road. But he had forgotten all about that dress.

Chrissy was wearing rubber boots on her feet because of the mud, and she had Justin cradled in her arms, but every man in the hardware store turned to stare at her in that midnight-blue dress when Reno opened the door and she walked through it.

Reno wondered how much of a sin it would be to take down each of his neighbors, some of whom were old enough to be his father. Of course, those two ranch hands from the Elkton spread were there, too, measuring out some nails for mending fence, and they were about Reno's age.

"Here, take this." Reno slipped out of his denim jacket and passed it to Chrissy.

He saw her start to protest, so he added, "It's not charity. It's just to keep you warm."

Chrissy looked at him and nodded. "Thank you, then."

Reno felt more pleased than he should that she had agreed to accept something from him. She was one of the most hardheaded women he knew when it came to her pride.

"Here, let me hold Justin while you put it on," Reno said next.

Chrissy handed him her baby, and Reno felt even more pleased. He hadn't had much holding time with the baby since they'd gotten to the ranch, and he missed it.

"Glad to see you made it to town to visit us," Elmer said from where he sat by the stove reading the Billings newspaper. He set the newspaper down on the floor and looked at Reno and Chrissy. "Didn't take you long."

Reno flushed. "We needed some supplies."

Elmer nodded. "I thought you might. Babies have a way of needing the craziest things. I remember when you were a baby. You had a special craving for applesauce. Your father used to have to make a special trip into Miles City just to get it for you."

"That was Nicki." The older citizens of Dry Creek had a tendency to confuse Reno and his sister. Fortunately, they had both heard the stories for so many years, they could usually set the record straight.

"Ah, well then." Elmer picked up the newspaper and settled back to read it. "I expect the little one won't be asking for that, then."

There was a moment of silence.

"Reno's not the baby's father," Chrissy announced—a little too loudly, Reno thought. "Even if Reno ate a tubful of applesauce, Justin won't be liking it, because they're not related."

The store got even quieter.

"I wasn't meaning anything by my words," Elmer said softly from where he still sat. "I was just remembering how babies are, and Reno and his sister came to mind—they were both cute as a button."

"He's lucky he can remember that far back these days," Jacob said from the other chair.

"My mind's just as sharp as it ever was." Elmer stood up from his chair as though to prove it. "Get out the checkerboard and I'll play anyone and prove it."

The silence inside the store eased, and Reno

heard the shuffle of feet as a couple of the men set the board up. Then the door opened.

"Ah, good, you're here," Reno said as Pastor Matthew entered the store.

Pastor Matthew worked as a relief clerk in the store in addition to preaching at the small church in Dry Creek. "You needed me? Store or church?"

"Store. Chrissy needs some new clothes. I was thinking maybe a pair of those farmer's overalls that you carry would work."

"Glory's coming right behind me. She's taken over the ordering of the stuff like the overalls, and she'll know right where to look for what you need."

Glory was the pastor's new wife. She was also an artist, and Reno had been hoping she would be around, so Chrissy could meet her. Not every small town in Montana had an artist.

Reno nodded in relief. "That would be good."

Chrissy liked the smell of Reno's jacket. Of course, it was probably because it smelled like the calves' feed supplements, and she was growing fond of the calves. They looked at her with big uncertain brown eyes, but she figured she could win them over after she held the milk bucket for them a time or two.

She was also fond of the smell of the tea she held in her hands. Elmer had offered her coffee, and

Jacob had said she should drink tea instead of coffee because of Justin, and so Elmer had made her a cup of orange herbal tea. He'd poured the hot water into a real china cup, even though everyone else, even the two men slowly counting large nails into a brown paper bag beside the far shelf, was drinking from disposable cups.

"You don't need to give me a real cup," Chrissy said. Jacob had already given up his chair by the fire for her, and Reno was holding Justin while she drank her tea. She hadn't gotten this kind of courtesy when she was pregnant.

"I wouldn't want you to think we don't have manners," Jacob confessed as he stood by the store's window. "It's bad enough I don't know how to dance—I won't have it be said that I don't know ladies like their tea in a proper cup."

"Oh, I've been planning to tell you I'm interested in your ad for a dance teacher, if you still want to learn," Chrissy said before she took a sip of the fragrant tea. Jacob was right. She did like a cup for sipping. "Just tell me when."

"I don't know how to dance, either," said one of the men counting nails as he looked up from the bag he was filling. "I'm interested in dance lessons if you're teaching them."

Chrissy didn't recognize the man who spoke up. She knew he was working on the Elkton ranch, but she hadn't talked with those ranch hands when she was in Dry Creek last fall.

"Since when do you need to know how to dance?" Reno said. He had been over by the counter, but he moved a little closer to Chrissy and frowned.

The ranch hand shrugged. "You never know when there's going to be a wedding. The last time I didn't know how to dance, and I felt I was missing out on the fun."

"No one's getting married in Dry Creek," Reno insisted.

Chrissy ignored Reno. She'd have to speak to him later about chasing away all her business. "I'm happy to teach you and Jacob at the same time. I'll even give you a group rate, since there's two of you. Does ten dollars an hour sound fair?"

"More than fair," Jacob said.

"I'd pay more than that to learn," the ranch hand agreed.

"I could use some brushing up, too," the second ranch hand said. "Count me in if you have space in your class. I don't think I've ever danced with a woman in a fancy dress like the one you're wearing."

"We're here to buy overalls for Chrissy," Reno said firmly. "That's what she'll be wearing if she teaches anyone to dance. Farmer overalls like Jacob over there wears."

Everyone in the hardware store turned to look at Jacob. Even Justin's eyes went in that direction.

Jacob was wearing well-worn denim overalls. The back piece snapped onto the front bib, at least on the right side of Jacob's front. He never kept the left side snapped into place because the metal hook had gotten bent in the washing machine and he hadn't taken the time to bend it back. "There's nothing wrong with my overalls."

"Actually, those overalls are kind of stylish." Chrissy glared at Reno. What was wrong with him today? "In fact, I've seen lots of women wear those overalls with halter tops, especially when it's hot outside."

"I hear the temperature is going to get into the seventies tomorrow," one of the two ranch hands said. "You might want to set a new fashion around here. Can't remember when I've last seen a pretty girl in a halter top."

Reno grunted. "She'll be wearing one of my work shirts with the overalls."

"Not when I'm dancing," Chrissy protested. She knew Reno was being protective of her, but he was going too far. "I'll teach dancing in a dress."

"Then it's the orange one," Reno said.

Chrissy looked up at Reno. His cap was pulled down, and it partially hid his face. But she didn't need to see his entire face to know that he was scowling at everyone. "You're going to scare Justin."

Reno looked down at the baby he held in his arms, and Chrissy saw his face visibly soften.

"He likes the orange dress, too, don't you?" Reno murmured as he shifted Justin in his arms. "The two of us, we both think you should wear the orange one."

"The orange dress is fine," Chrissy said. "That is, if it's dry by then."

"It'll be dry," Reno promised.

Ten minutes later Chrissy was in the back room holding up a pair of striped farmer's overalls in front of her and looking in the long mirror Glory had set in a corner of the storeroom. Chrissy had taken off Reno's jacket, and the overalls covered up most of the blue Vegas dress as she held them up to the mirror.

"I'm sorry that the blue striped is the only color that we have in the small size," Glory said as she rummaged through a box on a nearby shelf. "But if I can find you a navy bandanna to twist around your neck, it looks kind of cute with a white T-shirt."

"Reno thinks I should wear his work shirts with the overalls," Chrissy said as she measured the length of the bibbed overalls against her legs. "So I don't think he'll give me a T-shirt."

"Oh, he won't, huh?" Glory looked up from the

box of new bandannas and smiled. "Sounds like he wants to keep his competition down."

"Reno?" Chrissy stopped looking at the overalls. "He says we're almost cousins, so I don't think he's in the competition—if there is one."

"But you're not cousins."

"No, but he thinks so, and that's why he's being so protective. Garrett would be doing the same thing if he were here, and he *is* my cousin, so I guess that's really the way Reno feels."

All of a sudden shopping wasn't as much fun as it usually was for Chrissy.

"Besides, there's the church thing," Chrissy said before she realized she was talking to the wife of the Dry Creek church's pastor. "Oh, I'm sorry—I shouldn't have said—"

Glory waved away the apology with her hands. "Don't worry about it. So tell me, what's the church thing?"

"It's simple. He goes. I don't."

Chrissy stood on one foot so she could start to pull the overalls on under her blue dress.

Glory nodded. "I see. And you don't go because…?"

"I can take care of myself just fine. I don't need a group of church people trying to tell me what to do."

Glory laughed. "Well, I don't think I'd want that, either."

"But you're the pastor's wife." Chrissy looked at herself in the mirror. She had the overalls on up to her waist and the navy skirt of her dress bunched around her middle, making her look like some sort of exotic sausage that sparkled. "You're supposed to like all that church stuff."

"Oh, I do," Glory said. "But the church isn't there to tell people what to do. It's there because we all need God's help to live the life He wants us to live."

"Well, I don't need His help," Chrissy said as she prepared herself for an argument. "I can take care of myself and Justin."

Chrissy focused on looking at her chin in the mirror. She didn't want to see the look on Glory's face when she argued with her. Chrissy was already looking on Glory as a friend, and she didn't want to disappoint the other woman. But she had to be honest, too.

"I can remember the days when I used to think that about myself, too," Glory said as she held out a handful of bandannas to Chrissy. "Try one of the red ones, too."

"*You* thought that once? What happened?"

"A man tried to kill me," Glory answered calmly. "There's nothing like seeing a gun pointing at you to make you realize you need help from others and from God. Now—" Glory opened her hand so the bandannas were all visible "—you might want one of the green ones, too. And I think we have a small white T-shirt here someplace."

* * *

Reno hoped he had gotten his point across to Brad and Mark, the ranch hands from the Elkton place. "You can dance, but no hands below the waist or above the waist. And I better see a good twelve inches of daylight between the two of you at all times."

Reno had Justin cradled in his arms, and he was pacing back and forth in front of the two ranch hands as they finished counting out the nails they would need to mend the north fence later today.

"No one dances that way anymore," Brad protested.

Brad was the older of the ranch hands and too tall in Reno's opinion. Reno was a little under six feet himself, and he figured that was tall enough for anyone. But he knew some women measured a man by his height. He didn't know why. A tall man would never fit in Mrs. Hargrove's old car.

"You should probably dance in your socks, too," Reno said as he stopped his pacing a moment to look down at Justin. The baby was sound asleep. "Leave your boots off. And maybe bend down a little, so you aren't so tall."

"That's kind of hard to do when you're waltzing."

Reno thought a minute. "You're right. Maybe we should stick to line dancing."

"Line dancing?" Jacob protested. "What happened to my waltz lessons?"

"Line dancing is more fun anyway," Reno said.

"Well, can I put my boots on if we're line dancing?" Brad asked. "I don't relish the thought of having my toes stomped on by Jacob or Mark."

Reno nodded. This was going pretty well, and he was a fair man. "If there's line dancing, you can keep your boots."

"Good. My mother taught me it's polite to have my boots on the first time I kiss a girl."

Reno forgot about being fair. "There's no kissing. It's dance lessons, not kissing lessons."

"Well, now, she might want to kiss me," Brad said as he stood up. "Ever think about that? It's not like she's a shy young thing who's never been kissed before."

There was a moment of shocked silence in the hardware store before Reno grabbed Brad's bandanna and pulled his face closer. "Like I said, there's no kissing."

"All right, all right," Brad said. "No kissing."

"I mean it." Reno released the cowboy's bandanna.

"No problem." Brad adjusted his bandanna. "Don't know what your problem is, though. I don't see you dating her any."

"She only got here yesterday."

Brad smiled. "So, have you asked her out?"

"She only got here yesterday," Reno repeated.

Brad's grin widened. "I thought so. Coward?"

"He's not a coward," Jacob offered from where he sat by the fire. "He's her cousin."

"I'm not her cousin." Reno gritted his teeth. "I'm just a gentleman."

"Humph! If you were a gentleman, you wouldn't suggest she go dancing in farmer's overalls."

"I agreed to a dress." Reno decided it was time he took Chrissy over to the café for lunch. They might as well eat lunch in the café before they headed back to the ranch. That way, he could save his cooking skills for supper.

From what he could tell, he was going to have to do a lot of home cooking in the next few days if he wanted to avoid the men of Dry Creek. Why had he never noticed before that they all had only one thing on their minds and it was pretty women? He missed the days when they just talked about the mud outside and the price of cattle.

Chrissy had bought the white T-shirt on credit to wear with the overalls, and Glory was just giving the bandanna around her neck a finishing touch. Chrissy liked what she saw in the mirror. "This does look all right."

Glory nodded. "It's not quite as elegant as your blue dress, but it's cute."

"Thanks for giving me credit for the T-shirt. That way I won't have to borrow any shirts from Reno."

Glory nodded. "Don't want to do that, huh?"

"It just feels funny."

Glory smiled as she turned to hang up the other T-shirts that had come in the package of three. "Well, that's a good sign."

"Good sign of what?"

Glory turned around to look at Chrissy. "Let's just say that I'm guessing you wouldn't hesitate to borrow a shirt from Garrett."

"Of course not—Garrett's my cousin. More like a brother, really."

Glory nodded. "That's what I thought."

"What does that mean?" Chrissy asked. She was starting to have a funny feeling in her stomach. She couldn't be having those kinds of feelings for Reno, could she? Of course she knew he was an attractive man. But that was just because she had good vision. Any woman would know that.

"Don't look so alarmed," Glory said soothingly. "It probably doesn't mean anything."

"It's just that I don't want to be responsible for wearing one of his shirts in case I get it dirty when I feed the calves." Yes, that was it, Chrissy thought to herself. She was just a thoughtful borrower.

"I'm sure he wasn't going to give you one of his church shirts," Glory said. "He'd just give you one of his working shirts that he wears out in the barn."

"Oh." Chrissy frowned as she started to fold up

the blue dress. "I hadn't thought about that. You have to dress up to go to church."

Now, when in the conversation with Glory had she decided to go to church when she was in Dry Creek?

"The blue dress is fine."

"For church?" Even Chrissy knew she shouldn't wear a cocktail dress to church. "It glitters."

"Well, I have a dress you can borrow."

"I don't take charity." Chrissy put the blue dress over her arm and started to walk toward the door back into the hardware store.

Glory smiled. "I'll sell it to you."

"I don't have much money."

Glory stopped to push a box of nails back farther on a shelf. "Who's talking about money? I'd settle for an hour of rocking your baby some afternoon. The twins are getting a pretty good size these days, and they don't want to be rocked anymore. I kind of miss it."

Chrissy turned back to look at the other woman. "That doesn't sound like much to cover the cost of a dress."

Glory grinned. "If it's not enough, I'll cut the dress in half and sell you the skirt part."

Chrissy smiled, too. "I guess it would be all right to take the whole dress if it's an old one."

"We'll pick out the oldest dress in my closet,"

Glory said cheerfully as she opened the door back into the hardware store.

"Just so it's not orange." Chrissy stepped into the store.

"Sunday school is at ten. Reno will know the routine." Glory turned out the light in the storeroom and followed Chrissy into the store.

Chrissy heard a long, low wolf whistle when she stepped into the main room of the store. She automatically looked over to where Reno stood holding Justin, but his lips weren't puckered in a whistle. His face had a frown, though.

"You're looking good," one of the cowboys who stood next to Reno called out. "I'm going to enjoy those dance lessons."

Chrissy gave the man what she hoped was a businesslike smile. "Tonight at seven. In the bunkhouse at the Redfern Ranch." She looked over to Jacob. "If that time works for you, too?"

"I'll be there."

"So will I," Reno said as he scowled at the two cowboys.

"You're going to take dance lessons, too?" Chrissy asked as she looked over at Reno. With his natural grace, she had assumed he already knew how to dance.

"If I have to," Reno said grimly.

"I don't know if I can give four lessons at the

same time." Chrissy thought a minute. "I guess maybe two of you could pair up and dance together."

"What?"

Chrissy didn't know who looked more shocked, Reno or the two cowboys. Even Jacob looked a little whiter than before.

"I'll partner with Justin here," Reno said as he lifted up the baby. Justin gurgled in delight, as if he'd been lifted up high before and liked it.

"And leave me with Jacob?" one of the cowboys protested.

"I ain't dancing with you—you can dance with Brad there," Jacob said. "I'll get me a broom."

Chrissy left the men to their discussion and turned back to Glory. Only the two of them were standing beside the counter as Chrissy took a ten-dollar bill from her purse. "I'll have the rest of the money for the T-shirt for you next Friday."

Chrissy didn't like to be indebted to anyone.

Glory seemed to understand, and she spoke low so only Chrissy could hear. "That's fine. And stop by the house next to the church before you leave town. We'll pick out a dress."

Chrissy nodded. "Thanks."

Chrissy wondered if she had made the right decision. She hadn't even thought about deciding to go to church here in Dry Creek—she'd just been drawn to the people. She hoped they wouldn't expect too much if she came. She wasn't quite ready to jump into anything like religion.

Chrissy could still hear the men arguing on the other side of the store. "I can't sing, you know. I'd be no good in the choir."

Glory smiled. "I'm not in the choir, either."

"And I could never do any kind of public speaking. I don't really see that I'd be any good to the church."

"Don't worry about it."

"I don't even have any money to put in the collection plate. Well, until I get my check from my last job."

"You don't need to give anything, and I'd expect you to let us know if you need our help."

"I guess I could pour coffee sometime."

"Pour coffee where?" Reno said.

Chrissy had not seen him walk over to the counter.

"Nowhere," Chrissy said.

Reno eyed her suspiciously. "I hope you're not planning to be the one going around and pouring coffee at Jacob's big party. The coffeepot's too heavy, and the cowboys tend to be a little too friendly with the coffee pourers."

"Really? I never noticed," Glory said.

Reno nodded. "Remember that chef who catered the big dance Mrs. Buckwalter gave last spring? She poured coffee, and look what happened."

"She got married," Glory said. "The last I heard, she's expecting their first child."

"Yeah, well, I think she got a couple of proposals that night she poured coffee—and they weren't all from that rich man she married."

"Well, you don't need to worry about me getting married. I'm too busy taking care of Justin."

"Oh." Reno frowned as he looked down at the smiling baby in his arms. "He doesn't take that much work."

"Remember, I get to hold him for a while some afternoon," Glory said. "I could even drive out to the ranch and take care of him when you're working outside."

"Maybe when I feed the calves," Chrissy said. "Reno said he'd watch him, but I know he has other things to do."

"It's no trouble for me to watch him," Reno said

"That'll be perfect," Glory said. "What time this afternoon?"

Chrissy looked at Reno.

"Make it three o'clock," Reno said.

"See you then," Glory said as she reached out to give Chrissy a hug. "I'll look forward to it."

"Me, too," Chrissy said as she returned the hug. She felt as if she'd just made another friend. She'd never had so many friends in her life before.

"Here, don't forget your dress." Glory handed a

large paper bag to Chrissy as she started to walk toward the door.

"Thanks." Chrissy turned to take the bag.

Reno opened the door for her, and Chrissy stepped out onto the porch ahead of Reno and Justin.

"Thanks for taking care of Justin while I tried on the clothes," Chrissy said to Reno. "But I can hold him now."

The air was warmer than it had been earlier in the morning, and it looked as if the mud was finally going to start to dry.

"He's my buddy. I can carry him over to the café," Reno said as he stepped off the porch. "He's settled in."

Chrissy could see Justin was happy. The baby was gurgling up at Reno as if he were talking.

Chrissy frowned. Justin didn't have to be so friendly to the man.

Although Chrissy could not blame her son too much. There was something very charming about Reno. Maybe it was the way he scowled when he thought something was threatening her or Justin.

"So, what was that all about? With you and Glory?" Reno asked as they started walking across the street.

In the middle of the gravel road was a big puddle. But it didn't worry Chrissy. She had her farmer overalls tucked into the rubber boots she had borrowed from Reno before they came to town. She could ford a small stream if she needed to. It all gave her a sense of confidence in being able to meet whatever challenges lay ahead. "I'm going to church."

"Here?" Reno looked dumbfounded.

Chrissy thought he didn't need to look so surprised. "Of course here. Sunday. There's a church, isn't there?"

"Of course." Reno started to smile. "So you're going to church?"

Chrissy nodded. "But I won't be singing any hymns or anything. I'll just be observing."

"Of course."

Reno's smile became even wider. Chrissy hoped he wasn't getting any ideas about what this all meant. "I think it'll be good for Justin."

Reno's smile turned into a grin. "Me, too."

Chrissy hoped she wasn't making a big mistake. She'd never gone to church before. Well, at least not where the people knew who she was. She was only getting a start in Dry Creek. Going to church might ruin everything, if the people treated her the way church people had treated her mother twenty years ago.

Chapter Ten

Reno decided he would ask Garth Elkton to take his place as an usher this next Sunday in church. Reno wanted to be sitting beside Chrissy in the pew throughout the entire service.

"Does Linda go to church?" Chrissy asked as she and Reno took the steps up to the porch outside the café.

Reno nodded. "She sings in the choir."

"So I won't be able to sit with her?"

"You can sit with me." Reno had never considered she would want to sit with someone else. He opened the door to the café. "I can help hold Justin."

"I don't think holding Justin is going to be a problem in this town. So far, everyone wants to hold him." Chrissy stepped into the café.

Reno's eyes had to adjust to the darkness inside.

It was already eleven o'clock, and the sun was starting to slide into its noon position. The clouds were gone for today at least, and the sun had already managed to dry up some of the mud.

There was no one in the front part of the café, but Reno could see through the open door into the kitchen area. Linda was leaning against the wall and talking on the phone. The air smelled of spaghetti sauce.

"I hope you like garlic," Reno said as he used one arm to pull a chair out so Chrissy could sit at one of the tables. He still held Justin in his other arm.

Chrissy lifted up her arms to Justin, and Reno could feel Justin squirm in recognition of her.

"I suppose I have to give him up." Reno bent to hand Justin to Chrissy.

The baby snuggled into his mother's arms, and Chrissy smiled down at him. It was all Reno could do to resist the temptation to stroke Chrissy's hair as she sat there. He could see why all the old masters used to paint pictures of the Madonna and Child. Chrissy was beautiful looking down at her baby. Her hair was a chestnut-brown that gradually grew lighter until it was blond at the tips. All her energy was focused on her baby.

Reno wondered what it would feel like to have all that love focused on him.

The faint scent of perfume floated up to Reno. "Gardenia."

Reno was pleased that Chrissy had worn perfume

for her drive to town with him. He hadn't expected it, but it was nice. A woman didn't put perfume on to impress a man she thought of as a cousin. Maybe he had a chance with her after all.

Chrissy looked up and then glanced down at the brown bag she'd set on the floor by her chair. "Oh, the gardenia was Jared's favorite. I used to wear it all the time for him. It's no wonder the scent is still on the blue dress."

"Oh."

"I think the bottle burned in the fire at my mother's house."

"If you like it, we could buy you another bottle."

"Thanks, but I don't wear perfume anymore."

"Oh."

Well, Reno decided, a man didn't get a clearer message than that. He wasn't one to talk about every emotion in the book, but sometimes a man needed to take a chance and speak up. "There's no reason to give up on men just because of someone like Jared. He wasn't half good enough for you, anyway."

Chrissy looked up at Reno with a wistful smile, and for one long heart-stopping minute Reno thought she was going to say something wonderful to him. Something like that she agreed with him and had no intention of giving up on men, especially him. Her rosy lips were moist, and her green-gray eyes were full of tenderness. She was almost going to speak.

Then the kitchen door slammed, and they both heard Linda at the same moment.

"Boy, do we have trouble." Linda didn't even hesitate to come walking out to the middle of the café where Chrissy sat and Reno still stood. "I'm glad you're both here."

"Is there something we can do?" Chrissy asked a little more politely than Reno figured he would have.

Reno did his best not to scowl. *This better be about something more important than burned spaghetti sauce or no Parmesan cheese to sprinkle over everything.*

"I just got a call from Jacob's nephew, David. He's going to be here in a few hours and wanted to get directions."

"I thought he already called," Reno said. Something wasn't right here, and he was glad Linda had the sense to be dramatic about it.

"No, he didn't call. That's the whole problem. He said he didn't call. He doesn't have a cell phone. And—" she paused "—he doesn't even know who Mrs. Robinson is—in the song."

"So that wasn't him who called the other day?" Chrissy asked.

Reno noticed that just the tiniest shadow of a frown was starting to form on Chrissy's face.

"That doesn't mean it was the guys who were around your mom's place the night of the fire," Reno said to reassure her.

"You don't think they started the fire there and are coming up here, do you?" Linda asked, aghast. "They might burn down the whole town."

Well, Linda might be a little too dramatic, Reno decided. "Nothing's going to burn around here. If the rain doesn't stop the fire, the mud will."

"I guess so." Linda nodded.

"Besides, millions of people have cell phones. There's no reason to assume the man who called is even coming here." Reno hoped his words made everyone relax.

"There might be millions of people with cell phones, but how many people drive a black car and play that Mrs. Robinson song? It's not even popular anymore." Chrissy wasn't easily convinced.

Reno noticed that Chrissy's knuckles were white as she clutched the blanket that was wrapped around Justin.

"We don't know the man who called was driving a black car. And that song—it could be playing on a radio anywhere."

"Maybe," Chrissy admitted.

Reno noticed her hands were relaxing. "Even if

someone did come here, they wouldn't get close to you. The final road into Dry Creek is a private gravel road. I can put a roadblock up if you want. That way no one can come or go over the road."

Chrissy smiled a little sheepishly. "Well, maybe after my dance students leave tonight. I'll feel safe as long as they're there."

"And I'll watch the road during the day," Linda promised. "A car has to drive past here if it's going to go out to the Redfern Ranch."

"I forget how much different this is than Los Angeles. There's no way to block much of anything off down there."

"Strange cars are noticeable here, too. We all know everyone's cars and pickups, so we know if a strange one is around," Linda added.

"And there's a long driveway into the ranch," Reno said. "My dog, Hunter, always knows when someone's coming. There's no reason to worry."

Just to be on the safe side, Reno planned to tell Sheriff Carl Wall about the problems with the lawyer and the suspicious fire in Los Angeles. But Chrissy didn't need to know about that conversation.

"I'll try not to worry," Chrissy said.

"Good." Reno nodded.

"I just need something to distract me," Chrissy added.

"You could have lunch," Linda suggested as she

pulled her order pad out from the pocket of her waitress uniform. "If that's what you came in for…"

"You have a uniform on," Chrissy said as she looked at Linda. "I thought you hated uniforms and swore you'd never wear one."

Linda leaned down. "Jacob's nephew wanted formal service for the party he's giving for his uncle. If he's willing to pay for it, I decided I could wear a uniform. He promised there'd be a big tip, too." Linda looked at Chrissy. "I got another uniform in case you want one. I figured you can use a big tip as much as I can."

Chrissy shrugged. "Sure. I've worn worse uniforms when I've been working."

Reno nodded. "The ones in Vegas."

"I meant the orange one from Pete's Diner," Chrissy said. "The Vegas dresses are beautiful. They just need a dry cleaning to take the perfume scent out of them, and they'll be as good as new."

"If you want to help get the cake and the appetizers ready, you can come by tomorrow afternoon, too." Linda looked over at the baby in Chrissy's arms. "I suppose it's awfully expensive to raise a baby, isn't it?"

"It doesn't matter how much it costs," Chrissy said a little defiantly. "You can't put a price tag on a baby."

"I know," Linda whispered as though stricken.

Her voice rose as she talked. "That's what I keep telling—people."

Linda's words ended on a hiccup of a sob, and she turned and ran back into the kitchen.

"Here. Hold Justin," Chrissy said as she stood up and handed her baby to Reno. "I've got to go find out what's wrong."

Reno couldn't help but notice that Justin didn't snuggle into his side the way he did when his mother held him. When he was on Reno's lap, the baby just stared up as if he expected to be entertained. "Yeah, well, I'd tell you what was going on if I knew a blessed thing to say about it all."

Justin gurgled up at him.

Reno smiled. "Well, I think it's going to be a while before lunch, so I guess I could tell you about the little pigs that went to market—but I need your toes."

Reno unwrapped a corner of Justin's blanket. "Now, the market that these little pigs went to wasn't like the grocery stores you see today. It was more like the hardware store. Remember when we were over at the hardware store? Well, that's the kind of place this market was that the pigs went to. It was a place where everyone kind of stayed around and talked."

It took Reno almost fifteen minutes to exhaust his store of nursery rhymes. He'd even thrown in the recipe for instant oatmeal so the baby would be able to cook for himself when the day came.

"No sense in thinking you won't need to cook," Reno said. "Women don't stay in the kitchen anymore, so if you want to eat, you'll have to know how to cook. Trust me. Fried potatoes get old after a while."

Now, when had Reno gotten tired of bachelor cooking? He never used to mind. For the first time since his sister had gotten married, Reno wondered if his father would have given them the same advice not to marry if he hadn't already been married and had the two of them. Eating every meal alone out at the ranch sounded less and less appealing as the days went by. Granted, Nicki and her husband were on the ranch property. But they were in their own house, and he couldn't eat every meal with them. No, it would just be him when Chrissy and Justin left. Him and his fried potatoes.

"Well," Reno said to Justin, "no sense in fretting about it. I can learn to cook something else. Starting with supper tonight." He looked down at Justin. "Maybe I can make something to impress your mother."

Reno looked around the café. There were tables and chairs and several water pitchers on the small serving table at the back. But he didn't see any menus.

"Of course, menus don't have the recipes with

them anyway," Reno said. "Maybe it's better just to sit and think. Unless you want to tell me what your mother likes to eat?"

Reno looked down at Justin. The baby apparently didn't have any suggestions for supper.

"I also make a mean chili, but I didn't put out any beans to soak." Reno thought aloud. He wondered if Linda might have a frozen casserole that she would sell him. They had some funny Italian stuff they served sometimes. A little of that should impress Chrissy.

The door to the café kitchen opened, and this time both Chrissy and Linda came out. Even though they were smiling, Reno could tell they had both been crying. "Everything okay?"

"Everything is fine," Linda announced with her head held high. "I just don't think like a man."

Reno could tell he was in dangerous territory. "Good. I think."

"Men can be so stupid," Chrissy added cheerfully as she started walking back toward the table where Reno sat.

"I don't think Justin should be hearing this," Reno protested. He wasn't so keen on hearing it himself.

"Oh, not in the mental way," Chrissy said.

"What other way is there?" Reno didn't know if he should go on with this, but it seemed a little late to change the topic of conversation to the mud outdoors.

"There's such a thing as being stupid in the heart," Chrissy said as she stood beside Reno and held out her arms for Justin. "Come to Mama."

"Oh. What does that mean?" Reno lifted Justin up so Chrissy could hold him again.

"It means that not all men see how good it can be to have a baby," Linda explained as she came closer to the table, as well. "It doesn't matter if babies cost money, they are wonderful."

"Well, I certainly agree." Reno decided he finally knew how to make his way through this conversation. Women tended to worry about things like this, he supposed. Well, they shouldn't have worried. They should just have asked him. "Take Justin—in time, I could love him like he was my own son. I wouldn't care how much money it took to raise him."

There was stunned silence in the café.

"We weren't talking about Justin," Linda finally said softly.

"Oh." Reno thought a minute. "But he's the only baby around."

Linda looked at him as she pulled her order book from the pocket of her uniform. "And he'll probably *be* the only baby around since Jazz is so hardheaded he absolutely refuses to have a baby if we get married. He says they're too much money."

"Oh." Reno decided he'd already said too much.

"That's why Linda called the engagement off," Chrissy explained as she looked down at Justin. "She always assumed they'd have children."

"What man doesn't want to have children?" Linda continued, and then added with half a sob, "His parents had children. I always just assumed he would want them, too."

"Well, the two of you have been engaged a long time. I'm sure you can work it out. Maybe he didn't mean exactly *no* children," Reno said. "Maybe if you talked to him again—"

"No!" both women said in unison.

"He needs to be the one who comes to Linda," Chrissy explained. "That's the way it works."

Reno wondered how men and women ever got together. "But he might not know that's the way it works. Maybe he's waiting for her to come to him."

"Well, he'll wait until the day he dies, then," Linda said calmly as she reached into her pocket and brought out two small menus that she set on the table in front of Reno. "Now, can I take your order?"

"Did I smell spaghetti sauce?" Reno asked as he picked up a menu and looked at it. He was glad the conversation was returning to questions he knew how to answer.

"The spaghetti sauce burned."

"Oh. How about a cheeseburger?" Reno looked at the four remaining items on the menu.

"We're out of buns."

"I could have some pancakes."

Linda shrugged. "No milk to make the batter."

"The soup of the day?" Reno asked.

"It won't be ready until tomorrow. The beans are still soaking."

Reno finished looking at the menu. Chrissy was patting Justin on the back and she didn't look worried about what to eat. "That leaves the liver and onions."

"We don't really have that," Linda confessed. "Jazz just put it on the menu so it would look like we offered more things. We didn't think anyone would ever order it."

Reno closed the menu. "Do you have anything to eat?"

Linda thought. "Not really. Jazz was the one who did the ordering and the cooking, and he's been gone for three days now."

"I see."

"We do have some imported mustard and a couple of frozen hamburger patties. I could fry you up a couple of those."

"Sounds good," Reno said.

"Or we could wait for Mrs. Hargrove to get here,"

Chrissy offered. "Linda called her before we came, and Mrs. Hargrove said she'd bring over some of the meat loaf she had left over from supper last night, along with some bread for sandwiches."

"She's bringing some rice pudding, too. With raisins and cinnamon in it," Linda added. "And then I'm going to put the closed sign up for a few hours this afternoon and go into Miles City and stock up on supplies. It isn't easy running the café if you're only one person."

"Well, Jazz shouldn't have just left like that," Reno protested. What was Jazz thinking? It wasn't like him to be that irresponsible.

Linda blushed. "I sort of told him to leave."

"Ah." Reno thought a minute. "So *you're* the one who told him to leave, but he's supposed to know that *he's* the one that needs to come back and apologize?"

"Of course." Linda looked at him in surprise. "I would think that's obvious."

"Do you happen to know where he's staying these days?" Reno decided it wouldn't hurt to give Jazz a clue about what these rules were that men didn't know about.

"We put a down payment on the Jenkins place. So he's out there, I would imagine."

"You finally managed to get the down payment money!" Reno knew that they'd been working for over a year to pull that money together. "Congratulations!"

Someone knocked on the door of the café and Linda hurried over to open it.

"Mrs. Hargrove!" Linda held out her arms. "Here, let me take some of that so you can come inside."

"Oh, I don't have time to stay," Mrs. Hargrove said from outside the door.

"The baby's here."

"Oh." Mrs. Hargrove stepped inside the café and looked around. "Chrissy's baby?"

Mrs. Hargrove had a large, foil-wrapped packet in one hand and a loaf of bread in a plastic bag in the other hand. She set both of them on a table beside the door and stood there. She wore a blue gingham dress with her black sweater over it and a four-cornered scarf on her head.

Chrissy's heart started beating fast. She knew Reno had said Mrs. Hargrove wanted her here, but he could be wrong. He might have just been polite when he said that. "Hello, Mrs. Hargrove."

Mrs. Hargrove walked closer and whispered, "He's not sleeping, is he?"

Chrissy looked down at Justin. His eyes had closed. "Maybe a little bit. He sleeps a lot."

"Babies do that." Mrs. Hargrove nodded as she walked closer still. "I'd forgotten how tiny they are. How old is he now?"

Chrissy blushed. "Eight weeks."

Justin stirred in his sleep and yawned.

"Don't you think he's a little small for his age?" Reno asked with a frown. "I think we should take him to Dr. Norris and have him weighed."

"He's just about perfect," Mrs. Hargrove said as she looked down at Justin. "Besides, his mother is small boned. Maybe he takes after her."

Chrissy couldn't stand it. "He doesn't have a father to take after. Well, I mean, of course he has a father. Everyone has a father. It's just—" Chrissy took a deep breath. "He doesn't have a father in the legal sense."

Mrs. Hargrove smiled as though that fact didn't bother her at all. "What's done is done. I'm just hoping you'll let us make up for that and do some of what a father would."

"Huh?" Chrissy figured she hadn't heard right.

Mrs. Hargrove said, "We'd love to help take care of your baby."

"You don't care if I'm not married?"

"Well, of course I'd love to see you get married." Mrs. Hargrove looked at Reno. "To some fine young man."

Chrissy swallowed. She couldn't even look at Reno. "Am I on some kind of list at the church? Is that why you're being nice to me?"

Mrs. Hargrove laughed. "The only list we have

is a prayer list. Besides, no one needs a reason to be nice to you."

Chrissy wasn't so sure about that, but she didn't think she'd figure out anything by asking more questions. Maybe when she went to the church she would find out what the deal was. She'd die of mortification if a prayer that she would get married was written out somewhere.

"Now, I hear you need some lunch," Mrs. Hargrove said as she stepped back to the packages she'd left on the table. "Let me get the meat loaf to the back while it's still warm. It makes a wonderful sandwich with grilled toast, and I think Linda already has the toast going."

"I've never seen anyone bring food to a restaurant before." Chrissy looked over at Reno. He wasn't frowning, so that must mean he hadn't seen the look Mrs. Hargrove had given him when she mentioned that Chrissy should be married.

"There are some good things about being in a small town," Reno said. "I mean, meat loaf might not be gourmet, but it's filling."

Chrissy wondered if it was the smell of that meat loaf that had kept Reno distracted. "I love meat loaf."

"Good, because we're having it for supper tonight, too."

"Sounds fine."

Justin moved again and woke up, so Chrissy looked down at him. "He doesn't look like Jared much at all."

"Good." Reno nodded.

"Well, maybe around the eyes he does a little."

"The color of his eyes will change as he grows," Reno said.

"Have you been reading baby books?" Chrissy asked in surprise. Reno never ceased to amaze her.

Reno shook his head. "I just know from watching kittens and other animals."

Chrissy nodded. "And the calves."

"Oh, their eyes mostly are always brown."

"I bet they're getting hungry again," Chrissy said.

Chrissy had watched Reno feed the calves this morning, but this afternoon he had promised to let her hold the bucket. She was looking forward to it.

Chapter Eleven

Chrissy was glad she had her overalls and boots to wear. She was in one of the corrals on the Redfern Ranch, and all twelve calves wanted to butt against her legs. She didn't know what they would have thought if she'd been wearing her Vegas blue dress. They'd probably be trying to eat the sequins right now. A couple of the bigger calves pushed their way closer to her, trying to get their heads near the bucket she held even though she had told them clearly that it wasn't their turn and that other calves were eating at the moment.

"They just don't listen," Chrissy said as she looked over at Reno. He'd stepped a few feet closer to the fence, saying he wanted her to see what it was like to be alone with the calves.

The afternoon had turned sunny, and Chrissy

thought that might be why the calves were so playful. The clouds had gone away as she and Reno drove back from Dry Creek, and the sun was warm enough that neither one of them needed a jacket.

Chrissy was glad that Glory had driven out to sit with Justin today, because she wanted Reno's full attention to be on her while she fed the calves for the first time. When a calf nursed at the rubber bucket spigots, he tended to push the bucket around with his head. It was all Chrissy could do to keep control of the bucket. Calves, she learned, didn't have any sense of etiquette.

When one of the calves finished all the milk in the bucket, Chrissy would swing around and grab a full bucket from the shelf that ran along the edge of the barn. If she wasn't fast enough, the calves would start to nudge her.

"You'll probably need to push that big one away, the one with the white spot on his forehead," Reno said. "He always wants to eat. I call him Piggy."

Chrissy giggled. Reno had a name for each of the calves. "Don't you think he'll get confused about what kind of an animal he is?"

"Him? He's not very philosophical. He doesn't care what he is as long as he's well fed. He'd probably rather be a pig."

"Ahh, he's not a bad calf," Chrissy said as she reached out to pat Piggy. The calf turned his head, however, and she ended up patting his wet tongue. The calf had been hoping she had something to eat in her hand. "Ugh, Piggy."

Chrissy wiped off her hand.

"See?" Reno had moved a step closer, but not close enough that the calves gave their attention to him. As long as Chrissy held the feeding bucket, she was their favorite.

"Be careful of Graceful there," Reno added.

Chrissy looked down at the small calf with the big brown eyes that was standing close to her right side. Graceful, Reno had told her, liked to come in close and, because she was small, could slip in around the other calves. Of course, to get that close, she had a tendency to step all over the toes of whoever was holding the feeding bucket.

"How do you think of all these names?" Chrissy asked.

Reno shrugged. "The same way anyone thinks of a name. How did you come up with the name Justin?"

"I named him after my father," Chrissy said as she gently shoved Graceful away from the bucket.

"Really? I didn't think you knew who your father was." Reno came closer and pushed Piggy to the outskirts of the calf herd.

"I don't," Chrissy admitted as she looked up at Reno and gave a small smile. "I just thought I knew the name for a while. I went through a period where I begged my mother to tell me my father's name. A couple of times I thought she started to say his name, but all that came out was 'Just—'. Of course, I decided his name was Justin."

"Well, wasn't it?"

Chrissy shook her head. "Turns out my mother was going to say 'Just stop asking me' or 'Just forget about it' or something. But I'd already started calling my father Justin in my mind, so I decided to continue. After all, he had to have a name."

Chrissy kept her eyes focused on the calves while she answered Reno's question. She wanted him to know about her father and she hoped he would understand, but she didn't want to look him in the eye in case he didn't quite see it her way.

"Of course he needed to have a name," Reno said indignantly. "You needed something to call him, and Daddy sure wasn't it."

Chrissy winced. How did he know that had been a sore place in her heart?

"One of the hardest things I ever did was call Lillian 'Mother' again after she came back last fall," Reno continued. "It had been all I could do to call her Lillian for all those years when she was gone. I didn't want to name her at all."

Chrissy nodded. So that was how he knew. "Your mother is sorry about hurting you and Nicki when she left—at least, that's what she's said. She used to talk about her children when I knew her in Vegas."

Reno nodded. "I know she's sorry. It's still hard for me to call her Mother."

"Yeah," Chrissy murmured. "I wonder if parents ever think about how it is for kids."

Piggy pushed to be closer to the bucket at the same instant that it all flashed in Chrissy's mind. "What's Justin going to call his father?"

"He won't be worrying about that for a while." Reno stepped in closer still and put his hand on the feeding bucket next to where Chrissy held it. "He can't even talk yet. You've got plenty of time to figure it out."

"Maybe I should let his grandmother raise him," Chrissy said. "At least then he'd get to hear all about his father. It's important for a boy to know who his father is. Really, maybe even more important than knowing who his mother is."

"I don't know about that," Reno said slowly. "Mothers are pretty important."

Chrissy let Reno take full control of the bucket so she could think. "I thought telling my mother about Jared was hard. Wait until I have to tell Justin about him."

"Kids are pretty understanding."

"Were you?"

Reno didn't know how to comfort Chrissy. "No, I

guess I wasn't very understanding. But I grew up all right. Every kid has to make his peace with something."

Chrissy reached up and gathered her hair into a twist at the back of her head. "But usually they only need to make their peace about the fact that the Easter bunny isn't real and the tooth fairy isn't going to leave a dime under their pillow every time something painful happens."

"So Justin will turn out stronger than most. He'll be loved. That makes a big difference."

"I don't know if I can be enough for him."

Chrissy looked more scared than Reno had ever seen her, even on the night when they were racing back to the fire at her mother's house. Her shoulders were hunched, and she didn't even notice that Graceful was stepping on her toes.

"You won't be alone with Justin," Reno said. "You don't have to be everything to him. You've got people who care."

Chrissy had never had people, outside of her mother, whom she could count on. "I thought Mrs. Hargrove was just being polite when she said she'd help."

"She wasn't," Reno said. "And I'll be there and Garrett will be there."

"And I can really handle most things myself," Chrissy added. "All I'll need is a little help."

"And we can give you more than that."

Reno saw the old Chrissy emerge as she talked. She was confident and smiling again. "As long as I'm in Dry Creek, we'll be fine, then. I'll just have to stay."

Reno was speechless. Chrissy had just said she was going to live in Dry Creek. He had never wanted to hear any words as much as he wanted to hear those. But it wasn't right. "You don't need to stay because you're scared of what will happen if you leave. We'd all still be there for Justin no matter where you live."

"Don't worry. I won't expect this job to last forever. I know these calves will be able to eat grass pretty soon— or hay, or whatever it is you're feeding the others."

"It's not about this job," Reno protested. "I want you to stay in Dry Creek. I'm just worried you'll—" Reno stopped himself. He hadn't meant to say all of this out loud, but maybe he needed to. "It's just that Dry Creek isn't like Las Vegas."

Chrissy was frowning at him. "Well, of course it's not."

"We don't have any shops where you can buy those fancy dresses. We don't have any beauty salons. We don't have any gourmet restaurants. And you think you can live without them now, but you're wrong. All women like those kinds of things."

Chrissy's frown turned to a smile. "You're brilliant. That's absolutely right."

"What?" Reno hadn't thought she would agree so easily. And she didn't need to look so happy about it. She could at least have pretended to think about staying in Dry Creek, as she had said she was going to do. "Shouldn't you at least think about Justin a little more? We have lots of fishing around here. And horses. Little boys love to ride horses."

"Justin can't even walk yet. He's too young to ride horses." Chrissy finished feeding the last calf and swung the bucket up on the shelf. "I need to go inside and talk to Glory. I'll come clean the buckets a little later, before the guys come for a dance lesson."

Reno figured he might as well clean the buckets. He hoped Nicki and Garrett came back from their trip soon. He didn't understand women at all, and now that Nicki had found love, maybe she could help him out.

Chrissy lined her lips with the darkest red lipstick that she had. Jared had called this her "kissing lipstick," although he had never kissed her when she had it on because he said it made his lips look red, as well. Still, she looked very dressed up when she wore it with blush and eye shadow and her diamond-chip earrings.

She already had the blue dress on, so she'd just need to sweep her hair up into a French braid to have exactly the look she wanted. She had looked at the orange dress as it hung on the hanger and couldn't bring herself to wear it. Tonight, she told herself, was important. She wanted each of her dance students to go back and report to everyone else in town that she looked beautiful.

A report like that would make it much easier to put her plan into action. When Reno was describing Dry Creek to her earlier this afternoon, she'd realized he was absolutely right. There was no beauty salon for women in Dry Creek. And the women wouldn't want just a beauty salon. They would want a place to visit and buy soaps and perfume. The men had the hardware store. The women needed a place, too.

Chrissy wasn't totally naive. By now she had figured out that half, or maybe all the jobs on that job board in the café were fake. Oh, someone was willing to pay her to do what the ad asked. It was just that the ad wouldn't be there at all if she didn't need the work.

It was a kind gesture from many people in Dry Creek. But she couldn't build her future on feeding Reno's calves or doing Elmer's mending. She needed to have a real job.

Or, better yet, she needed to have a business—

and a beauty shop could be it. She had wanted to go to beauty school after she graduated from high school, but Jared had wanted to move to Las Vegas, and she'd thought it wouldn't hurt to work as a waitress for a year or so before they settled down.

But now, when she looked at her life, she knew she needed to have a plan.

Chrissy snapped a hair clip into place and smoothed a few strands of hair off her neck. The first step to her plan would be to impress her dance partners. To do that, she should be ready when they came to the door.

She looked out the window. The night was dark on the Redfern Ranch, but she saw the lights of a pickup as it drove down the long road into the main part of the ranch. That would be her students. The two cowboys from the Elkton Ranch had said they'd stop in Dry Creek and pick up Jacob on their way.

Well, she was ready for them.

She had Reno's coffeemaker plugged in to the outlet by the table in her makeshift kitchen. She also had a plate of cookies Mrs. Hargrove had given her as a welcome gift before she and Reno left Dry Creek earlier today. Justin was dozing in the crib by her bed. She hoped to keep the music down low enough that he would sleep through the lessons.

Chrissy went over to the CD player that Linda had lent her for the lessons. Linda said the player was only taking up room on the counter in the back of the café and that Chrissy was welcome to use it until Saturday night. The café advertised music with dinner on Saturday night.

"It used to be live music," Linda had said. "But since Jazz isn't here to sing and play his guitar, I hope people will be happy with some CDs. I have a pretty good selection of music."

Linda had lent Chrissy some waltz music, and Chrissy was planning to give her a few dollars after she collected the fees from her students tonight.

Chrissy sighed. She'd been so determined to be independent and not take charity from anyone, but it seemed as if she was getting help from everybody. She really should get a notebook and write it all down, so she could pay it back when she was able.

"Anyone home?" Reno's voice called out softly as he knocked on the door.

Chrissy went over to the door and opened it.

"Oh." Chrissy had never seen Reno in a suit. He was freshly shaven and smelled of something herbal. The suit was black, and his shirt was snow-white and open at the collar. She could see his throat as he swallowed.

"Am I early?"

"Ah, no." Chrissy knew she was staring. But she had just never expected Reno to look like this. She knew he was handsome, of course. But she'd always thought his good looks were of the kind that were at their best in blue jeans and flannel shirts. She'd never thought of what he would look like in formal clothing. Now she knew.

"Is something wrong?" Reno asked.

Chrissy blushed. "I just never thought you'd look like this in a suit."

"I can change it. It's just what I wear dancing."

"You look very nice. I was just surprised, that's all."

"Oh." Reno smiled. "Well, you look very nice, too."

"Thank you." Chrissy realized they were still standing on the porch. She stepped to the side. "Oh, I'm sorry, come in. The others will be here in a minute."

Chrissy could hear the sounds of the pickup as it made the final turn into the road that led to the main ranch house. It would have to make another turn to come down to the bunkhouse.

"I was hoping if I got here early, there'd be time for a dance before the others started," Reno said.

"Oh, I couldn't possibly. I mean, it's just the lessons."

Chrissy wasn't sure she'd feel right about dancing with Reno all alone in the bunkhouse. It made her breath come up short just thinking about it.

Reno shrugged. "It's just that I hate to make a fool of myself in front of the other guys."

"Oh, I see." Chrissy told herself she needed to forget about Reno's startling good looks. Tonight he was just a student who needed a little extra practice. She went over to push the button on the CD player. "I can see how you wouldn't want to do that."

The sounds of an instrumental waltz played softly in the kitchen.

"I'm trying to keep the music down so that Justin can sleep," Chrissy said as she stood in position to dance with her first student.

"We don't need much in the way of music," Reno said as he reached behind his back and turned off the switch to the main overhead light in the bunkhouse. Only a lamp in the far corner by the bed gave off light as he put his hand on Chrissy's waist and drew her to him so they could waltz.

"We should leave the big light on."

"Hush, we don't want to wake Justin. Leaving the light off will help him sleep."

Chrissy supposed he was right.

Reno's life was complete. He hadn't known it would feel so good to hold Chrissy in his arms, even if she was counting in his ear and trying to lead. She had pulled her hair back and put it up in some kind of an elegant braid. If it weren't for the few rebellious strands of hair that escaped the braid, she would look so perfect he'd think she wasn't real.

It was those strands of hair that were his undoing. He couldn't help but lift them off her neck. The skin of her neck was like warm silk. Her hair was even softer. And there, right at the base of her throat, he could see her pulse fluttering like a butterfly.

"I didn't have any pins," Chrissy said as she stopped dancing and looked up at him.

It took Reno a second to know what she was talking about. "You don't need pins for your hair. It's beautiful like this."

Once Reno had smoothed back her hair, he noticed the small wisps around her ear and he tucked those back, as well. When his hand rested against the side of her neck, he could feel her pulse.

Chrissy was looking up at him.

Reno knew he shouldn't kiss her. But his life to this day seemed long, and all the days following this moment seemed short. Sometimes a man just needed time to be frozen for a second so he could think.

Reno forgot his hand was still resting along the side of Chrissy's throat until he felt her pulse with his fingertips. The beat of her pulse was increasing. And she was looking at him with eyes that waited.

Reno bent his head slowly. He wanted her to have time to signal him that she wasn't ready for a kiss. He would have stopped at the last minute if it killed him rather than force her into a kiss.

But no signal came, and his lips met hers. Suddenly the days that had seemed so short spreading before him now began to seem long, because nothing in them would match this moment of time.

A small circle of soft light came in the window of the bunkhouse.

Chrissy was the first to pull away. "That's the lights from the pickup. The others are here."

Reno nodded. He couldn't speak yet.

Chrissy swallowed. "I don't usually kiss men on the first date—" She stopped. "Not that this is a date or anything."

"It could be," Reno said. "We could tell the others the lessons are off. I could take you to Miles City, and we could see a movie or something."

For the first time in his life Reno thought that the home he'd surrounded himself with was too small. He needed to think bigger. For a moment he wished he lived in a big city. If he did, there would be someplace he could take a woman like Chrissy on a date that would show her how important she was to him. Everything around here seemed too ordinary. "We could even drive down to Las Vegas and see one of the entertainers there. Something with fireworks."

"Las Vegas." Chrissy looked startled. "We just came through there."

"I know. But just because we're in Dry Creek

doesn't mean we can't drive someplace else for some excitement."

Chrissy frowned and touched his lips with her fingers. "I didn't mean to get lipstick all over. Let me get something to wipe off the lipstick."

"Forget my lips for a second." Reno heard the sounds of heavy footsteps on the steps that led up to the porch of the bunkhouse. He didn't have much time. She wasn't even really listening to him. "I've even thought it would be fun to go to Paris some day."

"Paris! You've never mentioned Paris."

Now he had done it, Reno thought. Chrissy was looking at him with more suspicion than longing in her eyes. She must think he wasn't serious.

Chrissy had found a tissue somewhere and wiped his lips with it.

"A man doesn't need to stay on the same piece of land he was born on," Reno said when he could. "Sometimes he needs to reach for more."

It sounded as if an army was knocking on the bunkhouse door.

"I better let them in," Chrissy said as she reached for the door handle.

Brad was the first one through the door, and his eyes went straight for Reno. "What's going on here?"

"I was just giving Reno a little extra help with his

dancing," Chrissy said as the three men all stepped into the room. "Hi, Jacob. Brad. And Mark, isn't it?"

Brad grunted and grinned at Reno. "Need extra help, do you?"

Reno nodded. It certainly looked to him as if he could use some extra help. Not that he trusted Brad to be able to give it to him.

No, Reno decided, what he needed was a little divine intervention. He felt a little odd asking God to give him enough money to take a girl someplace so he could impress her. Reno had grown up learning to be content with what he had and pretending some things, like having a mother, didn't matter. After all, he had a sister and a father.

Reno was good at knowing the limits to how much he could expect. He'd always thought that was what God wanted. No, it wasn't likely He would okay a trip to Europe. God would probably tell him that a good marriage proposal didn't require Paris anyway.

Oh—Reno stopped himself. When had he decided to ask Chrissy to marry him? Surely that wasn't a good idea. The two of them? He stamped down the hope that rose in his throat. That was clearly outside the limits. Wasn't it?

Chapter Twelve

Reno sat on the rocker on the bunkhouse porch and cradled Justin in his arms. The baby had woken up after about two rounds of waltzing, and Reno was relieved to be able to take him outside on the porch and rock him. Of course, Reno positioned the rocker so that he could see through the window and watch Chrissy conduct her lessons.

"She's good," Reno admitted to Justin as they sat in the darkness.

Chrissy was taking her teaching seriously. Even Brad was frowning and trying to match his steps to some tape she'd put on the floor.

The golden light from inside the bunkhouse filtered out into the darkness of the porch and Reno could hear the faint sound of music with a strong beat. The Montana night was dark and moonless.

Reno's dog, Hunter, had curled up at the foot of the rocker and was lying there just as though he'd forgotten he was part wolf and shouldn't be so happy to be domesticated.

"Must be more clouds up there," Reno said to Justin by way of information. He'd already introduced him to Hunter and explained about dogs. "You remember clouds? Those big white things in the sky that look like pillows."

It was amazing all the things a baby had to learn.

Until he'd had Justin around, Reno had never thought about what he would be missing if he didn't have a child. He liked to hold Justin and think of all the things that he could share with the boy as Justin grew older. There could be fishing trips and baseball games.

"And some cooking lessons, too," Reno reminded him. "Some of these jobs are equal opportunity now. We won't just leave it all to your little sister. And the laundry, too."

Reno knew he was dreaming. But what could it hurt to dream for a night? The desire to marry Chrissy and have a family with her had taken hold in him, and he deserved at least one night of wondering what it would be like before he actually said anything to her and heard her answer.

He knew he didn't have a chance. And it wasn't just that he really couldn't afford to take her to Paris.

After all, Chrissy seemed to be enjoying her time in Dry Creek, but he still didn't think she would stay for long. She was visiting.

Of course, she'd surprised him already when she'd made her decision to go to church this next Sunday. She'd talked about where to sit and what to wear enough so he knew that she fully intended to go, and not as a visitor. No, she was trying to find where she fit with the church and with God. He hoped that meant she intended to give God a fair chance in her life.

But even if she made her peace with God, it didn't mean she would want to stay in Dry Creek.

Reno knew the reason Chrissy was in Dry Creek was that she was scared. But she had told that fire captain her suspicions about Mrs. Bard's attorney and had given him Jared's phone number in Las Vegas. Reno expected that someone had at least questioned the attorney by now. The authorities might even have talked to Jared.

The custody issues with Justin would calm down soon. When the fire authorities started to ask the attorney questions, Reno knew the man would stop his harassment and Chrissy would feel free to go anywhere. Reno would be happy when that day came except for one thing—if Chrissy was free to live anywhere, she wouldn't choose to stay in Dry Creek.

Reno wondered where Chrissy *would* choose to live. He looked down at the baby looking up at him. "My guess would be Los Angeles, wouldn't you say, sport?"

Reno had decided that Justin was a long name for a baby and he had experimented with nicknames. He'd tried out "Jus," but that sounded like an old man. He'd moved on to "sport." It wasn't quite right, but it was closer.

Hunter moved slightly at his feet, and Reno looked down. The dog had tensed up as though he heard something.

Reno turned from the window and looked out into the dark night away from the bunkhouse. He could see the tall outlines of the trees around the main house and the angles of the barn. He'd left the yard light on, so he could see the circle of packed dirt between the bunkhouse and the main house that everyone used for parking. There were no strange cars there. Just the two pickups—his and Brad's.

Everything looked normal, but Reno trusted Hunter's instincts, so he stood up and moved out of the light from the window so he could see better. He let his eyes adjust and looked over at the barn. There was always a little noise on the ranch. A cow might be mooing or a chicken scratching at the ground.

Reno looked around the corner of the bunkhouse

so he could see the long road that led into the ranch. He didn't see any lights of approaching vehicles. He had never fully relaxed since Linda had said that the man who had called the café asking for directions to Dry Creek wasn't Jacob's nephew. But unless someone was crawling on his belly through the pasture directly in front of the bunkhouse, no one was around who shouldn't be here.

"Is it maybe just a rabbit?" Reno asked the dog standing at his feet. Hunter didn't always care whether the intruder was a six-foot human or a six-inch rabbit. Either way, he went on alert.

"Or do you feel something coming?" Reno frowned into the darkness. Hunter seemed to sense when a car was coming. Reno had often wondered if the dog felt vibrations from the distant vehicles before they even turned onto the drive that led up to the Redfern Ranch.

Whatever it was that Hunter had heard, the dog must have decided it was all right, because he went back and lay down beside the rocker again.

"Well, we should probably go inside before too long anyway," Reno muttered as much to himself as to Justin. "You need your sleep, and those lessons should be about over."

Reno would feel better if the ranch hands left and he could go put up the roadblock he'd nailed together late this afternoon. The roadblock was a bunch of wooden sawhorses and some metal sheeting he'd had in the barn.

Even though someone could get past the roadblock, he would make enough noise to wake Reno as well as Hunter. Especially since Reno intended to sleep in the barn on the cot he kept for calving season. That way, he could hear anything coming down the road better than if he was in his cozy upstairs bedroom in the main house.

Chrissy knew her breath was coming in soft, quiet gasps. "The boys," as she'd referred to them all night, had decided to teach her how to do a down-home cowboy line dance as a thank-you for teaching them how to waltz. They didn't have a CD with the right music, so the three of them took turns calling out a beat.

The furniture in the bunkhouse was already pushed to the wall or moved out to the porch, but it still hadn't seemed as if there was enough room for all the swirling and stomping.

Chrissy had had to hold up the long skirt of her blue dress when it came to some of the stomping sets, and she realized she must have looked a sight with all her sequins sparkling and her hair falling out of the French braid on her head. She would have done better in a cotton square-dance outfit, but she was glad she'd decided not to wear the orange dress.

"Now, that's a man's dance," Jacob said in satisfaction. He was breathing hard, too, and he had a big smile on his face. "I think it must come from Ireland or somewhere."

The main light in the room gave off a bright light. Reno had turned it on when the three men arrived. Since Justin had already woken up with all the pounding at the door earlier, Chrissy had decided to leave the light on.

Not that it mattered now anyway, since Justin was out on the porch with Reno. Of course, she doubted Justin was sleeping, even though there were no bright lights out there to disturb him. Justin never seemed sleepy when he was with Reno. He always seemed to want to stay awake and see what was happening.

"It's not a man's dance," Brad protested as he leaned against a wall so he could put his boots back on. Brad was wearing a white shirt with a black cowboy tie and what he had said earlier were black snakeskin boots. "If a man's going to go to the trouble of getting all dressed up for dancing, he likes to hold a woman when he's dancing, and in that one you only twirl her around."

"Oh, let me get you a chair." Chrissy looked around. Where were her manners? A man shouldn't have to stand to put on his boots. Had they put all the chairs out on the porch? She'd had two chairs at the table earlier.

"I'm fine." Brad waved the offer away. "I don't want to bother Reno. At least, not now that I'm getting my boots back on."

Brad smiled when he said that, and the other two men nodded and chuckled.

"Why would he care if you have your boots on or not?" Chrissy wondered if she was missing some cowboy humor.

"I told him a gentleman only kisses a lady when he has his boots on," Brad said with a long, lazy drawl to his words and a new something in his smile.

Chrissy blinked.

"Not that a gentleman even brings the subject up," Jacob said with a frown at Brad before turning to Chrissy. "I wouldn't want you worrying about him. He's just got a peculiar way of joking. Don't pay him any attention." He turned back to Brad. "For some fool reason he thinks all woman want to kiss that ugly mug of his."

"Who are you calling ugly?" Brad demanded to know with more energy than he'd put into the rest of the conversation.

Chrissy was relieved to see that, in truth, Brad would rather argue with Jacob than kiss her. She decided there must be something about this dark Montana night that made men want to take up kissing. She shouldn't think it meant much.

As she recalled, Linda had told her stories last fall

about the old days at the Redfern Ranch when the cowboys had held a kissing auction or two. It must be something about this ranch area.

Chrissy looked up to see the door to the bunk-house opening.

"Someone's coming," Reno announced as he stepped into the bunkhouse. He decided he was grateful the other three men hadn't left yet. If there was going to be trouble, all three men would be good to have around. "I don't know who it is, but Hunter noticed someone was coming first and I can see the lights coming down the road."

"Who'd be coming here?" Jacob asked. "We're almost finished with the dance lessons."

"I'm sure they're not coming to dance," Reno said as he felt Justin squirm. Without thinking much about it, Reno shifted Justin in his arms so the baby could see better.

Reno was glad he'd left the yard light on. At least he'd be able to see what kind of vehicle was coming down the driveway.

"Well, maybe it's just a neighbor coming by to visit," Chrissy said.

"Maybe," Reno said. He didn't tell Chrissy that neighbors around here didn't drop by to visit someone this close to midnight. Everyone was in bed at this hour. Of course, if there was an emergency, that would be a different matter. But then they'd usually call first.

"I don't suppose anyone heard the phone from the house ringing earlier?"

Jacob shook his head. "We wouldn't have heard a phone even if it was down here in the bunkhouse."

Reno nodded. Now that it occurred to him, he hadn't checked the answering machine in the house since breakfast. He and Chrissy had been in town, and he'd been busy after that. "Maybe someone called earlier to say they'd be over this evening."

"Your neighbor Lester did say he was feeling lonely these days. Maybe he's coming over to talk," Chrissy said.

"Lester?" Jacob said in astonishment as he walked over to the window and looked out. "He doesn't even say much in the middle of the day. What would he need to say at midnight?"

"Whoever it is, you can't see them out that window yet." Reno heard his sister's horse, Misty, neigh from the corral by the barn. Even the chickens sounded as though they were flapping around in their coop. Whoever was coming up the drive wasn't bothering to be quiet about it.

"That's Big Blue," Chrissy said. "I'd recognize those gear changes anywhere."

"Garrett's truck? He wouldn't be grinding his gears like that." Reno's new brother-in-law was a legend in trucking circles, and he would no more grind the gears on his big rig than a cowboy would shoot his favorite horse.

"I don't think it's Garrett driving," Chrissy said as she walked toward the door of the pantry and looked out that window. "Yeah, it sure looks like Big Blue from here. The lights are up high and running around the cab of the truck. I'll bet it's Nicki driving."

Reno nodded. Nicki always did have a heavy hand with grinding gears. She'd learned to drive on a tractor. She'd made the gears on their father's truck grind almost the same way. Of course, that'd been fifteen years ago. She was a pretty good driver these days.

Jacob shook his head. "That man must be crazy in love to let his wife drive like that."

"I hear that's the way it is," Brad said. "First they get you all married up, and then look what happens. You can't even drive your own truck."

"Hush about the driving," Chrissy said as she walked back to where everyone else was standing. "I remember Nicki, and she wouldn't be driving that way, either, unless something was wrong."

"I hope no one's hurt." Reno had looked out for his sister all his life. He felt a sudden guilt that he'd hardly thought about her much at all since that letter had arrived at the post office in Dry Creek. He hadn't even called Nicki and Garrett when they were down in Denver. Of course, they hadn't called him either.

The sound of the truck was louder now that it was turning into the yard of the Redfern Ranch.

"Well, no point in us standing here wondering about it. Let's step outside and see what's going on," Jacob said as he walked toward the door.

"Let me put Justin in his crib," Reno said. No one knew for sure it was Nicki and Garrett out there, and Reno wasn't taking any chances. He turned to Chrissy. "Is there a rattle or something that he likes to play with so he doesn't cry?"

"Justin hardly ever cries," Chrissy protested.

Jacob and the other two men walked out on the porch.

"I know," Reno said as he handed Justin into Chrissy's arms. "It's just that now would be a very good time for him to be quiet so that no one knows he's here."

"Oh," Chrissy said. "Sorry. I wasn't thinking."

"It's Nicki," Jacob called from outside.

Chrissy stood on the side of the porch. She had laid Justin down inside in his crib, and she could hear him from the porch. She had thought about wrapping the baby up in his blanket and taking him out with her to greet Nicki and Garrett, but something stopped her.

Chrissy realized Nicki and Garrett didn't know she was here. She was sure of Garrett's welcome, but not of Nicki's. Nicki had seemed very friendly when Chrissy was here before, but Chrissy figured there was a difference between being friendly to someone who was staying for only a few days and someone who looked as if they had moved into your bunkhouse.

Reno knew something was wrong the minute his sister stepped down out of the cab of her husband's truck. For one thing, she didn't appear to have her husband with her. For another thing, she didn't appear to have much of her hair, either.

"Welcome home, sis," Reno said as he stepped forward to welcome Nicki with a big hug. Nicki had never paid much attention to fashion before she got married, but even then she'd never had her hair in a short, shaggy, bizarre cut like this with one side shorter than the other. "It's good to have you back."

Nicki walked into his arms before she started to sob.

"It's just horr—horren—awful," Nicki wailed.

Jacob and the two ranch hands milled around with their hands in their pockets. Reno could see they wanted to be helpful but weren't sure what was wrong.

"I guess this isn't them guys you were worried about earlier at least," Mark, the quiet ranch hand, finally said. "That's good. No need to worry."

Nicki pulled herself back from Reno's arms and took a deep breath. "I'm sorry if I worried you driving in like that. It's just that I've had a—" Nicki took a deep breath "—a horrendous experience." Nicki smiled at Reno to show she'd learned yet another word.

"Was it lice?" Jacob asked in concern.

"What?"

"I thought it might be lice on account of the way you've chopped off your hair."

"My hair happens to be the latest fashion you can find in Denver," Nicki said with her chin in the air. "It is not odd—or even unusual I think is the word Garrett used."

"So you cut it that way on purpose?" Jacob asked.

"Nicki looks great in any hairstyle," Reno said swiftly, with a look at Jacob to let him know that the haircut had, obviously, been intentional.

"Thank you." Nicki smiled. "I knew you would stand by me even when Garrett wouldn't."

"Wait a minute." Reno didn't want to take sides in a marital argument, not that he wasn't surprised that Nicki and Garrett were even having an argument. It must be a first for them. "I'm not sure now's the time—"

"Oh," Nicki gasped as she took another step back and looked at Reno more closely. "I didn't notice. Did someone die? Oh, my, it wasn't anyone I know, was it?"

"Of course no one died."

"Then why are you wearing your suit?" Nicki asked. "You shouldn't scare a person like that. I thought you had been to a funeral."

Brad started to chuckle. "No, ma'am, he was just dancing, is all."

"Dancing?" Nicki looked as startled as she would have if someone *had* died. "Here?" Nicki looked around the yard. "There's no place here to dance."

"There's the bunkhouse," Jacob offered.

"Oh, I get it," Nicki finally said. "You're practicing a skit for something. Like the time Lester dressed up like Elvis and paraded into the café. That was a good one. So who are you guys going to be? The Three Stooges?"

"It's not a crime to learn how to dance," Reno said. He didn't like the looks that were developing on the faces of Brad and Mark. They hadn't liked being compared to the Three Stooges.

"Ladies like a man who can dance," Brad said stiffly.

"I just want to have some fun at the next wedding," Mark added.

"Oh." Nicki thought for a minute. "Yeah, that makes sense. What—do you have some kind of an instructional video or something? You could use the VCR at our house if you want."

"We don't need a VCR," Jacob said. "We have us a dance instructor."

"A pretty one, too," Brad said with more confidence.

Reno could see Nicki running through all the pretty women in Dry Creek and deciding against each one. He might as well come out with it. "Chrissy Hamilton is here."

Nicki looked around again.

"In the bunkhouse," Reno said.

"Well, why didn't you say so?" Nicki asked. She sounded as if she had forgotten all about her hair. "Does she have the baby with her? I told Garrett she didn't need to keep it a secret. I've been dying to see her and the baby! How are they?" She turned to Reno. "You know, I think I'm second cousin to Chrissy. Isn't that something? I always thought you and I would have such fun with a cousin, and now we have one."

"She's not *my* cousin," Reno said. "You're the one who married her cousin. Not me."

Reno could have saved his words. No one seemed to care whether or not he was Chrissy's cousin except him. Nicki had already started walking down to the bunkhouse, and Jacob and the two ranch hands were still looking confused.

"Wonder why she'd do that to her hair?" Jacob finally asked.

"What I wonder is where she left that husband of hers," Brad said. "Do you think this means she's single again?"

"Of course not," Reno snapped. He should get down to the bunkhouse, but he didn't want to leave any confusion in Brad's mind. "Married people have arguments. It doesn't mean they're divorced."

"Oh, I know that," Brad said cheerfully. "I was just thinking that if she was to leave that man of hers, she might like some sympathy. I could take her dancing."

"She doesn't dance," Reno said as he started to walk away.

"I can teach her," Brad called after him. "Now that I've been taught myself, I can teach anyone."

"She's still married!" Reno shouted back.

One thing he knew for sure was that Nicki would never divorce her husband. Once she was married, she was married. Reno was like her in that regard. They'd both seen the pain of a divorce. Maybe that's why it had taken them both so long to think about getting married.

Chapter Thirteen

Chrissy gave up trying to get Justin to sleep. First Nicki had come down to the bunkhouse in a whirlwind of kisses and excitement. And then Reno had joined them just as Nicki mentioned that she should go up to the main house to see if there were any phone messages for her on the answering machine.

"Come with me?" Nicki asked.

Chrissy propped Justin up against her shoulder. That made him stop squirming, at least. "Of course. Do you think Garrett will call?"

Nicki had told Chrissy a little of their argument before Reno came into the room.

"Oh, I'm not waiting for Garrett's call," Nicki said with an unconvincing smile. "I'm curious about whether that order for cattle feed I called in before I left is finally ready to be picked up at the hardware store."

"I'm sure Jacob would have mentioned it," Reno said.

Chrissy frowned at Reno. Sometimes, she thought, men could be so dense. "It's worth checking anyway."

"Sure. Why not?" Reno said as he stepped closer to Chrissy and held out his arms. "But you better let me carry Justy here across the yard. It's still muddy enough out there to be slippery in places."

"Justy?"

"I'm trying to find a nickname for him, but I don't think that's it," Reno said as he glanced over at the door. "It's chilly out there, too. Better bring an extra blanket."

Chrissy held Justin out to him, and the baby went to Reno easily. Weren't babies supposed to cry when you handed them to strangers? she asked herself as she reached over to the bed and grabbed another one of Justin's blankets.

"Oh." Nicki stopped as she was walking toward the door and turned back to stare at Reno. "The baby's not crying or anything. He cried when I picked him up. He likes you."

"Well, you don't need to sound so surprised," Reno said.

"I've just never seen you with a baby before." Nicki looked at him.

Chrissy could see where this was headed. They had been down this road before in the past couple of days. "Reno's not the baby's father."

"Well, of course not." Nicki looked startled now. "Who said he was?"

"Oh, I forgot, you didn't see the letter. You must be the only one in Dry Creek who hasn't."

"What letter? Did Reno write you a letter?"

"It's not from Reno. We may as well go up to the other house. I think Reno still has the letter there someplace. You can read it for yourself," Chrissy said as she walked toward the door.

"And take a jacket for yourself, too," Reno called back to Chrissy from the porch. "Use that denim one of mine if you need to—"

"I can use a blanket," Chrissy said. The blankets weren't hers any more than the jacket was, but they felt more like hers, and she wanted to borrow only as much as was absolutely necessary.

Reno and Nicki were waiting for her on the porch. Reno frowned at the blanket, but he didn't say anything. "Here, hold on to one of my arms. You should have worn my extra pair of boots down here. With a couple layers of socks, they would have been fine."

"My shoes are good enough for dancing," Chrissy said as she held on to the elbow he had bent. "Besides, your feet are a size twelve. It'd take more than a couple of pairs of socks to make them fit."

Chrissy had no sooner put her hand in the crook of Reno's arm than he pulled his arm closer to his side and her hand with it, forcing her to walk even closer to him.

"Well, you can have all my socks, then," Reno said.

Chrissy didn't have the courage to look at Nicki directly, but she did glance over at her. Reno's sister was staring at the two of them as though she'd never seen a man offer a woman his entire sock wardrobe before.

"I'm going to buy some boots with my first check," Chrissy said to Nicki, hoping it would help. "It's not like I'm a complete charity case."

"Well, of course not," Nicki said decisively as she finally started to walk toward the house. "I forgot. Reno always helps family."

Chrissy nodded. She had suspected as much. Garrett would have helped her, too.

The walk across the yard wasn't nearly long enough for Reno. The night had turned a little warmer than it had been when he was outside rocking Justin earlier, and Reno liked the feel of Chrissy's hand tucked close to his side. With Justin in his arms and Chrissy walking close to him, he was a contented man.

The night was dark except for the yard light.

"I'll go ahead and open the door," Nicki said. She was already ahead of them in her walk across the yard.

"Put some water on for tea, too," Reno called after her.

"Tea?" Nicki turned back. "Since when do you drink tea?"

"Since coffee isn't good for Chrissy. Not now with the baby," Reno answered.

"Oh," Nicki said as she started up the steps of the main house.

"You don't have to drink tea because of me," Chrissy said.

"A man never died from drinking a cup of tea," Reno said. You would think it was a crime to change a habit, the way Nicki was looking at him tonight. It did a man good to change his ways every now and again.

"Here, watch this step," Reno said when they came to the porch.

Nicki had turned the light on in the kitchen by the time Reno and Chrissy came inside. Reno had thought Nicki's hair was an odd color when he'd seen it down in the bunkhouse, yet he hadn't been sure because the light wasn't very good down there. But under the kitchen light her hair looked almost orange. Of course, it was hard to tell, because it was so short.

"Now, where's the teakettle?" Nicki said as she walked over to the old stove. "Ah, there it is. Just give me a second to light a match, and we'll have it all set."

"Light a match?" Chrissy asked.

Nicki looked at Reno and Chrissy. "Which one of you is doing the cooking these days?"

"Men can cook," Reno said. "You don't need to assume that just because Chrissy is a woman she's doing the cooking."

Nicki shrugged as she picked up the teakettle and walked over to the sink. "I'm just surprised she likes your fried potatoes that well, that's all."

"We haven't had fried potatoes," Chrissy said.

"Well, then, what's he been feeding you?" Nicki asked as turned on the water and filled up the teakettle.

"We've had meat loaf," Reno said. "With baked potatoes."

Reno didn't add that Mrs. Hargrove had written down the recipe for baked potatoes when she slipped a couple of potatoes into the sack that held a piece of her foil-wrapped meat loaf.

"And canned corn," Chrissy added. "It was all very good."

Nicki brought the teakettle back to the stove. "Sounds good to me."

"We have to have good meals for Chrissy." Reno

defended himself, even though his sister hadn't said anything more. "Because of Justin."

Nicki struck a match and lit a burner on the gas stove. "We should all eat good meals. It keeps a body healthy."

Nicki set the teakettle on the burner. "Now, while this water gets hot, I think I'll go into the living room and listen to the messages."

Reno watched his sister leave the kitchen. By now he'd realized that the message she wanted to check for must be from Garrett, and he wanted to give her the privacy she needed.

"I wonder what they fought about," Chrissy whispered when Nicki left the room.

"I thought she already told you," Reno whispered back. He could hear the soft mumble of the answering machine playing back messages.

Chrissy shook her head. "She kind of left that part out. Mostly she just said Garrett didn't like her hair."

"Yeah, that's probably not enough of a reason for this bad of a fight," Reno agreed. "Garrett seems like the kind of a guy who could get used to any kind of hair."

"Oh, Nicki doesn't like her hair either," Chrissy said. "She already asked me if I can fix it for her."

Reno would never understand women. "Well, if she doesn't like her hair, why does she get so upset if someone else says something about it?"

"I think it's just Garrett who upset her."

The mumble of the answering machine stopped, and both Reno and Chrissy became still.

They didn't even bother to look uninterested when Nicki came back to the kitchen.

"Well," Reno asked, "was there a message for you?"

Nicki shook her head as she held out a small sheet of notepaper. "Not for me. But a Mrs. Bard called. She said something about being very sorry for hiring some attorney and that she wanted you to know she was telling him to stop everything he was doing." Nicki held out the piece of paper. "She left her number and said she'd be very happy if you'd call so she could say how sorry she was to you in person. Although she also said she'd understand if you didn't want to."

"Mrs. Bard called?" Chrissy was still taking it in. "Are you sure it was Mrs. Bard?"

"That's who she said she was. The message is still there, if you'd like to replay it."

Reno was standing. "Thanks for saving it. I think we would like to listen to it again."

Chrissy nodded. "I can't believe she'd call. Not now."

Reno knew what she meant. He couldn't believe it either. He wondered how long Chrissy would stay now that she would feel safe in leaving.

* * *

Chrissy sliced a red bell pepper into thin strips. Nicki was chopping onions, and Linda was peeling some cloves of garlic. They were all standing around the counter in the kitchen of the Dry Creek Café. The midday air was sticky and humid. The sky outside was overcast and gray. They had the door to the outside propped open so they could get the breeze.

"Jazz should be here helping," Linda said. "But there's still a lot of mud up on the flats where the Jenkins place is, and he can't get out unless he drives the old tractor the Jenkinses left when they moved to Florida."

"And if it rains again today—which I think it will—he won't get out even with the tractor. The rain always hits that area the worst, and it feels to me like thunderstorm weather today." Nicki blinked. She had been blinking more and more as she cut the onions, but so far Chrissy hadn't seen any tears. Nicki looked over at Linda. "But don't worry. We'll get by without him just fine. I kind of like chopping these onions."

"Besides, aren't you mad at him?" Chrissy asked.

Linda's lips formed a thin line. "Mad or not, he should be here. He's just lucky that Jacob's nephew stopped in Miles City and picked up the waitress uniforms for tonight, or I'd have to be doing that today. It's too much for one person. We're partners in this café, and this catering job is a first for us. We've never cooked for a hundred people before."

"We'll do fine," Chrissy said to reassure her. "You've got the grill all set up, and the potatoes bake themselves. Besides, people won't even notice the rest of the food once they try this salsa. Once we're finished with the salsa, we're home free."

Chrissy still ached from her night of dancing last night, so she was grateful to stand in one place and slice peppers. She would let Jazz deal with the mud. Reno had offered to keep Justin with him out at the ranch so Chrissy could help Linda today.

Linda nodded. "I guess the salsa is the only complicated thing. Jacob said a party isn't much of a party without something hot and spicy, so he wanted this salsa even though he can't eat any of it himself on his steak."

Nicki shook her head. "Men."

Chrissy shared a look with Linda. So far, Nicki hadn't really talked about her argument with Garrett, but she certainly was chopping the onions on her cutting board with unusual vigor and blinking her eyes often enough that she could be crying.

"They're just never happy with things the way they are," Nicki continued as she halved a big white onion with a single swipe of her knife. "There's nothing wrong with plain steak."

"I must confess I like a little steak sauce myself," Linda said.

"And I'm going to try the salsa," Chrissy added.

Nicki grunted. "Well, I'll probably try the salsa, too. I have to see how my onions taste."

Chrissy looked at the pile of chopped onions that were in the bowl beside Nicki's cutting board. "If it's any consolation, Garrett usually likes his steak plain."

"Plain," Nicki grunted. "At least it's not red, like everything else he likes."

"Maybe you'd like to talk about what happened?" Chrissy suggested.

"Yeah," Linda agreed softly with a twinkle in her eye. "We're running out of things to chop."

"There's still the chives for the baked potatoes," Nicki said, but then she smiled. "I guess I should just spit it out. It's not such a big thing, really—it's just that when we were in Denver Garrett wanted to test-drive this red convertible. I said it sounded like fun and so we did. But I never thought he'd buy it." Nicki paused. "Can you imagine—a red convertible?"

"That doesn't sound like Garrett," Chrissy said carefully. "Did he ask you if you wanted him to buy it?"

"Well, of course, but I said yes," Nicki snapped. This time a tear did roll down her cheek, and she swiped at it with her sleeve. "What kind of wife would tell her husband he can't buy something when it's his own money? I didn't earn any of that money. It's his. He can throw it out of an airplane if he wants."

Linda frowned. "So you're worried that he's wasting money?"

"No, I don't care about the money." Nicki paused and turned to look at the other two women directly. "It's just—well, look at me. Am I the kind of woman a man takes riding in a red convertible?"

A thousand light bulbs went off in Chrissy's head. "Is that what happened to your hair?"

Nicki nodded miserably. "I was going to surprise Garrett and become a blonde. I thought that would fit in with the red convertible. But the beautician did something funny with the color, and we tried to fix it and it didn't work, so I said she should cut it off, and then—" Nicki gestured to her hair. "Finally I just left, and she hadn't even finished. Now look at me."

"It's not so bad," Linda said kindly.

"I know some women can carry off the bald look," Nicki said with a sigh. "Maybe I'll have to try that. I think there's some old sheep shears somewhere on the ranch."

"Don't you dare," Chrissy said. "Besides, I think I can fix it. When we finish getting everything ready for tonight, we'll set you in the chair over there, and I'll go to work."

"Do you really think you can fix it?" Nicki asked hopefully.

Chrissy nodded. "I didn't spend all those years in front of cosmetic counters for nothing. I've been made over so many times I know most of the tricks."

"Oh, that would be wonderful. I thought about going to a beauty salon, but the only one I know about is Darlene's Place in Miles City."

"She closed her shop last winter—turned the building into a video arcade," Linda said. "Now that she's retired, she just sits home and collects her quarters. There's no place closer than Billings now. I've been needing a permanent, too, but I don't know where to go."

"Why, that's wonderful news," Chrissy said.

Both Nicki and Linda looked at her as if she hadn't been listening.

Chrissy smiled. "I'm not telling anyone else yet, but I'm thinking about going to beauty school, so I can open a place in Dry Creek."

"That's great," Linda said. "Women are always asking about a place to get their hair cut. I think you'll have lots of business."

Nicki nodded. "You'll pull in women from east of here, too—it's closer for them than driving to Billings."

"Well, I have to go to beauty school first, so I

thought I'd move back to Los Angeles for a few months so I could do that. But don't tell anyone yet. I haven't decided for sure."

Chrissy didn't want to have everyone know her hopes yet, because they still felt so new to her. Besides, staying in Dry Creek was her dream, and she needed to make it happen herself. First she'd go to school. Then she'd see about renting a place to set up her salon. Then—and this was where her dream merged into pure fantasy—she'd see about finding a house for her and Justin to live in. Maybe a house with chipped appliances that required coaxing before they'd work and a hat rack hanging on the kitchen wall that held a dozen green caps, all with bright yellow tractors on them.

Chrissy stopped the dream right there. She was almost seeing the face of the man sitting at the kitchen table, and that would never do. She knew who the man was. That wasn't the problem. The problem was she couldn't love him. If she ever did get married, it would have to be to a man she didn't need. She had done fine without Jared, and if she ever did marry, it would be to someone who would not devastate her when he left. That would never be Reno. She had a feeling that if she ever started loving him, really loving him, she wouldn't be able to go on when he left. And of course he would leave. All men did.

Chrissy looked around. She didn't have to look far to see women who were unhappy in love.

"A woman can care too much, can't she?" Chrissy asked. "I mean, in a relationship with a man."

"She sure can," Nicki said as she cut through the onion on her board. "That's all I've got to say about it."

Linda looked more uncertain. "I guess it depends. You both need to care to make it work. And you both need to be strong to be a team. I mean, you can't just both be off doing your own thing like…" Her voice trailed off. "Like Jazz and me."

Well, that answered Chrissy's question. She didn't want to be crying like that in a month or two.

"Ah, don't worry." Chrissy put her hand on her new friend's shoulder and lied with all her heart. "It'll be all right—someday—somehow…" Finally Chrissy felt she should tell the truth, so she whispered the last. "Maybe."

A loud clap of thunder sounded outside, and all three women looked toward the door.

"Look at that rain come down," Nicki said.

The rain beat a steady tune on the roof of the café, and one look out the open door showed that it was already making puddles outside.

"Jazz will never get out now," Linda said.

"We'll be fine," Chrissy said.

Chapter Fourteen

Reno held Justin on his lap—and that was no easy task when a dozen grandmothers all wanted to hold the baby. Reno was sitting on a folding chair in the Elkton barn that stood on the edge of town. The barn hadn't been used for years except for town celebrations like this. Reno had his back to the wall and a stack of damp dish towels on his right. Dinner was over and the dancing had started a few minutes ago.

The only reason that no one was pestering Reno to hold Justin right now was that Reno asked anyone who came up to be his substitute at the coffeepot for a few minutes first. So far he had two takers. Even Brad had wanted a turn at baby holding, and was over at the coffeepot now. Reno had poured at least ten big two-gallon pots of coffee, and he wanted to take a few minutes to hold his…partner.

No, Reno thought to himself, that was not the name for Justin that he was looking for, either. The problem was that the one name that kept coming back to his mind was one he couldn't use. He wanted to call Justin "son."

"Yes." Reno lifted Justin up just for the pleasure of hearing the boy squeal in excitement. "You're really something, you know that?"

Justin smiled back at him. Chrissy might say babies that young didn't smile, but Reno refused to believe it. Babies were a lot smarter than people gave them credit for.

They also listened better. Justin had been a very attentive audience this afternoon when Reno had practiced the question he was going to ask Chrissy tonight. The more Reno rehearsed what he was going to say, the more the wild hope grew inside him that maybe Chrissy would agree. After all, he couldn't give her everything. But he could give her some important things. A home. His love.

Reno looked out at the dance floor in the middle of the barn. So far, about a dozen couples were waltzing to the music, but a lot of people were still standing around the edges.

Linda, Nicki and Chrissy had done a great job with the barn. They had green and blue streamers hanging from some rafters and huge birthday banners on one wall. Jazz had driven into town on a tractor just before the whole party started with a gunnysack full of wild roses. They made the whole barn smell sweet.

The night outside was dark, and the rain was finally letting up. There would be plenty of mud to fight when people tried to get home, but for now everything was magical. The night chill made the inside of the barn feel cozy. And with the roses and the sound of the music, it was very nice.

Of course, the barn was not Paris, but Reno figured this was where he'd have to propose. Now that Mrs. Bard had talked to the attorney, Chrissy had no reason to stay in Dry Creek. He needed to ask his question before she thought about leaving. He knew they'd still have issues to resolve even if she said yes, but he trusted God to help them figure everything out.

Reno was not aware that he had sighed until Nicki sat down in the chair next to him. "Poured a lot of coffee already, huh?"

"Yeah," Reno said. "It's not good for people, you know."

Nicki grunted. "I plan to drink a whole pot of it tonight."

"I thought you said Garrett might get here tonight if he drove through."

"Yeah," Nicki said. "That's why I need the coffee."

Reno could see that Nicki's hair looked better.

Somehow she'd managed to get it back to her natural color, and now the short tufts were smoothed out so they looked wispy instead of deranged. "Nice hair."

Nicki nodded. "Thanks. Chrissy fixed it."

Reno could already see Chrissy. She'd been coming back and forth between the café and the barn for a while now. But he'd been counting, and this was the last trip.

When Chrissy had said she was going to wear a uniform tonight, he'd thought she was going to pull out the orange dress. But Jacob's nephew had picked up uniforms in Billings, and both Linda and Chrissy looked like French maids, with black dresses and ruffled white aprons.

Reno frowned. Aprons in Dry Creek had never looked like those. That's why Reno knew he needed to time his request for a dance carefully. If he waited too long, Chrissy would be whirled off to dance with someone else. With her hair swept up into that braid she wore, Chrissy was beautiful.

"She's got a way with hair," Nicki offered by way of conversation. "Plus, I like her."

This time Reno was the one to grunt. "I expect she'll be leaving before long."

"Really? She told you about her plans?" Nicki turned to him and asked.

Reno's heart sank. "No, she didn't need to…"

"But—" Nicki began.

"Could you hold Justin for a minute?" Reno interrupted his sister as he stood up. Chrissy had just folded the last tablecloth. Reno turned around and held Justin out to his sister. "If Brad comes back, he's next in line to hold the baby. Right now I've got to do something."

Chrissy was tired until Reno asked her to dance. "I thought you might want to practice some more. You didn't get your full lesson the other night, because you had to take care of Justin."

When the dancing started, Jazz had hung some brass lanterns with candles in them from the rafters and then turned off the overhead lights. The candle-light and the smell of wild roses turned the barn into a grand ballroom.

Reno guided Chrissy to the quietest corner on the barn floor and started to dance with her.

"You don't need lessons," Chrissy finally whispered as she arched back from Reno so she could see his face better in the shadows. Reno continually surprised her. She had always assumed he was so dedicated to his ranch that he didn't socialize enough to know how to dance like this. But if he danced like this… "You must have been on some pretty fancy dates."

"None that compares with this one." Reno guided her closer to him and started dancing again.

"Oh."

"In fact, I'm thinking it will have to do instead of Paris."

"Oh." Chrissy had a funny feeling in her stomach that was interfering with her breathing. Reno sounded different. As if he was about to make an announcement or something. "Are you planning to fire me?"

"What?" Reno sounded startled.

"Well, I've only been able to feed the calves once so far, and that's my job. I wouldn't really blame you if you needed to fire me."

"No one's firing anyone," Reno said firmly. "I don't care about you feeding the calves."

"Well, but I'm living in the bunkhouse and everything. If you want me to leave, I'd understand."

Chrissy didn't know why she was rattling on like this. Anyone would think she wanted to be fired. It was just that she was having a hard time thinking. Maybe she was allergic to the roses.

"I don't want you to leave. In fact—" Reno took a deep breath and stopped dancing so he could look down at her "—I want you to stay."

"Oh."

"And just so there's no misunderstanding, I'm asking you to marry me."

Chrissy couldn't breathe. She wondered if she was going to pass out.

Reno paused as if he expected an answer, but when he didn't get one, he started talking again. "I've given it a lot of thought, and there are advantages for you in marrying me. I've got a house and a steady income. Granted, the house needs a new kitchen, but we can work on that. Besides, Justin needs a father, and I'd like to be his father. I could look after both of you, and you wouldn't need to worry."

"Oh." Chrissy found it was remarkably easy to start breathing again. Although she was having some trouble with her vision being blurry. She blinked. "So you want to marry me so you can take care of me and Justin."

Reno nodded in relief. "Yes."

"I'm sorry, I can't," Chrissy said as she blinked again. "It's kind of you, but I don't take charity."

"It's not—" Reno started to say, but Chrissy had already turned to walk away. She needed a breath of fresh air. It was the roses. That's what it was. She really must be allergic. It was affecting her eyes and everything. She kept her head down as she walked toward the door.

Reno decided he'd lied to himself all night. He'd told himself he was prepared for Chrissy to say no, but he wasn't. He'd had to ask, but he'd never reconcile himself to her answer.

The chatter of the couples talking as they danced and the sounds of someone moving a tray of coffee cups slowly filtered into Reno's mind. Chrissy had gone toward the door so fast she hadn't seen that Garrett had stepped through it only minutes before she had.

Reno heard Garrett call Chrissy's name, but he could see she didn't stop.

And now Garrett was frowning and walking toward Reno.

"What'd you do to upset my cousin?" Garrett demanded when he finally stood before Reno. "She's crying."

Reno looked over at Garrett. His new brother-in-law looked as if he hadn't slept in days and hadn't smiled in even longer. The man was itching for a fight.

"Probably the same thing you did to upset my sister," Reno said as he braced his feet so he could take a punch if one was coming. He figured he could give Garrett as good as he got if it came to fists.

Garrett's anger deflated. "I don't know what I did to upset your sister."

Reno relaxed his muscles. "Yeah, well, I don't know, either."

The other couples on the dance floor danced around Reno and Garrett as if they were part of the decorations.

Garrett shook his head. "I don't think I understand women very much."

Reno grunted. "Welcome to the club."

Garrett was silent.

"I think it was something about her hair," Garrett said finally. "All I said was that it was sure short." Garrett paused. "And a little orange."

"Yeah, well, all I said was that if Chrissy was with me, she wouldn't need to worry," Reno said.

"Worry about what?" Garrett looked up. "Is something happening? She got this strange message on the answer machine at the ranch house from a Mrs. Bard saying that the attorney hadn't been able to get his message through and that she should be careful."

Time froze for Reno. "You mean tonight?"

Garrett nodded. "I thought Nicki might have left me a message, so I stopped at your house to see. I didn't actually listen to the message. Mrs. Bard was leaving it when I was there, and I overheard it."

"So she just left the message?"

"What does it mean?"

"It means we keep our eyes open and hope we don't see a black strange car around here." Reno looked over at the people by the coffee table. He saw Nicki talking with Mrs. Hargrove, but neither one of them had Justin in their arms.

"That wouldn't be a fairly new black car with

tinted windows? Four doors? Rides low like it's
been modified somehow?"

Reno's attention came back fully to Garrett.

Garrett continued, "I saw a car like that when I
was starting up the road to the ranch. It was coming
out. I thought maybe someone had been to visit you
and found you weren't home."

Reno started to walk across the room, and Garrett
followed. Something about them made the couples
stop dancing as the two men walked through.

"What's wrong?" someone said.

Reno didn't turn back to answer whoever had
asked the question. He was close enough to Nicki
to ask his own question. "Where's Justin?"

Nicki looked up. "Brad has him, remember? It
was his turn to hold him."

Reno looked up and down the people sitting in the
row of chairs on the side of the barn. He didn't see
Brad.

"Brad! Brad Parker!" Reno turned and called.

"Yeah, what's the matter?" Brad stepped out of
the circle of people who had been dancing. He had
his arm around one of the Baldwin girls.

"Where's Justin?"

"Oh, I gave him to the next guy on the list."

Reno's heart stopped. "What guy? What's his
name?"

"I don't know his name. He was hanging around

the coffee table after you started dancing, and when I said I was in line to hold Justin, he said he was next."

"You gave a baby to a man, and you didn't even know the man's name!" Reno knew half the reason he was so angry was that he shouldn't have left Justin himself. No matter what it took, Reno should have held him all night.

"Well, the girls were all coming over to see the baby, and we got to talking and then I thought I should dance with at least one of them and—" Brad slowed down and swallowed. "I'm sorry. I thought you weren't worried about those bad guys any-more."

"Did you see where he went?" Reno asked, and then turned to face the rest of his neighbors. "Did anyone see where the man went who was holding the baby?"

Reno heard a gasp by the doorway and looked up. Chrissy was standing there, white-faced and still. How was he ever going to face her? He'd just told her she wouldn't have to worry if she stayed with him, and look what had happened!

One of the ranch hands standing by the door cleared his throat. He'd just come in from the porch. "I saw a man with a baby get into a black car a little bit ago."

"Which way did he go?"

"He headed east from here, but then he took a turn up toward the flats." The ranch hand coughed. "I noticed it because I knew he'd be back in no time. A car like that will never make it through the mud up there."

"That's for sure. I can't get through that mud in my pickup," another man said.

"My tractor will make it through," Jazz said. He was standing quietly beside Reno. "That's why I drove it in instead of my pickup. That old tractor will go anywhere up there, even off the road if you need."

Reno nodded. "Let's go."

Reno's eyes were still on Chrissy. She looked as if she was going to faint.

"I'm in," Garrett said as he stepped next to Reno, and then looked at the ranch hand who'd seen the car leave. "How many guys were in that car?"

"Just two of them," said the ranch hand who'd seen the car leave.

"I'll come, too," Jazz said. "In case the tractor starts acting funny."

Reno caught Mrs. Hargrove's eye and silently mouthed the words asking her to go stand beside Chrissy. The older woman hadn't taught Sunday school for all those years without being able to read lips in a crowd. She nodded when she understood, and started walking over to Chrissy.

"Here, take some of these," Nicki said.

Reno turned his gaze back just as Nicki handed him a bunch of long barbecue forks. They'd used them in grilling the steaks.

"Those guys might be armed," Nicki explained.

Jazz turned a little white. "I hope they don't have guns."

"Those forks are pretty sturdy," Nicki said as she bent one slightly and nodded in satisfaction. "Sturdy and sharp. A poke with one of these would let someone know you're serious."

Reno took the forks. He didn't have time to argue. He started walking toward the door. Garrett followed.

Nicki nodded. "I'm taking one of the forks for me, too."

"Where do you think you're going?" Garrett, turning back, demanded to know.

"I know those flats better than any of you," Nicki said as she started toward the door, too. "I ride my horse there all the time. Besides, I know how to stand on a tractor without falling off."

"You can fall off a tractor?" Garrett sounded surprised. They were at the door now. "Maybe we should take my car."

Nicki grunted. "That little tin can convertible wouldn't make it past the first turn."

"I thought you were the one who wanted that

convertible," Garrett said. "If you didn't like it, why didn't you say so?"

Chrissy watched all four of them walk out the door. Mrs. Hargrove had her arm around Chrissy and she felt some of the chill leaving her. Chrissy took a deep breath. She had to think. "I need to go get Justin."

Mrs. Hargrove squeezed her shoulders. "I don't know if there's even room for all four of them on that tractor. They can't take any more people."

"I'm not going with them," Chrissy announced. She should never have allowed herself to get soft. Since she'd been in Dry Creek, she'd forgotten her own rule. She could depend only on herself. That was the way it had been all her life and that was the way it was now. She'd have to go for Justin.

"But there's no way to get a car or a truck up on those flats. Jazz is right about that," Mrs. Hargrove said gently.

"Then I'll walk," Chrissy said. Yes, the warmth was returning to her arms. She felt as if she could do anything she had to do. "Reno has some old boots in his pickup that he uses in the mud. I'll put them on and walk up there."

Mrs. Hargrove nodded as though she was thinking. "All right. Then I'm coming with you."

"But you can't—" Chrissy stopped short of offending Mrs. Hargrove. "I mean, it's a long way over to those flats, and it's not good for everyone to get that kind of exercise."

Mrs. Hargrove stood up straight. "I may be old, but I'm in good physical shape. Besides, you'll need someone to show you the way, and the only one who knows those flats better than Nicki is me. I used to live up there years ago."

Chrissy nodded. She could use a guide. "Then I'll pay you, of course."

"What?" Mrs. Hargrove looked even more offended than she had when Chrissy had suggested she was old.

"That's the way it has to be," Chrissy said. "I take care of my own."

Mrs. Hargrove pursed her lips. "We'll talk about it later."

Since they were both already standing close to the door, it was a simple thing to slip out without anyone seeing them leave. Everyone else had crowded toward the middle of the barn, exchanging stories about seeing the man in the black car and wondering if they should call the sheriff.

The boots were cold, but Reno had a couple of jackets in his pickup, as well. Chrissy slipped one over her maid's uniform and handed one to Mrs. Hargrove.

"I don't suppose we should take a wrench or anything," Chrissy said. "With all this talk of weapons, I'm wondering if we should have something with us to help."

"God is our help," Mrs. Hargrove announced decisively as she stepped away from the pickup and pointed herself toward the flats.

"Well, I'll just have to pay Him, too," Chrissy said before she realized she'd spoken aloud.

Fortunately, this time Mrs. Hargrove wasn't offended. In fact, she laughed. "You sound like you're not used to accepting help from anyone."

"I'm not," Chrissy said as she started to walk. She could see the outline of the tractor as it moved up the road. "It's always been just me and my mother."

Mrs. Hargrove nodded as she matched her steps to Chrissy's. "And now it's just you and Justin."

"Yes," Chrissy said. She swallowed a sob. "Just the two of us."

Chapter Fifteen

Chrissy had cold gray mud on her arms and her legs and her face. And if that wasn't bad enough, she had slid down the latest slope and was now sitting in mud. It had stopped raining completely since she and Mrs. Hargrove had walked out of Dry Creek. After it stopped raining, a half-moon appeared in the sky. When they started out, they could find their way only because they could see the fence posts that lined the land on the flats. Now the moon gave them some light, unless it went behind a cloud.

"Well, at least we know we're on the right road," Chrissy said as she put her hand down to give herself leverage to stand. "I can see the wheel prints from the tractor when I'm down here."

"That's good." Mrs. Hargrove turned to look down the road. "I expect they've already gotten to

Justin. I keep thinking we should see some lights from the tractor."

"How much farther to where Justin is?" Chrissy said as she stood. She knew Mrs. Hargrove didn't know the answer, but she just wanted to hear her say some more reassuring words.

Mrs. Hargrove had stopped to pray periodically as they walked, and each time the older woman thanked God for the tractor and for a strong young man like Reno to go after Justin. Chrissy relaxed more and more each time the older woman prayed. Mrs. Hargrove prayed with such conviction Chrissy almost came to believe it would be all right.

"Well, I don't know." Mrs. Hargrove smiled. "Maybe it's not as close as you'd like. But don't worry. It's in God's hands. And remember, we've both agreed that no one would hurt Justin. They must have orders not to hurt him."

Mrs. Hargrove had led the way for a long time now, and Chrissy had followed.

"I never should have let you come out here," Chrissy said. "But I'm so glad you did. I would have been crazy by now, and you keep reminding me that Justin will be all right."

Mrs. Hargrove nodded. "It's good to have someone help you over the rough patches."

"I—" Chrissy started to repeat the phrase she must have said a dozen times tonight. She knew now the words weren't true. "I guess I do need the help of others sometimes."

"We all do," Mrs. Hargrove said as she started walking forward. "That's what makes a church."

"There's not a church out here, is there?" Chrissy peered into the darkness. She'd be grateful for some steps to sit on for a minute or two.

"No." Mrs. Hargrove chuckled. "I mean the people part of the church."

"I haven't actually gone to the church yet," Chrissy cautioned the older woman.

"But you will," Mrs. Hargrove said. "In your time."

"Maybe," Chrissy said as she matched the older woman's steps. Something about the darkness made it easy to talk to Mrs. Hargrove. "Reno asked me to marry him tonight."

"Ah." The older woman stopped and looked at Chrissy.

Chrissy shrugged. "He doesn't love me or anything like that. He just wants to take care of me and Justin."

"I see." Mrs. Hargrove started to walk again.

Chrissy thought she saw a small smile on the woman's face in the moonlight, but she must have been mistaken. The moonlight was gone almost as soon as it appeared, and when Chrissy looked again there was no smile.

"I guess that's why he would want to take care of us, huh?" Chrissy said. "Sort of a mission for the church."

"Oh, I doubt it's that. Not if I know Reno," Mrs. Hargrove said.

"Well, he is awfully fond of Justin."

"And I've seen how he looks at you."

Chrissy didn't answer. Mrs. Hargrove was right about a lot of things, but not about this. "All I know is that the more he wants to give me, the more nervous I get. Why—he even wanted to give me his socks! All of them."

"That is an unusual gift," Mrs. Hargrove agreed.

"Well, it was so I could wear a pair of his boots and not have to worry about ruining my shoes in the mud."

"I see. Very sensible of him, then," Mrs. Hargrove said as she peered ahead. "I think I see a light."

Reno peered into the darkness. The tractor pulled and groaned as it crawled ahead. Its headlights didn't shine too far into the night, so Reno had to squint and pray to keep on the old road. Of course, the tractor wasn't made for taking a midnight drive. Most ranchers didn't drive their tractors anywhere at night except maybe out to their fields.

Still, even as hard as it was to see, Reno was a happy man. There was a thick chain stretched out behind the tractor, and at the end of the chain was a late-model black car.

Inside the car, Jazz sat in the driver's seat where he could keep an eye on one of the gentlemen who used to drive the black car. Reno used the term "gentlemen" loosely. What he really meant was that the two men had obligingly worn expensive silk ties with their equally expensive suits. The ties made it so much easier to keep the two men's hands firmly behind their backs. The other man was in the back seat squeezed between the door and Garrett. On the other side of Garrett sat Nicki, holding Justin.

Not only was Justin well, the baby seemed to think they were taking him on this outing for his pleasure.

Fortunately, the thick mud had so thoroughly discouraged the kidnappers that Reno thought they were almost happy to see them coming. The two had both been outside the car looking and pointing at their wheels that were buried halfway up the hubcaps in mud.

Well, the kidnappers had been relieved until Nicki jumped off the tractor and pointed two of her barbecue forks at them. They'd looked a little startled then, and one of them offered to turn in the attorney to make a better deal for himself.

Reno had assured them both they would meet with the law soon enough and that they could propose their deals at that time.

Reno turned around to look behind him. He could see Garrett and Nicki talking in the back seat of the car, and it didn't look like they were arguing. That was a good thing. Nicki deserved a happy marriage.

Reno had held Justin for a long minute after he pulled him out of the black car and scolded the kidnappers for not having an infant car seat.

"Yeah, well, those babies are nothing but a big pain," one of the kidnappers had said. "They don't care if you're the one in charge."

Reno realized he was going to miss having a baby around. He couldn't picture himself married if it wasn't going to be to Chrissy, so he'd never have any children of his own. Reno decided it was a good thing Nicki had gotten married, so he could at least have some nieces and nephews.

Reno had been lost in thought, so it took a moment to figure out that there was some white thing flapping in the darkness ahead. Of all the peculiar things. It looked as if some cowboy had left a white apron on the fence along the road. Reno leaned farther forward. No, that couldn't be right. The apron looked to be moving like a flag.

Chrissy watched the tractor come into view, and she saw the car that it pulled. "Is Justin all right?"

Chrissy knew her voice was loud, but she didn't expect the tractor to jerk to a stop at the sound of her voice or for Reno to climb down off the tractor and take such huge strides toward her and Mrs. Hargrove.

"Yes, he's fine." Reno stopped when he was about three feet away. "But what are the two of you doing out here?"

"Strolling out to meet you," Mrs. Hargrove said, just as if anyone could stroll in this kind of mud. "It's kind of you to stop for us."

"Stop for you?" Reno seemed dumbfounded. "Of course I'm stopping for you. You're in the middle of nowhere. There aren't even cows out this far! I thought the two of you must be a mirage."

"Doesn't that only happen in the desert?" Mrs. Hargrove asked.

"It *should* only happen in the desert," Reno agreed. "But nothing seems to be happening right tonight."

"Well, we don't know that, do we? The night's not over yet," Mrs. Hargrove said as she walked toward the car. "Do you suppose there's room for me in there?"

"I don't know," Reno said. "There's five people already. Six with Justin. I guess we could get two more in."

Mrs. Hargrove bent to look in the window that Jazz had rolled down. "Hi, everyone. Mind if we hitch a ride?"

Chrissy walked over to the window, too.

"Of course not," Nicki said as she opened the back door next to where she was sitting.

"Justin!" Chrissy cried out as she held out her arms for her baby.

Nicki lifted the baby up to her.

Reno joined everyone by the window and frowned. "I don't know if we're going to have room for everyone inside."

"Oh, well, Chrissy is too muddy to ride in here anyway," Mrs. Hargrove said. "She'd ruin the seats."

Mrs. Hargrove, Chrissy and Reno were all standing around the one open window.

"Oh, I can put a blanket under me." Chrissy looked up from her baby. "It'll be fine."

"But it's such a nice night out," Mrs. Hargrove continued. "And you've never had a tractor ride before. This is your chance."

"I'm not sure—" Reno started before Mrs. Hargrove stepped on his foot.

"Chrissy would like to take a tractor ride, wouldn't you?" Mrs. Hargrove said.

"Uh, yeah. Sure," Chrissy said.

Reno didn't have to look at Chrissy's face to know that she was just being polite. It was hard to say no to Mrs. Hargrove. Chrissy bent to give Justin back to Nicki.

"It's kind of bumpy," Reno warned her.

Mrs. Hargrove stepped on his foot again. Reno figured he better shut up if he wanted to keep his toes.

Chrissy started walking toward the tractor.

"What do you think you're doing?" Reno turned to whisper to the older woman.

"Just be charming," Mrs. Hargrove hissed back as she started bending to sit inside the car. "I must say, you used to be better at this in the first grade."

Chrissy decided they should outlaw tractors. She'd never realized there was nowhere for a passenger to sit on a tractor. At first she thought she could stand on that big round thing that went between the wheels. That was what she climbed on to wait for Reno.

Reno climbed up on the other side of the tractor. "You'll fall off if you stay there."

Chrissy looked around. Reno had left the lights going on the tractor, but they gave more of a soft glow than any kind of real light. "Don't they have some kind of fold-down seat for passengers?"

Reno grunted. "They have one seat. Made out of tin. And it bounces."

"Well, where did Nicki sit?"

"Nicki likes to ride the wheel." Reno sat down in the one seat and pointed to the huge metal piece that rose out above the big tires. "But that's an acquired skill. I wouldn't recommend it for your first tractor ride."

"Well, where *would* you recommend?"

Reno bent and adjusted the metal seat so it moved back a few inches and then patted his knee. "Here."

"On your lap?" Chrissy swallowed. "But I'm all muddy."

"Mud doesn't bother me." Reno remembered it was mud that Chrissy thought was keeping her out of the car. "In fact, I've grown fond of mud lately."

"You're sure?" Chrissy asked as she slid toward him.

"I see you have my boots on." Reno knew the importance of talking softly to someone who was nervous.

"I hope you don't mind," Chrissy said as she put her foot on the floor beneath Reno's foot.

"Not at all." Reno held out his hands and lifted Chrissy onto his lap. "Did you remember to use extra socks?"

Chrissy shook her head. "I think that's why I'm getting a blister."

"Oh, well," Reno said as he felt Chrissy start to relax on his lap. "You'll remember next time."

Reno didn't need to start the tractor again, but he did need to put it in gear to move forward. He thought they were about a mile off the main road into Dry Creek. It could take the old tractor ten minutes to go a mile if he kept it in first gear.

Reno drove the tractor with one hand and kept the other hand around Chrissy's back.

"I'm sorry I didn't watch over Justin better." Reno didn't know how to say it other than to say it straight out. "If anything had happened to him, I would never have forgiven myself."

"I know."

"I wouldn't blame you if you never trusted me with another thing."

Reno couldn't see Chrissy's eyes because of the darkness, but he could see the slight smile that moved her lips in the light of the half-moon.

"Oh. Well, I was going to ask you to help me with a few things," Chrissy finally said.

"Really?" Reno knew Chrissy never asked anyone for help. If he hadn't been so surprised, he would have answered her sooner. He didn't realize the pause was long until he felt some stiffness in her back.

"That is, if you're willing to help me," she added.

"Of course I'll help you." Reno felt her back relax.

"You haven't even asked what it is."

"I don't need to know. You'll tell me when you're ready."

The tractor growled low and deep as it moved

toward the main road. Reno tried to think of something charming to say. Why was it that when he most wanted to say something compelling, he had no words at all?

"I was thinking," Chrissy said hesitantly.

"Yes?"

"Well, if you were to help me with a few things, would that be enough? I mean, I don't think you should marry someone just so you can be there to take care of them."

"What?" Reno growled in rhythm with the tractor. "I didn't ask you to marry me just so I could take care of you…"

"Oh?"

Reno took a deep breath and forced his voice into a whisper. "I asked you to marry me because I love you."

"Oh."

Reno wasn't sure, but he thought *that* "oh" sounded a little happier. "I don't have much to offer except my love and the ranch, but that's what I meant to say."

Reno figured he would spend the rest of his life thinking of more charming ways to say what he was about to say. "Since I didn't make it clear the first time, I'm going to ask again. Chrissy Hamilton, will you marry me?"

"Maybe."

"Maybe?" Reno ground the word out as the tractor pulled into Dry Creek. "What do you mean 'maybe'?"

Although the windows in the houses of Dry Creek were all dark, someone in the barn saw them coming down the road and shouted out that they were back. But Reno wasn't paying any attention. The night was just light enough he could see Chrissy smile as she said, "Well, probably. But I have a few things to do first. Can you wait?"

"I'll wait all my life if I need to."

Reno figured he had just enough time to kiss Chrissy before the whole town descended upon them.

Epilogue

Six months later

A few snowflakes fell here and there on the main road in Dry Creek, but winter was only beginning and it was still warm enough to be outside, especially if a man—or a woman—had a cap on.

Reno and Chrissy were both wearing green tractor caps, even though, as Chrissy said, they should upgrade to a big-league sports cap now that she'd become a licensed beautician.

Reno disagreed. He said tractors had served them well.

What could Chrissy do but smile and agree?

Chrissy was a happy woman. She and Reno were leaning against the hood of his pickup and looking through the big window into the Dry Creek hardware store. The pickup was parked far enough away that the people inside the hardware store didn't see them watching.

Not that they would have cared. She and Reno had waited inside for a little while for the mail to be delivered and then decided to wait outside where they could be together. Only Mrs. Hargrove knew they had left the store, and that was because she was the one holding Justin.

Reno had leaned against the pickup first and then opened his arms so that Chrissy could lean against his chest instead of the cold metal of the pickup hood.

"I still mean to take you to Paris someday," Reno whispered in her ear once Chrissy had settled against him.

"Someday," Chrissy agreed as she looked down the street to see if the mailman was coming.

She didn't see the mailman's truck, but she did let her eyes linger on the church building. She sometimes wondered these days why it had taken her so long to accept that God cared about her. And not just God; other people cared, too. She was so well loved, she no longer tried to do everything herself. Not that she wanted to be dependent, either. She still planned to open that beauty salon and have her own business. Reno was her biggest supporter in that dream.

"Here he comes," Reno said softly in her ear.

"I wonder if it will be here today."

"We mailed it in Billings yesterday. It should be here."

The mailman drove his truck next to the door of the hardware store and parked. He picked up a leather bag full of mail before stepping out of the truck and walking up the steps. The man looked as if he was in his usual hurry, and he pulled out several banded packets of mail and set them on the counter inside the hardware store before placing one single letter on top of all the bundles.

Chrissy smiled. Jacob was sorting the mail again, and he held the first envelope up and stared at it for a minute. Then he called over to Elmer. In the meantime, Lester came over to look at the envelope. Lester gestured for Mrs. Hargrove to come. With everyone gathering around the envelope, Glory and Pastor Matthew came over, too.

Finally there were so many people standing around and staring at the envelope that Reno and Chrissy could no longer actually see it.

"Who do you think will open it first?" Reno asked.

"Mrs. Hargrove," Chrissy said. "She'll figure it out in a minute or two."

Mrs. Hargrove didn't actually open the envelope herself, because she had Justin in her arms, but Chrissy could see her urging Jacob to do it. Finally

Jacob tore the end off the envelope and pulled out the paper.

Jacob waved everyone away from him so he'd have space in which to read the letter aloud to them.

Chrissy heard Reno whisper the words along with Jacob as the older man read them inside. "Reno Redfern and Christine Hamilton cordially invite all of their friends and neighbors to attend their wedding this coming Christmas Eve in the sanctuary of the Dry Creek church. A reception will follow."

Chrissy heard the roar of approval coming from the hardware store at the same time as Reno squeezed her closer to him.

* * * * *

Dear Reader,

I remember reading about a holy man who was asked for the secret of his obviously contented spiritual life. He said the answer was easy. First, you keep to the Bible, and second, you deal with yourself and others with kindness.

I thought a lot about kindness while I was writing about a young woman who had made a mistake and is then surprised that people do not react to her unkindly. It has always been easier to judge a person than to bolster him or her up with kindness.

While that is particularly true for the strangers around us, it is also often easier to be harsh to ourselves than it is to be kind.

My hope is that *A Baby for Dry Creek* will remind all of us to be kinder to ourselves and to others.

Janet Tronstad

A DRY CREEK CHRISTMAS

For every one that exalteth himself
shall be abased; and he that humbleth
himself shall be exalted.

—*Luke* 18:14

In memory of my dear friend
Judy Eslick

Chapter One

Millie Corwin squinted and pushed her eyeglasses back into place. The night was full of snow clouds and there were no stars to help her see along this long stretch of Highway 94. Millie was looking for the sign that marked the side road leading into Dry Creek, Montana. She could barely see with the snow flurries.

What had she been thinking? When she had told the chaplain at the prison that she would honor Forrest's request, she hadn't thought about the fact that Christmas was in the middle of winter and Dry Creek was in the middle of Montana so she would, of course, be in the middle of snow.

She hated snow. Not that it made much difference. Snow or no snow, she had to be here.

Millie saw a sign and peered down the dark road

that led into Dry Creek. Only one set of car tracks disturbed the snow that was falling. Hopefully that meant most people were home and in bed at this time of night. She planned to arrive in Dry Creek, do what she had to do, and then leave without anyone seeing her.

Millie turned the wheel of her car and inched her way closer to the little town.

She wished, and not for the first time, that Forrest had made a different final request of her while he was dying.

She met Forrest three years ago. He'd come into Ruby's, the coffee shop where she worked near the Seattle waterfront, and sat down at one of her tables. Millie must have taken Forrest's order a dozen times before he looked her in the eyes and smiled. There was something sweet about Forrest. He seemed as quiet and nondescript as she felt inside. He was restful compared with all of the tall, boisterous, loud men she'd learned to ignore at Ruby's.

It wasn't until he had been arrested, however, that she knew the whole truth about Forrest. He'd been a criminal since he was a boy and had, over the years, gotten deeper and deeper into crime until he'd eventually become a hit man. His last contract had been for someone in Dry Creek.

When Millie got over the shock of what Forrest was, she decided he still needed a friend. She had visited him while he was in prison, especially this past year when he'd been diagnosed with cancer. The odd thing was the sicker he got the more cheerful he became. He told her he'd found God in prison.

Millie was glad enough that Forrest had found religion if it made him happy. She smiled politely and nodded when he explained what a miracle it was that God could love a man like him.

Personally, Millie thought it would be a miracle if God loved anyone, but that it had more to do with God than the people He was supposed to love. However, since Forrest was sick, she supposed it was good if Forrest thought God loved him and so she nodded pleasantly.

But when Forrest added that God loved her as well, she stopped nodding.

Of course, she kept smiling. Millie didn't want to offend either Forrest or God.

Then Forrest added that he was going to pray for her so she would know God's love, too. Millie could no longer keep smiling; she could barely keep quiet. She'd always kept a low profile with God and she figured that was the smart thing to do.

If God was anything like the other domineering males she'd seen—and there was no reason to think otherwise—then He looked out for His own interests first. If He noticed a person like her at all, it would only be to ask her to fetch Him a glass of water or another piece of toast or something else to make Him more comfortable.

Millie had grown up in a foster home where she was the one assigned to do chores. Usually, the chores consisted of cooking, doing laundry and taking care of the five boys in the home.

Millie didn't know if it was because she was easier to order around than the boys or if her foster mother really believed males were privileged, but—whatever the reason—she soon realized she was doing all of the work for everyone in the house and, instead of being grateful, the boys only became more demanding.

By the time Millie left that home, she'd had enough of dealing with loud, demanding males.

And those boys were mere mortals. She figured God would be even more demanding. No, it was best if God didn't even know her name. She didn't want anyone mentioning her to Him. She had no desire to be God's waitress.

Still, Millie wasn't good at telling people what to do or not to do, and she certainly couldn't tell a dying friend to stop praying. So she changed the subject with Forrest and asked what kind of pudding he had had for lunch. She would just have to hope Forrest came to his senses on his own.

He didn't. Every letter he wrote after that said he was praying for her.

When Forrest died, the chaplain at the prison forwarded a final letter Forrest had asked him to mail.

In the letter, Forrest said he had tried to right some of the wrongs in his life. He hadn't done anything about Dry Creek, however, and he asked Millie to go to the place and try to restore the little town's innocence.

"I fear I've made them distrust strangers and I regret it," he wrote and then added, "Please go there, without telling them who sent you, and do something to restore their faith in strangers. And when you go, go at Christmas."

Millie winced when she read that line in the letter.

Even though Forrest had gone to Dry Creek at Christmas himself, Millie knew it was more than that that made him suggest the holiday. Forrest knew Christmas was a lonely time for her.

Not that she didn't like Christmas. It was just that she always felt like she was on the outside looking in when it came to the holidays. She'd made Forrest tell her several times about the little town with the Christmas pageant and the decorations. It all sounded like a picture on one of those nostalgic calendars.

In the foster home where Millie grew up, they had never done much to celebrate Christmas. Her foster mother always said she was too busy for that kind of thing. Millie had tried to make a fake Christmas tree one year out of metal clothes hangers and tin foil, but the boys had laughed at it and knocked it down.

Millie had never had a Christmas like the one Forrest witnessed in Dry Creek and now, it appeared, he wanted her to have one.

Even though the thought of spending Christmas in Dry Creek held a kind of fatal attraction for Millie, she would never have agreed to Forrest's request if he were alive and she could tell him face-to-face why his idea wouldn't work.

For one thing, Forrest was asking her to make the little town trust strangers again, and she wasn't the kind of person who could do something that would make a whole town change its mind about anything. Forrest knew that.

Even more important, Millie suspected that if the people in Dry Creek knew who had sent her they wouldn't trust her even if she did manage to sound persuasive. After all, Forrest had tried to kill a woman in their town two years ago. The people certainly wouldn't welcome a friend of Forrest's, let alone want to celebrate Christmas with her.

But Millie couldn't tell Forrest any of those things when she got the letter, because—well, he was dead. So she did the next best thing. She called the chaplain who had mailed the letter and tried to explain why she wasn't the person to fulfill Forrest's last request. The chaplain listened and then told her Forrest had said she might call and that Forrest wanted her to know his request was important or he wouldn't have asked her to do it.

All of which was why Millie was here in the dark. She couldn't let Forrest down.

Of course, she couldn't do exactly what he wanted, either. Therefore, she made her own plan. She decided she would do what she could to restore Dry Creek's trust in strangers and she would do it at Christmas, but she would do it without actually talking to a single person. In fact, she'd do it without even seeing another person's face.

Forrest would have to be content with that.

Hopefully, she'd be able to do what she needed to do tonight, Millie told herself as she saw a few house lights ahead of her. She had gone down the road that led into Dry Creek. It was Saturday, December 22. If she left her presents in the café tonight, the people of Dry Creek would discover them on Monday, Christmas Eve Day.

By Christmas, the people of Dry Creek should all be talking about the kindness of the stranger who'd come to town in the middle of the night to bring them a wonderful surprise and who then left without even waiting to be thanked.

Maybe they'd call her the Christmas Stranger.

Millie rolled her tongue over that phrase. Christmas Stranger. She rather liked the sound of that, she decided.

Brad Parker shoved his Stetson further down on his head and squinted as he tried to read his watch in the dark. Snow was falling outside and the heat from his old diesel engine barely kept the ice from forming on the windshield of his pickup. It was a sad night in Dry Creek, Montana when a thirty-four-year-old man ended his Saturday evening hiding out in his pickup without even a woman beside him to make it look like he had a reason for being there.

The worst part was, he'd already been parked behind the closed café for the past half hour, well off the road so no one could see him, and wondering when it would be safe to go back to the bunkhouse at the Elkton Ranch.

The last time he'd gotten back to the bunkhouse before dawn on a Saturday night was because of a tooth that was so infected Dr. Norris had insisted on opening the clinic to fix it even though it was Sunday—and everyone in the whole county knew Dr. Norris never missed a Sunday church service if he could help it.

Brad had been in enough pain at the time that he'd said yes when the good doctor asked him to come to church some Sunday morning. And, Brad told himself, he meant to do just that—someday. No one would be able to say Brad Parker didn't keep his word, even if they could say he was a fool to make a promise like that in the first place when he didn't own a tie and would rather have the root canal all over again than actually go to church.

Brad ran his tongue around his teeth. They all felt fine to him. He did an internal check for other pain and found none. He appeared to be in fine health. Which was a pity, in a way, because the guys would understand him making a short evening of it if he had reason to suspect he was dying or something.

If he wasn't dying, though, they were sure to guess the truth, and that was why Brad was sitting here in the cold. It was bad enough that he knew he always got depressed around Christmas. He didn't want to have to hear about it from the other guys in the bunkhouse, as well.

He'd left the poker party early because he was heading out to another game on the other side of town. He got halfway to the game and decided he didn't want to play anymore. All he wanted was to go home. Since he was already on the road, he just kept driving until he pulled into Dry Creek.

That's when Brad realized he couldn't show up at the bunkhouse yet. If Charlie hadn't stopped going to Billings on Saturday nights, no one would even be in the bunkhouse to hear him slip in early. But Charlie fancied himself the grandfather of "his boys," and he was sure to make a big deal about Brad and Christmas.

Brad shook his head. He never should have told the guys that his parents had been killed in a car accident just before Christmas when he was small. It had been five years ago that he'd mentioned it, and every year he still caught one or two of them watching him with a certain look in their eyes just before Christmas. He didn't know why they made such a big deal about it.

It wasn't a crime to get depressed at Christmas anyway. Brad made it through the other fifty-one weeks of the year just fine. If he wanted to feel sorry for himself one week out of the year, the rest of the world should just let him.

Still, as long as he was going to bed early tonight, he might as well get up early tomorrow morning. Maybe, since his week was already shot because of Christmas, he should just keep his promise to Dr. Norris and show up in church.

Yeah, Brad thought to himself grimly as he tried to make himself comfortable on the old seat of his pickup, he'd just get all of the bad stuff out of the way and start the new year fresh. No point in wasting a good weekend next year by going to church.

That's what he'd do. Get rid of Christmas and

church in one fell swoop. But first he'd give Charlie another half hour to go to bed just in case the old man might surprise Brad and actually be asleep when he got home.

It was sure going to be some Christmas, Brad said to himself as he leaned back against the seat of his pickup and closed his eyes. Yeah, it was going to be some Christmas.

Chapter Two

Millie held her breath as the shadows of Dry Creek came into view. The little town was just as she had pictured it when Forrest told her about it. The clouds had parted and the moon was shining even though a few flakes of snow were still falling. There was one street lamp, and it gave off enough light that the flakes looked like glitter floating over the darkened town. A lone pair of tire tracks had packed down a thin path of snow on the road into town, but else-where snow sat soft and fluffy alongside the dozen or so buildings.

Millie could see the church with its steeple. The house next to the church had lights in the second floor windows and filmy white curtains. That must be the parsonage where the woman whom Forrest had been sent to kill lived. At the time, the woman had just been passing through Dry Creek when two little boys decided she must be an angel, and therefore just what they needed for the town's Christmas pageant.

Forrest always shook his head when he told Millie about the little boys who thought they'd found their own personal angel. Forrest had never known that kind of innocence in his own life. Of course, he hadn't been sent to kill the woman because the boys thought she was an angel. The woman had witnessed a crime, and that made some big guys nervous enough to want her out of the way.

Forrest was particularly glad he hadn't succeeded in that job.

The woman, Glory Beckett, was now married to Matthew Curtis, the man who was pastor at the church. The pastor also worked at the hardware store down the street, and Millie wished she could see that building more clearly. Millie's favorite memory of Forrest's Dry Creek stories was the part about the old men who sat around the woodstove in that building. If she were coming into town like a regular person, she would like to sit with those old men some morning and listen to them argue about cattle prices. It all sounded so peaceful. She truly wished—

Millie shook her head. She couldn't afford to dwell on those kind of wishes. A life around a cozy wood stove in Dry Creek wasn't meant for someone like her. She had her tables at Ruby's. They might be filled with scruffy men who wanted more coffee, but that was what she had for the time being.

Millie dimmed her lights when she pulled close to the café. No one was around, but she didn't want her lights to shine into the windows of any of the houses farther down the road. She didn't pull in too close, because the snow wasn't packed down that far off the road and she didn't want to get stuck. She checked the mirror behind her as she turned off her lights. No one was coming.

Millie opened her car's door. Forrest had told her stories about the café, and so she knew the spare key was sitting under a certain rock on the porch. With any luck, she would be in the café and have her surprises delivered in less than ten minutes.

Brad wasn't sure what woke him up. It might have been the lights on the car that was driving into Dry Creek. Not that the lights themselves would have woken him up. It was when the driver dimmed the lights that something stirred his sleeping brain. When he heard the thud of a car door quietly shutting, he opened his eyes. Even then half of his brain was thinking that Linda was coming in early to open up and maybe he could get a cup of coffee.

He discarded that theory as soon as he thought

it. Linda had closed the café for Christmas week so that she could go visit that boyfriend of hers in Los Angeles. Linda had said the town could use the café if anyone wanted to cook a Christmas Eve dinner like she had in the past, but so far no one had agreed to do the cooking. In any event, Linda wasn't even in the state of Montana.

Brad slid open his pickup door and woke up completely. The cold air pushing into the pickup was enough to get a man's attention. He wished he didn't have to go and investigate, but he saw little choice. Everyone knew Linda was gone, and if someone had mischief in mind, now was the time they would do it.

The snow softened Brad's footsteps as he walked along the side of the café. He looked in the corner of the window and saw a figure moving around inside. Whoever it was had thought to bring a flashlight, and the beam of the light was flickering around inside. The flashlight sealed the argument for Brad. No one who had any business being in there would bother with a flashlight when the light switch was right next to the door.

It must be some kid, Brad thought to himself. He could see the boy's shadow and judged him to be around eleven or twelve. Brad figured a boy that young would be more nuisance than trouble. Brad looked over at the car parked in front of the café. He

didn't recognize it, but it was a kid's car all right—
a beat-up old thing the color of crusty mustard. It
looked like it was held together with rubber bands
and bubble gum—but it was still a car. Which meant
the boy was probably at least sixteen.

With any luck, Brad could deliver the boy back
to his parents and that would be the end of it.

Millie's fingers were so cold she had a hard time
keeping the flashlight steady. She had set the bag of
flannel Santa socks at her feet and the other bag, the
one with the hundred-dollar bills, on the table in
front of her.

It was the perfect thing to do with the money
Forrest had given her before he left for Dry Creek
two years ago. Millie had tried to give the seventy-
five hundred dollar bills to the police, but they didn't
want them because they couldn't prove they were
connected to a crime. She didn't want them because
she couldn't prove they *weren't* connected to a
crime. She had been poor all her life, but she'd never
knowingly profited from the misery of others.

Millie had fretted about what to do with those
bills until she'd realized they were the solution to
her problem in Dry Creek. She'd give a bill to each
person in Dry Creek along with a note saying the
money was from a stranger. That would make them
all trust strangers more, wouldn't it? A hundred

dollars would do that to most people in Millie's opinion. It sure would have caused a stir with those boys in her old foster family.

Besides, she'd be able to get rid of the money and fulfill Forrest's request at the same time. It was brilliant. And the best part of all was, she wouldn't have to actually open her mouth and talk to anyone.

Millie supposed she should have pre-stuffed the socks and written her notes, but she had decided she would do that in the café. She wanted to think about how excited each person would be when they opened their socks and saw the money.

It had not been easy, but Millie had remembered the names of most of the people who lived in Dry Creek. Forrest had sprinkled his stories with a surprising number of names and, fortunately, they had stayed in her head. She'd written names on most of the socks. In her opinion, a present wasn't really a present unless it had a person's name on it.

Some of the names might be misspelled, but she was sure each stocking would find its owner. She even had a few labeled "Anyone," for those she might have missed. Most nights last month, after she finished at the coffee shop, she'd pick up the glue gun and personalize the Christmas socks. Before the glue dried, she sprinkled glitter on the writing.

She was proud of the socks. The money might be from Forrest, but the socks were from her.

Millie didn't know what made her think something was wrong. Maybe it was the fact that the air inside the café was suddenly a couple of degrees colder. Or maybe it was the darkness inside had grown just a shade deeper, like someone was blocking the moonlight that had been coming through the open door behind her. Whatever it was, she didn't have enough time to turn around before she felt the arms close around her.

Woosh. Millie felt her breath leave her as panic rose in her throat.

"What the—?" Brad revised his opinion of the juvenile delinquent he was apprehending. The boy might be small, but he wasn't puny. He had stomped on Brad's foot with all his might. The kid was wearing some kind of wool coat that made grabbing him difficult, but Brad had roped calves for the last twenty years and knew a thing or two about handling uncooperative creatures.

Brad grabbed the boy around the middle and hoisted him up in the air where his feet could do less damage. The boy gasped in outrage, but Brad didn't let that stop him.

"If you want me to put you down, you have to stop kicking," Brad finally said as he shifted his arms so that the kid was hanging on Brad's hip like a bag of grain. Brad had his arm hooked around his captive's stomach, and the boy's head was facing toward the café door. He wore enough wool to clothe a small army, and it bunched up around his middle. Brad was having a hard time keeping the boy from wiggling out of his arm so he could walk back to the light switch.

The boy must be deaf, because he sure wasn't doing what Brad had politely suggested. Which was what Brad would expect, considering the whole night had gone from bad to worse. Well, Brad decided, he'd had enough.

He took his other hand and pushed the wool coat up high enough so he could get a firm grip on the boy's stomach. The boy's shirt had come untucked in the struggle, and Brad figured his hand was firmly anchored around the boy's stomach.

"That's better," Brad said. The boy had gone still in his arm.

Brad took a couple of steps over to the light switch even though something was beginning to make him think he'd got a few things wrong. The boy must be even younger than Brad had figured.

His stomach was softer than anything Brad imagined you'd find on a boy of fifteen who lived around these parts. Maybe that was the kid's problem. No one had taught him to ride horses or wrestle calves. Brad doubted the boy had even done any summer farm work. That belly had never been scratched by lifting a hay bale or sliding under a broken-down tractor.

The boy gasped again when Brad flipped the light switch, but Brad was ready for him. This time he tipped the kid upright so they could face each other.

"Oh." Brad still had the boy in his grip, or rather—he corrected himself—he still had her— *her*—in his grip.

"You're a girl!" Brad could see she was more like a woman, but he was only starting to sort things out, and "girl" would do for now. He never should have left those poker games tonight.

The girl-woman just glared at him. She had green eyes and wispy blond hair that settled in soft curls around her face. And her face—she looked solemn and scared all at the same time. The only muscles that moved on her face were her eyelids. She kept blinking.

"You dropped my glasses," she finally said.

Brad looked back and he saw where her glasses had fallen to the floor. He also saw a brown paper bag with a long tear in it on top of one of the tables. Through the tear he saw money.

Brad whistled. "I guess I don't need to ask what you're doing here."

The woman went even stiffer in his arms.

"I'm not one to judge people," Brad continued as he carried her over to the brown paper bag. He began to wonder if the woman had been getting enough to eat. She sure didn't weigh much. He could carry her around on his hip like this for hours without tiring. "I figure you're poor enough that stealing some money from a cash drawer is tempting, but you'd be much better off getting a job."

The woman relaxed some. "I have a job."

"Now, there's no need to lie to me," Brad continued patiently. "No one's blaming you for needing help. But in this town we ask for help, we don't steal from each other."

"I'm not stealing."

For such a little bit of a woman, she sure was stubborn. Brad looked at the bag more closely and frowned. Why had Linda kept that kind of money in the café? Even though break-ins were rare around here, there was no point in tempting folks.

"What's your name anyway?"

"You don't know me. I'm a stranger."

Something about the way the woman said that irked Brad. "I wasn't planning to sit down and socialize or anything—I just asked your name."

"Oh. My name's Millie."

"Millie what?"

"Just Millie."

Brad sat down in the chair next to the table. As he folded all six foot four of himself onto the chair, he shifted Millie so she sat on his knee.

Brad almost sighed. No wonder he had thought she was a kid. Even with her sitting on his lap, he still didn't meet her eye to eye. Which was a pity, because he'd been wondering if her eyes weren't more blue than green, and he'd been hoping to have another look. Of course, it wasn't because he was personally interested. It was just so he could answer the questions if he had to describe her for a police report. Looking down, he saw the top of her head. "How short are you anyway?"

That statement at least made Millie look up at him. Her face was no longer pale and scared. It was more pink and angry now. Of course, that was probably just because he'd been carrying her sideways.

"I'm just under five feet *tall*, not *short*," Millie said. "And I don't see what business it is of yours anyway."

Brad grinned. He'd always liked green eyes that threw spit darts at him. "Lady, everything about you is my business. At least until I can get the deputy sheriff to come pick you up."

That seemed to take Millie's attention away from him. She twisted around on his lap and looked at the door.

"Don't even think about making a run for it," Brad said. Until he said that, he had half a mind to give her a few dollars out of his own pocket and send her on her way. But he figured he should at least wait until she said she was sorry and promised to stop stealing from people.

"I don't run away," Millie announced.

Brad believed her. She sat as still as a stone on his lap, as if she was resigned to the worst. He didn't want to scare her. "Well, it's not like they'll probably lock you up or anything—you didn't even make a getaway."

Brad reached down and picked up Millie's glasses off of the floor, then gave them to her.

Millie took the glasses from him and settled them on her nose.

Brad frowned. Those glasses not only hid the golden tones in Millie's green eyes, they hid her face, as well. Without them, she was pretty in a quiet sort of a way. Her face was pale with freckles scattered across it. With her wispy blond hair and those solemn green eyes, she looked like pictures he'd seen of young girls living on the sun-bleached prairie a hundred years ago.

She didn't look like his ideal woman, of course. Her hair might be blond, but it didn't have any of the brazen look he preferred. He liked women with red lipstick and sexy laughs who knew how to flirt.

But still, for a quiet kind of a woman, she was pretty enough. Until she put those glasses on. The glasses made her look like a rabbit.

Of course, how the woman looked was not his problem. Brad stood up and wrapped Millie under his arm again. "Sorry I don't have any rope to tie you up with. So we'll just have to make do until I get the sheriff on the phone."

Brad sat down again once he reached the phone at the back of the café. He settled Millie back on his lap. This time it seemed more like she belonged there. Like he was getting used to her. "You don't really need those glasses, do you?"

"That's none of—"

"—my business," Brad finished for her. Well, she was right. She was too serious for the likes of him anyway. He needed a woman who liked a good time and would leave it at that. A woman like the one sitting on his lap would turn her green eyes on him and expect him to make a commitment to her. He didn't need any of that. Especially not when he was depressed anyway. He reached for the phone and dialed a number. The phone rang and rang. No one answered.

Brad sighed. It was time someone dragged Sheriff Carl Wall into the twenty-first century and got him a cell phone. What were law-abiding citizens supposed to do when they apprehended a thief in the middle of the night?

Brad looked back over at the bag of money on the table. The bag was small, more of a lunch bag than anything. Still, it was stuffed full. If she'd only been stealing twenty bucks to make it to the next town, he'd probably let her go.

But seeing that bag of money gave him pause. The side of the bag was split and he could see the bills. He wasn't close enough to see the denominations, but there were probably a few hundred dollars there. He wasn't doing anyone any favors if he let a thief like that loose in the night.

"I guess I'll just have to take you in," he said finally. The Elkton bunkhouse wasn't the fanciest place around, but it was built solid and all of the locks worked. He could just lock her in his room for the night, and get the sheriff to come out in the morning.

In the meantime, Brad would throw a tablecloth over that bag of money and lock the café door. It should be safe enough until morning when he and Sheriff Wall could come back and investigate. As he recalled, the sheriff was particular about the scene of the crime, and Brad wanted to be able to tell him that he hadn't touched anything.

For the first time that evening, Brad had a happy thought. He might not need to go to church tomorrow morning after all, not when he had to clean up after a crime. Even God and Dr. Norris had to understand that keeping the law was important.

And, Brad decided, because he had fully

intended to go to church, that should count as keeping his promise even if he didn't actually get there. He told himself it wasn't his fault someone had been stealing from the café.

Chapter Three

"Get in," Brad said as he held the door of his pickup open. The passenger door had a tendency to stick, and he'd had to put Millie down so he could open it. He'd kept one arm hooked around her stomach while he'd swung the door open with his other hand. "Get in."

"I never ride with strangers," Millie said as she braced herself.

Brad sighed. He could feel the woman tense up. He never knew a thief could be so particular about the company she kept. "Don't worry. No one's a stranger for long in Dry Creek—"

Well, that made her relax, Brad thought.

"Really? So you're not worried about strangers around here?" she asked as she turned around to face him. "You trust them?"

The woman sounded downright cheerful. Brad wondered why for a moment before he remembered. "We're not so trusting that we don't lock our doors, of course."

Brad lifted the woman up into his pickup and settled her on the seat. He knew he was lying a little, but he figured it was allowed under the circumstances. Some people did lock their doors when they went away for a trip—if they could find their keys, of course.

Brad figured he should drive his point home just so she knew she wasn't in some nostalgic Rockwell painting where everyone was easy pickings for any thief who might come driving by. "We've had our share of crime here. Why, we had a hit man come to town two years ago at Christmas. He tried to kill the pastor's wife."

"Oh." The woman was looking straight ahead as if there was something to see out the windshield of his pickup.

"Of course, we took care of him. Had him arrested and sent to prison." Brad congratulated himself as he shut the door on his pickup. That should let her know that the people of Dry Creek knew how to handle bad guys.

Brad walked around to the driver's side and got in.

"I'm sure he must have been sorry," Millie said.

"Who?" Brad put the key in the ignition.

"The man who tried to kill your pastor's wife. I'm sure he was sorry."

The woman's voice sounded a little hurt. Brad looked over at her. That's just what he needed—a sensitive thief. Ah, well. "You don't need to worry. The people of Dry Creek are big on forgiveness once you say you're sorry. If you just explain that you tried to take the money because you were hungry—"

"I wasn't hungry." Millie lifted her chin and continued to stare straight ahead.

Brad gave up. "Fine. Have it your way."

"I wouldn't steal even if I *was* hungry," Millie added quietly.

"Fine." Brad looked in the rearview mirror as he put his foot on the gas and eased the truck forward. He really shouldn't feel sorry for a woman that determined to be unreasonable. "But if you were hungry, say real hungry, that might explain why you had broken into the café in the middle of the night."

There, Brad told himself, he'd given the woman an excuse for being at the scene of the crime. She could say the money was just sitting on the table and she'd only been looking for a piece of bread. He wasn't sure she was smart enough to use the story, but he'd done what he could for her.

Brad turned his pickup onto the road going

through Dry Creek. The town sure was quiet at midnight.

After a few minutes of silence the woman said, "I'm not a thief."

Brad figured it was going to be a long night and an even longer morning with the sheriff. He was beginning to think maybe he wouldn't be getting such a good deal by skipping out on church to revisit the scene of the crime. What a night. He'd never imagined the day would come in the life of Brad Parker when church sounded like the better of two possibilities.

Millie's hands were cold. Ordinarily, she would put them in the pockets of her coat and they would be warm enough. But the man beside her made her nervous, and she wanted to keep her hands free. She didn't know exactly why, but it just seemed like a good idea. She'd never really liked big men, and this one had to be at least six feet tall. She could hardly see his face, not with the darkness and that Stetson he wore. Mostly, she could just see his chin. He needed a shave, but outside of that, his chin looked all right.

"I would think the jail would be back that way." Millie was trying to remember the map she'd studied before starting the drive from Seattle. The bigger towns were all west of Dry Creek. Going east, there weren't any towns of any size until you got to Minot, North Dakota. Leave it to a big man like that to have no sense of direction. Maybe he couldn't see very well with that hat on. If that was the case, she wouldn't criticize. She knew what it was like when a person couldn't see too well.

"I'm not going to the jail. I'm going home to the ranch."

"What?" Millie forgot all about being understanding. She knew she shouldn't have gotten into the man's pickup. That was a basic rule of survival. Never get into a car with a strange man. "You have to stop and let me out. Now!"

The man looked at her. "I told you I was holding you until I could get the sheriff."

Millie tried not to panic. The man was big, but he didn't look malicious. Still, what did she know? The only part of him that she'd gotten a good look at was his chin. "Usually, suspects are taken to a jail to be held for the sheriff."

"We don't have a jail in Dry Creek."

Of course, Millie thought, she knew that. "There's one in Miles City."

The man grunted. "You'd freeze to death in there this time of year."

"I have a coat." Millie put her hands in her pockets. She did have a good warm coat, and she was glad she'd brought it with her. "I'd really prefer the jail."

The man just kept driving. "I'm not driving back that direction tonight. The sheriff can take you there tomorrow if he wants. He's the one that has to okay turning the heat on anyway."

"They don't heat it?"

The man shrugged. "Budget cutbacks. They only heat it when they have someone locked up, so the sheriff tries to keep it clear this time of year."

Millie looked out the window. The night was black. It was even too cloudy to see any stars. She didn't see lights ahead that might have signaled a ranch house, either. Not that she was anxious to get to this man's ranch. "Is your wife home?"

Millie told herself to breathe. The man must be a local rancher. That meant he had to have a wife. If there was a woman around, she'd be all right. She trusted women.

The man grunted. "I'm single."

"Oh."

"Not single in the sense that I'm looking for a wife." The man reached up and crunched his hat farther down on his head. "Of course, I enjoy a date just like the next man. I'm all in favor of dating. You know, casual dating."

"Oh." Millie was trying to count the fence posts outside. How was she going to find her way back to Dry Creek when he stopped this pickup? She really wished the man had a wife. "Do you have a sister?"

"Why do you want to know about a sister?" The man's voice sounded confused. "Are you into double-dating or something? If you are, I could set up a date with one of the other guys—Randy is seeing someone pretty regular."

"Will she be there?" Millie felt her hands tense up.

"Where?"

"At your ranch."

"My ranch? Oh, ah, yeah. My ranch. I think so."

Millie relaxed. "Good."

Brad told himself he hadn't been this stupid since he was sixteen. He'd just lied to a woman to impress her. Why had he allowed her to think he owned a ranch? Hadn't she seen his pickup? It was an old diesel one. Did he look like he owned a ranch? He should have corrected her and said he worked on a ranch. Worked, not owned. Of course, he dreamed of having his own ranch, and he hoped to make that dream come true before long, but still—

And, to make it worse, the woman was a thief. It stood to reason she would only date a man with property. Of course, it wasn't like she was a bad criminal. Maybe he should tell her he was close to owning his own ranch. His ranch wouldn't be as big and fancy as the Elkton Ranch, but it would do.

Brad shook his head. Was he nuts? The last thing

he needed was to fantasize about dating a woman who was a criminal.

He usually didn't fall into the trap of lying about what he had in life. Of course, he usually didn't need to—women wanted to date him because he was fun to be with. There were lots of women who would like to date him—women, by the way, who didn't have a rap sheet.

Brad shook his head again. He didn't know what was wrong with him. He shouldn't even be having this conversation with himself. Maybe he was running a fever or something.

He looked at the woman out of the corner of his eye. She sat so close to the other door, Brad could have put two other women between them. Women, he might add, who would want to sit next to him. Millie, if that was her real name, sure wasn't the friendly type.

Besides, she had that little frown. He doubted she would recognize a good time if it came up and bit her on the backside. He shouldn't even care what she thought about him.

Brad turned the wheel of his pickup. The mailbox for the Elkton Ranch stood at the gravel road that led back to the ranch house. Fortunately, the boss was off spending Christmas with his wife's family in Seattle, so no one was home in the big house. The bunkhouse was just past the ranch house.

"I live here," Brad said as he eased the truck to a

stop in front of the bunkhouse. Anyone with any sense would figure out from that that he didn't own any part of this ranch.

Brad expected some question about why he lived in the small house instead of the big house, but Millie didn't seem to notice.

"Someone's home inside," Millie said. The relief in her voice made her sound happier than if they had stopped at the big house.

Brad looked at the windows and, sure enough, Charlie stood in the window looking out to see who had driven up to the bunkhouse at midnight. It wasn't until Brad saw Charlie that he realized his plan had a small problem. The bunkhouse didn't have many rules. Actually, there were only two. No wet socks by the woodstove, because no one wanted to burn the place down. And no women allowed past the main living room of the bunkhouse.

Sometimes the rule on the socks was bent. But the one about women? Never.

Charlie would insist Brad turn around and go find Sheriff Wall and deliver the suspect to him. He wouldn't care that it was twenty degrees below zero outside and Brad didn't even know where the sheriff was right now, or that the suspect in question was unfriendly and uncooperative and looked at Brad, when she had those glasses of hers on, like he was the one who had committed a crime.

Brad decided he had had enough for one day.

"Here, you might want to wear my hat," Brad turned around and set his hat square on the woman's head. The woman's glasses were the only thing that kept the hat from falling halfway down her face. "And there's no need for the glasses."

"What?"

Brad plucked the glasses off the woman's nose and hooked the top button on her black wool coat. There, she looked like a juvenile delinquent again. "Just give me a minute of quiet and I'll have you safe inside."

"Safe inside from what?" The woman's voice was rising in panic.

"Ah." Brad thought. "Spiders. The man inside keeps pet spiders."

Brad congratulated himself. All women were afraid of spiders. But just in case. "He might have some snakes, too."

Brad could feel her stiffen up, and he felt a little bad. He pulled her across the seat to his side. "You don't need to worry, though. I'm going to carry you through to a safe place. You just need to be quiet for a little bit."

"Why?"

"Ah, the spiders go crazy when they hear any noise." Brad opened the door. The wind almost froze his ears now that he didn't have his hat.

Brad stepped out of the pickup and picked up Millie again. It didn't seem right to carry her like a bag of grain now that he knew she was a woman, but he didn't want to make Charlie any more suspicious than he'd naturally be. The truth was, those glasses of Millie's had reminded Brad that Charlie couldn't see so well at night anymore, and Brad figured there was a good chance he could slip Millie into his room without Charlie even seeing them. And he could do it, too, if he used the side door to the bunkhouse.

The door squeaked, and Brad tried to be as quiet as he could. The rooms for the ranch hands were all lined up in a row, and each had a door going off of this long hallway. At the end of the hallway was the main room where Charlie was standing by the window.

Brad held his breath. His room was only two doors down from the side door, and it would take only a little luck to reach it before Charlie figured out that he wasn't coming in the main door.

Brad put his hand on the doorknob leading into his room at the same time that he heard Charlie cough. Brad pushed the door open anyway and put Millie inside. "Stay there a minute."

Brad only waited long enough to be sure Millie was standing upright before he stepped out of the room and closed the door.

"That you, Brad? What's that you have?" Charlie asked as he peered down the long hallway.

Brad put on his best smile. "Nothing."

"Nothing?" The old man frowned.

Brad kept his smile going. "Well, Christmas is coming, you know."

"That's right." The old man relaxed and smiled as he walked down the hall toward Brad. "I forgot it's the time of year when a person shouldn't be too nosy."

"That's right. All those Christmas presents." Brad figured by now Charlie would be expecting more than the new pair of leather gloves Brad had tucked away in his drawer for the occasion. Brad figured he'd need to get Charlie a shovel or something big. Maybe a ladder would do.

"I'm glad to see you're in the Christmas spirit," the old man said slowly.

"It's a joy to give." Brad kept smiling. He wondered when lockjaw set in on a man's mouth. He figured it'd be coming any minute now.

"That's good to hear." Charlie was talking the same, but Brad noticed the old man wasn't looking at him anymore. Instead, he was looking over Brad's shoulder.

Brad turned around. Millie stood in the doorway of his room, and she wasn't wearing his hat or her glasses. She was wearing the coat buttoned up to her neck, which, with her blond curls and timid face, made her look like she was about twelve.

"I see we have company," the old man said gently.

"I thought you were going to stay in the room," Brad said.

"I'm not afraid of spiders," Millie said to no one in particular. Her face went white when she said it. "Unless they're black widows, and then anyone would be afraid."

Millie couldn't see much without her glasses. Mostly it just looked like a long tunnel with a white light at the end of it and several large rocks along the way. The closest large rock was the man Brad.

"If you have spiders, you really should make them stay out in the barn," Millie suggested. She'd taken off the hat he put on her head and looked for her glasses. "You forgot to leave me my glasses."

"Oh."

Millie didn't know why he needed to sound so annoyed. She hadn't made any fuss about the spiders. "I would imagine they'll have spiders in the jail."

"No, they won't. Too cold," Brad said as he held out her glasses.

Millie could see the arm outstretched, and she reached for the open palm. Ah, there were her glasses.

She blinked when she put them back on. Usually,

she didn't blink so much. At first, she thought it was because of the light in the hallway. But that didn't make sense. Even though she couldn't see, her eyes had already adjusted to the brightness.

No, what was startling her eyes was the man. She hadn't had a good look at him until now. My goodness, he was handsome. Not that she was interested herself. The closest thing to a boyfriend she'd had in the last five years was Forrest, and he'd turned out to be a hit man. She didn't exactly have reliable sense when it came to men. But still, she'd have to remember what the man looked like so she could tell the other waitresses at Ruby's. They'd enjoy a story about a good-looking rancher who lived in a house full of spiders.

She took another good look at him so she'd remember. Brad's hair was dark as coal, she decided, and he kept it just long enough to curl a little at the ends. The hair alone made him look like a movie star. But it didn't stop there. He had the blue eyes of the Irish. No wonder his chin was strong. The Irish always had strong chins. They also generally talked a lot, and that was what the man was doing right now.

Brad had stepped closer to the old man and was whispering something to him. The inside of the room was made out of oak logs. There were beige curtains on the window and long leather couches around the room. The old man nodded several times while Brad spoke.

Then both men looked up. Millie heard the noise, too. Even with all of the snow outside, it sounded like a dozen pickups had screeched to a stop out in front of the bunkhouse.

Brad didn't bother to leave the shadows of the hallway. He wondered what had made the other guys rush home from Billings. He looked at the clock on the opposite wall. It was only twelve-thirty. "There must have been a fight. There'll be a broken bone or two."

The door opened and eight other ranch hands stomped into the bunkhouse.

"Okay, who's hurt?" Charlie demanded as he stepped into the main room from the hallway.

All eight of the men who had entered the bunkhouse stopped. "We're worried about Brad."

Brad stepped from the hall into the main room. "Why? I'm right here."

"Oh." The men flashed each other guilty looks and then stared at the floor.

Finally, Howard, one of the older men, cleared his throat and rubbed the beard on his chin. "We thought we'd check on you, that's all. Heard you hadn't made it over to the other game."

"Since when is it a crime to go to bed early on a Saturday night?" Brad was getting tired of apologizing for not spending his night gambling. Just because he didn't want to sit down with a bunch of smelly men and bet his week's salary against theirs, it didn't mean anything was wrong.

"It's just not like you," another of the men, Jeff, mumbled. Jeff was the only one who had taken his hat off when he came in the bunkhouse, and Brad could still see the snow melting on the man's shoulders.

"Whoa," Randy, the youngest ranch hand, said and then he whistled. "We take that back—it *is* like you. Going to bed early when you have company is an altogether different thing."

It took Brad a full ten seconds to realize what Randy was saying—or rather what he was seeing.

Brad turned around, but he already knew what he would see. Millie had left the hallway and was standing behind him. She was holding the neckline on her coat tight around her throat, and it made her look nervous and young. At least she had her glasses on so she didn't look as pretty as Brad knew she could.

"It's not what you think," Brad started.

"You don't need to say another word," Randy said as grinned and backed up toward the door.

"Yes, he does," one of the other hands, William, spoke up. William had been an accountant before he became a ranch hand, and with his thinning blond hair and long face, he still looked like he was always trying to balance the books. William had known Brad for the past ten years. He was looking at Brad now like he'd never really known him, though. "Isn't she too young?"

"Of course she's too young," Brad snapped back.

"I'm twenty-three," Millie spoke up.

Brad groaned. How could the woman be twenty-three and be so dumb? "She's young for her age."

William nodded, no longer upset. "Still, it's the age that counts. Sorry we bothered you."

"You didn't bother me. Nothing's going on."

Brad could see the speculation in Randy's eyes. Randy was only twenty-two or so himself, and he looked like he was realizing Millie was more his age than Brad's.

Randy swallowed and spoke. "Well, if nothing's going on with the two of you, then maybe you wouldn't mind if I—"

Brad felt his arms tighten. It had been a while since he'd taken down any of the other guys with his fists, but he could still do it. "She's not in the market. Besides, you already have a girlfriend."

Charlie cleared his throat. "Now, there'll be none of that." He looked at Brad. "That's the reason why we have the rule—no women allowed."

"She's not here because she's a woman," Brad said. "She's here because she's a thief."

Brad expected his statement to bring some

dignity to the situation. Instead, William looked at him like Brad was the one at fault.

"You don't need to lie. We're prepared to make some exceptions for you on account of—" William swallowed and stared at the floor "—on account of the time of year and all. If she eases the pain some, maybe we could let her stay with you for the night."

"What?" Brad was dumbfounded. Sometimes a man broke the bunkhouse rules, but never ever was anyone given *permission* to break them. How pathetic did they think he was?

"William's right," Charlie mumbled. "She could even stay with you through Christmas, since the boss isn't here. He'll never know. You've got your own bath and everything, so the two of you will be snug in your room. She'll make you happy."

Randy and the others just stared at the floor.

Brad snorted. "You're all hopeless. She doesn't make me happy. I caught her breaking into the café."

"Really?" William asked. He looked at Millie and smiled. "You're sure she wasn't just hungry? She's awfully small to be a thief."

"I'm not a thief," Millie said.

Brad looked over his shoulder. Millie stood in the hallway in that long wool coat of hers looking like a refugee. "Then what were you doing in the café with all that money?"

"I can't say."

Brad looked at the other men. "See?"

"Does anybody recognize her?" Charlie asked. He'd taken a step closer to Millie and was studying her. "Between all of you, I figure you know every woman over the age of sixteen in the whole county."

"Never seen her before," William said.

"I'd remember her if I had," Randy added.

"I'm a stranger," Millie said.

"A stranger who happens to be a thief," Brad added.

"Maybe," Charlie said thoughtfully. "She doesn't look like any thief I've ever seen, though."

"Well, we'll find out in the morning when I can get hold of the sheriff."

"The sheriff's not in his office tomorrow," William said. "It's Sunday—he'll be in church."

"Well, then," Brad said grimly, "that's where I'll need to go to talk to him."

There was silence in the room.

Finally Randy spoke. "You're going to church?"

Brad nodded. People went to church all the time around Dry Creek. What was the big deal?

There was more silence.

"Inside the building?" William finally asked. "Not just volunteering to shovel the steps like you sometimes do when it snows?"

Brad nodded. "Of course, inside the building—"

Randy whistled. "This'll be something to see."

"There's nothing to see. I'm going to just take Millie there to the sheriff and give her a chance to confess—"

"I didn't know they still did confessions in church," Randy said.

"I don't have anything to confess," Millie said. "Well, at least not about being a thief."

"Wow," Randy said. "This'll be something to see."

Brad was annoyed. "There's no reason to get all excited. There'll be nothing to see or hear in church tomorrow. I'm just going to tell the sheriff about the scene of the crime and—"

"You mean there's a crime scene?"

Brad shook his head. It was hopeless. "Anyone want to stay out here and chew the fat? Millie needs to go to bed and get her sleep, but I'll be sleeping on the couch out here and I'm happy to have some company for an hour or so."

"No, thanks." Randy grinned. "I think I'll be getting up early in the morning."

"Me, too," William added. "I haven't been to church in a while."

"You've *never* been to church," Brad said as he sat down on a folding chair. "You're as much of a heathen as I am."

"I was baptized as a baby," William protested as he turned to walk toward the hall. "That makes me a member."

Brad shook his head. "No, it doesn't."

"I think you need to pay dues to be a member," Randy added as he turned to the hallway, too.

"Just go to bed," Brad said.

Charlie nodded. "We all need our sleep."

Brad didn't know if it was sleep he needed. Maybe an aspirin would do him more good. He had a feeling he wasn't going to sleep at all tonight, and it wouldn't be because of the lumps in the sofa.

Chapter Four

Millie had been to church once when she was a child. Her foster mother had taken her to an Easter service because the child welfare representative was going to come the next day and there was always a question on the form the man filled out about church or other religious activity.

They had gone to an old church that had big stained-glass windows that showed pictures of Jesus in many different poses. Millie had been in awe. She liked the picture best of Jesus kneeling down beside a child. The child had been wearing a blue robe, and Millie had on a blue dress that day. She looked at the picture and pretended it was her that Jesus was smiling down at and talking to in such a friendly way.

When she left the church, Millie told her foster

mother about pretending that she was in the picture with Jesus. Her foster mother said she was silly. She said those pictures of Jesus were from thousands of years ago and had nothing to do with today.

Millie still remembered the disappointment she felt. It was the first time she'd realized Jesus lived such a long time ago. Somehow she had the feeling he was supposed to still be alive today.

That was the last time Millie had been inside a church.

She was surprised that the church in Dry Creek didn't have any stained-glass windows. Of course, she remembered looking at the church last night in the dark and she hadn't seen any, but churches had always seemed mysterious places to her, and she expected to step into the church in Dry Creek and see something dramatic like a stained-glass window anyway.

Instead, the church was humble. The glass was frosted because of the cold outside, but not decorated in any other way.

There was a strip of brown carpet going down the middle of the church between the rows of wooden pews, but the flooring on both sides of the carpet was the kind of beige linoleum that she had seen frequently in coffee shops. The only problem with that kind of linoleum was that there was a special trick to getting off the black scuff marks. Millie looked down at the floor. Everything was scrubbed clean, but the black marks were still there. She could tell someone how to fix that.

Not that she was here to talk about the floor, Millie reminded herself. She was glad Brad didn't seem like he was in any hurry to actually go inside the church, either. They both just stood in the doorway.

There were quite a few people in the church already, but they weren't sitting down yet.

"Do I look all right?" Brad whispered down at her.

Millie looked up. She was getting used to Brad's face. Well, sort of.

Maybe it was because she'd spent the night on his pillow and grown accustomed to the warm scent of him that lingered in his room even as he slept in the other room on the sofa. When you've been in someone's bed like that, she thought, handsome didn't seem to matter so much.

Besides, he didn't seem to care that he was handsome, so that helped some more. He was mostly worried about the tie he had around his neck. He'd had to borrow it from Charlie this morning, and Charlie only had two ties and said he needed one for himself. Charlie kept the black one, the one he called his funeral tie.

Brad had had to settle for a red tie with elves on it that Charlie had won in some bingo game at the senior center in Billings last year.

Millie nodded. The elf tie did go, in a way, with the green shirt Brad had borrowed from William.

"I feel stupid wearing dancing elves around my neck," Brad said.

Millie wasn't used to men admitting they felt stupid. "They look a little like drunken mushrooms."

"Really?" Brad seemed cheered by the idea.

Millie nodded. "At least I have my coat to wear."

Millie had bought the black wool coat years ago because it covered everything. She could have her waitress uniform on and no one would know. She didn't always like people to know she was a waitress when she rode the bus to work. Too many men felt they could flirt with any woman who was a waitress. Of course, the men were usually harmless. But still, she didn't want to be bothered.

Brad was frowning down at her. Millie wondered if maybe the coat wasn't too protective. She didn't want men to scowl at her, either.

"I could hold your glasses for you," Brad said finally.

What was his problem with her glasses? That was the second time this morning that he had suggested she not wear them. "My glasses are fine."

Brad nodded. "I thought they might fog up so you couldn't see. You might not know that. Glasses do that in the cold."

"I'm fine."

Brad nodded again, "Well, we might as well go in then."

There was a double door that led into the Dry Creek church, but only one half of it was open this morning.

Millie felt Brad take her elbow at the same time that they took a step into the church.

"Oh." Millie wished she had given her glasses to Brad. At least then she wouldn't see all the people who had turned around to look at them. There were tall people, old people, short people, and children. They all seemed like they were talking—until she and Brad walked into the church.

"Well, welcome!" A ripple of excitement went around the people standing in the church.

"Why, Brad Parker!" An older man stepped forward and held out his hand. The man was wearing a tweed jacket, and he smelled of old-fashioned after-shave.

Brad shook the man's hand. "Good morning, Dr. Norris."

"I'm glad you came." The older man wasn't content with a handshake. He slapped Brad on the shoulder, as well.

"I told you I'd come," Brad said.

Millie was glad Brad didn't move. She was also glad he was so big. She could almost hide behind him as long as he stood just where he was. Maybe no one would notice she was there.

"And welcome to you as well, young lady," the doctor said as he stopped looking at Brad and looked over at Millie. "We're glad you've come to worship with us."

"Oh." Millie gave a tight little smile. "I don't know if we'll be staying for—"

"Of course you have to stay for the service." An older woman stepped forward and beamed at Millie. "We're singing Christmas carols, and the Curtis twins are going to practice their donkey song—you know, the donkey who carried Mary to the Inn?"

"You mean the twins—Josh and Joey?"

"Why, yes," the woman said. The woman had her gray hair twisted into a mass of curls on the top of her head, and she was wearing a green gingham dress with a red bell pin. Millie knew who the older woman was before she held out her hand.

"My name's Mrs. Hargrove," the woman said.

Millie nodded and took the woman's hand. She never thought she'd get to meet Mrs. Hargrove. Mrs. Hargrove had written to Forrest several times while he was in jail. That's why Forrest knew so much about Dry Creek. And to think, Millie would hear the twins sing. Oh, she hoped Brad didn't want to meet with the sheriff before she could do that. "My name's Millie."

"How did you know about the twins?" Brad asked quietly.

Millie looked up at him and saw the suspicion in his eyes. She'd have to be more careful. "I thought you mentioned them last night."

"Me?"

"Well, maybe it was William—he brought me an extra blanket in case I got cold and stayed to talk for a little bit. Did you know he used to do the books for a restaurant in Seattle?"

"William what? I thought you were going straight to bed. That's what everyone was going to do."

"Well, I couldn't go to sleep if I was cold, could I?"

Someone started to play the organ, and Millie was relieved to see everyone starting to sit down.

Brad was still scowling. But at least he'd stopped looking down at her, Millie thought.

"I don't see the sheriff here," Brad said.

"He'll be here any minute," the older man, Dr. Norris, said, as he gestured to the pews. "You're welcome to sit anywhere."

"I think we should sit at the back," Brad said. "In case Sheriff Wall gets here soon."

The doctor nodded.

Millie was glad that the sheriff wasn't there quite yet. She and Brad walked to the last pew and sat down. Brad seemed to relax. He even loosened his tie.

Now that Millie was getting a good look around,

she noticed that someone had decorated the small church for Christmas. There was a short, stubby tree with tinfoil stars on it by the organ. Some of the stars were crooked, and they all looked like children had made them. Mixed in with the stars were some red lights that twinkled. Several poinsettia plants stood in front of the speaker's stand.

Some years at Ruby's they had poinsettia plants on the counter at Christmas. Once or twice the manager had given Millie one of the plants to take home after her shift ended on Christmas Day. They were hardy flowers and lasted almost till Easter.

"No one's wearing a tie, except for Pastor Curtis," Brad whispered in her ear. "I thought everyone wore a tie to church."

"This is sort of an informal church, I think," Millie whispered back.

Millie heard some sounds behind her and turned around. There stood all of the men from the Elkton Ranch bunkhouse, looking shy and out-of-place in the doorway.

"Welcome," the pastor said quietly from the front of the church. "Please take a seat anywhere."

The men filed into the back pew on the other side of the church, and the service started.

"I don't sing much," Brad whispered as everyone around them stood with a songbook in their hands.

"Me, neither," Millie said as she stood up. She

figured it didn't matter if you sang or not as long as you stood up at the right time and were respectful.

Singing wasn't as hard as Millie had thought. Some of the songs were Christmas carols that she knew from the radio that played at Ruby's, and she joined in the singing of those—quietly, of course.

The church service reminded Millie of a roller coaster she'd ridden once. She was scared at every turn of the corner, but she found she enjoyed it if she sat back and didn't try to fight the experience. Being in church was kind of like that.

There was a light behind the wooden cross in the center of the church, and Millie decided she could stare at that. She wasn't sure she was supposed to be listening to the sermon since she was just here to wait for the sheriff, so she didn't want to keep her eyes on the preacher. Of course, she couldn't help but hear the sermon. It was something about grace.

Millie wasn't quite sure what it all meant. The pastor had said grace was when you got something for free, but the only time Millie had heard of grace was at Ruby's when sometimes a customer would pray before they ate. One of the other waitresses said the people were saying grace. Millie wondered now if the people had been hoping they would get their dinners for free and not have to pay. She was surprised Ruby hadn't put a stop to people saying grace if that was the case.

No one got a free meal at Ruby's unless they happened to be really down on their luck. Then Millie sometimes paid for their meal out of her tips for the evening. Millie wondered if grace was something like that. When she gave out a free meal because another person was hungry and couldn't buy the meal for themselves. She'd have to ask the pastor if that's what grace was.

Of course, she'd have to wait until Brad turned her over to the sheriff and the sheriff turned her loose. She didn't suppose the pastor would want to talk to a woman who was in the process of being arrested.

Millie's favorite part of the whole church service was when the Curtis twins put on their donkey faces and sang a song about taking Mary to the Inn. They walked up and down in front of the church like they were on a long journey. Once one of the twins brayed like a donkey and pretended to fly. That had to be Josh.

Millie hadn't thought about how difficult it must have been for Forrest to learn so much about the people of Dry Creek in the few days he was in the little town. Even with Mrs. Hargrove's letters, there was a lot he learned himself. He said he'd talked to people in the café and even stopped at a few houses to ask directions here or there and had stayed to chat.

"People will tell you anything if you get them

talking," Forrest said to her once when she asked how he did it. "Everyone likes to talk."

Millie wished Forrest were here. He'd know what to do about the mess she was in. Of course, if he were here, he'd probably want her to continue on with her mission. She hoped Brad was right and that the people of Dry Creek did trust strangers. If they didn't, she sure didn't know how she'd get them to trust strangers now.

When the service was over, the pastor stood at the back door to shake hands. The men from the Elkton Ranch were the first ones in line. In fact, Millie suspected a few of them had tried to beat the pastor to the door so they could go through it before he even got there. But Charlie made them get in line.

Brad and Millie were right behind them.

"I'm glad you could join us this morning," Pastor Curtis said to Randy as he shook the younger man's hand.

Randy blushed and ran his finger around his necktie to loosen it. "We mostly came in to see the crime scene."

"What?" That was from Mrs. Hargrove. She was coming up to greet the men, too. "I know our singing isn't too good, but I'd hardly say it's a crime scene."

"No, ma'am." Randy turned even redder. "I mean the crime scene at the café."

A ripple of whispering went through the whole church until everything got silent.

"A crime! Has anyone seen a stranger?"

A gasp came from another corner. "Has anybody been shot this time?"

Millie looked around her. Forrest was right. He had taken away this little town's trust in strangers. She could see it in the faces around her. They were scared.

"It's nothing like that," Brad said gruffly. "Just a little bit of—well, maybe something was stolen."

"We have a thief?"

"I'm not a thief," Millie denied automatically. She wished she hadn't said anything when everyone turned to look at her.

"Well, of course you're not," Mrs. Hargrove agreed. "Anyone can see you're a nice young woman." The older woman smiled at Millie. "I was so pleased you were able to convince Brad to come to church with you."

Millie blushed. "Brad came to see the sheriff."

"Well, still—" Mrs. Hargrove kept smiling. "I can't believe you were stealing anything." The older woman looked up at Brad. "Are you sure she didn't just stop at the café thinking it was open and she could get something to eat? Maybe she was hoping to find a sandwich. Maybe she was hungry. Linda would have given her a sandwich if she had been there."

"That was a mighty green sandwich she was

taking out of there. I was hoping to catch up with the sheriff so I could show him where I left everything." Brad looked around. "I thought he'd be in church this morning."

"He had something to do in Miles City," Pastor Curtis said. "But he's planning to be at our house for lunch, so he should be here any minute."

Millie looked around. She saw skepticism on a lot of faces. "I wasn't taking the money. I was trying to give it away."

Brad nodded. "Give it away? Where'd you get it from in the first place?"

"I can't tell you where."

Brad snorted. "You're going to have to think of a better story than that if you expect Sheriff Wall to go easy on you."

"I think I hear the sheriff now," the pastor said. "Maybe we should go over to the café and get this settled."

Millie looked around. The faces that had been smiling weren't smiling at her anymore. They weren't exactly frowning, but she could see the caution in everyone's eyes. "I didn't do anything wrong."

"I'm sure you didn't," Mrs. Hargrove murmured as she patted Millie on the arm.

Millie noticed Mrs. Hargrove didn't look her in the eye when she said those words, however. Mrs.

Hargrove had obviously reconsidered her confidence in Millie.

It wasn't the first time since Forrest died that Millie wished she could have a few words in private with him. If Forrest could see her now, he would have to agree that she wasn't the person to make everything better with the people of Dry Creek. She was going to make it worse. Even Mrs. Hargrove didn't believe her.

"He should have sent an angel," Millie muttered. Dead people could do that, she figured. There were supposed to be lots of angels up there.

"What?" Mrs. Hargrove looked startled.

"Who's 'he'?" Brad bent down and asked. "Do you have an accomplice?"

"How many of them are there?" someone else asked.

"It's me. Just me," Millie said. She had never felt more alone in her life.

"It's best if you tell the truth." Brad frowned down at her. "I should have figured you had someone else in this with you. He probably sent you in as bait and—" Brad whistled "—I left the money right there for him."

Brad took Millie's elbow. "Let's go."

Millie had to almost run to keep up with Brad's long steps. The air outside was cold, and she hadn't had time to put the collar up on her coat. She could feel the air all the way down as she breathed it in. "You don't need to hurry."

Brad only snorted and kept walking. A dozen other people were trailing after them. "Don't know why it took me so long to figure it out—of course, a woman like you has a man around. Even Randy figured *that* out. With those eyes of yours, of course there's a man around."

"I don't—" Millie started to protest and then decided to save her breath. He wouldn't believe her anyway. They'd soon be inside the café, and he would see for himself that the money was still there and there was no man in sight.

Millie wondered how she had made such a muddle of Forrest's request. The people of Dry Creek would be even more suspicious of strangers after she left. Millie looked up at the determined set of Brad's chin and corrected herself. She should have said if she left. If she was able to.

The rancher didn't look like he'd let her leave anytime soon. She almost wished she did have some man someplace who would come get her. Although, as she looked at the rancher again, she didn't know what man she'd ever known in her life that she would put up against the one in front of her.

She looked at Brad again. Had she heard right? Did he think her eyes were pretty?

Chapter Five

Brad turned the handle on the door to the café before he remembered he had pushed the button on the other side of the handle and locked the door when he left last night.

"The key's under the rock," Mrs. Hargrove offered as she stood at the bottom of the steps. "The third rock on the porch there by your foot."

"But I have—" Millie said softly.

Brad didn't listen to Millie. Instead, he let go of her arm and bent down to turn over the rock. It was a piece of granite from the hills in the area, and snow was lodged in its crevices. It looked like Linda had hauled half of the mountain down here to place around her café. Some of the rocks outlined a dormant flower bed, but the rest of the rocks were just scattered here and there on the wide porch.

Brad decided that, when this was all over, he was going to ask the sheriff to do a public service talk on how to lock a door and keep it locked. Someone needed to pull Dry Creek into the modern age. What was the point of locking a door when a person left the key under a rock a mere four feet away? Except— "There's no key here."

"—That's because I have it," Millie said as she put her hand in the pocket of her coat and pulled out the brass key.

"You have it." Of course, she had it, Brad told himself as he took the key she offered. He hadn't asked himself last night how Millie had gotten in. "I suppose you turned over every rock on this porch hoping to find a key."

Even as Brad said that, he looked at the other rocks. They were all covered with snow. No one had moved them in the last few days. Which meant Millie hadn't turned over every rock to find the key; she'd turned over only one. "How did you know which rock it was under?"

"Someone told me."

Brad didn't know how a voice as quiet as Millie's could give him such a splitting headache. He supposed he had begun to hope that she wasn't really the thief he had first thought her to be. That she was just going inside the café to get out of the cold and maybe to fix a sandwich for herself. He was even beginning to think that Linda might have left the money there in a brown paper bag and that Millie was just counting it.

The rock took away all of those comfortable illusions. "Someone must have scouted out the town. The whole thing was planned and premeditated."

Millie frowned. It wasn't much of a frown, but Brad noticed that the tiny lines in her forehead made her nose smaller, which made her glasses slip a little bit. When she spoke, her voice sounded hurt. "I wasn't going to do anything bad. 'Premeditated' makes it sound like murder or something."

Brad heard the gasp at the bottom of the stairs. He knew the whole congregation had followed him and Millie over to the café, so he wasn't surprised that everyone was listening. The gasp came from one of the Curtis twins. It was Josh. The boys were six years old and fascinated with the usual boy things. "Did she say murder?"

"Nobody is going to murder anyone," Brad said firmly, turning around. He didn't want the rest of the people to start thinking in that direction. "This is Dry Creek. We're not like Los Angeles, where they have murders on every street corner."

"We almost had a murder here," the Kelly girl reminded him as she twisted her ponytail. She stood off to the side of the porch in an old, worn parka.

Brad wished he could remember her first name.

All he knew is that she had two older sisters that he sometimes saw in the bars in Miles City. He knew *their* names, not that it did him a lot of good with this girl. He'd just have to take a guess. "Now, Susie—"

"I'm Sarah," the girl corrected him. "Remember there was that hit man that came here? So you can't say it never happens." The girl turned her eyes from Brad and stared at Millie. "Maybe she's one, too."

Josh gasped again and turned his blue eyes up to Millie, as well. "Does she have a gun?"

"Of course she doesn't have a gun," Brad said automatically before he remembered that he hadn't really checked. "At least, I don't think she does—"

Brad was remembering that coat Millie wore. She could have a cannon tucked in the corner of that thing and the wool was so heavy it wouldn't even make a bulge. But she hadn't been wearing that coat the whole time, had she? Surely, he would have noticed if she was armed. She was too skinny to hide anything without the coat. Unless, of course, it was in the pocket of the coat.

Brad wished he'd just taken Millie to the jail last night. This was all getting out of hand. Where was the sheriff anyway? Brad ran his finger under his collar. It took him a minute to think of something to reassure the kids. "If she had a gun, she would have shot me by now."

"Some man came and tried to shoot my mom," Josh said to Millie. Josh was missing a front tooth, and he leaned toward Millie when he spoke. "That was before she was my mom."

"It happened at Christmas time, too," the Kelly girl insisted. "Right after the Christmas pageant. And we're having another pageant this year—I wonder if someone will be shot this year."

"I don't have a gun." Millie knelt down so she could look Josh in the eye. "You don't need to worry."

Brad snorted. He figured worrying was the only smart thing they *could* do, given the state of affairs. He took a side step closer to Millie and looked down at her. He really should find out if she had a gun. "I should frisk you."

"What?" Millie said as her eyes looked up to meet his.

Brad had a sudden vision of running his hands up and down Millie's coat. The problem was, the coat was so bulky he'd have to run his hands under her coat. He wasn't sure he should do that in full view of everyone. At least not with the kids around. Maybe if she wasn't wearing that coat, he could see if she was armed. "You should take your coat off."

"But it's cold."

Brad nodded. He'd tried. "We'll leave it to the sheriff. Where is he anyway?"

"I hear him," Mrs. Hargrove said. "He's using the siren."

Millie cleared her throat and turned so she faced the people waiting at the bottom of the porch. The air was cold, but most of the coats she saw were unbuttoned and unzipped. Everyone was looking at her so intently; they didn't even seem to notice the cold. Millie wasn't sure this was an ideal moment to try to explain, but sometimes a woman had to deliver her message any way she could. "Just because a man's a hit man, it doesn't mean he's a bad man."

"What?"

Millie figured the bellow behind her came from Brad. It was close enough to cause her ear damage, but she continued. She smiled at Josh and Sarah both. "Maybe the hit man was real sorry for the things he did and wished he could do something to make it all better."

Millie stopped there. She'd done her best. She hadn't gone against Forrest's wishes and said she knew him, but she'd come close. Surely, someone in the crowd would read between the lines and understand what she was trying to say. Mrs. Hargrove was puzzling something out. Surely, *she* would understand.

Millie figured she'd been understood when Mrs. Hargrove stepped up on the porch looking like she'd puzzled her way to some conclusion and was ready to speak.

"Are you a reporter?" the older woman demanded to know.

"Me?" Millie asked, aghast. "I could never be a reporter." Millie could think of a hundred reasons why she wasn't a reporter. "I don't even know how to type."

Mrs. Hargrove bent over slightly and looked at Millie's hands. "You've got a tiny ink stain on one finger. Maybe you write in longhand."

"Well, I write, but it's not the news," Millie protested. Didn't Mrs. Hargrove know that shy people never became reporters? They would have to talk to people. All kinds of people. The woman could just as well have asked if Millie was an astronaut who flew to the moon. "It's more like—well, I take orders for things."

Millie could tell by the faraway look in Mrs. Hargrove eyes that she wasn't listening anymore. She was, however, thoughtful. "Now that I think of it, I'm surprised we haven't had more reporters snooping around doing some kind of a sequel to the story they did back then—they were quite interested in our hit man and the angel. I must admit it was a good angle. And here it is Christmas again. People might be interested in seeing what had happened to the town where it all took place."

"I swear I'm not a reporter." Millie raised her

hand. She'd place her hand on one of those Bibles people were holding if they wanted her to. "I don't even know any reporters."

"Well, let's hope you know a lawyer or two," a man's voice came from the back of the crowd.

Millie looked up. That must be the sheriff. He wore the uniform and—everything. She gulped. He had a gun.

Millie blinked and pulled the collar of her coat closer around her neck. "I don't know any lawyers, either."

The sheriff nodded. "I expect the county will have to get you one then. Not that they'll be happy about it. They don't even want to pay for heating the jail this time of year."

The sheriff stepped in closer and looked at Millie intently. She felt like a bug under a microscope.

"Unless, of course, you have money to pay for your own attorney," the sheriff added hopefully. "That would be good. My cousin over in Miles City works cheap. You might be able to hire him."

Millie thought of the remaining tip money she had in her purse and shook her head. "I used all my money driving here. I just have enough to get back."

"Where are you from?" the sheriff asked casually.

"Seattle."

"Lady, are you crazy?" Brad asked as he turned his back on everyone and jabbed the key into the lock on the door. "Driving all that way to rob us in Dry Creek? Let me tell you, the odds weren't great that you would find much money just lying around anywhere in town."

Brad shoved the door to the café open.

"I already told you. I didn't find the money here. I brought it with me."

Brad was tall enough that his shoulders filled out the doorway as he stood and turned on the light. "Yeah, and I'm the tooth fairy."

Millie took a deep breath. With a little bit of patience, she could explain everything to the sheriff. She could still keep Forrest's identity secret. She could just say that someone wanted to repay the people of Dry Creek, and she was the delivery person.

Millie heard Brad's low whistle before she stepped into the café, too.

"Don't touch the crime scene," the sheriff said as he stepped past Millie.

Brad had removed the tablecloth that he'd draped over the money last night.

"But look at these!" Brad had bent down and pulled one of the flannel Christmas stockings out of the sack on the floor. He had a look of horror on his face as he held it up. "I didn't get a good look at these last night."

Mrs. Hargrove and the pastor stepped ahead of Millie, too.

"Someone made them," Mrs. Hargrove said.

"I didn't have a pattern for the stockings," Millie said a little defensively. What did they expect? She'd relied on glue and hand-stitching to finish the stockings. Fortunately, she'd found several large remnants of red felt at a fabric store.

"It has Elmer's name on it," Mrs. Hargrove said, turning to tell everyone.

By now, half of the town of Dry Creek had come through the open door.

Mrs. Hargrove held another sock that Brad had pulled out of the sack. "This one says Jacob."

Millie could hear the murmur.

"I could see how a person might guess the name Jacob," someone in the back said. "But Elmer? I bet there's not fifty people left in the world with a name like Elmer."

"And here's Pastor Matthew and Glory." Mrs. Hargrove held up two more stockings.

The sheriff turned to Millie. "How do you know our names?"

Millie closed her eyes. "I was just doing a favor for a friend. He wanted to do something nice for Dry Creek, and he asked me to help him. That's all."

"We don't even have a phone directory anymore that lists everyone," Mrs. Hargrove said as she looked at all of the stockings on the table. "I'm not even sure I could sit down and write out everyone's name—not without a picture or something in front of me."

"My friend had a very good memory," Millie said. "He knew everyone's name."

"Is your friend Santa Claus?"

Millie looked down at the last question. Little Josh was looking up at her with hope in his eyes.

"I want a train," he said. "One that runs on the tracks and has a whistle. My dad says they're expensive, but I'm sure Santa Claus has one."

"My friend's not Santa Claus," Millie said softly as she knelt down to look the boy in the eyes. "But if he knew you wanted to have a train, he would have sent one to you. My friend's dead."

"Is he in heaven?"

"I—ah, well, I—" Millie didn't believe in heaven, but the little boy was looking at her with such innocence that she couldn't tell him that. And who knew? Maybe he was right. She certainly didn't know anything about it.

"My mother's in heaven," the boy said. "It's real nice there. I bet they have lots of trains. Maybe your friend could send one down from there—a superduper flying train. Do you think they have flying trains in heaven?"

"I—ah—I wouldn't know," Millie finally managed to say.

"Me, neither," the boy agreed. "You have to die to go to heaven."

Millie nodded. "That's what I've been told."

"Looks like you've been told a lot of things," the sheriff said. His voice was not friendly like the young boy's. "Mind if I ask some questions?"

Millie rose to her feet. She supposed it was too much to ask to be left alone so she could keep talking to Josh. "Go ahead."

"First, where are you from?"

"Seattle."

The sheriff wrote something in the black notebook he'd pulled out of his shirt pocket.

"That hit man was from Seattle," said an older man who had entered the café late.

"What brings you out this way?"

"I was doing a Christmas favor for a friend."

The sheriff looked a little interested in this, even though he didn't write anything in his notebook. "And who would that friend be?"

When Millie didn't answer, the sheriff looked over at Brad.

"Oh, no, it's not him," Millie protested. She didn't want anyone to suspect him of anything. "I don't even know him—not really. He was just doing his duty when he took me to his ranch last night—"

"His ranch?" The sheriff frowned. "You mean the Elkton place?"

"Is that your last name?" Millie turned to Brad. It was funny, she thought, that she hadn't heard his last name after all the time they had spent together. Of course, the time was hardly social, so she supposed it wasn't surprising. "I saw the name on the mailbox this morning."

The sheriff snorted and turned to Brad. "Did you tell her you owned the place?"

Millie saw the red creep up Brad's neck and said the only thing she could think of. "I think maybe I'm the one who assumed it was his place."

"But I didn't correct her," Brad said.

The sheriff shrugged. "Well, I suppose that doesn't matter. I guess it stands to reason you'd try to impress a pretty girl."

Millie pulled her coat a little tighter around her. She didn't much like it when Sheriff Wall said she was pretty. "We came to church this morning to see you."

The sheriff nodded. "Sorry I wasn't there. Now, answer me this—did you plan to take this money away from the café?"

Millie relaxed. "No."

The sheriff frowned. "So you're maintaining your innocence? You're saying you weren't in here last night planning to steal this money?"

"No, I was giving the money away."

Mrs. Hargrove gasped. "Don't tell me it's charity!"

Millie looked over at the older woman. She seemed more upset than she had been all morning.

"I bet it's that church in Miles City." Mrs. Hargrove was nodding emphatically as she turned to look at the rest of the townspeople. "Remember last year they wanted to give us food baskets? I told Pastor Hanks we didn't need their pity."

"Of course, we don't need any pity," the older man at the edge of the group said. "We can take care of each other."

"It's not charity," Millie said softly. "It's a gift from someone who cares about each of you."

"Maybe it's from Doris June," the old man said as he looked over at Mrs. Hargrove. "You told me she was doing pretty good at that job of hers in Alaska now that they gave her that big raise. Isn't she making another ten grand a year now?"

"Even if she is, my daughter knows better than to throw her money away like this."

"I wasn't throwing it away," Millie protested. "I was trying to do the right thing."

Sheriff Wall put up his hand. "No sense in anyone getting all stirred up until we find out where the money came from. Mrs. Hargrove, do you have that telephone number for Linda down in Los Angeles?"

The older woman nodded. "It's at home."

"Well, would you mind calling Linda and asking her how much money she had in the cash register when she left?"

"I'll be back in a minute." Mrs. Hargrove turned around and started toward the café door. "And while I'm there, I'm going to call that Pastor Hanks and give him a piece of my mind. Charity—we don't need charity. The people of Dry Creek are doing just fine."

She slammed the screen door on her way out.

"Now—" the sheriff looked around at everyone in the room, "—I'm going to ask everyone to step outside. Until we know otherwise, this is a crime scene in here, and I intend to keep it pure."

Millie looked around. The day was warming up, and sun streamed in through the windows. Most people kept their coats open, so they must be comfortable in the café even though it wasn't heated. They were all standing around the tables.

Millie thought the old man who was at the side of the room, the one who had been talking earlier, might be Elmer. And the couple sitting down at a table were probably the Redferns. The woman looked pretty enough to have been a cocktail waitress in Vegas, and she was holding a baby who looked like he was a year old. Forrest hadn't met her when he was in Dry Creek, but he'd heard about her in a letter Mrs. Hargrove had sent to him.

The people started walking toward the door. Millie turned to join them.

"Not you," the sheriff said as he put his hand on

Millie's arm. "You stay with me. I need to ask you some more questions."

Millie nodded. She supposed she'd have to expect questions. At least until Mrs. Hargrove was able to talk to Linda and find out that the money hadn't been left in the café when Linda went away.

"In the meantime, why don't you count that money?" The sheriff nodded toward Brad. "Give us some idea of what we're talking about here. Misdemeanor or felony."

Millie was glad that Brad wasn't leaving with the others. She didn't feel exactly comfortable with the sheriff, not when he was asking her all of those questions. She wasn't sure that Brad believed that she wasn't a thief, but she did feel safer with him around.

Brad looked up. "They'd give her a hard time if it was a felony."

The sheriff nodded.

"I don't think she intended that much harm," Brad said as he walked over to the table that held the bills. "She probably just wanted some traveling money. That car of hers looks like it'd fall apart if someone sneezed in it. She probably needs to repair it, and I'd guess that'd take a fortune."

"There's nothing wrong with my car," Millie said before she remembered the ping in the engine. And the hiccup in the carburetor.

"That car needs to be taken out and given a decent burial," Brad muttered.

Millie frowned. She was slowly figuring out that the reason she felt safe with Brad was because he saw her as a kid instead of as a woman. Not that she wanted him to look at her like he wanted to kiss her or anything. But it was annoying to be around him and realize he was so totally immune to her charms.

Of course, she wasn't exactly swooning over him, either. Granted, he was tall and powerful. She supposed most women would fall at his feet. Fortunately, he wasn't her kind of man at all.

She'd always thought that if she was going to be attracted to a man it would be a man who was quieter. Someone who didn't always require attention and service. Someone who would be content to blend into the background with her. A man like Brad didn't blend at all. He stood out and demanded attention.

No, she shook her head, Brad wasn't even close to her ideal man. She should be grateful he didn't notice her. And if he wanted to treat her like a kid, so much the better. She'd just treat him like a—a— Millie sighed. She couldn't treat him like anything but what he was. The most gorgeous man she'd ever seen, with or without her glasses on.

Chapter Six

"Well, how much money is there?" the sheriff asked.

Millie had sat down on one of the chairs and loosened her coat. The sun was shining in through the windows and had warmed up the café considerably. The red-and-white floor gave the place a cozy feel. There were a dozen small tables in the place. Millie wouldn't mind working in a small place like this if she ever left Ruby's.

Brad grunted in answer to the sheriff's question. He had sat down at a different table and counted the bills.

Millie didn't need to hear Brad's answer to know that there were seventy-five hundred-dollar bills in that sack. She supposed that was more than enough to be a felony. She wondered how far she should carry Forrest's request to not let anyone in Dry Creek know she was his friend. Surely, he wouldn't want her to actually be arrested.

"It's not as much money as it looks like," Brad said slowly. He didn't look at either Millie or the sheriff. "I didn't quite get it all counted, so I don't have an exact count. But I'd guess it's under a thousand."

Millie sat up straight at Brad's answer. "There's more than that."

Brad wanted to put his head down and bang it against the table. Here he was trying to keep Millie out of jail, and she was doing nothing to help him. He clenched his teeth. "I'm sure there's not enough here to warrant felony charges."

"Oh," Millie said.

Finally, the woman looked like she was coming to her senses. At least she didn't argue with him again about the amount of money on the table. What was Linda doing with all that money anyway? Business at the café hadn't been *that* good.

Brad wondered if Linda and that boyfriend of hers had managed to sell the farm they had just bought. Brad rather hoped not. He had his eye on that place himself, and almost had enough saved to put a good down payment on it if it came on the market again.

"Well, it's fine with me if it's not a felony," the

sheriff said. He'd picked up a few pieces of paper with tweezers and placed them in a bag. "I'd just as soon not do the extra paperwork."

Brad nodded. "Looking for fingerprints?"

Sheriff Carl Wall nodded without much enthusiasm. He was a decent sort of guy. He wouldn't be any more comfortable than Brad would be if they had to send Millie away on felony charges.

Brad looked over at Millie. The woman should sit in sunlight more often. The light filtered through her short blond hair and made her look almost angelic. She just didn't look dishonest, and that fact made Brad hesitant.

Brad had always thought he was a pretty good judge of people. A thief should look like a thief— at least when he looked in her eyes. Brad had been looking in Millie's green eyes and not seeing anything that made him think she was lying.

"Not that it'll do much good even if I do find fingerprints," Sheriff Wall continued. "This is a public place. People can have their fingerprints all over here and it's not a crime. Besides, Millie didn't actually take the money off the premises. Don't know if I'd have enough to ever get it to trial. Plus, there weren't any witnesses."

Brad nodded. "I sure didn't see anything."

Brad decided he'd done more than his share of good deeds for the day. He'd gone to church and stayed through the sermon. He'd even sung a hymn or two. Then he'd had mercy on a poor woman who obviously needed someone to take care of her. "I guess it's sort of like grace."

Millie looked up at him and blinked.

Brad stood up and walked over to where the woman sat. "You know, the pastor in church talked about grace. That's how it is for you—not having to go to prison and all. We'll just call your sins forgiven."

Brad sat down in a chair across the table from Millie. He was pleased with himself. Maybe he should go to church more often. He seemed to have a flair for making moral points.

"I didn't ask for forgiveness," Millie protested softly, and then bit her lip. "I don't have anything to be forgiven for—at least, not with the money. The money is mine to give away."

Brad frowned. Well, maybe he wasn't so good at making those points after all. But then the woman looked tired. Not that she wavered in what she said. He had to admire the fact that she had stuck with her story. She was tenacious for such a little thing. He was kind of growing to like her. "Do you ever flirt?"

Millie looked startled.

"I was just wondering. You're always so serious." Brad had never been attracted to a serious woman until now. He supposed it must have something to do with the Christmas season. He was all out of whack around Christmas.

"Men don't respect you when you flirt with them."

Brad shrugged. "Sometimes it's just a way of being friendly."

Millie was quiet for a moment, and then she looked down at the top of the table. "That's what some of the other waitresses said. And then they told me I'd get more tips that way."

"You're a waitress?" Brad was surprised. Usually waitresses did know how to flirt. Millie's co-workers were right—they did get more tips that way. He knew he always gave a little extra to someone who had entertained him with a joke or two.

Millie looked up at him. "What's wrong with me being a waitress?"

Brad spread his hands. "Nothing. Some of my favorite people are waitresses."

It was odd, Brad thought. When Millie looked so serious, those glasses somehow suited her face. She was as solemn as a Madonna, but she looked good. Maybe it was just the sun in her hair and the defiant look in those eyes of hers.

"I can flirt," Millie lied. What was it about that man that made her want to prove him wrong on everything? It was a good thing he didn't ask her if she could fly.

Maybe it was the arrogant way he sat there and seemed to assume someone should pay attention to him. He was the kind of man she usually didn't want sitting at one of her tables at Ruby's. Not that he'd probably be worried about that. He wouldn't starve. If he ever did get to Ruby's, the other waitresses would fight over bringing him his order.

"I just don't think it's honest to flirt with someone so they give you a bigger tip. A tip is for the service," Millie finished.

"And the smile," Brad said and paused. "I know a nice smile has cheered me up when I've been discouraged. I think that's worth something."

"Well, yes, of course. It's always good to be friendly."

Millie knew she sounded about as prim as a country schoolteacher. The truth was that she couldn't flirt with men because men, real men, scared her a little. Of course, she couldn't admit that to someone like Brad. "I flirt with short men."

Brad frowned at that. "How short?"

"Shorter than me."

"But you're not even five feet tall."

Millie nodded. "Short men need encouragement, too."

"I'm pretty short," Sheriff Wall offered. He had been quiet, and Millie had forgotten he was there, but he had obviously been listening. "Maybe a bit more'n five feet, but short enough to need encouragement."

"You're the sheriff. That's encouragement enough," Brad said.

The sheriff walked over to the table. "Maybe, but if the lady likes short men, I thought I should put my hat in the ring. She's not going to find any men around here who are shorter than me."

"She doesn't like short men."

Sheriff Wall smiled. "Just because you're six-four, there's no reason to be cross. Plenty of women like tall men. You should leave a few for the rest of us, especially if they like short men."

Millie figured the sheriff was right. Plenty of women did like men as tall as Brad. Somehow the thought wasn't as comforting as it should have been. She looked over at Brad. "I suppose you have someone special anyway."

Brad grinned. "I'm free as a bird."

Millie blinked. She couldn't believe she actually cared.

Brad heard the knock on the café door before it became a pounding. He was enjoying the pink that was covering Millie's face, though, and he didn't much want to get up and answer the door.

It was slowly occurring to Brad that Millie might have cured his Christmas blues. He hadn't had a discouraging thought since he'd met her. Of course, that might be because he'd been busy trying to figure out whether or not she was a thief.

Maybe he should do something like this every Christmas. He didn't suppose, though, that he could count on the café to provide him with a thief just before Christmas every year.

"Are you going to answer that?" Millie finally asked.

Brad looked at Sheriff Wall. "You're the public servant."

Sheriff Wall snorted. "That doesn't mean I get the door."

Still, the sheriff stood up and walked over to the door. Halfway there, he stopped and looked back at Millie. "Just remember, Brad's too tall for you."

Millie blushed a bright red.

Brad smiled. Now she looked like a Madonna with a sunburn.

Millie turned to look at the door. Maybe if she ignored Brad and his teasing, he would stop looking at her like that—like he knew something that she didn't, and it was causing him to smile like a simpleton.

"I'm not really six-four," Brad whispered to Millie. "If I take my boots off, I'm only six-three. I'm shorter than you think."

"I don't care how tall you are."

Millie turned all of her attention to the doorway.

It wasn't difficult to do, because Mrs. Hargrove was waving something at the sheriff and trying to talk.

"Let me get my breath," she finally said.

Mrs. Hargrove was standing in the doorway and taking deep breaths. She looked like she'd been running or, at least, walking fast. Her gray hair was a little disheveled and her coat was unbuttoned.

"You should have taken it easy getting back," Sheriff Wall said as he helped Mrs. Hargrove to a chair. "We're not in any rush."

"But—the money's—not Linda's," Mrs. Hargrove said as she sat down.

Millie could see the sheriff frown.

"Did you say it's not Linda's?"

Mrs. Hargrove took a deep breath. "No one left any money in the café. I talked to Linda, and she cleaned out the cash drawer to buy her plane ticket. She also said she wished she hadn't, but that's a different matter."

"So that means…" the sheriff began thoughtfully.

Everyone was silent for a moment.

"How about that church?" Brad asked. "You know, the one with the Christmas baskets."

Mrs. Hargrove shook her head. "I called Pastor Hanks. He thought I was nuts. He said they don't have that kind of money to give away in Christmas baskets, especially this year. They're giving canned green beans and some of those fried onion rings, so people can make a Christmas casserole. Then he said it had been a hard year and asked *me* for a donation. I told him I'd send him five dollars."

Everyone was silent for another moment. Millie kind of liked the silence she found in Dry Creek. There wasn't any traffic noise. There were no airplanes flying overhead. There weren't even any barking dogs, although she supposed that was only for the moment.

"So the money was hers," Brad said finally as he looked at Millie.

Mrs. Hargrove beamed. "That means she's innocent."

"Still, something's funny," the sheriff said as he scratched his head. "For one thing, she made an unlawful entry here even if it was because she was hungry or something."

Millie swallowed. She'd forgotten about using the key to get inside the café. That had seemed like the least of her worries.

"Not that that's worth locking her up over," the sheriff continued. "Not with the heating problems over at the jail and all. It costs fifty bucks a day just to keep a prisoner in jail this time of year, and the café is open to everyone."

"I'm sorry about the breaking and entering," Millie offered.

"See, she's sorry," Brad added.

Millie looked at Brad. He was looking at her like she'd just passed some sort of test and he'd guided her through it. If she wasn't mistaken, the man actually looked proud of her. Millie couldn't remember the last time anyone except Forrest had been proud of her.

The sheriff nodded. "Still, we have to do something. We can't have strangers thinking they can come into town and break into a place of business and nothing happens."

"I could pay a fine," Millie offered. Now that the money was hers again, she could use one of the hundred-dollar bills to pay the fine. She could take it from one of the extra stockings. "If it's a small fine, that is. I don't have too much extra."

"How far are you planning on driving?" Brad asked incredulously. "That money in there would take you to either coast."

"The money's not for me." Millie realized the people of Dry Creek had not suspected she was going to put the money in their stockings. Which meant that she just might pull off a Christmas surprise after all.

The sheriff shook his head. "I'm not doing some kind of fancy fine. It'd be one thing if it was a traffic fine, but I'd have to drive into Miles City just to get a form for a special-circumstance fine."

"Well, you give parking fines all the time," Brad said. "Charge her with one of those."

Sheriff Wall looked at Millie. "Might be better to just give her some community service to do."

Mrs. Hargrove brightened. "We do have a lot of work left to get ready for Christmas."

"Christmas?" Brad frowned. "I was thinking community service would involve something like picking the litter off the roads or something. I could help her with that. But Christmas—"

"No one can do litter removal with all this snow unless they have a bulldozer," Mrs. Hargrove said. "Besides, we've always done a good job of celebrating Christmas in Dry Creek." Mrs. Hargrove looked at Brad. "Just because you don't like Christmas, it doesn't mean it's not a good community-service project. Besides, it's time you got over your problems with Christmas anyway. It'll do you good."

Brad stared at her. "Who told you I have problems with Christmas?"

"Everybody knows." Mrs. Hargrove shrugged. "Why do you think we let you park behind the café last night and didn't bother you?"

"You knew I was there?"

Mrs. Hargrove looked at Brad. "Christmas can be a hard time when you have memories you would rather forget. But as far as I know, the only remedy is to make new memories."

"I don't have any memories," Brad protested, and

realized it was true. And that's what bothered him most about Christmas. Other people could talk about the happy times they had shared with their families at Christmas. But he couldn't recall any. He was five when his parents were killed in the car accident, but he didn't remember any Christmases before that. Surely, he should have some memories of Christmas.

"What would I do for Christmas?" Millie asked.

Brad thought she looked a little too eager for someone facing community service. Brad turned to the sheriff. "It's not supposed to be fun, you know. She can't just decorate a Christmas tree or something."

"She could help get ready for the church service," Mrs. Hargrove said.

"I could help you get those black streaks off the floor," Millie offered.

"You know how to do that?" Mrs. Hargrove asked.

Millie nodded.

"Then you're an answer to my prayers."

"Well, I can't just let her run around free, either," the sheriff said as he looked at Mrs. Hargrove. "I don't suppose you would—"

"I'll be happy to keep an eye on her."

Brad snorted. "She'd sweet-talk her way around you in no time."

Mrs. Hargrove's eyes started to twinkle, and she nodded to Brad. "Maybe you should join us then."

"What?" The sheriff frowned. "Oh, I don't think that will be necessary. I planned to keep an eye on her myself."

Brad grinned. Mrs. Hargrove might be old, but she understood a young man's heart. It didn't always need to be the short man who got a break with the new woman in town. Brad turned to the sheriff. "Don't you have to be on duty?"

Sheriff Wall grunted. "No more than you do."

"Things are slow at the Elkton Ranch this time of year. I'm sure they can spare me for a little civic duty."

Millie was bewildered. It sounded like both of the men actually wanted to spend time with her. And they'd have to watch her mop a floor to do it. That didn't sound like any fun. "You'll get your shirt dirty standing around."

"I have some old shirts," Brad said.

"And I have some extra scrub brushes just waiting for a volunteer," Mrs. Hargrove said. "We've tried everything on those black streaks."

"I'll bring some coffee for a break when I come by in the morning," the sheriff said. "No point in anyone starting today. Besides, it's Sunday."

Brad turned to Millie. "I have some extra old shirts. You'll probably need one, too. I'll get you fixed up when we get back to the bunkhouse."

Sheriff Wall frowned. "I don't know if she should stay at the bunkhouse."

Millie agreed with the sheriff. "I don't mind the jail."

"Oh, you can't stay in the jail, dear," Mrs. Hargrove said. "It's cold this time of year. Besides, I think the bunkhouse might be just the place. Charlie will keep an eye on things."

"She can have my room. I don't mind sleeping on the couch."

"Well, it's all set then," Mrs. Hargrove said as she pointed to the money and then looked at Millie. "I guess that's all yours then. Keep it in a safe place."

"The bunkhouse is safe."

The sheriff nodded and looked at Millie. "Just don't go spending it too fast. I plan to make a couple of inquires just in case there've been any other thefts recently in the area. I should hear back today."

"Just as long as you know by Christmas," Millie said. She would want to have the stockings ready before Christmas Day. She was glad that things seemed to be working out. She didn't mind spending a couple of days in Dry Creek.

Millie looked at Brad. He was still smiling.

"Does everybody here drink the same water?" Millie asked. Maybe there was some kind of mineral in the water around here that made people smile a lot. She'd heard about places where the population was a little below average in intelligence because of a tainted water supply. She supposed a mineral that got into the water supply could have a similar effect on emotions.

"I guess we do," Mrs. Hargrove said. "We all have our own wells, but it comes from the same water table."

Millie nodded. "I was just curious."

Brad couldn't help but see the change that came over Sheriff Wall. The sheriff had been leaning against the wall by the door, and he straightened up. The smile left his face. His eyes narrowed like he was thinking.

"What kind of stuff do you figure you need to clean those black streaks off the floor?" he finally asked Millie.

Brad wondered why the sheriff was that inter-ested in floor cleaners and then realized the man probably wasn't. Something else was going on here.

"I thought I'd get some baking soda," Millie said.

Mrs. Hargrove nodded. "That might work."

The sheriff was silent for a moment. "I've got baking soda at the office. I'll bring some out for you tomorrow. No point in buying any new."

"Oh, I don't mind," Millie said. "It won't take long to get some. And, if that doesn't work, I know another trick or two."

"Best to use county supplies since it is a public building."

"I wouldn't call the church a public building,"

Mrs. Hargrove protested. "I mean, it's open to the public, but we're independent."

"Still," the sheriff said, "I think it's best."

He turned toward the café door and motioned to Brad. "Mind if I have a word with you before we head out? You know, to explain your duties and all."

"Sure." Brad got up. He wasn't sure what was making the sheriff look older than his years, but he expected he would soon find out. He was pretty sure it was related to this floor-cleaning project.

Brad had scarcely stepped out onto the porch and closed the café door behind Sheriff Wall than the sheriff started to talk.

"I don't like it," Sheriff Wall said. "All them chemicals and cleaners—who knows what she's up to? Especially when she's asking about our water supply."

"You're not worried she's planning to do something to our water?"

"Well, not the water. It'd be hard to hit all the wells. But I didn't like the fact that she was asking," the sheriff said. "The way I figure it, that money could be payment for doing something—maybe the something just hasn't happened yet."

"Oh, I don't think—" Brad began to protest, but then he remembered. Dry Creek wasn't the same place that it had been before the hit man had come two years ago. He could no longer just assume that

the only crimes in town were kids being mis-
chievous.

Sheriff Wall nodded. "All I'm saying is that we
need to keep an eye on her until we know how she
came by that money."

"Maybe she saved it," Brad suggested. He didn't
like to picture Millie as a criminal.

The sheriff shrugged. "Even if she saved it,
what's she doing carrying it around in a brown
paper bag? Most anyone I know who saves that
kind of money keeps it in a bank or gets a cashier's
check or something."

Brad had to admit the sheriff had a point. What
would a waitress be doing with that kind of cash on
her? And all in hundred-dollar bills. It wasn't her tip
money, that was for sure.

"I'll keep a close eye on her," Brad said. He felt
another headache coming on. The only good thing
was that he figured this Christmas would be one
he'd always remember.

Mrs. Hargrove thought he needed memories.
Well, it looked like he was going to have them
whether he wanted them or not.

He couldn't help smiling a little. He guessed he
did want them, especially if the memories included
a little bit of a woman with green eyes.

Chapter Seven

Millie drove her car back to the bunkhouse at the
Elkton Ranch thinking the rest of the day would be
spent in Brad's little room. Not that that was bad.
She supposed it was better than a jail cell. The room
was warm, and he had lots of books that she could
read. She wouldn't mind dipping into a mystery
novel or taking a nap.

Brad had driven his pickup right behind her all
the way to the bunkhouse. He said it was so he'd be
sure she didn't get stuck in a snowdrift, but she
knew he was also making sure she didn't drive off
now that she had the money.

Millie smiled to herself. All in all, it hadn't gone
so badly. She hadn't been forced to tell anyone that
she was in Dry Creek because of Forrest. Now if she
could just avoid any other questions, she would do

fine. The more she thought about it, a quiet afternoon all alone in Brad's room sounded perfect.

Millie hadn't stepped all the way into the bunkhouse before Charlie came trotting over to the door.

"There you are!" Charlie said as he held out his hand for Millie's coat. "I was hoping you'd get back soon."

Millie looked up. Charlie was looking directly at her. "Me?"

Charlie nodded. "We need a woman's advice about the Christmas tree."

"Christmas tree?" Brad asked. He had followed right behind Millie through the bunkhouse door. "Since when do we put up a Christmas tree?"

"We decided this year should be different since we have company," Charlie said as he smiled at Millie. "Mrs. Hargrove called to tell you to dress in old clothes when you go down to clean the church tomorrow."

"Oh, I will." Millie slipped out of her coat and gave it to Charlie.

"Mrs. Hargrove is the one that said you'd be staying with us through Christmas," Charlie added as he turned to walk to the corner closet.

Brad decided the world had gone crazy. Charlie had shaved off his beard, and he usually didn't do that until spring. In addition, he was carrying Millie's coat to the corner closet as if they didn't always leave their coats in a pile on the one chair.

And, unless Brad missed his guess, Charlie was also wearing his church shirt, and here it was the middle of the afternoon! Granted, it was still Sunday, but Charlie usually couldn't wait to change into his working clothes whenever he came back to the bunkhouse.

Plus, Brad took a tentative sniff, he could smell cinnamon.

Brad looked around. The smell was coming from the black woodstove that stood in the corner of the bunkhouse living area. He didn't have to walk over to see the tin can sitting on the stove. "Who's cooking cinnamon?"

Charlie was back from the closet and had the decency to blush. "I saw it on TV—you put a stick of cinnamon in some water and boil it. It makes the air fresh for holiday company."

Brad needed to sit down. He walked over to a straight-back chair that was sitting next to the stove. "I thought that's what coffee was for."

"I wasn't sure Millie liked coffee," Charlie said anxiously. "I didn't see her drink any at breakfast."

"Of course she likes coffee," Brad said. He had to move a bowl of popcorn so he could sit down. "She's a waitress."

Brad held the bowl of popcorn on his lap.

"Don't eat any of that!" Charlie ordered. "That's for the tree."

Brad looked down at the popcorn. "We're really having a tree? A live tree? Not just one of those tinfoil things that they sometimes give away at the diesel fuel place in Miles City?"

Charlie nodded emphatically. "Of course we're having a real tree. We've got to have a proper Christmas tree if we have company."

Millie blinked. She had never been someone's Christmas company. Charlie said it like it was an honor. A sliver of panic streaked through her. "I've never helped with a tree before."

Brad looked up from his popcorn and frowned. "Never?"

Millie shook her head. "I think they're pretty, of course. But I usually just got myself a poinsettia plant or something like that. A tinfoil thing would be just fine with me."

"Didn't your family celebrate Christmas?" Brad asked.

Millie blushed. "My foster mother was always too tired."

Brad gave a low sympathetic growl.

"Not that I minded," Millie said quickly. "I didn't need to have Christmas."

"Well, don't you worry about a thing, we're going to have just as much Christmas as we can right here," Charlie said. "And we're starting with a tree. How hard can it be to do a Christmas tree? That lady on television gave a few pointers. I'm sure we can figure it out."

"But there's a lot to having a tree. For one thing, you have to have decorations, and we don't have any," Brad said. "Everyone knows you need decorations."

"Well, Jeff's gone to Miles City to look for decorations," Charlie said. "All we need to do is get the stand ready for the tree, so that when he gets back we can go chop one down before it starts to snow again."

Brad frowned. "Where are you going to find pine trees this far down from the mountains?"

"We'll find something," Charlie said. "As I recall, there's a few pines on the north side of the ranch near that gully."

"But those trees are the windbreak for the north pasture," Brad protested. "The boss will have our hides if we chop them down. Besides, the cattle won't have any shelter then."

"Well, we wouldn't chop them all down. All we need is one little Christmas tree. The cows won't miss that. Then we'll get the popcorn strung and see what other decorations Jeff brings back."

Millie felt like she'd fallen down the rabbit hole and entered a whole new world. She was surprised she didn't have visions of sugarplums and reindeer dancing in her head. Actually, come to think of it, she did seem to have a little ringing in her ears. "Do you have any aspirin?"

Charlie looked over at her and thought a minute. "I think they'd be too small for decorations, but they are white, so maybe we could glue them on to something red."

"The aspirin's not for the tree," Millie said. She was beginning to feel the responsibility of being the Christmas company. No wonder so many people came to Ruby's for Christmas dinner. All they had to do then was pay for dinner. They didn't need to provide inspiration. "And—ah, speaking of the tree, I hope you're not doing anything special just because I'm here. I don't mind not having Christmas. Really. I usually don't do all the Christmas things anyway."

"Don't you worry about Christmas," the old man protested at the same time as he turned to scowl at Brad. "And don't think that we're going to let you mope around this Christmas, either. That's okay when it's just us guys here. But it's not okay when you have company."

Millie decided she really needed that aspirin. Or she would if she had to listen to Brad say one more time that she wasn't his company, wasn't his girlfriend, wasn't his date—wasn't his anything.

"You're right," Brad said simply. "I do need to cheer up and stop thinking about myself."

Millie looked at him skeptically.

Brad smiled at her slightly.

Millie looked at him and frowned a little.

Brad grinned and just kept looking at her.

"No one said where there was an aspirin," Millie finally said.

"I've got some right here." Brad handed her a small tin.

"I never take aspirin," Millie said as she snapped the tin open. Half of the eight tablets were already gone. She took out two of the remaining ones and handed it back to Brad.

"Neither do I," Brad said as he picked out two tablets for himself. "Neither do I."

Brad decided he was going to do Christmas right if it killed him—which, in this case, it just might. If he had a brain in his head, he would drive Millie back to town and let the sheriff take over guarding her. Let the county pay a few bucks to heat the jail. He'd even bring her a tinfoil tree to set in the window.

Brad no sooner thought of it than the picture of Millie spending Christmas in jail passed by his mind and he knew he couldn't do it, not even if he went in and sat in the cell with her and the little tree.

No, he had to make Christmas special for her. He had thought he was the only one who had never done any of the usual Christmas things, but it seemed like Millie might have him beat. She seemed more clueless about Christmas than he did. And he would have to be blind not to see the wistful look on her face when someone mentioned the Christmas tree.

"Can't we just tie the tree to that pole lamp or something? You know, the cast-iron one with the bear?" Millie asked as she watched him carefully select two pieces of lumber to make a Christmas tree stand. They were out in the barn and the wind was blowing in the open door. Millie was sitting on a bale of hay. Brad had the light on even though it wasn't more than three o'clock in the afternoon.

"The tree would be all crooked that way," Brad said. Ever since he'd decided to celebrate Christmas, he was determined to not take any shortcuts. Not that the lamp idea was a bad one. Charlie had won that lamp at some senior bingo party, and it would bear the weight of a tree—it just wouldn't keep it straight.

Still, it was kind of sweet of Millie to sit there with that little frown on her forehead and worry about how to save him the time and effort of building a stand. "Besides, it's not a problem. I can make a tree stand in no time."

Brad had built line shacks and corrals. He knew a little about engineering and carpentry. A tree stand wasn't even a challenge, but he wasn't in any particular hurry to finish the task and head back inside where all the other guys were sitting around stringing popcorn.

"Well, I guess if it's a small tree, it'll work," Millie said as she stood and walked over to look down at the lumber. "It will be a small tree, won't it?"

"It'll have to be. A large one will be too big for the horses to drag."

"Horses?" Millie stepped back. "Aren't we going in the pickup?"

Brad shook his head. "Too much snow this time of year. The horses are a better way to get there."

"But I've never ridden a horse."

Brad looked up at her. She looked a little scared and nervous and he decided that her look must be growing on him, because he didn't consider all of the other options that they had. "Then you'll have to ride double with me."

Brad held his breath. He wasn't at all sure that she would want to ride double with him. She might not know it, but riding a horse double was almost a date in Montana. After all her talk about short men and flirting, he'd gotten the distinct impression that she didn't want to date anyone and, if he was honest, she especially seemed not to want to date him.

"I don't know…isn't it cold?" Millie asked.

"You can wear my parka. It's down-filled and good for twenty below zero."

Brad didn't add that the lining was some kind of special silk and he'd spent a month's salary on it.

"But what about you?" Millie looked up at him, and her green eyes were full of concern.

"Don't worry about me. I'll keep warm," Brad promised. He was slowly realizing he'd like nothing better than to have Millie lean into him as they rode his horse back to the ranch. He'd ride without a shirt or a coat if he had to, just to have her trust him like he was picturing in his mind.

Millie still had that little frown on her forehead.

"I can borrow one of the spare coats," Brad added, and watched as her frown lifted. He congratulated himself that she cared about him and his comfort.

"You wouldn't be able to drive the horse if you got too cold," Millie said.

"Oh." Brad decided maybe she didn't care as much as he'd hoped. Brad drove a nail into the lumber he had set for the tree stand. There was no need to prolong the task. He drove in another nail. "You don't need to worry. The horse knows the way back to the ranch anyway. Even if I couldn't ride him, he'd make it back to his stall."

Millie nodded.

Brad hammered the final nail into the lumber and stood up. "Here. We've got us a tree stand."

Brad opened the barn door for Millie and followed her out into the yard of the ranch. Snow covered most of the ground, although it had been pretty well stamped down from all the feet that had walked over it. The air was cold, and Brad saw Millie put her hands in the pockets of her long black coat. "I'll lend you some gloves, too."

"I can just put my hands in the pockets of your coat," Millie said.

"Not if you plan to stay on the horse."

Brad regretted his words the moment they were out of his mouth. He could tell Millie was worried, so he added, "Don't worry. I won't let you fall off."

Millie knew something was wrong the minute she and Brad stepped inside the main room of the bunkhouse. There were two long strings of popcorn garland running between the bear lamp and green recliner. There were Christmas carols playing on a small CD player. What there wasn't any sign of was peace on earth and goodwill toward men.

All of the men in the room were hunched over something on the floor by the stove, and they were clearly arguing.

"I tell you it's wrong," Charlie said as he studied what looked like a large piece of white paper. "It doesn't look like any angel I've ever seen."

Millie walked over to the men. Someone had drawn a crayon picture of an angel—at least she thought it must be an angel. "Are those wings?"

"See, she can tell those are wings," Randy said triumphantly.

"She was *asking* if they were wings," Charlie protested. "That's a big difference."

Randy looked up at Millie. "It just didn't seem right putting wings on an angel like it was some big chicken or something. I mean, what's something like an angel doing with chicken wings? I think their wings should look more like a horse's mane. You know, rows and rows of curling hair. Now, hair is nice. It's got class. It's fitting for someone who lives in heaven."

"I notice the wings are blond," Brad said from behind Millie's shoulders. "You always were partial to blondes."

"That's an angel you're talking about," Charlie said. "Show some respect."

"Well, she's not an angel if she doesn't have wings," Brad said. "She's just a good-looking woman in a white nightgown with lots of blond hair. Lots and lots of hair."

"She kind of looks like that country-western singer with the big—" William began and then looked at Millie and blushed "—with the big hats."

Charlie cleared his throat. "I hope you're not

planning on putting any—hats—on the angel. We run a respectable place here."

"We're a bunkhouse," Brad protested.

Charlie lifted his chin. "As long as we have Christmas company, we're a home, and a home has certain standards."

Brad was speechless.

"Wow, that's kind of nice," Randy said. "It's good to have a home at Christmas."

Brad looked over at Millie. How was it that one woman could make their bunkhouse a home for Christmas?

Come to think of it maybe that was why he got so depressed at Christmas. Christmas was a time for families, and every year when the holiday came around it reminded him that he was alone. All he had to do was listen to a song on the radio or pass by a display in a store to know that Christmas was for families. That must be it.

Brad was almost relieved. It was all because of decorations and ads that he was depressed. Everyone had to face the advertising world at some point and realize that just because someone in an ad had something it didn't mean he had to have it.

No, he just needed perspective. He certainly didn't need to change his being single. All he had to do was get through these few days each December.

He just needed to remember that Christmas was

only one day. He still had the other 364 days left to enjoy his bachelorhood. The advertising world didn't make so much of families the other 364 days.

Yeah, he had the good life. Once he got past Christmas, his life would be normal again. He'd be worrying about a poker hand instead of popcorn garlands. It would all be fine. Christmas would be here and gone soon. Maybe even quicker if he could hurry it along. "We better go see about that tree."

"I rigged up a sled for the tree," Randy said as he stood up and brushed his hands off on his jeans. "My horse can pull that easy enough."

"I figured I could bring the ax," William offered.

"But you can't just leave the Christmas drawing," Millie protested.

"Oh, yeah," Randy said as he bent down and rolled the paper up. "I'll need to finish it after we get the tree up so we can put it on top."

Brad nodded numbly. It shouldn't surprise him that they were going to have an angel who looked like a Vegas dancer sitting on top of their Christmas tree.

"I'll have some cocoa waiting for when you get back," Charlie said as they all started to look for their coats. It took a minute for everyone to realize Charlie had hung the coats up in the closet. No one ever hung up the coats.

Brad almost shook his head. He wasn't the only

one who was going crazy at Christmas. Randy was drawing angels and Charlie was turning into Little Miss Homemaker.

It was going to be a miracle if they all survived this Christmas without turning into city gentlemen with manicured nails who refused to change the oil in their car. Before long, they'd all be useless.

And it was all her fault, Brad thought as he looked at Millie.

How could one woman who looked so small make such a big difference in this old bunkhouse?

Chapter Eight

Millie felt like she was in a snow globe as she rode behind Brad's saddle. The sun was setting, but there was still enough light to see the snowflakes fall. The air was so cold it felt brittle, but Millie found the steady sway of Brad's horse comforting. The landscape dipped into a long gully and then rose to small hills all around.

Millie couldn't remember the last time she'd been in a landscape with such openness. She didn't see any houses or roads or telephone poles. All she could see were stretches of white snow and the hoof-prints the horses had made on their way into the gully where the pine trees stood.

Charlie was right. The cows wouldn't miss the small tree they had cut and strapped onto the sled that Randy pulled behind his horse.

They had debated which tree to cut until they saw the little tree. The branches on the tree were crooked, and William, after studying the ground around it, said they were doing the poor thing a favor by cutting it down. It was surrounded by taller trees and wasn't getting enough sunlight to grow properly.

The tree reminded Millie of that tree she'd tried to make long ago out of tinfoil and metal hangers. The tree was spindly and deformed, but somehow it tugged at her heart.

Millie turned her head around. It was getting dark, but she could still see Randy and William following behind them. She quickly turned her head back. The gap between her and Brad's back when she turned let cold air between them. Millie shivered. She was glad she had Brad's back to block the wind that came with the snow flurries.

"Sorry," Millie whispered. She suspected the borrowed coat Brad was wearing wasn't nearly as warm as the parka he had lent her, so she leaned against him as closely as she could so that at least his back would be warm.

"No problem," Brad mumbled.

All of the horses kept their heads down as they walked into the wind, and Millie knew Brad kept his head down and had his wool scarf tied around his mouth. A bandanna kept his hat tied down and his ears warm.

Millie settled into her place on Brad's back. She rested her cheek against his one shoulder and wrapped her arms more securely around his waist. She had to lift the edge of his coat in order to hold tight to his waist, and she worried that in doing so she left room for a draft of cold air. She had offered earlier to put her hands on the outside of his coat, but he had declined, saying she'd freeze her fingers.

Millie could feel the snaps on Brad's shirt, and she kept her hands clasped around the snap just above his brass belt buckle. Her hands had made a warm spot against his stomach, and they were cozy there.

Millie wondered why she felt so comfortable pressed against Brad's back this way. Well, maybe "comfortable" was the wrong word. It was more a feeling of belonging than comfort. It must be because, with her hands clasped around his stomach, they had started breathing to the same rhythm. Or maybe it was because she could be so close to him and she didn't have to worry that he was going to turn around and want to talk or anything.

Millie sighed. It wasn't easy when you were a shy woman to spend any time around an outgoing man like Brad. She'd been a waitress long enough to know men like him weren't happy with simple conversation; they wanted witty remarks and flirta- tious comments. The few times Millie had gone out with men like that she'd learned she wasn't what they were looking for in a date. Those dates had been disastrous, and she wouldn't care to repeat them.

It was too bad, she thought. There was something about Brad that she was growing to like, especially now as they rode through the darkening night. If only they could ride like this forever and not have to talk.

"You can see the lights of the bunkhouse," Brad said through his muffled scarf. "We're almost home."

Millie nodded and snuggled a little closer. Brad pulled on the horse's reins and she could feel his muscles ripple down his back. She thought for a second that she would have to remember to tell the other waitresses about this ride, but then she realized she never would. This night belonged only to her. Even though she could hear the hooves of the other horses behind them stepping on the snow, it felt like she and Brad were alone outside.

"I don't mind if you take it slow getting back," Millie whispered.

She felt Brad's muscles tense. He probably thought she was crazy.

"It'll be easier on the horses," she added. She didn't want to be pushy. "They must be cold."

"They're fine," Brad said.

Millie nodded.

Brad had never been so glad to see the shape of the Elkton Ranch barn come into view. And that was counting the time he'd almost frozen to death rounding up strays during the bad winter about ten years back. Brad needed to end this ride and he needed to end it soon.

If it didn't, he was going to go way over the deep end. He didn't know what was wrong. Millie wasn't the kind of woman he should be thinking about dating. Who was he kidding? He'd stopped thinking about dating a mile back there and had gone right on to thinking of the big time.

He needed to end the ride. For one thing, she deserved someone more permanent than him. He wasn't ready for the *big* time. He was the kind of guy women looked to if they wanted a *good* time. And that was the way he liked it. He steered clear of women like Millie who made a man think of settling down and having babies.

He didn't know what was wrong. Millie didn't even wear lipstick, and yet he'd been one breath away from starting to whistle the wedding march. He barely knew the wedding march and, besides that, his lips were near frozen from the cold.

Brad shook his head. It must be something about the way she laid her cheek against his back that made him want to take care of her.

Of course, he knew it was only the Christmas craziness, but if he started whistling some wedding song, he'd make a fool of himself for sure.

"Yeah, we're almost there," Brad repeated himself as his horse walked into the edge of the ranch yard.

Millie thought she must be frozen to the back of Brad's saddle. "I can't move."

Brad had ridden into the barn and swung out of the saddle easily enough himself. But Millie was stuck. Her legs felt like they were permanently glued to the saddle.

The air was warmer inside the barn and the horse was standing politely beside the feed trough waiting to be given some oats. Randy and William had ridden over to the bunkhouse so they could unload the tree from the sled, but Brad and Millie had gone straight to the barn to dismount.

Millie tried to move her toes, and she felt the muscles tighten in her boots. At least she didn't have frostbite.

Brad took the reins of his horse and led the animal over to a small pile of hay. "You're just sore from all that riding. I didn't know we'd be gone that long."

"I'm never going riding again," Millie said, and then gave an exaggerated groan for emphasis.

Brad chuckled.

Oh, my word, Millie thought, *I almost made a joke. And he laughed.* She couldn't remember the last time she'd joked with a handsome man. Usually she only felt relaxed enough to joke with her women friends and men like Forrest who were shy themselves.

"It might help if you take the coat off," Brad said. "That'll help you move easier."

Millie pulled her left arm out of the parka and then finished pulling it off her right arm. She handed the coat down to Brad, and he set it on a hay bale. Millie shivered. It was cold, but she could move easier.

"Here," Brad said as he held his arms up to her. "Now let me swing you down, and you can sit on these bales."

Millie pushed against the back of Brad's saddle and tried to get her leg to properly swing itself over the horse. It didn't work. Finally, she just tilted her whole self over and let the leg come if it wanted.

Brad held his arms out to catch Millie. She fell into his arms and grabbed him around the neck. Usually when a woman had her arms around his neck, Brad recalled she also had a certain inviting look in her eyes.

Brad could only see one of Millie's eyes because he was actually facing her ear instead of her face, but he was pretty sure the look he hoped for wasn't there. Her eyes showed panic.

"Don't worry. I've got you," Brad whispered.

If it was possible, she looked even more alarmed.

"I can stand," Millie said.

Brad noted she didn't relax her grip on his neck, and her glasses were perched precariously on her nose.

"I think my leg just went to sleep, but it'll be fine when I put some weight on it," Millie added.

Since Millie wanted to stand, Brad shifted her, hoping to get her in a position where she could. He regretted it the minute he did it.

Instead of looking at her ear, Brad was now looking at those green eyes of hers. Both of them. Her glasses had fallen completely off, and he saw them resting on her shoulder. Without glasses, Millie's eyes went soft and dreamy. She relaxed in his arms.

Brad supposed Millie might have become calm because she couldn't see, but he told himself it was just possible that it was because she was caught up in the magic of the moment, as he was—and that she was thinking how close they were to kissing, and if he just moved an inch or two this way and she moved an inch or two that way, they would meet in a kiss.

Brad took a deep breath just like the one he took every time he climbed into the chute at the Billings rodeo. He was an amateur at bull riding, just like he was an amateur at kissing. He'd never realized before, though, that a kiss could take every bit as much courage as climbing on the back of a two-thousand-pound bull.

"Oh," Millie said softly as Brad moved a little closer.

"May I?" Brad asked. He looked carefully at Millie's eyes. He didn't expect her to give him a verbal okay, but he did expect to see in her eyes if she was okay with a kiss.

"Oh," Millie repeated even softer.

Brad didn't see any refusal in her eyes. He looked twice to be sure. Then he took a deep breath and kissed her.

Millie thought her heart was going to stop. Failing that, her brain was going to melt. And it was all because her glasses had fallen off and in all the surrounding blur Brad was kissing her like he thought she was a fragile china doll.

Millie had been kissed before, but never like she was precious.

"Oh," Millie said when he pulled away a little bit.

Brad was smiling and, for some reason, he didn't look nearly as tall as he had before. It must be because his face was a little blurry and fuzzy. Millie decided she should go without her glasses more often if it made men like Brad look so very nice.

Millie heard the barn door open even though she couldn't actually see the door open. She could, however, see the big blocks of gray color that moved inside, and then she heard the neighing of a horse.

"Hey, there."

Millie recognized Randy's voice.

"What's happening here?" That was William. He sounded suspicious—like he'd added up the columns and wasn't sure they matched.

"I need my glasses," Millie said. If she was going to answer questions, she needed to be able to see.

Brad handed her the glasses.

"I was just helping Millie get off the horse," Brad said. His arms were still around Millie's shoulders.

William snorted. "Looked to me like you were helping her with a whole lot more than that."

Millie put her glasses on, and everything became clear. She could see through the open barn door that the night was almost fully dark now. The light Brad had turned on inside the barn gave the walls a yellow glow. Hay bales were stacked in one corner of the barn and horse stalls lined another wall.

William and Randy were both sitting on top of their horses and leaning forward as they looked at her and Brad. Randy was grinning, but William was looking stern and worried.

"My leg went to sleep," Millie explained. "I couldn't get off the horse, and Brad was helping me."

William looked directly at Millie. "You just be careful of him. He's a heartbreaker, he is."

"Oh." Millie blinked. Of course. She knew Brad was a flirt even if she had forgotten it for a moment. Men like him kissed women all the time for no good reason.

To be fair, women probably kissed Brad all the time for no good reason, too. He was certainly worth kissing if all of his kisses were like the last one. It wasn't his fault that Millie was the kind of woman who liked a reason for a kiss. A reason being maybe she was becoming a little special to the man kissing her.

Brad looked up at the other two ranch hands in astonishment. "Since when am I a heartbreaker?"

Brad always made very sure the women he was dating had no illusions about him. No one's heart had ever been cracked as far as he knew. Certainly, none had been broken. He didn't date the kind of woman who would be serious. "Besides, last night you were willing to let her sleep in my room with me because I was feeling a little down about Christmas. And now I can't kiss her!"

"That was different," William said firmly. "We didn't know Millie back then. Now, well—anyone can see she's the kind of woman who deserves a guy who's going to make a commitment."

Brad wanted to argue with that, but he couldn't.

He didn't know much about Millie. He didn't even know for sure that she wasn't a thief or that she wouldn't leave tomorrow without saying goodbye. But one thing he did know: she did deserve one of those husbands mothers always wanted for their daughters. She deserved a man who could give her a home and financial security. Brad might have that someday, but today he didn't. He had nothing to offer a woman like Millie except his diesel pickup, and he had a feeling that wouldn't do.

"Well, then, we'd best get to the bunkhouse," Brad said. William sure knew how to bring a man down to earth. "It's cold enough out here to spit ice."

William nodded and smiled. "Charlie wasn't kidding about the cocoa. That'll warm you up. We could smell it when we took the tree inside."

Brad nodded. He supposed he would have to be content with that.

"Does he have marshmallows?" Millie asked.

Brad looked down at her. Her short blond hair was sticking out in all directions because she'd pulled off the wool cap he'd given her earlier. Her glasses were still a little crooked on her face. Her cheeks were red from the cold, and her lips were warm from his kiss.

Brad would have promised Millie the moon—the least he could do was get her some marshmallows. "If he doesn't, I'll go get some."

"Where?" William stopped midway through stepping down off his horse and turned to stare at Brad. "Where would you get marshmallows way out here in the middle of the night? And it's Sunday. Even the stores in Miles City are closed by now."

From the expression on William's face, Brad would have thought he'd offered to bring Millie the moon after all. "I could borrow some marshmallows from Mrs. Hargrove. She always keeps things like that on hand."

William finished stepping to the ground before he gave Brad another peculiar look.

"She's a well-prepared woman—Mrs. Hargrove is," Brad said for no reason other than to try and stop the look that was growing and growing on William's face.

"You don't have a temperature, do you?" William finally asked as he took a step closer to Brad. "I hear the flu this season makes people a little light-headed."

"I don't have a fever." Brad said. He couldn't swear that he wasn't light-headed, but he was pretty sure his temperature would log in at a normal 98.6 degrees.

"Well, we should get these horses taken care of and get inside anyway," William said. He gave Brad another curious look before he turned back to his horse. "No sense in hanging out here in the cold when we can be inside decorating the Christmas tree."

Brad nodded. He had forgotten about the Christmas tree. He had the whole Christmas thing yet to do. There would be the tree and more cinnamon on the stove. And that was only tonight. Tomorrow night would be Christmas Eve, and that would be even worse. He wondered if Charlie would want them all to go to the Christmas pageant at church. Brad had a feeling this was one holiday he would never forget.

At least when he thought of Christmas in the future, he could look back to this evening ride with Millie. If that wasn't Christmas magic, he didn't know what was.

Chapter Nine

The warm air in the bunkhouse made Millie's glasses fog up.

She stepped to the side of the doorway so that she wouldn't block the way as Brad and the other two men came inside the bunkhouse. The air inside smelled of chocolate and fresh pine. Empty cups ready for cocoa were sitting on a small table by one wall. The ranch hands were gathered around the small tree that was lying on the floor next to the black stove.

Millie rubbed her hands. The wood burning in the stove kept the large room heated. Her fingers had stung a little from the cold when she first stepped inside the room, but they were already starting to warm up. She was grateful for the prickly feeling in her hands as the heat reached them. That small tingling distracted her from The Kiss.

Millie stole a look up at Brad. He might be accustomed to a kiss like the one they had just shared,
but she sure wasn't.

Brad was looking over at the group of men inside
the room so Millie took her time and studied him
carefully. He was handsome as usual. He still wore
his hat, but she could see his face beneath it and it
all looked normal. He wasn't wearing any tiny smile
or dreamy expression on his face.

Millie frowned. She knew William had said Brad
was a heartbreaker and she supposed she shouldn't
be surprised that he didn't look any different, but she
had secretly hoped he would. Not that she'd
expected him to be smiling like an idiot or anything,
but shouldn't he have some sort of funny look on his
face after a kiss like that? He didn't look like he was
affected at all. He certainly didn't have the stunned
look she knew she was wearing.

She watched as Brad said a quick hello to the
guys in the bunkhouse and then as he wiped his
boots lightly on the rug by the door. He took his hat
off and brushed the snow off it before he put it on a
rack next to the door. He still had a few snowflakes
melting on his cheek and his face was a little red
from the cold.

Outside of that, Millie couldn't detect anything
different about him. There was no sign Brad's heart
had been beating in an irregular rhythm or that he

was remembering a particularly sweet moment. In fact, he had paid more attention to his hat than he had to her since they'd come inside.

If Millie had been wearing a hat, she wouldn't even have remembered she had it on after that kiss. She felt like her own heart had been dipping and fluttering as if it belonged to a crazy woman. She'd even been trying to remember all she'd ever heard about flirting so that she'd know what to say next.

But now, seeing Brad, she hoped the sputtering happiness she felt inside hadn't shown on the outside. She was grateful she hadn't tried to say anything on the walk back to the bunkhouse. She didn't want to embarrass Brad by gushing over him when the kiss seemed like it was just routine to him. He probably kissed every woman who couldn't manage to get off a horse by herself. Maybe he meant it to be kind, like kissing backward children on the forehead to console them for their clumsiness.

Millie blinked and told herself it wasn't a tear that she felt in the corner of her eye. It was just moisture from the sudden heat of the room.

"I'm a little tired," she said as she gave a small yawn and an apologetic shrug. That should get rid of any doubt that she was still excited about a kiss that had happened a full five minutes ago. She didn't want anyone to think she was gullible enough to think that kiss mattered.

"Here, let me look at you," Brad said as he turned his full attention toward her. He bent his head and peered at her critically.

"I'm fine, though," Millie hastened to add. She didn't want to overplay being tired. Charlie would insist she go lie down, and she didn't want to miss any of this time taking a nap. Even if the kiss was nothing to remember, she wanted to remember every minute about this evening.

"How tired?" Brad asked as he took hold of her wrist and began to raise her hand up.

Millie blinked. Was he going to kiss her hand?

Brad stopped raising her hand and put his thumb on her wrist to feel her pulse.

"Being tired can be a sign you got too cold out there," he said. His blue eyes had deepened with worry. Millie started to hope maybe he did care, until he added. "People usually go to sleep just before they freeze to death."

"I wasn't that cold—and I'm not really that tired." Millie decided Brad was looking at her now like she was a sick bug at the bottom of a microscope. That wasn't the kind of attention she wanted. "I'm just—fine."

There had been many times in her life when Millie wished she were clever, but during none of those times did she wish it as fiercely as she did now. She felt as if she only knew how to flirt and be bold, she would know how to capture Brad's interest. Even a bug that knew how to flirt could capture his attention when he was standing so close.

Well, Millie guessed that technically she had his attention, but it was only because he thought she might be overly cold and on the verge of death. Brad probably didn't want to deal with the sheriff, which he'd have to do if he let her die while he was supposed to be watching her.

Unfortunately, all of the advice on flirting from other waitresses that she had listened to at Ruby's hadn't left her with a clue on how to flirt with a man when he was standing right in front of her counting out her pulse to make sure her heart was beating normally so she'd be able to pay for any crime she might have committed.

Of course, Millie thought optimistically, a woman didn't need to know how to flirt to be friendly. And the first step in being friendly was to find out more about the other person.

"You know, I never did get your last name," Millie said as she looked up at Brad. She smiled a little to show she was friendly, but not so much that he would think she was *too* friendly. It was the best she could do.

Brad looked down at Millie. She was smiling politely at him like she was a cashier at the grocery store and was asking him whether he wanted a plastic bag or a paper bag to carry home his potatoes. He had just kissed the woman. Shouldn't she at least look a little moved by the experience? "It's Parker. Brad Parker."

Millie nodded at him.

Brad expected her to ask about the weather next, and he didn't think he could hold his temper if she did. It was downright humbling to a man to know his kiss could have so little effect on a woman.

If he wasn't a little off-center because of everything that was going on, he would be able to think of something to say to make Millie smile at him like a woman ought to smile at a man who had just kissed her.

He could tell her that her eyes looked like emeralds when she laughed or that her skin was as soft as velvet, but Millie didn't look like the kind of woman who would like any of those words. Even he knew they were clichés. Unfortunately, in her case they were also true. Not that that would matter. Women always liked something that they hadn't heard before. Brad couldn't think of one thing to say that didn't sound like it had been said a thousand times already.

How did a man describe a woman like Millie?

"I see Charlie has the tree all ready to go," Brad said finally as he finished taking her pulse. "Your heart rate seems healthy."

At least her heart seemed to be doing better than *his,* Brad said to himself as he turned to face the other men in the bunkhouse, who were all gathered around the little tree they had chopped down.

Brad was glad none of the men were paying any attention to him and Millie. He suspected that wasn't because of good manners but because they'd finally gotten a steady look at the tree. It had been half dark when Randy cut it down, and sometimes things looked different when they had some light on them.

"It's kind of small," William said as he tipped the tree upright. The tree barely made it to William's belt buckle. "And it's got a bald spot where it didn't get enough sun. At least, I think that's its problem."

William turned the tree around so everyone could see the place where there were no branches.

"It's beautiful," Millie declared as she reached out and tried to coax a nearby branch into covering the bare spot. "It just needs a little help, that's all."

Millie didn't get the branch to cooperate and she stepped back.

"I guess we could stick it in the corner behind the lamp—if we angle it just right no one will see the bald spot," Charlie said hesitantly as he measured the tree with his hand. "And then maybe if we put some extra lights on it right there—"

"I only got one string of lights," Jeff interrupted

as he handed a plastic bag to Charlie. Jeff had been leaning against the wall, but he stood up straight to deliver his lights. "And I was lucky to get those—the stores in Miles City are all sold out. Vicki at the grocery store had to get that strand from the back room. I owe her dinner some night next week."

Charlie reached into the bag and pulled the strand of lights out. He looked at them for a moment. "But these are pink."

Jeff nodded. "Well, Vicki said they were Easter lights—they used them around the store windows in April—but I figure lights are lights. There's no reason Christmas trees can't have pink lights."

There was silence for a moment.

"Maybe they'll turn sort of red when we get them on," Millie finally said. "Sometimes things look different when they're on a tree."

Brad didn't care if the lights were purple. Millie was looking at the tree the way he wanted her to look at him. "They'll look just fine. The thing is that they're lights."

Millie turned and looked at him gratefully. "That's right, and I've always liked lights."

Millie still wasn't looking at him with quite the adoration that she had for the tree, but Brad felt he was making progress. It was a sad day when he had to compete with a tree for the affection of a woman. Brad looked at the tree. To make it even worse that was one pathetic tree. He'd swear it had two bald spots instead of just one.

Brad reached up and patted his own hair just to reassure himself. It was damp, but all there. No bald spots for him.

"Did you get any ornaments?" Millie asked Jeff as she walked over to where the man stood.

Brad followed Millie over. He'd compete with the tree if he had to, but he wasn't about to compete with Jeff just because the man had a few fancy ornaments in his hand.

"Wait, let me get my camera," Charlie called out as he limped across the floor to the shelf on the wall. "I want to get pictures of the tree decorating from start to finish."

"Since when do you have a camera?" Brad asked.

Charlie never took pictures. Not even the time William rode the calf backward down the loading chute. Charlie always said a man should rely on his memory when it came to things he'd seen in his life.

"Jeff brought me back one of them box cameras—you know, they're made out of cardboard so if a cow steps on them or something you're not out a lot of money," Charlie explained as he picked up the disposable camera from the shelf. "I'm thinking of starting a Christmas memory scrapbook for the bunkhouse here."

Brad wasn't even stunned anymore. If the truth

were told, he wasn't even listening. "That sounds nice."

Brad had stopped listening and just concentrated on looking. He wished he had a camera of his own, so he could take a picture of Millie. How did she manage to look twelve and twenty-three all at the same time? She had her head tilted to the side and was watching Jeff reach into the bag in front of him just like he was Santa Claus and the bag held the treasures of the world.

"Didn't your mother ever take you to see Santa?" Brad stepped a little closer so he could ask her the question and not risk it being heard by everyone in the room. He thought all mothers took their kids to see Santa Claus. He'd always imagined that, if his mother had lived, she would have taken him.

Millie looked up at him. Her eyes held on to the excitement of the tree as she shook her head. "I had a foster mother."

Somehow, Millie let him know all about her foster mother just by the flatness of her voice.

"I'm sorry." Brad was surprised by how much it disturbed him to know that someone had neglected Millie. She would have been the kind of little girl who should have had a mother who cared about her.

"It's all right," Millie said.

Brad scowled. No, it wasn't all right, but there was nothing he could do about it. Except perhaps get those ornaments for her. "If we need more things for the tree, I can drive to Billings tonight."

Charlie frowned and looked at his watch. "Even if the roads were good, the stores would be closed by the time you get there."

"They have that new place that's open twenty-four hours," Brad said. "What's it called—the some-thing Mart?"

"Isn't that too far to drive?" Millie asked softly.

"It is when it's starting to snow like this." Charlie frowned again and shot Brad an incredulous look. "You've driven that road enough to know about that one place where it always drifts closed in a few hours after this kind of snow—now, I know you'd get to Billings, but you wouldn't get back before Christmas."

There was a moment of silence. Charlie stood holding his cardboard camera. He hadn't even taken one picture yet. William was still holding up the pathetic tree by its top branch. Jeff held the bag with whatever ornaments he'd found. Randy sat on the floor with a string of popcorn in front of him. They had all stopped what they were doing to look at Brad.

"Unless that's what you want," Charlie finally said quietly. "Not to be here for Christmas."

Brad was speechless. He had been ten kinds of a fool. Here he had spent years mourning the fact that he'd never had a family Christmas, and he'd had family who wanted to celebrate with him all that time. The guys in the bunkhouse weren't worried about his Christmas depression because it meant he wasn't his usual cheerful self. They were worried because they cared about him.

"There's no place I'd rather be for Christmas than right here with all of you," Brad said. His voice sounded heavy, so he gave a cough at the end of his speech. He wouldn't want anyone to think he was sentimental. It would be better if they thought he was coming down with something.

"Well, good then," Charlie said with a cough of his own. He set his camera down on a chair and pulled a big red handkerchief out of his jeans pocket to wipe at his eyes. "I think someone must have put some green wood in that stove—it's started to smoke a little and it's getting in my eyes."

"I don't see any—" Randy began, then stopped when William jabbed him in the ribs with an elbow. "Well, maybe a little smoke—"

Everyone was silent for a moment.

Finally, Millie spoke. "The tree doesn't really need decorations. It can still be a Christmas tree."

Brad could have hugged her for bringing them back to a safe topic.

"But I have some decorations," Jeff offered as he pulled a package of shiny red balls out of the plastic bag. There were six ornaments. "It might not be enough, but that's all they had left on the shelf."

"Well—" Charlie cleared his throat and put his handkerchief back in his pocket "—I don't want anyone worrying about decorations. I've been watching that television show, and that woman said you could make Christmas decorations out of anything you have around—old hair curlers or those cardboard things from toilet paper."

Randy frowned. "It doesn't seem right to have toilet paper on a Christmas tree."

"It's not the paper, it's the cardboard rolls."

"Oh." Randy still looked unconvinced. "I guess I just can't quite picture it."

"Well, do you have any old hair curlers lying around?" Charlie asked in exasperation.

Randy shook his head. "I guess toilet rolls are all right."

Everyone took a minute to look at the tree.

Brad was the first to hear the sound of a car—or maybe it was two cars—driving up to the bunkhouse. Charlie was the one who limped over to the window, however, and opened the curtains a little so he could see.

"Looks like we got company," Charlie announced. "Good thing I made lots of cocoa."

Millie walked over to the window, and Brad followed.

"Who'd be coming to see us?" Randy asked.

Brad had asked the same question. He knew every one of the men in the bunkhouse knew lots of people and went lots of places. But most of the places they went were bars, and the kind of people they met there weren't the type to come calling on a Sunday evening, especially when it was a long drive from the highway to the Elkton Ranch bunkhouse. When it was snowing, a person had to have a reason to come calling to the bunkhouse.

"Maybe it's Christmas carolers," Charlie said. "It looks like they've got a red light going—"

"It's the sheriff," Brad said. He doubted Sheriff Wall was coming to bring them a Christmas fruitcake.

Brad moved closer to Millie until he stood directly behind her as she looked out the window. The sheriff wouldn't be able to see Millie when he came in the door if Millie stayed right where she was. Brad knew he couldn't hide Millie from Sheriff Wall if she was wanted for a string of crimes, but that didn't stop him from wanting to try anyway. He told himself it was just because she was so little that he felt so protective of her. He didn't know why he had to get all mixed up with a woman who was probably a thief—and not a very good thief at that.

"What's the sheriff doing here?" Charlie said. Brad noticed the older man wasn't moving over to the door to open it.

"Maybe he found out something about Millie's

money," William said with a frown. He wasn't moving toward the door, either.

No one was moving. Everyone just stood there worrying.

"Maybe it's not the sheriff," Jeff finally said. "Maybe he lent his car out to someone for the night and they got low on gas."

Brad snorted. "He wouldn't lend that car to his mother. No, he's here about the money."

"There's nothing he can say about the money," Millie protested softly. "It's just regular money."

Brad didn't even bother to answer her. There was nothing regular about a stack of hundred-dollar bills in this part of the country. He suspected there was nothing regular about it in Millie's life, either.

Chapter Ten

Millie had never seen so many silent men standing and looking at each other. Brad stood in front of her, and she wouldn't have even been able to see anything but his shirt if she hadn't moved to the side. She had no sooner moved than William stepped in front of her, and so all she saw was William's back.

Even Charlie, who had just opened the door, was still standing beside the open door like he was waiting for the sheriff to turn around and head back out of the bunkhouse. It took Charlie two minutes to close the door. By then the temperature inside the bunkhouse had fallen ten degrees.

Even when the door was closed, no one moved.

Finally, the sheriff spoke. "I thought I should check in."

He stood on the mat just inside the door, and the

snow on his tennis shoes had not begun to melt. He hadn't smiled since he stepped inside. "Just doing my duty, you know."

No one answered.

"Well, you've checked in," Brad said finally.

Millie had never been a chatty waitress, but she knew that many fights had been avoided by a few friendly words, and sometimes it was as simple as finding a safe topic of conversation. She quietly stepped out from behind William and looked toward the sheriff. "Did you have an easy drive out from town?"

The sheriff turned to look at her. For her, he smiled. It was quick and humorless, but it was a smile. "Yes, I did."

Millie tried to smile back. "Good."

Brad shifted himself so he was in front of Millie again, but Millie didn't care. She had done what she could to start a regular conversation.

No one else offered any topics of conversation. Millie swore she could hear the frost growing on the windowpanes. Finally, she decided she needed to make one more attempt. She moved out from behind Brad again. "We've got a tree to decorate."

"I heard." The sheriff grunted. "That's why I'm here."

"You came to decorate our tree?" Brad asked in amazement.

Millie was glad she wasn't still standing behind

Brad. She wouldn't have been able to see the astonishment on Brad's face if she had been. He was cute when he was dumbfounded.

"Not exactly," Sheriff Wall said. He finally took his cap off and held it in his hands. "I came to check out the story I heard that you rode horses back into the gullies to get the tree."

"Of course we rode horses," Brad said. "None of the pickups would have made it in all the snow back there."

The sheriff nodded. "I'm afraid I'll have to ask you to keep the barn locked then."

"What?"

Millie wasn't sure which of the men had asked that question. Maybe it didn't matter. They were all looking at the sheriff like he had forgotten where he was. Or maybe who he was.

"The barn doesn't have a lock," Charlie finally spoke.

"Oh," Sheriff Wall said as he looked at Millie and then studied the floor. "Well, then, I guess you'll just need to be sure that you keep a good eye on the— ah—the suspect so she doesn't steal a horse and ride out of here while she's under surveillance. I can keep an eye on the road through Dry Creek. But if she steals a horse and rides across the land, I'd miss her."

"Me?" Millie figured she was as astonished as

the men now. "Steal a horse and ride it away? Across fields and everything?"

"She can't even get off a horse by herself," Randy said from the sidelines. "Probably can't get on one, either."

"She did just fine for a beginner," Brad said. "Nobody knows how to do anything the first time they try it."

"Me?" Millie still couldn't quite believe it. No one had ever accused her of doing something that adventurous before. "Do you really think I could do that?"

Brad figured he must have had a premonition about his life and that was why he never truly liked Christmas. People sure weren't themselves today, and the only thing that was different was that Christmas was the day after tomorrow. He couldn't believe Millie stood there looking at the sheriff like he had handed her a prize compliment.

"He's saying you would be running from the law," Brad said so she would understand there was nothing complimentary about it.

"Well, technically, it would be *riding* from the law," Sheriff Wall said. He'd stopped looking at the floor, and now, when he talked, he flashed a quick grin at Millie that made him look ten years younger.

Brad snorted. He could see the sheriff liked the look in Millie's eyes. She was looking at him like he had said something very clever. Brad would have been the first to congratulate Sheriff Wall if he had said something useful. But he hadn't. And it didn't matter how young he looked at the moment, the sheriff was too old for Millie.

"Could I learn how to ride a horse that quick?" Millie asked.

Brad started to feel uneasy. Millie looked a little too eager for his comfort.

"It's not about learning anything fast," Brad said. He looked at the sheriff. "You don't have to worry about Millie. Even if she knew how to ride a horse, she'd have more sense than to ride off by herself at this time of year across the fields. It's freezing out there."

"It's not so bad out," Sheriff Wall said as he started to take his jacket off. He still hadn't stopped grinning.

Brad frowned. He was finally getting a good look at the sheriff, and he was realizing what was wrong. He was wearing tennis shoes. That was part of the reason he looked so young. "What happened to your boots?"

"No sense in wearing them today in all the snow."

Brad snorted. "You've worn them in snowdrifts up to your hips. You're not wearing them now because they make you look taller—that's why. They add a good two inches to your height."

The sheriff shrugged. "There's nothing wrong with being short. I'm just being who I am."

Brad grunted. Who did Sheriff Wall think he was kidding? "I don't think many people are going to vote for a sheriff who doesn't wear boots."

"It's not election year for another two years."

"Time goes fast around here."

Millie figured Brad had that all wrong. Time didn't go fast at all. It fact it didn't even seem to crawl. It was frozen now that all the silence had come back.

"Maybe we should have some cocoa," Charlie finally said. He looked at the sheriff. "You're welcome to stay now that we know you've really come courting and not to make things difficult for Millie."

The sheriff looked like he was going to protest, but finally ducked his head in a nod. "Thanks."

"Courting!" Brad protested until Charlie cut in.

"A man's got a right to go courting," Charlie said firmly. "And the sheriff here is a good prospect for some woman. He's got a home—"

"He lives in the Collinses' basement," Brad said. "And that's only in the winter. I don't even know what he does in the summer when the water table rises and the basement's too damp."

"I'm looking around to buy a house," the sheriff said.

"And he's got a good public service job," Charlie continued, just as if Brad had not even spoken.

"A badge doesn't make a man any better," Brad said.

"I'm ready to get married," the sheriff said. "I'm not just looking for a good time, like some men."

Brad figured he was beat. Sheriff Wall was ready to make a commitment. Brad knew most mothers would look at a man like the sheriff and hope their daughters had sense enough to be interested.

Brad didn't like to be rushed. If he ever did get married, he wanted the marriage to be because he wanted to live with that particular woman and not because he had just arrived at some time in his life when he wanted a wife. But that kind of decision took time. The sheriff was as ready to marry as Brad was to date. Brad could never compete with Sheriff Wall if a woman was anxious to get married. And Millie, if she had any sense, would have to see that marriage to a man like the sheriff would solve all her problems.

Brad looked over at Millie. The smile on her face hadn't changed much since the sheriff started talking. Still, if she was smiling, that had to mean she was interested. Brad wondered if maybe he hadn't been too cautious about marriage in his life.

Millie didn't know why Brad had turned polite. He'd been arguing away with the best of them, and then he stopped and put a tight smile on his face and became quiet.

"Well, how many want cocoa?" Charlie said as he started walking to the small room off the back of the main room. That was Charlie's kitchen.

"I'd like some," Millie said. She turned toward Charlie. "And let me help you."

"No." Charlie shook his head. "You're our company, and the day I put company to work in the kitchen is the day that I retire as cook." Charlie looked around at the men in the room before looking back at Millie. "You sit and visit with the sheriff. Brad can help me."

Millie would have rather helped Charlie with the cocoa than sit and talk with a strange man. She didn't have anything in particular to say to the sheriff, especially since he had announced he was looking for a wife. He might be a little shorter than the other men in the room, but Millie couldn't picture herself being married to him all the same.

Of course, she still had to talk to him. The sheriff had walked over to the tree with her, and they were both looking at it.

"It's not always how big the tree is that counts," Millie remarked. That tree was looking shorter and shorter to her each time she saw it. She looked over at Randy. "You're not cutting more off the bottom, are you?"

"I'm not cutting anything off anywhere," Randy said.

"Maybe the branches are drooping when they

thaw," William said as he walked over to look at the tree, too.

"Maybe we can set the stand on a box," Millie suggested. "I'm sure it'll look fine as long as it's up higher."

"And we don't have the decorations on it yet," Jeff chipped in as he carried his plastic bag over to the tree. He pulled out the string of lights again. "I tested these, and they're ready to go."

"But they're pink," the sheriff said as he looked at the lights. "Aren't you worried they'll make everything look a little strange?"

"The lights might look red when they're on the tree," Millie said. "You need to give them a chance."

Sheriff Wall looked at Millie. "You're right. That's the way we do it in Dry Creek. We always give everyone a chance."

Millie thought she might be turning a little pink herself. Not because she was embarrassed, but because she was annoyed. "You don't need to give me a chance. I didn't do anything wrong."

Brad held the mugs of cocoa a little higher. Good for Millie. She wasn't falling for the sheriff. She just stood there beside the tree looking a little fierce, like she was ready to defend something.

"Cocoa?" Brad offered one mug to Millie. "I put extra marshmallows in it for you."

Brad would have dumped the whole bag of

miniature marshmallows in the cup if he could have.
As it was, the melting tower of marshmallows only
stood a half inch over the rim of the mug.

"Thanks." Millie took the cup and gave him a shy
smile. "That's the way I like it."

Brad felt like he might be in the running after all.
Just to make sure, he added, "That tree is looking
pretty good."

"Do you really think so?" Millie looked up at him
anxiously. "I'm hoping the decorations will make it
look better."

"We've only got six ornaments," Jeff reminded
everyone as he pulled one of the shiny red balls from
the bag. "There won't be enough to cover the tree."

Everyone looked at the ornament Jeff held up. It
had a scratch on one side of the ball, and silver
showed through. The ornament was about two inches
in diameter and hung a little lopsided from Jeff's
fingers.

"I'll make some ornaments," Brad said. He regretted his words the minute they left his mouth. How was
he going to make ornaments? Then he remembered
a glimpse of a long-forgotten scene. He was with his
father, and his father was showing him how to make
cowboy ornaments for the Christmas tree. Brad must
have been only four years old at the time.

"You will?" Millie's face was lit up. "You'll
make ornaments?"

The look on Millie's face must have been what his own face looked like all those years ago, Brad thought.

"No one's getting me to make anything out of toilet-paper rolls," Jeff muttered. "I don't care what they call those ornaments."

"And this popcorn has too many kernels to string right," Randy added. "I keep poking myself with the needle."

Brad kept looking down at Millie. "All we need is a whole bunch of empty tin cans."

Brad thought he was looking at the prettiest Christmas ornament there was. Millie's smile lit up her whole face, and Brad stopped noticing her glasses altogether. She was beautiful.

"That's one thing we've got is tin cans," Charlie said. He was holding two more mugs of cocoa and gave one each to Randy and Jeff. "We can empty more if we need them."

"We have some old paint in the barn, too." Brad was reluctant to stop looking at Millie, but he figured he'd better. He knew she didn't like a lot of attention coming her way, and he didn't want to spook her off just when he was beginning to think the two of them might have a chance.

"I'm planning to buy a farm in the spring," Brad said, only half realizing he had spoken his words instead of just thinking them.

Everyone turned to Brad and looked puzzled.

Brad cleared his throat. "I had thought some of that old paint might come in handy when I buy my place, but it's better to use what we can now."

Brad was relieved that his explanation seemed to make enough sense to everyone that they didn't pester him anymore about what he had meant. He wasn't ready to answer questions about anything. He hardly knew himself what the tumble of emotions inside of him was about. He was forgetting who he was. He was Brad Parker. He liked women who liked a good time. He wasn't the kind of a man to make a commitment.

Brad stopped for a moment. He'd forgotten the most important thing: Millie. He didn't know much about her, but he did know that she hadn't had an easy life. She deserved a man who was better than Brad Parker and the sheriff combined. She deserved to marry a saint.

Brad looked at her. Everyone in the room had turned their attention back to the Christmas tree. Millie was frowning slightly at it.

"Maybe if we just move this branch," she finally said as she reached out and gently bent one of the branches.

Brad knew the tree was a hopeless cause. He also knew that it was a cause that was important to Millie. He might not be saint enough to marry her, but he sure could do his best with that tree of hers. "I've got some twine we can use if we need it."

Millie smiled gratefully up at him. "Do you think it will work?"

Brad nodded his head. He'd make it work even if he had to nail more branches on that tree. He was going to give Millie a good Christmas if he had to use every nail and tin can on the Elkton ranch.

Chapter Eleven

Millie let go of the sigh she was carrying. Randy had tied his picture angel to the top of the tree, and Charlie had turned off the last of the lamps in the bunkhouse. Everyone was standing in a circle around the tree. Millie decided there was no doubt the scraggly pine was a Christmas tree now that it was all dressed up.

Brad had used a hammer and a nail to pound holes into the sides of dozens of tin cans, and when he put a small candle in the middle of each tin, the candlelight shone through the holes and made hundreds of tiny twinkling stars. The cans themselves had been painted dark red, and some of them had white trim.

Jeff and William had tied the cans to the tree with haying twine before adding the decorations Jeff had bought. The strand of pink lights circled the tree a couple of times, and with the red of the tin cans, the lights actually looked like they belonged.

"It's beautiful," Millie said.

Brad let go of the sigh he was carrying. It had occurred to him when he was halfway through emptying out all of the soup cans in the kitchen that the tree would look homemade with the ornaments he was making. Tin cans couldn't really compete with ornaments a person could buy in the store. He didn't want Millie to be disappointed in the tree. If it wasn't too late to get to Billings and back, he would have dug his way past the drift that usually stopped people and gone out to buy more ornaments right then. Even now he wasn't sure. "You really like it?"

Brad wondered how it could be that, with five other men hovering around the tree, Millie smiled up at him like those tin cans were filled with diamonds instead of holes and it was all due to him.

"It's just like I've always pictured a Christmas tree should look," Millie said softly. "It reminds me of a starry night."

Brad swallowed. The light from the candles flickered over Millie's face in the darkness and then left her in shadow. "I'm glad you like it."

The other men were silent except for the sounds of swallowing or coughing or clearing their throats.

Charlie was the only one brave enough to bring out his handkerchief and dab at his eyes.

"That smoke's still hanging around," Charlie muttered after he put his handkerchief back into the pocket of his overalls.

Each of the men had their faces turned toward the Christmas tree. The tree itself was standing on a wooden crate that Jeff had pulled in from the barn. Charlie had donated a few white dishtowels to cover the tree stand and the crate. Millie had arranged the towels so they looked almost like snowdrifts.

The clock was ticking in the corner of the room, and the fire was crackling a little as it burned in the corner stove, but otherwise it was a silent night.

"It's too bad Mrs. Hargrove isn't here," William said finally. "She'd have us all singing a carol or two—"

Brad wished the older woman were here with them. She'd enjoy the tree.

"Oh, that reminds me," the sheriff said as his hand went to his shirt pocket. Sheriff Wall was wearing a white shirt with broad gray stripes and a black leather vest. "She asked me to give you something when she heard I was coming out here tonight."

The sheriff pulled several blue index cards with printing on them out of his shirt pocket. "These are the visitor forms for the church. In all the commotion, she forgot to have you fill them out this morning, and she felt bad about it."

Charlie frowned. "I didn't know you had to fill out a form to go to church. Is it like voter registration?"

"Nah," Sheriff Wall said as he fanned the cards out and held them out to everyone. "It's just a new program Mrs. Hargrove volunteered to do. I don't really know much about it—I've only gone to church the past month or so, and they didn't have them back then. I think it's just to give Mrs. Hargrove your address or something so she can send you another postcard."

"Mrs. Hargrove knows where we live," Charlie said, but he took one of the cards anyway. "Still, I guess it's only polite to thank the church for having us, so I guess I'll be filling one out."

After Charlie took a card, he gave a stern look to those around him. Finally, William took a card. Then Randy and Jeff each took one. Brad held his breath when he put his hand out and took one. Millie even took one.

Everyone just looked at his or her card.

"Mrs. Hargrove said something about handing them back to her when Millie comes to town tomorrow to do her community service," the sheriff said. He looked pleased with himself that he had delivered all of the cards. "I'll be happy to come by tomorrow and pick Millie up so she can get started."

"Millie and I will be in town at eight," Brad said. He put the card in his shirt pocket. He was perfectly able to see to Millie. "There's no need for you to drive all the way out here."

"I don't mind," the sheriff said before he shrugged his shoulders and looked at Brad. "Don't suppose it matters, though—I will see you and Millie at eight. I thought maybe we should meet in the café."

"I thought we were going to the church," Millie said. "To take care of the black marks on the floor."

"We'll start out at the café," the sheriff said as he walked toward the closet that held his coat. "We'll be wanting some coffee and the county runs a tab there. Linda showed me where everything was before she left—even her flavored creamers."

"Linda trusted you with the stuff in her café?" Charlie asked. The older man was frowning.

"Yeah," Sheriff Wall said as he opened the closet door and reached for his coat. "Of course she trusts me. I'm sworn to uphold the law."

"That wouldn't have made any difference to Linda a year or so ago," Charlie commented as he walked over to the door. "I guess she's finally growing up. She always struck me as someone who'd rather put poison in a lawman's coffee than creamer. I don't suppose she sits down with you while you drink it, though, does she?"

The sheriff grinned. "Now that you mention it, she does. I guess we all grow up sooner or later."

Sheriff Wall he put his coat on and walked toward the door before turning to the others in the room. "We'll see some of you tomorrow."

Millie smiled. "We'll be there."

"I'll wish the rest of you a Merry Christmas then," the sheriff said as he tipped his hat to the group. "Be sure and watch that tree of yours, or you'll burn the bunkhouse down."

"We'll be fine," Brad said. He had seen the flicker of worry in Millie's eyes. "There's enough snow outside to stop a forest fire anyway."

"That's true," Millie said.

Brad didn't bother to wave to the sheriff as the man opened the door and stepped into the night darkness. Sheriff Wall could find his way home all right. Brad was much more interested in Millie.

"I could bring some snow in if you're worried," he offered. He figured the candles would burn for another half hour or so. He wanted Millie relaxed while she watched it. "Just so it's handy if we need it for anything."

Millie was happy. She was having the kind of Norman Rockwell Christmas that she'd imagined. Granted, Christmas Eve wasn't until tomorrow, but she was sitting here with a group of people who had actually decorated a tree.

Millie had always known she could decorate a tree for herself when she was in Seattle. One year she'd even bought some tinsel and lights. But when it came time to get a tree, she didn't. Part of her Christmas dream was to decorate a tree with other people.

"We've got more cocoa," Charlie said as he sat down on one of the leather couches that Jeff had pulled closer to the tree. "It's self-serve in the kitchen."

Millie walked over and sat down on the couch next to Charlie. "You make great cocoa."

Charlie beamed as though she'd handed him a hundred-dollar bill. For the first time that night, Millie remembered what she was doing in Dry Creek. She had a mission, and it had nothing to do with tin-can lights and cocoa.

Millie looked around the room. She didn't feel like a stranger anymore. She wondered how she could fulfill Forrest's request or if it was really necessary.

"The community service won't be hard," Brad said as he sat down on the couch next to Millie. "No one really expects you to work."

Millie had to stop herself from scooting over to sit pressed against Brad.

"*I* expect me to work," Millie said. Her voice was a little sterner than she had intended. She didn't care what Sheriff Wall thought about her and her community service, but Millie hadn't been a slacker before she came to Dry Creek, so there was no reason to start now.

Brad smiled slightly. "I guess I'm not surprised at that."

"We can't all be prima donnas," Millie continued. She didn't want Brad to think she was boring, but she just couldn't summon up the effort to pretend to be carefree. She was a person who obeyed the rules in life, and that was just the way it was.

Brad smiled wider. "No chance of that happening. You won't even let me wait on you."

"You got me cocoa," Millie protested. She wasn't used to a man wanting to help her with her coat and that kind of thing. She was used to doing this for herself *and* a table of other people at the same time. "Besides, I don't need help with much."

Brad stopped smiling. "I scared you with all my talk of spiders before. I'm sorry I did that."

Millie didn't know who had moved, but she was sitting closer to Brad on the sofa than she had been before. She looked around the room. Charlie had gotten up from the sofa and was over by the table. Jeff and Randy had left the room, and she could hear them in the kitchen. William alone sat near the tree.

If Brad only knew, it wasn't spiders she was scared of right now.

"It's okay," Millie said as she tried to move away from Brad without being obvious about it. She was afraid she had been the one to move closer in the first place, and she didn't want him to think she was—

"Oh." Millie realized that as she moved away, Brad moved closer. Maybe she wasn't the one who had moved on the sofa after all.

William got up and left his place beside the tree. Millie looked around. She and Brad were alone in the room. "Everyone's in the kitchen."

"Probably more cocoa." Brad doubted it was a sudden thirst for cocoa that had made the other men give them some privacy, but Brad was glad for the kindness they were showing him.

He wasn't sure if it was good news or bad news that Millie looked so nervous around him all of a sudden. He wished he had another month or two to get to know her before he kissed her again. But he didn't have a month. She would be gone by then for sure. He tried to slide down into the sofa cushions a little more. Maybe she really *didn't* like tall men.

Brad pulled the blue form out of his shirt pocket, more for something to do than because he even remembered what the form was for.

"I wonder what they send you," Millie said. She was looking down at her own form intently.

The Welcome Visitors form was as basic as they came, Brad figured, but he was grateful for it. Even with all of the lamps in the room off, there was enough light from the tree to see what was on the card. There was a graphic of a church on one corner and several printed questions in the middle of the card. One question asked if you would like someone from the church to visit you. The other asked if you had a prayer request. At the bottom, the church said they'd send a special gift to anyone who returned the card with his or her address. That must be what Millie had just read.

"It can't be much," Brad said. "The church doesn't have money to buy people anything. They've been raising money for the past year just to get a new organ for the place."

"Money's tight around here, isn't it?"

"Not so tight that we don't get by," Brad said. He didn't want Millie to think they were poor in Dry Creek. "And when money *is* tight—or someone has a health problem or something—we all chip in and help them over the hump."

Brad wished he'd paid more attention to the accountant he'd paid to do his taxes last year. Brad was so close to having enough to buy a place of his own that he had wanted to ask the man a few questions about buying property in addition to the usual questions about his taxes. "We're not rich by any means, but no one has lost their place or not had enough for some medical care—at least, no one that I've known of, and I've lived here for ten years."

"You mean you haven't always lived here?" Millie asked.

Brad could swear she was surprised. He tried real hard not to be offended. He knew some women put great stock in men who had traveled and been lots of places. Some of the waitresses he'd known thought travel was the measure of a man. Of course, that might be because they were used to truckers, and a trucker wasn't really a trucker until he'd been to both coasts a few times. But Brad had never had any desire to move around.

"I was born in Illinois," Brad said, "but I like Dry Creek. I don't expect I'll be moving from here."

"But surely you travel?" Millie insisted.

"Not if I don't have to," Brad said. He figured the woman might as well know him. He was a basic kind of a guy. No particular flash. He wasn't one to fly a woman over to Paris for her birthday. Now, he *might* drive her to the coast or up to Canada for a long weekend or something.

Millie didn't seem to have anything to say in response to him not traveling so Brad just sat there on the sofa. He figured his chances were about zero.

"Does anyone in Dry Creek travel?" Millie asked. She was suddenly realizing that she would need to leave in a couple of days. After she completed her community service, there would be no reason to stay in Dry Creek. And she couldn't stay. Once she gave out her Christmas presents, she would be broke. She'd have to go back to work. She accepted that, but she'd hoped that she might see some of the people in Dry Creek again. She'd hoped at least some of them occasionally went to Seattle.

"Mrs. Hargrove flew up to Alaska to see Doris June a couple of years ago," Brad said. "She liked the moose—they walked right down the streets in Anchorage just like they owned the place."

"Does anyone else go anywhere?"

Brad was silent a minute. "The sheriff goes to conventions every year—he gets around pretty good."

"Oh." Millie blinked and looked down at the card in her hand so that Brad wouldn't see the tears in her eyes. She supposed she was silly to have gotten so attached to the people in this town. Millie looked out of the corner of her eye at Brad. He was sitting a little awkwardly, like he was trying to push himself into the sofa cushions. He had a frown on his face, and he was staring straight ahead at the tree. But Millie wished he was the one who went to conventions. If he went to conventions, he was bound to come to Seattle once in a while.

"I went to a rodeo once," Brad offered.

"Really? Where?"

"Cheyenne."

"Oh." Millie realized that she had never heard of anyone having a rodeo in Seattle.

Brad swore he didn't know how to please a woman. He'd finally realized he could offer a wife some excitement, and Millie sat there looking like it was nothing to her. Of course, he supposed it didn't matter to her where he took any future wife. "Rodeos can be good entertainment."

Millie nodded. "Now that I know more about riding a horse, I can appreciate them more."

Her response certainly didn't ring with enthusiasm. Brad figured he could have suggested a trip to the dentist and gotten the same response. He told himself it was probably just as well. If excitement and travel were important to Millie, it was good that he knew it now.

"I should have gone and gotten some better decorations for the tree," Brad said. The poor thing looked a little forlorn to him just now, even though the candles were all still burning brightly and he had arranged branches so that he'd covered the bald spots on the tree. Why had he thought that tin-can ornaments could compete with the shiny new balls that people expected on their trees these days?

"I love that tree," Millie said fiercely.

"Really?"

Millie nodded firmly. "It's beautiful."

"Yes," Brad agreed, even though he'd stopped watching the tree and was watching Millie watch the tree. The candlelight reflected off her glasses and cast a golden glow all over her face. When had her face become the only one he wanted to look at? Her hair still didn't have any more brass in it, and she still didn't wear any of the makeup that he'd thought looked so good on most women. But she was beautiful.

Brad moved a little closer on the sofa. Millie didn't move away. He took that as a sign of encouragement and moved closer still. Millie did look up at him when he did that. But she didn't move away. Instead, she gave him a shy smile.

Brad moved all the way closer and put his arm on the sofa behind Millie.

Millie forgot about how much she would miss Brad when she left. She forgot about the fact that she was a cautious woman and not at all the kind of woman men like Brad wanted to date. All she could think about was the moment she was living.

Brad had his arm around her, and they were looking at the most beautiful Christmas tree she had ever seen. The light from the candles danced between the pine branches of the tree and reflected off the bottoms of the tin cans. The pink lights added a softness to the shadows the branches cast.

Millie was having her Christmas. The Norman Rockwell one Forrest had wanted her to have.

"I owe him an apology," Millie spoke without thinking.

"Who?" Brad said as he moved his arm from the back of the sofa to her shoulders.

Millie felt enclosed and happy. "Just a friend."

Millie took a good look around her. She wanted to remember this Christmas for the rest of her life. She hoped she'd remember the feel of Brad's arm around her as well as the flickering light of the candles on the Christmas tree. She'd never experienced anything like it yet in her life, and she wasn't hopeful enough to expect another one to come along. But she sure would be grateful if it ever did.

Chapter Twelve

Millie could smell the coffee the minute she stepped out of her car in front of the café in Dry Creek. It was only eight o'clock in the morning, but she felt like she had been up for hours already. She hadn't slept well and had to admit she was feeling annoyed with life in general. She didn't know what was wrong with her today.

Well, maybe she did know, she thought as she shut her car door. But there was nothing to be done about it. Last night had shown her what Christmas was all about, and the experience had made her feel more alone than she'd ever felt in her life.

No wonder her foster mother had never bothered with Christmas.

A sentimental Christmas wasn't worth it when a person had to go back to her real life. And for her,

Millie thought, real life consisted of waiting on tables of complaining, demanding people at Ruby's cafe.

"I guess the sheriff is here."

Millie looked up at Brad when he spoke. He had driven behind her into Dry Creek after she had refused his offer to ride in his pickup with him. For some reason, she wanted to be alone in her old car. She certainly didn't want to be sitting next to Brad. The wind made his lips white and his face red, but he didn't seem in any hurry to step past her and go into the café.

The morning itself was dreary. The sun was hidden behind thick gray clouds, which probably meant snow was coming later today. The snow that had fallen yesterday was tramped down around the café and didn't look as clean as it had yesterday. A film of dirt had settled over everything.

"I hate snow," Millie announced.

Brad only grunted. "Everybody can't live at the beach."

"I don't live at the beach," Millie protested. She rented a small apartment so close to the docks that she perpetually smelled fish. She tried hard to convince herself the neighborhood was charming. "It's the waterfront, and that's altogether different."

Now that Millie thought about it, she didn't know what she had against snow. The weather on the docks in Seattle could be just as wet and almost as cold as Montana in winter. Maybe she had just always hated snow because it reminded her of all those days she'd spent with her foster family in Minnesota. She had moved to Seattle five years ago to start a new life. Some days, though, it felt like her new life was just a repeat of her old life. All that had changed were the people sitting around the tables that she waited on.

"It's all by the water," Brad said. His lips were pressed into a line that could not be mistaken for even the smallest of smiles. "I know there's fancy prices at the coast, but living by the water doesn't make a man a better man. There's nothing wrong with a bit of snow. Lots of good men live in the snow."

Millie didn't have a chance to answer because Brad started walking up the steps to the café. His boots stomped on each step, one at a time, until he reached the top.

Brad figured he had ruined any chance he'd ever had with Millie. But, he said to himself as he opened the door, it was probably just as well. There was no point in imagining how much fun he and Millie would have on a real date when he knew the price he'd have to pay when she left. The simple fact was, they had no future and he was wise to realize that.

Brad stood to the side and held the door for Millie.

He smelled cinnamon on her when she walked by. Millie had helped Charlie prepare an early breakfast this morning, and Brad couldn't help but notice she had been not only civil, but downright nice to Charlie. In fact, Millie had had a smile for all of the men in the bunkhouse…except for him.

Brad wondered when everything had changed with him and Millie. She'd seemed to like his arm around her last night. She had even snuggled up against him the little while they sat and looked at that tree.

It was the tree's fault, Brad decided. No good ever came from taking a pathetic little pine tree and dressing it up like it was something to stare at. It gave rise to all kinds of hopes in a man's chest that just simply weren't going to come true. Maybe there was a good reason he'd never liked Christmas, Brad told himself as he followed Millie into the café. Maybe he didn't like Christmas because he had the sense to be content with his lot in life and wasn't given to empty dreaming.

Christmas was nothing but a promise that hadn't come true in his life. Maybe it did for some people, but it hadn't for him.

"Good morning," the sheriff called out in greeting to Brad and Millie, just as if he were blind and not able to see they were miserable. "Looks like it'll be a good day."

"It's overcast," Brad said. "It'll probably snow later, unless it's too warm to snow—then it'll be some kind of icy slush."

Brad didn't know how any man could be optimistic with the thought of slush falling on him later in the day, though the sheriff seemed like he could be. At least he didn't flinch when Brad informed him of the prospect.

"I got the coffee ready for you, but I'm going to need to go into Miles City. I have some official work to get done," Sheriff Wall said as he started to put his coat back on.

Brad could see that several cups, napkins and spoons had been set out on one of the tables. Someone had even folded the napkins, and Brad was sure it hadn't been the café owner, Linda, because the corners were all crooked. When Linda bothered to fold napkins, she got them straight.

"Thanks," Brad said, even though he figured the sheriff wasn't listening to him since he was looking at Millie. Sheriff Wall was as pathetic as he was, Brad figured by looking at him. Maybe the sheriff was worse, Brad decided. At least Brad hadn't tried folding napkins to impress Millie.

"Did you sleep all right last night?" the sheriff asked Millie just as though he cared.

Millie nodded. Brad had to give her points for knowing to be cautious about the sheriff. Of course, he then took some points away when she smiled at Sheriff Wall as she said thank-you. A simple thank-you would have been enough. She didn't need to smile at the man. The lawman would be out folding more than napkins if Millie didn't tone down those smiles.

"I'll be back in a few hours," the sheriff continued. "Might even make it back for lunch. Mrs. Hargrove promised to make us her special meat loaf with black olives—it's her Christmas special."

Millie longed with all her heart to have a special Christmas recipe that people knew about. Since she usually worked on all of the holidays, her Christmas special was whatever the chef had made for the day. And the only reason people asked her for it was because she was their waitress. Most of them didn't even know her name.

"Maybe I'll ask for her recipe—unless it's a secret." Millie looked at Brad. "Do you think it's a secret?"

"I doubt it. It's hard to keep anything a secret in Dry Creek."

Millie didn't point out that *she* still had a secret. Maybe that's why she was feeling so cranky today. She had a secret and she didn't want to keep it a secret. She wanted to tell Brad what she was doing and why she was in Dry Creek.

"Well, I guess I better get going," the sheriff said

as he nodded his head at Millie. "Besides, I see Mrs. Hargrove coming, so you guys will be getting down to work in no time."

Millie smiled goodbye to the sheriff. She guessed the spilling of secrets would have to wait until she got the floors in the church all scrubbed.

Thinking of the floors made Millie feel more cheerful. There was nothing like getting rid of black marks to make a person feel like they had accomplished something in a day. She might not have a special Christmas recipe, but she did have a special cleaning method.

"Aren't you worried about what she's going to put on those floors?" Brad asked the sheriff, just to remind the man that it hadn't been that long ago that he thought Millie was planning some kind of a crime. The sheriff had made that remark about the water supply and hadn't followed up. Brad wondered what kind of a lawman the sheriff was.

"Naw," the sheriff said as he waved goodbye. "I ran her through the system and got enough information on her to put my mind at ease. Besides, I have a buddy on the Seattle police force."

"Does that mean I don't have to do the floors?" Millie asked.

The sheriff stopped with his hand on the door. "Well, you still broke into the place…"

Brad held his breath. If Millie didn't have to do

the floors, she didn't have to stay at all. He thought he at least had today to convince her to stay. He was glad she had the community service. If there was one thing he knew about Millie, it was that she didn't take the easy road anywhere.

Millie nodded. "I would do them anyway. I just wanted to know if anything was going on my official record."

The sheriff went a little pink at this.

"Don't worry," Brad said. "Unless I miss my guess, the sheriff didn't even file the report. He hates paperwork."

Sheriff Wall left the café as Mrs. Hargrove entered it, and they nodded to each other.

"Good, the coffee's on," the older woman said as she unwound a wool scarf that she'd worn around her head. "There's nothing like a cup of coffee to get me going in the morning."

Mrs. Hargrove drank her cup of coffee while she was standing on the welcome mat in the front of the café. "I got snow on my boots coming over here, and I don't want to track up this clean floor. We have enough to do with getting one floor clean. No point in adding another floor to the list."

Millie looked at Mrs. Hargrove. She was wearing a navy parka over a pink gingham dress. Forrest had told Millie that Mrs. Hargrove usually wore a gingham dress in some color or another.

"You don't want to get your dress dirty," Millie said. "Brad and I brought lots of old clothes if you'd like to borrow some."

When Millie left the bunkhouse, Charlie had insisted on giving her old flannel shirts to take with her and several pairs of men's overalls.

"They're full of holes," Charlie had said when he handed the two bags to Millie. "So you might want to wear a couple of the shirts at the same time— mostly the holes aren't in the same places."

Millie looked at the older woman. "I've got the old clothes in the trunk of my car. I thought I'd take them over to the church and put them on there."

"Makes sense, since the church is heated. Pastor Matthew said he went over and turned the heat on at seven this morning, so it should be comfortable by now. And don't you worry about these dresses of mine—they all wash up fine," Mrs. Hargrove said. "I haven't met the stain yet that I couldn't figure out—except for the black marks on the church's floor. I'm anxious to see how this baking soda idea of yours works."

"Oh," Millie remembered. "The sheriff didn't leave me the box of baking soda he said he had in his office."

"Don't worry," Mrs. Hargrove said as she patted the pocket of her parka. "I brought a small box that I had. It's brand-new—never been opened. Don't know if that makes a difference or not, but I'm not taking any chances. Those black marks have been bothering me for years now."

Millie knew how easily water splashed, and that was why she had worried about Mrs. Hargrove's clothing. She'd never once expected the woman to help her clean the floor. But it was clear when she, Brad and Mrs. Hargrove walked up the steps of the church ten minutes later that the older woman expected to scrub.

"Oh, no," Millie said as she took the final step up to the church. She had her purse strapped around her neck, and her hands were free. Her long wool coat kept her warm even though the air was cold. Millie stopped to take a breath. "You don't need to get down on your knees or anything. There's plenty of cleaning you can do without that."

"Maybe you could dust the rails of some of the pews," Brad suggested. He had carried up both bags of old clothes even though Millie had protested.

"You mean sit down while the real work is going on?" Mrs. Hargrove asked as she turned the doorknob on the church's outer door. "Nothing ever got cleaned by someone sitting down and taking a swipe at a little bit of dust. Besides, the pews will be cleaned later this morning. The twins do that when it's the Curtis family's turn at cleaning. I think they pretend the pews are dragons."

Millie knew the twins liked dragons. What she didn't know was that they cleaned the church. "Aren't they too young?"

"Too young. Too old," Mrs. Hargrove said as they stepped into the church. "Sometimes it seems that all of the work at the church is being done by the people you wouldn't expect."

Millie and Brad followed Mrs. Hargrove into the church.

"Of course, that's the beauty of it," Mrs. Hargrove said as she stood in the entryway to the church and unwound the scarf from her head again. "The Bible talks about the weak being made strong and the slave being made free. I figure that since the very beginning, the church has been surprised by what people can do and be."

"But that was a long time ago, wasn't it? The beginning, that is." Millie was remembering the time when she'd gone to church with her foster mother and the woman had told her that Jesus lived thousands of years ago and so had no meaning for today.

Mrs. Hargrove shrugged her shoulders. "God says a thousand years are but a day to Him. The way I see it, we're still in the early days with God and will be for a long time at that rate."

"You said there were scrub brushes around?" Brad asked. Just because God had all day didn't mean Brad did. He figured if he got the floor cleaned in the church before lunch, then maybe Millie would agree to go riding horseback again with him this afternoon. If he could get her leaning into him on the horse again, maybe he could talk to her and he could ask her to stay in Dry Creek for a little longer.

Brad decided he needed his head examined. Women didn't just stay in Dry Creek while they waited for some man to get to know them. No, he needed a better plan than that.

"Brad?" Millie asked for the second time. Brad was standing there, muttering to himself and frowning. He hadn't even heard her the first time she said his name.

"Huh?"

Brad focused on her, but she couldn't help but notice that his face turned a little pink at the same time.

"Mrs. Hargrove said the brushes are on the shelf above the sink in the kitchen. Do you know where that is?"

"Yeah, sure," Brad said as he started to walk toward the small room on the side of the church. "I was just going to get them."

When Brad stepped into the kitchen, Millie turned to Mrs. Hargrove. "I hope he's okay."

The older woman chuckled. "Oh, he's okay, all right."

"He seems a little distracted."

The older woman chuckled even harder. "I'd say that's a fair bet."

Millie frowned. She'd hoped to have another conversation with Brad like the one she'd had yesterday, and that didn't seem too likely if he was going to be distracted by something as simple as brushes.

"Is there a restroom where I can change?"

"Right through there, dear. The second door on your left."

Millie ended up wearing two flannel shirts and one of Charlie's old coveralls. She needed some twine to belt the overalls tight to her waist so they didn't flap around too much, but outside of that, everything had adjusted to her.

Millie decided it was a good thing she'd changed when she first got to the church. If she'd waited ten minutes, she never would have changed. That's when Pastor Matthew and his two boys came over to the church.

Millie had already started to scrub the first black mark. If she hadn't already been on her knees, the sight of Pastor Matthew would have put her there.

The minister wore an apron. Well, maybe it wasn't so much an apron as it was a dishtowel tied around his waist. But Millie could hardly believe what she was seeing. "He's going to start cleaning."

"I thought I told you it was the Curtis family's turn to clean the church this week," Mrs. Hargrove said. The older woman was sitting on one of the pews near Millie sorting through a box of crayons from one of the Sunday School classrooms. She had finally agreed to observe instead of scrub, since there were only two scrub brushes and Brad insisted he was going to take one and scrub beside Millie.

Millie had her scrub brush in one hand and water stains on her overalls. She'd clipped her hair back as best she could with the barrettes she had in her purse. She still couldn't believe it when she saw Pastor Matthew go into the kitchen with a mop. "But he's the minister!"

"I hope you're not saying that men can't scrub floors," Brad said. Millie looked over at him. He had speckles of black on his face and his forehead was damp. He had been working on some black marks about ten feet away from her, and Millie had to admit he was doing a good job.

"Well, ah, no, I wasn't saying that exactly." Millie wondered what she *had* been meaning to say. Of course, she knew that some men worked at cleaning. She'd seen janitors before. But, somehow, even with the janitors, she'd always assumed that they never cleaned or helped out at home.

"I'm just surprised that a minister would be doing the cleaning," Millie finally said. "Isn't he the boss?"

Mrs. Hargrove chuckled. "He'd be the first to tell you that he's not."

Millie couldn't figure it all out.

"When was the last time you did this?" Millie demanded as she sat back and looked straight at Brad. Even he must not clean regularly.

Brad stopped scrubbing. "Me?"

Millie nodded.

"I've never done this before," Brad said.

Ah, Millie thought to herself, she was right.

"At least not here," Brad continued. "But I do my share of cleaning up after other people. Just ask Charlie. We all take turns."

Millie frowned. This isn't what she expected. But even if Brad was willing to clean something on occasion, that didn't explain why the minister would.

"I thought ministers told people what to do," Millie said finally. She was puzzled. She had always thought that getting close to God would mean that she'd be run ragged doing errands for Him. He was powerful and He was male. That meant there would be no end to doing things for Him. "He should tell somebody to scrub the floor."

Mrs. Hargrove nodded. "I know it seems like that's the way it would work. But God has turned everything upside down."

Millie felt like she was the one who'd been turned upside down. Why would someone who could order others around do anything? "And where's Glory?"

"I think she's painting a scene for the pageant," Mrs. Hargrove said as she put the blue crayons in a plastic bag and tied a knot in the bag. "Everyone decided to try a simpler pageant this year, but we still wanted it to be nice."

Millie wasn't so sure she wanted to talk about God, but she wanted to talk about the Christmas pageant even less. It seemed like every time anyone brought up the Christmas pageant, they also brought up Forrest. When Millie thought of Forrest, she remembered those Christmas stockings in her trunk and wondered if she'd ever be able to fulfill Forrest's final request.

"But who does all the praying if the minister scrubs the floor?" Millie asked. She remembered the blue card in her pocket and pulled it out. "It asks for things to pray about here—I thought the minister would do all that."

Millie figured the church must pull in lots of prayer requests each week. It would keep the minister busy praying for all of them.

"Well, he certainly does some of it. But we all pray," Mrs. Hargrove said as she looked at the blue card. "I'm glad to see the sheriff got the cards to you. Have you filled one out yet? I'm happy to take yours and put it with the others."

"I'll do it when I finish scrubbing," Millie put the card back in her pocket. She hadn't been going to fill one out. She had told herself there was no point. She thought God didn't care about her or the things that worried her. But now she was beginning to wonder if she had been wrong. Maybe He did care.

"Can I put down a secret request?" Millie asked. She didn't know how to name some of the longings she was starting to feel. But if God were as smart as everyone seemed to think, He would know what she meant.

"Of course." Mrs. Hargrove nodded. "That sounds fine."

Millie went back to scrubbing.

"The baking soda is working," Millie said as she rinsed off the piece of floor she'd just scrubbed. Millie leaned back on her heels and stretched her back.

Mrs. Hargrove stood up and walked over to where Millie had scrubbed. "Why—my goodness— it sure is! What a blessing!"

"I'm glad it's working."

Millie liked looking around the church when it was almost empty like this. Brad had moved over by the pulpit to scrub the floor there, and Mrs. Hargrove still stood next to where Millie was scrubbing. The Christmas tree Millie had noticed on Sunday looked even more humble as it stood beside the pulpit.

"We decorated a tree last night, too," Millie told

Mrs. Hargrove. "It's a homemade one like the one here. It's beautiful."

Mrs. Hargrove nodded. "Sometimes they're the best ones. The Sunday school classes made the decorations for the tree here."

"Brad made our decorations."

Brad looked up from where he was scrubbing. His knees ached, and they felt stuck to the wet floor. But even with all that, his knees went weak when he saw the look on Millie's face as she talked about the decorations. She was describing their tree to Mrs. Hargrove, and it was apparent that any annoyance she might have felt toward him this morning was not felt toward the Christmas tree back at the bunkhouse.

Millie loved that old pathetic Christmas tree.

Brad was watching Millie and didn't pay any attention to the shadow that was passing beside him.

"So, that's the way it is," Pastor Matthew said quietly.

Brad looked up. "It's the tree she likes. She doesn't have much use for me."

Pastor Matthew smiled. "Well, we don't know that for sure, do we?"

Brad figured he did know, but he didn't want to contradict the man. Brad just waited for what he was sure was coming next. A minister was supposed to say something about faith and God and how everyone should reach for the impossible. But the minister didn't say anything, so finally Brad added, "I wouldn't think there's any point in praying about something like this."

Brad waited a minute for the pastor to disagree with him. Finally, Brad could no longer contain his feeling of hope. "Is there?"

Pastor Matthew smiled. "God cares about love, if that's what you're asking."

"I wasn't thinking that—" Brad swallowed and then stopped. "I mean it wouldn't be right to ask God something like this—I mean, He doesn't cast love spells or anything, does He? Something that would make Millie stay around awhile so she could get to know me."

Pastor Matthew smiled. "Maybe not love spells, but He can work miracles, and less than that seems to be required here. After we finish, stop by my house for a few minutes, and we'll pray about it. Glory's over painting the scenery for the pageant and we can have some privacy. That is, if you want it to be private."

Brad glanced at Millie. He sure did want it to be private. He didn't know what she would think if he said a prayer about her staying in Dry Creek. Come to think of it, he didn't know what he thought about it himself. He'd never prayed about anything before that he could remember.

"God might not know me." Brad thought he should mention the fact to the minister. "We don't exactly talk."

Pastor Matthew nodded. "I figured that might be the way it is."

Brad looked around the church. It wasn't just Millie who might find it odd if he decided to pray. The guys in the bunkhouse would never understand. Brad looked back at the minister. "This is confidential, right? I mean, seeing a minister is like seeing a lawyer, isn't it? You can't tell anyone, can you?"

Pastor Matthew smiled. "My lips are sealed."

Brad nodded. That was good. He didn't need a rumor going around that Brad Parker was in such deep trouble with his love life that he had to ask God to help him. Because, of course, he wasn't in deep trouble. Not really. Was he?

Chapter Thirteen

Millie had heard about the old barn that the town of Dry Creek had turned into a community center. There hadn't been cows in the barn for years, and someone had added heaters to the building when they had the Christmas pageant inside it a couple of years ago. The wood plank floor of the barn was scrubbed clean, and the unfinished wood had a weathered look to it.

The middle of the barn was the stage, and chairs had been set up all around the walls of the barn. High, tall windows let light into the area and several bales of hay were pushed against the far wall. The faint scent of paint thinner filled the cold, moist air inside the barn.

Millie looked up and saw the pulleys on the rafters that allowed the angel to swing down over the audience during the pageant. When Forrest had tried to kill the angel, he had waited until after she made her swing out and back. In fact, the pageant was over when he'd pulled out his gun. Forrest had been able to hide behind some tall screens that had been placed around and, at first, no one had seen that he had his gun pointed at the angel.

There were no screens anymore. In fact, as Millie looked around, she saw a shiny new lock on the back door to the barn and there were no places to hide behind screens or curtains or large chairs. Even the hay was pushed firmly against the wall.

Forrest would have been saddened to see how his actions had made the people of Dry Creek feel unsafe. The lock on the barn wasn't the only new lock Millie had seen as she walked over to the barn from the church.

The day was still cold and Millie didn't have any snow boots to wear, so she had walked in the path of several tire tracks to avoid the loose snow that was lying on the ground. Brad had said he needed to discuss something with the minister and had gone off with him, telling Millie he would meet her later over at the barn.

Millie was glad to have a few minutes alone and lingered in the doorway to the barn for just a minute. The snow that was predicted for today was still not falling. The clouds had gotten grayer, though, and the air felt weighted. Something about the day matched her restlessness—like she was carrying around something cold and heavy inside of herself and she needed to let go of it just like the clouds needed to let go of their moisture.

It was those Christmas stockings, she said to herself. When she put the money in them and delivered them, she would have done all she could in memory of Forrest. She would be released from the guilt she felt on behalf of him.

When that was done, she would be able to leave Dry Creek, she told herself. The tie she felt holding her here would be gone. Her life would go back to the way it was, and she would have to try and be content.

Millie stepped all of the way inside the barn and quietly closed the door. The day was so overcast that someone had turned on the electrical lights that were attached to some of the rafters.

The pastor's wife, Glory, was kneeling in the middle of the stage area and painting what looked like a trellis. Old newspapers were spread around underneath wooden figures. Several open cans of paint sat around on the newspapers.

"May I take a look?" Millie asked.

Glory looked up from her paints and smiled. "You can take more than a look. You're welcome to pick up a brush and join me."

Millie walked over to where Glory was painting.

Large wooden cutout figures were lying on the floor beside Glory. Some of them had been painted and some of them were still raw wood. Millie counted three sheep.

"Is that a dog?" If the cutout had been any less like a dog, Millie would have assumed it was supposed to be a sheep.

Glory nodded. "I'm afraid that over the years, our pageant has picked up some additional characters that you won't find in the Biblical account of the Nativity. One of them is a dog named Chester. He's supposed to be a sheepdog, but everyone knows Chester just shows up anywhere in the pageant."

Millie knelt down and sat the same way Glory was sitting with her legs crossed. "I thought Chester was a real dog."

Millie remembered Forrest telling her about the dog that chased the chicken in the Christmas pageant he had seen two years ago.

Glory nodded. "He is. This is the committee's way of compromising. They decided not to have any live animals in the pageant this year, but they did ask that we make a cutout of Chester just like we have a cutout of the sheep. It's to keep the children happy. They all like having Chester in the pageant."

"It seems like in a barn you would have real animals," Millie said.

Glory nodded. "It was a difficult decision to cut back this year. But people just didn't seem to have the heart to put on a full-scale pageant. Usually we invite some of the area churches, but this year we're just doing it simple and for ourselves."

Millie didn't want to ask why the people of Dry Creek were having a difficult time. She was afraid she knew.

"It's the economy," Glory added. "Everybody just seems a little more worried this year than last."

"Oh, the economy," Millie said. That wasn't so bad. "It's tough all over."

Glory looked up from her painting and smiled. "Is that what happened to you? Did you lose your job?"

Glory was friendly and her questions didn't have any sting in them.

Millie shook her head. "I still have my job. I'm on a break. It might not be much of a job, but it's waiting there for me when I go back in a few days."

"Well, that's good," Glory said as she picked up a brush and dipped it into a small can of black paint. "It seems like around here everyone is looking for work. It's always worse at Christmas. My husband keeps thinking about adding another part-time person to the staff at the hardware store just to give someone a little help."

"That's nice of him," Millie said as she looked

over the brushes. If she wasn't careful, she would be telling all of her worries to Glory, and she didn't want to do that. She would keep Forrest's secret until she could fulfill his request.

Millie nodded her head at the cutout animals. "Would you like me to paint one of the figures? If there's something simple, that is."

"Take any one of the sheep," Glory said. "Just paint it all white, and then we'll go back and paint on the hooves and the face."

Millie ran out of white paint after she painted two of the sheep.

"I think they had black sheep back then," Glory said as she passed the black can of paint. "At least it's a better color than the brown we're using for the donkey."

"There wouldn't be a black sheep at the Nativity scene, would there?" Millie asked dubiously.

Glory chuckled. "I don't know why not—the church always seems to specialize in black sheep."

Millie picked up a brush and dipped it into the black paint. She was beginning to think that the church was nothing like she had ever thought it would be.

The afternoon light had darkened by the time Millie finished all of the sheep.

"This one looks a little hungry," Millie said. Glory had given her suggestions on how to paint the sheep's faces, but then had left it up to Millie. "I hope the children don't mind."

Each of the cutout animals had straps on the back where a child was going to hold it during the pageant.

"The twins have already suffered their own disappointment. They wanted me to make some dragons, but I drew the line. I said I'd do Chester, but that was it. No dragons." Glory gave Millie a rueful look. "I think they wanted to surprise the angel when she comes out and says 'Behold, I bring you glad tidings.'"

Millie had never actually read the Bible. "There aren't…?"

Glory shook her head. "No. But the twins swear there should have been. I think they figure if Mary and Joseph had come in riding a dragon, the innkeeper would have given them better accommodations."

"That's kind of cute."

Glory sighed and stood up. "Yeah, they're hard to say no to. In fact—" Glory walked over to the bales and picked up two cutout figures that had been lying on top of them "—I made them these little ones for later—after the pageant."

Millie smiled at the two little dragon figures Glory had made. They were both still unpainted.

"Mrs. Hargrove is going to flunk us all in Sunday school if they use these in the pageant," Glory said.

Both Millie and Glory heard the voices of the men and looked toward the entrance of the barn. Pastor Matthew and Brad opened the door and stepped inside the barn.

"How's it coming?" Pastor Matthew asked.

"Good," Glory said.

Millie nodded and smiled.

Pastor Matthew walked over to Glory and gave her a kiss. Brad walked over to Millie, and she had a moment's panic that he meant to kiss her, as well.

"I painted a black sheep," Millie blurted out, and turned to walk back to where the animal cutouts were.

Well, Brad thought to himself, he guessed Pastor Matthew was right when he said God didn't hand out any love potions to people. Millie hadn't gazed up to him with anything near the look of adoration that Glory had on her face when she turned toward her husband.

Of course, Brad decided, it might be too soon for Millie to feel that settled, married love that Glory seemed to feel. Maybe a love potion would start out different—maybe there'd be a tingling sensation or something.

"Are you feeling okay?" Brad asked as Millie walked away from him. "Not dizzy or anything?"

"My one leg has a cramp in it," Millie said as she turned to him and then sat down. "It must be the way I was sitting. How did you know?"

"Oh, ah, there's a lot of paint fumes in here. I figured they might be affecting everyone."

"I don't think they'd give me a leg cramp," Millie said and stretched her leg out in front of her. "Unless it's some kind of slow-acting poison or something."

Brad had to congratulate himself. He'd just witnessed the opposite of a love potion. Millie wasn't even smiling at him now. In fact, she was frowning at him. He couldn't have done a worse job of it if he'd tried.

Brad sighed. He wasn't the kind of man who could be subtle. He'd just have to plough forward and hope that Pastor Matthew's God would have mercy on him.

"I wouldn't worry about it—the fumes aren't poisonous. I'm sure they haven't affected you at all. And that's good you're able to be around the paint fumes and not get sick," Brad said. He needed to get it out there before she started thinking she had the plague. "You know there's a job that's going to be opening up soon at the hardware store. Probably working with paint some. It might be a natural fit for you."

Brad decided Millie was looking at him like he'd sprouted another ear. "Some people really enjoy working in the hardware store."

"I've always worked in restaurants."

"Well, maybe Linda needs someone to help her

out in the café," Brad said. She wasn't making this easy for him.

"The café's closed."

"Well, now it is, sure—but it'll open again when Linda gets back from Los Angeles."

Brad didn't know how a man could break a sweat when the air in the barn was cold. Maybe he was the one getting sick from the fumes.

"Do you think she'd hire me?" Millie asked. Brad swore he saw a flare of hope in her eyes before it died. "After all this fuss about me breaking in and all. I mean, she might think I was planning to rob her."

"Oh."

"Of course I wasn't robbing her," Millie added. "It's just that—"

Brad nodded. He needed another prayer session with the pastor. After they'd talked and prayed, Brad had begun to have hope that Millie would stay in Dry Creek long enough for the two of them to have a proper courtship. He didn't think Millie was the kind of woman who would get engaged after knowing a man for only a day or two.

No, he needed some time to show her they would be good together. It didn't seem like it was such a big miracle for God to perform. It didn't require bringing someone back to life from the dead or parting a sea or anything. All Brad needed was a little time.

"How's your car doing?" Brad asked. That car might be his best hope. If the thing broke down, Millie would be around for at least a week while they sent away for parts.

"Fine," Millie said.

Brad nodded. He'd pray about that car of hers. He wasn't even sure you could call it a miracle if the car broke down before she left Dry Creek. In fact, it would probably be a miracle if it *didn't* break down. All he needed to do was have her drive it around until it died. He might not even need any prayer to pull this off. A full tank of gas might be all he needed.

Millie decided Brad was right about the paint fumes. They certainly seemed to be affecting him. One minute he was frowning, and the next minute he looked perfectly happy.

"I'll go open the door," Millie said as she stood up. The air outside was cold, but it was better to be a little cold than to be affected by those fumes.

When Millie opened the door, she saw that it was starting to snow. Tiny flakes were drifting to the ground. "It's snowing."

"We should get your car back to the ranch before the roads get slippery," Brad said as he walked over and stood behind her.

"I could ride back with you," Millie said.

"Really?" Brad looked happy and then he looked

stern. "No, it's better if you drive your car back. Wouldn't want to leave it in Dry Creek. And your tank is almost full, isn't it?"

Millie nodded. She knew to fill her tank in Miles City. Brad was right. She did like to have her car close by just in case. Besides, she still had those stockings in the trunk.

"You might want to drive it out to the barn when you get back to the ranch, too. Get some more practice driving in the snow. And then you'll want to drive it back tonight for the pageant."

Millie nodded again. She definitely needed her car tonight. It was nice of Brad to realize that, especially since he'd seemed so intent this morning on keeping her car off of the roads.

Chapter Fourteen

Millie stood outside the bunkhouse of the Elkton Ranch and stared down at the contents of her car's trunk. The sun was setting and light snow was still falling. It had been snowing for several hours, but Charlie had said the roads were not in danger of being blocked.

Charlie seemed particularly pleased that there was no reason to worry about the roads. He'd already convinced all of the men in the bunkhouse to drive into Dry Creek tonight to see the Christmas pageant.

It was the Christmas pageant that was causing Millie's frown. She had just slipped a hundred-dollar bill into each of the red stockings she'd made, and she'd stacked the stockings alphabetically in two neat piles in the trunk of her car. She was all ready to deliver the stockings, but she didn't know how to do it now.

At first, she had thought she would go to the barn before the pageant and lay the stockings around the room on the chairs. But then she realized it would create a lot of fuss, and she didn't want to take anything away from the pageant.

No, she decided, she'd have to deliver the stockings after the pageant. Maybe she could just leave them inside the barn door on the bench where people sat when they needed to take off their snow boots. Everyone would see them on their way out of the barn.

When Millie made her decision, she expected the heavy feeling inside of her to lift. She had almost completed her task. It hadn't gone as Forrest probably thought it would, but she would be able to deliver the hundred-dollar bills and finish what she had started. She should feel good, not sad.

After all, things were working out. Millie figured she was still a stranger to most people in Dry Creek—at least as much of a stranger as Forrest had been when he had been here. He'd only been in the little town a few days, as well. When she left, even the people she had met would eventually forget her name and what she looked like.

She would truly be a Christmas stranger.

And that, Millie finally admitted, was why she

was sad. The people of Dry Creek might forget her, but she would never forget them. Not Glory, or Charlie, or Mrs. Hargrove. And especially not Brad.

Of course, Brad would forget her, Millie decided in a burst of irritation. The man couldn't wait for her to get in her car and drive off somewhere. He didn't even seem to care where she was going. She could have suggested she drive to the moon, and he would have encouraged her to do it. Just to please him, she'd already driven up and down the driveway into the Elkton ranch several times this afternoon.

Millie looked over toward the bunkhouse. The last time she'd parked her car this afternoon, she'd deliberately parked so she could see in the big window in the living room. Frost had edged the window, but she could still see the little Christmas tree on the opposite wall.

That tree would always be her favorite Christmas tree, even though Millie vowed she would decorate one for herself next Christmas. Something about this Christmas had changed the feeling she had inside that she needed to be on the outside looking in at Christmas.

Maybe it was going to church here and seeing the people all work together. Or being Christmas company at the bunkhouse. Or even riding out to get the Christmas tree with Brad.

Maybe it was all of it. She supposed it didn't

matter. What mattered was that she no longer felt so alone. Not even, she swallowed, when she was leaving.

There, she thought to herself, she'd said it. She was leaving Dry Creek.

She really had no choice. She knew the job at the hardware store was a charity job and was meant for someone in Dry Creek. The pastor hadn't created the job to give it to someone who had just come into town. It might be an option to work at the café, but Linda was gone and there was no one to ask about working there.

It wasn't the stockings in the trunk that were bothering her, Millie finally admitted. It was her small suitcase that was sitting next to them. Millie had slipped the suitcase out of the bunkhouse earlier this afternoon without anyone seeing her.

She needed to be ready to leave Dry Creek. The longer she stayed, the harder it would be to leave.

Millie wondered if Forrest was looking down from heaven and seeing what a mess she'd made of her version of the plan. She knew now that Forrest had wanted her to meet the people of Dry Creek.

She had wanted to sneak into town and leave before anyone saw her. She would have succeeded, too, if Brad hadn't been parked behind the café.

For the first time it struck her just how odd that was. What had Brad been doing parked there? He couldn't have been having trouble with his pickup, because the old thing had started right up when he turned the ignition. And, if he'd had a flat tire, he wouldn't have been parked behind the café. Brad must have been sitting there for a long time, because she knew he hadn't driven back there while she was inside.

There was only one reason Millie could think of for Brad to be there, and she didn't like it.

Millie slammed the trunk of her car and headed back to the bunkhouse.

The main room of the bunkhouse was empty, but Millie heard someone in the kitchen.

Charlie stood at the stove stirring a big pot of something. Whatever it was, it smelled good, but Millie hardly noticed.

"I have a question for you," Millie said. She couldn't think of a subtle way to ask what she needed to know. "Around here, when you see a car that's pulled off the road at night, what do you think?"

Charlie looked up from his stirring. "Car trouble."

Millie shook her head. "There was no car trouble."

"Maybe it's late and no one's in the car," Charlie suggested.

Millie shook her head again. "Oh, someone was in the car all right."

Charlie smiled. "Well, if there's two someones in the car, then you have your answer. There's nothing quite as romantic as sitting together under the stars."

Millie nodded her head. She didn't know what had happened to the woman that had been in the pickup with Brad. "Do people around here ever drive into Dry Creek and leave their cars at the café before they go into Miles City?"

"Sure, if they're going to drive together most of the way." Charlie looked at her quizzically. "You worried about your car dying or something? If you are, anyone would be happy to give you a lift anywhere you need to go."

Millie shook her head. "No, my car is fine. Thanks."

Charlie shrugged. "Well, if you need anything, let me know."

Millie nodded. What she needed wasn't something Charlie could give her.

Millie walked back into the main room of the bunkhouse and sat down on a sofa. What she needed was to leave Dry Creek and Brad Parker before the cracks that were starting in her heart caused it to break in two.

Brad stopped and scraped his feet before he entered the bunkhouse. He'd been forced to drive back from Miles City all by himself. You'd think the other guys had never smelled women's perfume before. Brad had been determined to find the perfume that suited Millie best, and how was he supposed to tell what each one smelled like if he didn't have the sales clerk spray the air in front of him?

The other guys had gone together and bought Millie a wool scarf and some mittens, but Brad wanted a special gift, and that was a challenge in the small department store in Miles City.

Finally, Brad had settled on something called "Snow Angel" that the salesclerk swore was light and sounded, from everything he had told her, like it would be perfect for Millie.

Brad saw that Millie had been looking at the Christmas tree before he came in. When she heard him, she turned around.

"Sorry to let the cold air in," Brad said. When he had opened the door to the bunkhouse, a gust of wind had followed him in. "The wind's blowing out there."

"You must be cold," Millie said as she stood up. "I could start the coffeepot."

Brad shook his head. "I'll just warm up by the fire."

Brad had the bottle of perfume in his pocket. The clerk had wrapped the perfume for him, but he decided to wait until after the pageant to put the box under the tree. He didn't want Millie to think she needed to give him a present, so he didn't want her to know about the box.

Millie sniffed the air. The closer she walked to Brad, the more she could smell the perfume. It wasn't some kind of cologne for a man, either. No, the perfume was definitely the kind a woman would wear.

"I thought you were out with the other guys," Millie said.

"Oh, I was," Brad said. Millie thought he looked a little guilty, but he continued, "We had some business to take care of."

Millie wondered what the woman's name was. Not that it was any of her business, she reminded herself. "Well, that's good then, I guess."

Just then the rest of the ranch hands came into the bunkhouse. Millie noticed as each one filed through the door that none of them smelled of perfume. Which meant that, wherever Brad had been, he hadn't been with them.

Millie decided, as she blinked a few times, that it was just as well that she was leaving tonight after the pageant.

Chapter Fifteen

The pageant was scheduled to begin at seven o'clock, and by then the sky was completely dark. The snow flurries had stopped an hour earlier, and the clouds had parted enough to allow a few stars to shine through the blackness. The lights inside the barn showed through the high windows, and Millie could see into the barn each time someone opened the main door.

Millie parked her car as close to the barn as she could. She was surprised that Brad had offered to give her a ride to the pageant. She almost asked him why he wasn't giving a ride to Miss Perfume. But she didn't. She couldn't ride with him anyway, because she had the Christmas stockings. The Christmas stockings were supposed to be a surprise, and she no longer felt any desire to tell Brad all her secrets.

Brad would know soon enough anyway. Millie had decided the town of Dry Creek should know that Forrest was sorry, and so she'd enclosed a note in Mrs. Hargrove's stocking explaining everything.

The air was chilly when Millie opened the door to her car, and she walked quickly to the barn. She'd come back later and get the stockings.

The light inside the barn was dim, and Millie could see the trellis in the middle of the floor that had a sign hanging from it saying Bethlehem Inn. From the sounds of the shuffling feet and giggles coming from behind a makeshift curtain at the end of the barn, the animals were getting ready to play their parts.

A stereo was set up in the barn and Millie could hear the muted sounds of Christmas carols. She also heard the sound of Brad's voice and saw him talking with a group of men gathered near a coffeepot in one corner of the barn. There was no one standing near him who might be Miss Perfume, but then, Millie reasoned, the woman might be one of the ones she saw helping the children get into their costumes.

Millie walked over to a place where there were several empty chairs. Walking through the people of Dry Creek wasn't as easy as it sounded. People smiled at her and greeted her every step of the way. She'd refused several offers of a chair by the time she reached the one she wanted.

Millie picked a chair that had empty chairs on

both sides of it. She didn't want to get to know any more people in Dry Creek. She'd just be leaving soon anyway.

Someone turned the music up louder and flicked the light switches. That must be the signal that the pageant was ready to begin. The people who weren't already seated started to move to the sides of the barn where the chairs were positioned.

"May I?"

Millie heard Brad's low question as he sat down in the chair next to her.

Brad didn't know why Millie had such a surprised look on her face. He'd followed her car into Dry Creek to be sure she didn't have any mechanical trouble on the way. He'd even sat in his pickup for a little bit after they both parked until it became clear that she was not going to go inside right away. The only reason he'd gone in ahead of her was because he was beginning to feel like a stalker.

She should have figured out by now that he was planning to sit beside her.

"You're wearing perfume." Brad noticed the fact as everyone around them was sitting down. He hadn't thought she had been wearing perfume before. The scent she was wearing now was light and fruity. Maybe she wouldn't like the perfume he had bought for her. He should have asked if she had a preference. "What kind is it?"

"It's not perfume. It's peach soap."

"Ah, soap." Brad didn't know if that meant she would like perfume or not. Well, it was too late now anyway. He planned to give her the perfume tonight when they got back to the bunkhouse. He could only hope for the best.

The lights were dimmed almost completely for a minute.

Brad assumed by the sounds that the children were getting in place for the pageant.

The donkey was the first thing to come out from behind the curtain. The donkey was followed by nine-year-old Angie Loden wearing a blue table-cloth wrapped sari-style around her. A pillow made her look awkwardly pregnant, but the look in her eye made her look like a schoolteacher.

Millie smiled when she saw the little girl in blue. She wondered if girls playing at being Mary always wore blue because they had all seen the same stained glass picture of Jesus talking to the little girl in the blue robe.

Millie heard the choked-back laughter as the girl started her walk. She obviously wasn't as worried about talking to Jesus as she was about correcting the boy who was playing Joseph. Millie could almost hear the girl scolding him in a low whisper as the boy tried to keep up with the girl and the donkey. The boy was having a hard time not tripping on the hem of his robe, until finally Mary reached over and adjusted the belt around the robe so that material bunched up around the boy's waist, making the robe shorter.

One of the Curtis twins was carrying the cutout figure of the donkey, and he was leading the girl along the path toward the makeshift inn.

The Christmas music was turned almost completely off, and another voice came from the loudspeakers. Millie decided the voice was from a tape, because she didn't recognize it from the voices she'd heard in Dry Creek.

"At that time, Augustus Caesar sent an order that all people in the countries under Roman rule must list their names in the register," the voice said, as Mary, Joseph and the donkey slowly walked toward the inn.

Millie had not realized the whole Nativity scene started because someone wanted to collect everyone's name. She thought of the stockings in her trunk. They made a more appropriate Christmas gift than she had thought. She'd had to collect all the names of the people, as well. She knew how much trouble that could be. It gave her a certain empathy with Augustus Caesar.

Millie sat back and decided to enjoy the pageant. She chuckled along with everyone else when the innkeeper looked uncertain about whether or not he had any rooms. Finally, Mary looked down some imaginary hall and said she could see his inn was filled with tourists, and so there were no rooms for those people who really needed a place to stay.

The angel didn't fly overhead like she had in other pageants, but a blond girl climbed a ladder and flapped her wings while shouting out "Behold!" with as much enthusiasm as the original angel must have had.

Chester, the real dog, chose this moment to run inside and shake the snow off of his coat.

Millie expected the adults to scold and ask who had let Chester into the barn, but they all just seemed to shrug their shoulders and turn their attention back to the unfolding pageant.

It must have been when the shepherds were coming in from their fields that Brad put his arm on the back of her chair. Millie could feel it on her shoulders. She'd been laughing at Chester's efforts to herd the wooden sheep, and she looked up at Brad.

Brad was happy. He'd moved his arm from the back of Millie's chair to her shoulders and she'd smiled up at him. Her face was still glowing from the laughter, and even though he wasn't the reason for her laughter, the delight she was feeling spilled over onto him.

Brad began to wonder if he was wrong about

how long it took for a man to fall in love. He'd thought he needed to get to know Millie. But he was beginning to think he knew all he needed to know right now.

If the sheep hadn't arrived at the inn just then, Brad would have whispered something silly in Millie's ear. But she'd turned her gaze back to the pageant, and he wanted her to remember every single moment of this night. He'd wait and whisper in her ear tonight after he'd given her the perfume.

Millie sighed when the wise men started walking toward the inn. The littlest of the boys had trouble keeping his crown on his head and had to set his golden box of spices down on the floor so he could adjust his crown. Chester, of course, had to come over and sniff at the spices until he sneezed. Whatever it was that was supposed to be myrrh scattered across the floor.

All in all, Millie thought when the lights were dimmed for the last time, the pageant had been de-lightful. It had also gone much too fast.

Millie looked over at Brad. She'd have to say goodbye to him later. Maybe she wouldn't have to leave right after she delivered the stockings. But, for now, she should make her move while the children all came back on stage to sing "Silent Night."

The air outside the barn felt sharply cold to Millie after she had been inside. Brad had thought she was leaving to use the restroom, or he would have come with her. Setting the stockings out for everyone was something she had to do by herself. Forrest had been her friend, and she would help him do what he could to make his actions up to the people of Dry Creek. She had left Mrs. Hargrove's stocking on top of all the others, since it had the note inside it.

Millie could barely hold all of the stockings in her arms, but she didn't want to make two trips. She planned to leave them on the bench inside the door. Now that the pageant was almost over, it wouldn't be long before someone turned and saw the stockings.

Millie had left the door slightly open so that she could just push it completely open with her arms. She managed to come back inside the barn and stand by the door without anyone noticing her.

Everyone inside the barn was looking at the children singing in the middle of the floor, and Millie could see why. With their crooked angel wings and dragging shepherd robes, the children were charming. Even Chester was sitting calmly beside the wooden sheep while they sang.

Millie set the stack of stockings down on the bench. There were mittens and scarves on the shelf above the bench and some rubber boots under the bench. But the bench itself was clear until Millie set down her stockings.

When children finished their last notes of

"Silent Night," Millie stepped back outside the door. She left the door cracked open so she could hear people's excitement. Within minutes, she heard the first exclamation.

"Look at these!" a woman's voice said.

"Don't touch them," a man's voice answered.

"Why, they're Millie's stockings," Mrs. Hargrove said.

Millie smiled. The older woman would convince everyone to trust that the stockings were okay.

"Look what's inside them!" That voice sounded like it came from a teenage boy. "It's hundred-dollar bills!"

"What's money like that doing here?" the man who had spoken earlier said.

"I wonder if the stores are still open. I'd love to get the kids real presents for Christmas and not just new mittens," a woman said.

"Maybe I'll get my train set," a little voice said.

Millie heard a chorus of excited whispers until the man spoke again

"But what's the money doing here?" the man insisted loudly. "If we don't know what it's doing here, we shouldn't touch it."

"It's from Millie," Mrs. Hargrove said. "She left a note."

Millie could hear the people crowding next to Mrs. Hargrove.

"Is it counterfeit?" someone asked.

"No," Mrs. Hargrove said slowly. "It's money from Forrest."

"Who's Forrest?" someone else asked.

"That's the name of the hit man," someone else answered. "But what's that got to do with that woman?"

"Millie was his friend," Mrs. Hargrove said. "And she writes that Forrest wanted us to know he was sorry for what he did here."

There was almost total silence on the other side of the door.

Finally, Brad spoke. His voice was low, but Millie could hear it clearly.

"She was friends with a hit man?" Brad's voice contained a world of confusion and disbelief. "What kind of person is friends with a hit man?"

Millie turned to walk down the stairs. She'd heard enough. It was time to leave.

The air was just as cold when Millie walked back to her car, but she didn't notice a thing. The cold outside didn't begin to compare with the cold inside of her.

She opened the door to her car and was grateful that the car started right up when she turned the ignition. She backed the car away from the barn before she turned on the headlights. She didn't want her car lights to shine into the windows of the barn.

She would leave Dry Creek as quietly as she had come.

Millie rolled down the window as she pulled away from the barn. She wanted to hear any last music that might be coming from the pageant. She thought they would turn the stereo on again with the Christmas carols, but she didn't hear anything.

Finally, she rolled her window back up. She'd have to listen to her radio instead.

Chapter Sixteen

Brad sat down on the steps outside the church. He wasn't planning to go to church this morning, but it had snowed last night, and he figured he'd shovel off the steps just to show God and Mrs. Hargrove that he didn't hold any hard feelings toward them. Well, not many hard feelings anyway. Which wasn't bad considering he had met the woman of his dreams and neither one of them had helped him to keep track of her.

Millie had slipped away from the barn on Christmas Eve, and Brad hadn't even known it for a full fifteen minutes. She'd said she was going to the restroom, and he'd believed her. By the time he realized she wasn't inside the barn, he'd gone racing outside only to see that her car was gone.

He'd gotten into his pickup and followed the road

all of the way into Miles City thinking he would find her. When he didn't see her, he figured she had gone the other direction out of Dry Creek, and he came barreling back and drove all the way into North Dakota before he turned around.

That old car of hers went faster than he'd thought possible.

Brad stopped shoveling and leaned on his shovel. The days had been gloomy ever since Christmas. He'd always dreaded Christmas. But now he knew it wasn't Christmas that was his problem. It was all of the rest of the days that stretched out after Christmas was gone that were going to give him grief.

Even with all of the excitement in Dry Creek these days, Brad was miserable. Every time someone talked about what they had spent their hundred dollars on, Brad thought of Millie. He'd thought of her through conversations about toy dolls and new tennis shoes. Mrs. Hargrove even informed him about the new ice-crushing blender she'd bought with part of her money.

Brad still had his hundred-dollar bill in his shirt pocket next to his heart.

Brad had wished a million times since that night that he hadn't been shocked Millie had been friends with a hit man. He shouldn't have even been surprised. He knew Millie would be loyal to her friends, and that she took up with the underdogs. It only made sense that she would stand by her friends if they were arrested.

He wished he could tell her, though, that it was her note that made the difference to the people of Dry Creek, and not the money. Just hearing that the hit man had been deeply sorry allowed people to start trusting in strangers again.

Brad started moving his shovel again. The thing he really regretted, however, was that he'd never asked Millie for her address. He was sitting here with his heart full of things to tell her, and he didn't even know how to find her. All he really knew was that she lived somewhere around the waterfront in Seattle.

Brad had finished shoveling all of the steps when he saw the pastor come out of the parsonage and start walking toward the church.

"Good morning," Pastor Matthew called out. "You're joining us this morning for church, aren't you?"

Brad grimaced as the minister came closer. "I'm not fit for polite company these days."

Brad ran his hand over his face. He hadn't shaved for a couple of days, and he figured he looked pretty rough.

"Having a hard time?" the pastor asked as he came closer to Brad.

Brad nodded. "Not much I can do about it though."

The pastor looked at Brad for a minute. "If you want to come to my office with me, I think I have something that might cheer you up."

"No offense," Brad said as he leaned against his shovel, "but this is something prayer can't fix."

"God might surprise you," the pastor said as he started climbing the steps.

Brad figured God had already had His chance to work on Millie and had missed His opportunity completely.

"What you might not understand is that I need concrete help," Brad said as he started to follow the pastor. "I mean prayer is nice, but I need, well, real help."

The pastor had walked up the steps to the church and opened the main door. Brad still followed him as the minister crossed the back of the church and opened a door into a small room.

Pastor Matthew went to his desk, picked something up and turned around to face Brad.

"Is this concrete enough for you?" the pastor held out a blue card.

"Millie filled out a visitor's form?"

The tightness Brad had felt in his chest all week started to loosen.

The pastor nodded. "Of course, it wouldn't be right for me to give the information on this card to just anyone."

"Oh."

"However, I figure that a representative from the church should be allowed to call on Millie, since she did mark the box that asked for a visit from someone from the church."

"I've been to the church twice now—if the Christmas pageant counts."

Pastor Matthew grinned as he held the card out to Brad. "All you really need to do is invite Millie to next Sunday's service. I can even send a church bulletin along with you, so you have all the information."

Brad understood why people throughout the ages had kissed the feet of holy men when they got their prayers answered. "Thank you."

Ruby's café was on the Seattle waterfront, and most mornings in January the air was cold. The floor at Ruby's was made of thick wooden planks and the walls were filled with large paned glass windows. Ruby believed in natural light, plants and strong coffee. It was the coffee that brought the customers in, but Millie suspected it was the plants that made them want to linger over their meals.

Not that Millie was worried about customers who wouldn't leave.

She had just mixed up the order on table seven. Instead of bringing the man coffee with cream, she had brought him tea with sugar. In all of her years at Ruby's she'd never made a mistake on an order until after she got back from Dry Creek. Since she'd gotten back eight days ago, however, she'd made thirty-two mistakes. The reason she knew the exact number was because the other waitresses were trying to guess the limit of Ruby's patience and they were counting.

Of course, the waitresses all knew Millie's job was safe because they were running shorthanded. The dishwasher had quit, and Ruby had no sooner put the Help Wanted—Dishwasher sign in the window than one of the waitresses had quit, as well.

Not that the other waitresses weren't also sympathetic. They'd cooed and fussed over Millie that first day back until she thought she would have to take to her bed and have herself a good rest just to get some peace from people's good intentions.

Millie had distracted the other waitresses from their sympathy by telling them about the Christmas pageant at Dry Creek. When she left Montana, she fully intended to entertain them all with stories about Brad. But she found the stories she had thought were so funny when they happened now only made her feel sad. Even the story about the spiders would have made her cry if she tried to tell it.

Millie had slipped once when she was talking to Louise and had mentioned that she'd stayed in the bunkhouse in the room of a nice man.

The waitresses at Ruby's weren't usually impressed with someone who was just nice, but they seemed to know there was more to Millie's stories than she was telling.

The door to Ruby's buzzed whenever anyone opened it and came inside. Ruby said the buzzer allowed them to have good customer control. No customer was ever supposed to wait more than five minutes at Ruby's before he or she was seated and offered a cup of coffee.

So it was only natural that all of the waitresses looked up when the buzzer sounded.

Millie's mouth dropped open. In all of the days since she'd left Dry Creek, she never thought she'd look up at Ruby's and see Brad Parker walk into the café.

"What are you doing here?" Millie walked over to the man and asked.

For the hundredth time that day, Brad wondered if his plan was a good one. It was a long drive from Dry Creek to Seattle, and he'd thought of a million clever things to say to Millie when he saw her. But then he'd decided to just be himself and be honest. When he saw how white Millie's face was, however, he wished he had thought of something to tell her that didn't contain the words "I came because of you."

"I came for the job," Brad blurted out. He'd seen

the sign in the window of the diner, and he was only beginning to see the advantages it offered.

"What job?" Millie frowned.

"Dishwasher," Brad guessed. He was almost sure that was what the sign said.

That seemed to leave Millie speechless. Finally, she swallowed. "Here?"

Brad nodded. "I think that's where the job is."

Millie just stared at him.

"I'm hoping they'll take me temporarily. For a few weeks," Brad added. "I could use a break from moving cattle."

Millie might be speechless, but Brad could hear the other waitresses start to chatter. Finally, one of them walked over to him.

Brad saw by the woman's badge that her name was Sherry. Ordinarily, she would be the kind of woman who would catch his eye. Her hair was all highlights and curls. Her fingernails were deep red and slightly pointed. Her smile was friendly and her uniform not buttoned up tight.

"I'm sure Ruby will hire you on the spot," the waitress said as she stepped closer to Brad. "I sure would."

"Back off, Sherry," an older waitress said. "This is a *nice* man."

Brad thought she said the word "nice" like it was a code.

"A *nice* man from Dry Creek, I believe," the older woman said as she gave Sherry a stern look.

Sherry shrugged her shoulders and turned away. "Can't blame a girl for trying."

Millie decided she better set down the coffeepot that she was holding. Come to think of it, she should just sit her whole self down.

Louise seemed to agree. She looked at Millie and said, "Now's a good time to take your break. We're not busy. There's no one on the patio."

Millie nodded as she turned toward the patio.

"Take your time. I'll send out some of those fresh donuts for you and your friend."

Millie walked out to the patio, and even though she heard his footsteps behind her, she was still surprised to see Brad himself behind her there when she came to the table and sat down.

"Mind if I join you?" Brad said.

Millie blinked. She hadn't noticed how nervous he seemed. She had always thought she was the only one who got nervous. "Please do."

Brad sat down at the small table across from Millie.

"What brings you to Seattle?" Millie finally asked.

"You."

Brad knew he'd been clumsy. He hadn't meant to rush Millie like that. "I mean, I came to see you because you asked for a visit from someone from the church."

Brad pulled out the blue visitor's card that Millie had filled out when she was in Dry Creek. The corners were bent because he'd kept it on the dash of his pickup all the way from Montana to Seattle.

"You came to invite me back to church?" Millie sounded incredulous.

"I came to invite you back to Dry Creek," Brad said quietly.

Millie didn't answer right away so he just kept on explaining. "I know it's too big of a decision to make right away. I know you've only known me for a couple of days. But you aren't going to get to know me better unless you're in Dry Creek or I'm here." Brad took a deep breath. "So I thought I'd stay here for a while so we can get to know each other."

Millie started to smile. She felt like someone had turned the sunshine on in the middle of an overcast day. "We're going to get to know each other?"

Brad nodded and started to smile himself.

"You're willing to wash dishes so you can get to know me better?" Millie still couldn't believe it. Most men she knew wouldn't wash dishes for any reason. "You know Ruby throws in the pots and pans, too. It's not just the easy stuff like glasses and silverware."

"I'd figured as much," Brad said as his smile turned into a full grin.

"You do get a share of the tips though," Millie added. "And meals—you get meals."

"I'd settle for a kiss or two from the right waitress," Brad said, and then he remembered something and reached in his pocket. "And I have a Christmas present for you."

Millie looked at the silver box with the red ribbon on it. No one had ever given her such a pretty gift.

Brad handed her the box.

"Go ahead, open it," Brad said.

Millie had half of the paper off when she started to smell the perfume. She recognized it from the fragrance that had surrounded Brad on the night of the Christmas pageant. *She* was the perfume woman in Brad's life! She had to blink a little to keep the tears away.

"You're not allergic, are you?" Brad asked.

Millie shook her head. She only had one problem at the moment. "I don't have a present for you."

Millie figured the hundred-dollar bill didn't count because that was really from Forrest. She hadn't expected to meet Brad when she went to Dry Creek, so she hadn't taken a present with her. And she hadn't expected to ever see him again when she left, so there was no reason to buy him one later.

There was only one gift she could think of that

might please him, and she couldn't think about it too long or she'd decide it wasn't grand enough.

Millie stood up and leaned across the table. Then she bent down and kissed Brad square on the lips.

Millie had to swallow a chuckle, because she knew she had startled Brad for a second. But the man adapted quick. Before she knew it, the kiss was making her head spin and her knees buckle.

"Oh, my," Millie said when the kiss had ended. She was leaning into Brad and she was halfway into his arms. He moved around the table and settled her on his lap.

"You know, I have a feeling I'm not going to mind washing all those dishes at all," Brad said.

Millie just smiled. She had a feeling she wouldn't mind him washing all those dishes, either.

Epilogue

Four Months Later

Millie smiled as she looked at her bridal dress in the mirror. She had been staying at Mrs. Hargrove's for the past two weeks while she and Brad received marriage counseling from Pastor Matthew and made final plans for their wedding.

She and Brad had been going to a church in Seattle, but they both wanted to be married in the church in Dry Creek, especially after Millie started receiving the notes of thanks from the people in town. She was pleased that the notes were as likely to thank her for letting them know that the hit man was sorry as they were to thank her for the money.

The people in Dry Creek were good, solid people. Millie and Brad intended to live their lives in Dry

Creek and wanted to make the church their home. Since neither one of them had ideal childhoods, they knew that church would be their family.

Millie marveled at how much her understanding of God could change in just a few months. She and Brad had both asked God to help them understand more about Him, and they'd been astonished at what they were learning.

Millie fingered the lace on her veil. She had never thought she would know a man who wanted to take care of her as much as she wanted to take care of him. Brad had put a down payment on a ranch just outside of Dry Creek, and that would be where they would raise their family.

"Are you ready?" Mrs. Hargrove called up the stairs. "The carriage is here to pick you up."

When the ranch hands had heard that she and Brad were going to get married, they had rigged up one of the ranch wagons as a wedding carriage. Millie had seen the wagon this morning. It was covered with cascades of spring flowers. Pinks. Lavenders. And blues.

Millie refused to ride in the wagon without Brad, even for the short distance to the church, so everyone had decided to forget all the usual traditions, and she and Brad were riding to the church together. After the reception, they'd ride to their new home in the wagon, as well.

It would be a good start for them, Millie thought as she gave her face a final glance in the mirror and then headed down the stairs to her own true love.

* * * * *

Dear Reader,

Do you ever feel that God is asking you to do somethin[g]
that is just too difficult? I do. Like Millie in the book,
I sometimes feel as if I am a humble waitress and am
being asked to do something that God should know
requires being a king—or at least an elder statesman.
The peculiar thing about God, however, is that He does[n't]
mix it up. He uses the most unlikely people to do what
He wants done.

Of course, while this is sometimes alarming and often
frustrating, it is also what makes life with God unique.
He isn't impressed with your credentials or stature; He
is impressed with your heart. If you are willing, He wil[l]
lead you—and heap blessings upon you in the process.

Sincerely,

Janet Tronstad

Love Inspired
HISTORICAL
INSPIRATIONAL HISTORICAL ROMANCE

Working as a respectable
schoolteacher is the
one second chance
Annie MacAllister never
expected. Even more
surprising is that she
finds herself actually
helping her students—
not to mention Trail
End's most intriguing
citizen, John Sullivan.
Together they will need
divine forgiveness to
reignite their faith…and
find a future together.

ook for

econd Chance Bride

y

ANE MYERS PERRINE

Steeple
Hill®

vailable January
herever books are sold.

ww.SteepleHill.com

LIH82803

Luke Harris grew up without a family, and now that's all he wants. Even more so when he moves next door to widowed mom Janie Corbett and her three kids. For the first time, he can imagine having a wife and children to call his own. But the once-burned-twice-shy Janie won't accept Luke's attentions…until he confronts his troubled past.

Look for

A Family for Luke
by
Carolyne Aarsen

Available January wherever books are sold.

Steeple Hill®

www.SteepleHill.com

LI8751

Love Inspired
SUSPENSE
RIVETING INSPIRATIONAL ROMANCE

WITHOUT A TRACE WITHOUT A TRACE WITHOUT A TRACE

When a single mother mysteriously vanishes, the only witness is her three-year-old daughter, Sarah. FBI agent Sam Pierce needs to question the girl, but child psychologist Jocelyn Gold will barely let him near Sarah–or herself. Sam and Jocelyn were involved in the past; their hearts haven't healed, but now they must join forces to protect Sarah.

WHAT SARAH SAW
MARGARET DALEY

*Available January 2009
wherever books are sold, including
most bookstores, supermarkets,
drugstores and discount stores.*

Steeple
Hill®

ww.SteepleHill.com

LIS44322

REQUEST YOUR FREE BOOKS!

2 FREE INSPIRATIONAL NOVELS
PLUS 2
FREE
MYSTERY GIFTS

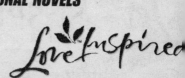

YES! Please send me 2 FREE Love Inspired® novels and my 2 FRE
mystery gifts (gifts are worth about $10). After receiving them, if I don't wish
receive any more books, I can return the shipping statement marked "cance
If I don't cancel, I will receive 4 brand-new novels every month and be bill
just $4.24 per book in the U.S. or $4.74 per book in Canada, plus 25¢ shippi
and handling per book and applicable taxes, if any*. That's a savings of ov
20% off the cover price! I understand that accepting the 2 free books and gi
places me under no obligation to buy anything. I can always return a shipme
and cancel at any time. Even if I never buy another book, the two free boo
and gifts are mine to keep forever.

113 IDN ERXA 313 IDN ER\

Name	(PLEASE PRINT)	
Address		Apt. #
City	State/Prov.	Zip/Postal Code

Signature (if under 18, a parent or guardian must sign)

Order online at www.LoveInspiredBooks.com

Or mail to Steeple Hill Reader Service:

IN U.S.A.: P.O. Box 1867, Buffalo, NY 14240-1867
IN CANADA: P.O. Box 609, Fort Erie, Ontario L2A 5X3

Not valid to current subscribers of Love Inspired books.

Want to try two free books from another series?
Call 1-800-873-8635 or visit www.morefreebooks.com

* Terms and prices subject to change without notice. N.Y. residents add applicable sal
tax. Canadian residents will be charged applicable provincial taxes and GST. Offer not va
in Quebec. This offer is limited to one order per household. All orders subject to approv
Credit or debit balances in a customer's account(s) may be offset by any other outstandi
balance owed by or to the customer. Please allow 4 to 6 weeks for delivery. Offer availab
while quantities last.

Your Privacy: Steeple Hill Books is committed to protecting your privacy. Our Privac
Policy is available online at www.SteepleHill.com or upon request from the Reade
Service. From time to time we make our lists of customers available to reputabl
third parties who may have a product or service of interest to you. If you would
prefer we not share your name and address, please check here. ☐

LIREG0

etermined to keep his
ter from eloping,
ade Porter hires wedding
anner Sara Woodward
arrange the wedding.
e might be the best in
e state, but she still finds
ade incredibly arrogant.
ter all, shouldn't his
ter have a say in the
ost important day of her
e? Not to worry, Cade
sures the lovely Sara…
e can plan *their* wedding
ght down to the day!

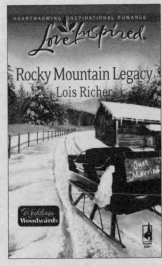

ok for

ocky Mountain

egacy

ois Richer

vailable January wherever books are sold.

ww.SteepleHill.com

Steeple
Hill®

LI87511

A SECRET PAST, A PRESENT DANGER...

HANNAH ALEXANDER

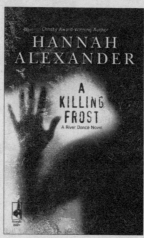

A terrible secret haunts Dr. Jama Keith. But she must return to her past—her hometown of River Dance, Missouri—and risk exposure. She owes a debt to the town for financing her dreams. If only she can avoid old flame Tyrell Mercer—but River Dance is too small for that.

When Tyrell's niece is abducted by two of the FBI's most wanted, Jama can't refuse to help—Tyrell's family were like kin to her for many years. The search for young Doriann could cost Tyrell and Jama their lives. But revealing her secret shame to the man she loves scares Jama more than the approaching danger....

Steeple
Hill®

A KILLING FROST

Available wherever trade paperbacks are sold!

www.SteepleHill.com

SHHA6